Changing
COURSE

Aly Martinez

Cover Design by Ashley Baumann at Ashbee Designs https://www.face-book.com/AshbeeBookCovers
Edited by Mickey Reed at I'm a Book Shark
http://www.imabookshark.com
Formatting by Stacey Blake at Self Publishing Editing Service

Prologue

"SARAH, DON'T DO this. Damn it! Stay with me." I reach over and gently brush the blood-soaked hair off her forehead.

Even in this horrific moment, I'm in absolute awe of how beautiful she looks. Bleeding and broken, unmoving in my arms, she is still the most mesmerizing woman I have ever laid eyes on. Deep down, I know this is just the husk of my wife. My Sarah would never have done this to herself. More importantly, she would have never done this to me. Maybe it takes this level of madness, but I finally realize that I have lost her completely.

Whether she lives or dies, Sarah is gone. This is not the woman who made me laugh more in seven years than the rest of my life combined. She definitely isn't the woman I spent years planning a future with, a future that now no longer exists. I feel a heavy weight in my chest at my silent confession, but oddly enough, I also feel a weight lifted off my shoulders. I have watched this woman disintegrate in front of my eyes for almost seven months. Every day, losing her a little more. The light in her eyes fading, while piece by piece and bit by bit, she lost grip of reality. Mentally, emotionally, and now physically, she's left me.

My Sarah died seven months ago on her way home from dinner, and I will never see her walk back into my life. Suddenly, I can't breathe. I'm terrified—and not only because Sarah might finally succeed in taking her own life. I'm paralyzed by the realization that my life is spiraling down in a free fall headed straight for misery, and the only thing I can think to do is anchor myself to this dying woman. I love Sarah with all my heart, but I am not clinging to the woman in my arms. Rather, I'm clinging to the life I thought we were going to have together. I have to accept that she isn't there anymore. Her heart might still be beating, but the bloody, confused, emotionally lost woman I am holding now is only the shell of my first and only love.

"Where the fuck is that ambulance?!" I yell as loud as my cracking voice will allow. Stroking the little bit of her unmarred skin I'm able to reach, I whisper in her ear, "Hang on, baby." Then I repeat the one sentence I have said almost daily since the tragic event that stole her from me. Maybe I say it for her, maybe just for me, but I know that it's the biggest lie I have ever uttered. "Just hang on, baby. It's all going to be okay."

Chapter ONE

Brett

I MET Sarah Kate Erickson seven years ago during a chance meeting at the local library. We were both reaching for the same William Shakespeare collection. Our hands brushed, sparks flew, and it was love at first sight. We dated for three years, got married, and had sex for the very first time on our wedding night. Well, at least that is the story she made me promise to tell our future children.

The truth is that I met Sarah in a bar while she was approximately one drop of alcohol away from spending the night praying to the porcelain gods. She had on some ridiculously tight red dress and the tallest pair of black fuck-me heels I had ever seen. It was whore-tastic, but damn, she looked amazing. She was already tall for a woman, but in those cock-hardening shoes, she towered over the other women. Her friends were dressed in similarly sexy and in somewhat coordinating outfits. A collaborative effort that was, no doubt, on purpose.

I watched as she asked for another drink from the bartender, who stood staring at her partially exposed breasts for a beat too long. She reached across the bar, pushed one finger under his chin, and guided his gaze back to her eyes while she ordered drinks. She then turned and leaned her elbows behind her, propping herself up on the bar and effectively thrusting her barely covered breasts into the face of every man in the room. It was then that I knew I needed to meet them—I mean her. I had to meet her.

Sure, staring at her was probably creepy as hell, but I just couldn't take my eyes off her. As cheesy as it sounds, there was just something about the tall blonde that commanded my attention. It didn't hurt that I got an insta-hard-on when I thought about those long legs wrapped around my waist. Okay, so maybe staring wasn't the only creepy part.

She continued to talk and laugh with her friends, swaying where she stood. It's a miracle she didn't fall over in those heels while she was so obviously trashed. Her friends seemed to be just as ensnared by her as I was. They listened intently as she spoke and laughed hysterically when she stopped. I had no idea what they were talking about, but if her overly animated hands and loud cackles coming from the group were any indication, it was one hell of a story.

A few minutes later, they started pointing out men—and women alike—as they walked by. They were rating the men on a one-to-ten hotness scale and bashing the women's clothing choices. I could tell they thought they were being quiet and sneaky, but everyone in the room who'd had less than fifteen drinks could hear every word they said. The three women finally paused their scrutinizing eyes on the man across the bar, and judging by their smiles and boob adjustments, they were definitely interested. *Lucky bastard.* I needed to make my move soon before he had the chance to make good on the eye-fuck he was throwing their way. Tossing back the rest of my beer, I decided it was time to hit the bar.

It's just my luck that, the one night I decided to go out without my boys, I met a living, breathing wet dream in heels. Women tend to run in herds, never straying far from each other. Fortunately for us, men work best as part of a team. One man approaching a group is difficult but not impossible. I had to be smooth or that group of piranhas would eat me alive. I needed to go over there, charm them all, and then ride off into the sunset with my leggy blonde. Well, her riding me until the sun set sounded like a much better option. But I was probably getting a little ahead of myself. I cracked my neck, shaking out my arms like some sort of prize fighter as I found the only positive I could see about this situation—at least I didn't have to argue with the boys over dibs.

"Can I buy you ladies a drink?" I ask when I get close to the three girls huddled together. *Real smooth, jackass! I'm sure they've never heard that one before.* I mentally chastise myself.

"Nope," says the shortest of the bunch as she turns around, ignoring me.

This is definitely not the usual response I get when I approach women. I'm not completely sure if she even looked at me before rejecting my offer. I'm a good-looking guy. I won't pretend I don't know it. I'm six foot five with brown hair and green eyes. I work out and take care of myself. All that shit women are supposed to like. I don't dress like the normal T-shirt-clad douchebags you usually see in this club either. Tonight, I'm wearing dark jeans, a fitted royal-blue button-down shirt, a black belt, and boots. It's not my best outfit, but seriously, Miss Shorty Shoot Down would be lucky to even get my attention.

I stand there for a minute, shocked by the rejection and trying to figure out a new plan of action. I refuse to walk away. Jerry Jerkoff from across the bar is not getting anywhere near my Red Dress.

"Hey, you're tall!" I hear slurred from beside me.

Turning, I come face to face with one of the sexiest women I have ever seen and the newest member of my mental spank bank.

"So are you," I reply into her ear so she can hear me over the music. I toss her a mischievous smile when I lean away, just so there is no mistaking that I'm interested.

"No, I mean you are reallllly tall." She sways backwards, making a dramatic show of craning her neck to look into my eyes. I laugh, nodding my head to agree with her assessment, while she grabs her friends, squealing, "Y'all, look how tall this guy is!"

I squeeze my eyes shut and adjust my pants as I hear the sweetest Southern accent roll off my drunken beauty's tongue.

"Hi. I'm Brett." I extend my hand out to her friend.

"Hi. I'm Regina Phalange," Shorty says, grabbing my hand.

"And I'm Anastasia Beaverhousen. Anastasia, as in the Russian royal princess. Beaverhousen, as in the house a beaver lives in." They all double over in fits of laughter.

"Right. Of course you are. So that would make you...?" I ask my girl when she finally stands back up and tries to wipe invisible tears from under her eyes.

"Oh God, I'm sorry about them. They have been drinking since noon, I swear. I'm Danika. Just Danika," she says without a single slur.

Interesting. Maybe she isn't as drunk as I first thought.

"Well, Danika, can I buy you and your drunk friends a drink?"

"Sure... Wait! Are you planning to drug any of us?" she asks in mock seriousness.

"Well, it wasn't the plan. But if you happen to have any drugs on you, I'd be happy to drop them in your drink when you aren't looking."

"Nah, I'm good. I roofied myself last weekend and it wasn't all that fun. I'll just take the drink," she jokes.

"Totally understandable." I nod, playing along.

"What do y'all want to drink? Brett here is buying this round!" she yells over her shoulder to her friends. "Oh forget it. They can't hear me. Just get us a Corona, Sex on the Beach, and a shot of tequila."

I flag down the bartender to order, adding a beer for myself. As I wait for the drinks, I alternate between chatting with the girls and staring down Jerry Jerkoff from across the bar.

"So which one is yours?" I ask as our drinks are placed on the bar in front of us.

"What? Oh, you mean the drinks? That depends. Which one do you think is mine?" she says, throwing her own flirtatious smile my way.

"Okay, let's see..." I rub my chin, pretending to be deep in thought. "You don't seem drunk enough to be drinking tequila shots tonight, so that's out. And you don't seem like the type of girl to order a fruity drink that comes complete with a cherry sword skewer and toy umbrella. Simple process of elimination. I'm going to guess the Corona is yours."

Staring at all three drinks in front of her, she waves her hand over them, making a show of reaching for each one. She finally reaches down, pulls out the umbrella and cherry skewer, and tosses them out of the fruity drink.

"Well, you were right about one thing. I don't order drinks with cherry swords and plastic umbrellas. I do, however, love Sex on the Beach," she says with a wink before chugging the drink and slamming it on the bar like she's hanging with Patrick Swayze at The Road House.

"Do you dance?" she asks, using the back of her hand to wipe her mouth.

"Why, yes, ma'am, Danika, I surely do," I reply in what can only be described as the perfect Southern accent.

"Wow. That was terrible. Brett, for your sake, I hope your dancing is better than your linguistic abilities," she says just seconds before slapping me on the ass and heading to the dance floor.

I know it is definitely too soon to be in love with this crazy woman, but I do know I'm in a shit-ton of trouble.

Chapter TWO

Brett

I SPENT the rest of the night glued to Danika's ass. I mean that both literally and figuratively. We danced, we laughed, and best of all, we got to know each other. She was beautiful in every way possible. She told me about her dreams to become a writer, and I told her about my decision to join the police force as soon as I finished college. I bought drinks and her girlfriends made toasts to absurd things like "vibrating butt plugs" and "bisexual men everywhere." While I might have been wrong about the amount of alcohol this woman could consume, I was absolutely correct about where her evening would end.

Three hours after meeting Danika, I sat in her bathroom, holding her hair while she threw up. It was quite possibly the most disgusting thing I have ever experienced. She puked until it was physically impossible for her to puke anymore. It was horrible, but I did what any man who wanted to have sex with a woman would do. I sat and stroked her hair while gagging and praying to God to keep myself from puking, too. By the time she finally finished evicting her organs into the toilet, I may have made an agreement with the powers above to name my first born Hephzibah just to make her stop.

I eventually woke up confused and hanging off the edge of an unknown bed. Opening my eyes, I immediately recognized the ocean blues of the beautiful woman standing over me.

"Hey," she says while walking around the side of the bed to sit down next to me.

"Jesus, it's early. How are you awake after the five-star puke show you put on last night?"

"Unless you want an encore, you seriously need to shut your mouth."

"Oh God no! I've been scarred enough. Do you want to get breakfast?

Or did you flush your stomach down the toilet last night along with the seventeen olives you stole from the bartender's garnish tray?"

"He left the tray wide open. He was asking for someone to steal his olives!" she says while trying to playfully punch me.

"Okay, okay, stop. I give up! I'm not awake enough for full-contact sports."

I grab her around the waist, dragging her down to lie on top of me. She freezes completely, and I realize that, while we were very affectionate with each other last night, she was drunk. I have no idea how much she actually even remembers from the night before. Releasing her from my arms, I sit up, taking her stiff body with me. I place her on the bed next to me and run my hands back and forth over my thighs just to keep myself from touching her again.

"Hey, let's start over. I'm Brett. I like football, long walks on the beach, beer, and golden retrievers. I'm terrified of scary movies, especially the ones made by Disney. I'm a Virgo, but don't worry. I act like a Pisces—or at least that is what my sisters tell me." I ramble, finishing with a closed-mouth smile, suddenly aware of our close proximity and my lack of a toothbrush.

"Well, hello, Brett. Nice to meet you...again." She winks.

"So, I'm guessing the wink means you remember last night?"

"Yep. I'm one of the unlucky few who never gets to forget a single drunken dance move. I'd be willing to give my first born to forget the ass I made of myself last night."

"His name will be Hephzibah," I answer matter-of-factly.

"What?"

"Nothing...just a little deal I made with the Lord last night," I mumble, dismissing the obviously bad joke with a hand gesture.

"Well, okay then," she says, confused. But she drops it, obviously not wanting to discuss last night any longer.

I stand, feeling uncomfortable about still sitting on her bed. "I better get going. I'm sure you have things to do today."

"Yeah, um, okay. Do you need a ride to your car?"

"Nah. We aren't far from my place. I can just walk and catch a cab to my car later."

"No, I don't mind. Really! Just let me just get dressed," she says just as awkwardly as I feel.

"Seriously, Danika, I can just walk. It's no big—"

"Sarah." She looks down at her feet while playing with the ends of her freshly showered hair.

"What?"

"Shit. My name. It's Sarah." She looks embarrassed and continues to avoid my eyes.

"Sarah? Really?"

"Yeah. Danika is the fake name I use when we go out. It's just something silly the three of us do. I'm horrible at keeping up with it. It always fails. Manda or Casey yells my real name across the bar, completely blowing my cover."

"I'm guessing I know Manda and Casey better as Regina and Anastasia?"

"Yep. That would be them. They picked club names from their favorite TV shows. I tried to use Blanche Devereaux for a while, but you would be surprised by the alarming number of men who watch Golden Girls. After that, I switched to my favorite future baby's name, Danika."

"Um, okay...Sarah." I purposely over-enunciate her name, pretending to be testing it on my tongue. "I'm going to head out. I'm glad you're feeling better. You should probably take some Ibuprofen and drink a gallon of water. I'm pretty sure there is nothing left in your body from yesterday." I look around, trying to remember where I took my boots off.

"Wow, you're tall." I hear the familiar phrase from behind me.

"So you've mentioned."

"No, I mean you are really tall!"

"Yep, you may have said that too." I raise my eyebrows, slightly annoyed at how such an awesome night turned into such an awkward morning.

"Look, I'm sorry. I'm not trying to be a bitch, I swear. I'm just not sure what to do in this situation." She steps towards me, trying to apologize.

I sigh, stretching, and scratch the back of my head. "How about you try introducing yourself with your *real* name then make me a delicious breakfast and point me towards your coffee maker." I smirk at her.

She pauses for a second before offering a heart-stopping smile of her own. "Hi. My name is Sarah, and there is no way in hell I am cooking you breakfast. I will, however, allow you to buy me some greasy food at the corner diner. And if you are desperate for coffee, I believe there is some decaf in the kitchen. I drink it when I need something warm in the horrible winters y'all have up here."

"I accept your offer, beautiful Sarah, for me to um...how did you so eloquently put it? Buy you some greasy food? But I really need to ask you a few things first. One, what the hell is the point in drinking decaf? Two, where exactly are you from that causes you to say 'y'all' every other sentence? And most importantly, why in God's name would you want to name a baby Danika?" I mock in horror before smiling, giving it every ounce of charm I have to offer.

"Oh, because Hephzibah is so much better?" she snarks over her shoulder as she walks into her closet, presumably to get dressed.

I grab my heart, feigning injury. "Touché, Sarah. Touché."

And just like that, I start to think that maybe I was wrong and it's not too soon to fall in love with this fascinating woman after all.

Chapter
THREE

Brett

"OKAY, EXPLAIN this to me one more time," I ask Sarah while we sit in a candy-cane-striped booth in a dive restaurant a few doors down from her apartment.

Sarah gives me a long-suffering sigh before repeating, "They put the bacon, egg, and cheese sandwiches together wrong. So I order a fried egg, two pieces of toast, four slices of bacon, and two pieces of cheese to make my own."

I lean forward, intrigued. "It's bacon, egg, and cheese on toast. How can anyone possibly make that wrong?"

"The proper way to make it is: bread, cheese, bacon, egg in the center, then bacon, cheese, and bread. It gives you the perfect bacon-to-egg ratio. When they make it for you, they stiff you on the bacon and the cheese. And then, it's really nothing more than an egg sandwich flavored with bacon and cheese."

"I don't think I have ever had a conversation where the word bacon was used more," I laugh at her.

"You obviously don't have very intelligent friends then. I've had an entire conversation with Manda about why bacon is superior to all other meats. I'm passionate about the things I love, and that includes bacon."

"How are you not fat?"

"Good genes. Oh, and stripping every Friday night really helps me burn off the calories, too," she says nonchalantly, taking a sip of her Mr. Pibb.

I try to cover my shock but obviously fail as I shout, "What?" loud enough to make all the other customers turn to look.

She dies laughing, falling over onto the bench seat.

"Wow. That was wrong." I pretend to be annoyed.

"No, that was hilarious. Oh my God, your face was priceless." She continues to laugh until the waitress shows up with our food.

"You sure you're feeling okay after puking all night?" I ask purposely as she lifts her first bite to her mouth.

"You did not just bring that up right now."

"Of course I did. Your face is priceless!" I say, mocking her as I dodge the pickle she throws at me.

OVER THE next hour, we finished the most entertaining breakfast imaginable. The conversation flowed easily, never lulling even for a minute. We swapped funny stories, laughing at all the crazy things we had done in our teens. At one point, we were so loud that the waitress came over and asked us to keep it down. Her warning did nothing to quiet us though. I was so enamored with this woman that half the time I forgot we were even in a restaurant at all.

After Sarah taught me the finer points of making the perfect breakfast sandwich, we finished up and headed to the register to pay. As soon as we were both on our feet, I reached down to grab her hand, craving the physical connection the table denied me during breakfast. In true Sarah fashion, she lifted my arm and twirled under it before wrapping it around her shoulders and leaning into my chest.

We walked back to her apartment wrapped in each other. I kept my arm around her shoulders, and she held my hand as it draped down her chest, her other hand tucked securely in my back pocket. Every so often, she would look up to give me one of her award-winning smiles, and in those moments, as silly as it sounds, I knew that my life was never going to be the same. I was ruined and wrecked and I hadn't even seen her naked yet.

"Give me a minute and I'll take you to your car," she says as we walk back into her apartment, releasing my hand only to search for her keys.

While I wait, I walk around her apartment looking at her pictures, studying each one for clues about Sarah Erickson. I stop on a picture of her in a bar, huddled together with Manda and Casey. Sarah is in the middle, leaning down to their level, arms thrown around them. The girls are all looking in different directions, but Sarah is staring directly into the camera. She's dressed almost exactly as she was last night. Different dress, same black heels. Her hair is sweaty, and her eye makeup was starting to run. I can almost guarantee it was from a night spent on the dance floor.

Less than twenty-four hours ago, I would have told you that she looked ridiculous. Now, I can honestly say that I have never seen a more beautiful woman in my life. I have an overwhelming desire to steal the picture, but I'm sure I'd never hear the end of it if she caught me trying to escape with it shoved down my pants.

"You ready?" she asks, wrapping her arms around my waist from behind.

I turn in her grasp, reaching up with both hands to tuck stray hairs behind her ears and peering into her clear blue eyes.

"How weird would be if I said no?" I ask honestly and kiss her on her forehead.

"How weird is it that I want to ask you to spend the day with me?" she responds, standing up on her toes, kissing me chastely on the lips.

"How weird is it that I want to spend the rest of the day kissing you?" I kiss her a little longer, sucking her bottom lip into my mouth, grazing it with my teeth as I pull away.

"How weird is it that I want to do far more than just kiss you for the rest of the day?" she says, grabbing the back of my head and pulling me down to gain access to my neck, licking and sucking her way up to my ear.

"How weird is it that we keep saying 'how weird is it'?" I joke, groaning as she bites me.

Reaching down, I roughly grab her ass, grinding into her with my hard-on, causing her to let out a growl. My lips land on hers just seconds before I thrust my tongue into her mouth. Her tongue meets my every stroke, twisting and dancing with mine. Suddenly, I lose all sense of control. I'm desperate for her and completely unable to keep my hands in the respectable territory anymore. After I push her ten steps backwards, she falls onto the chair across from her couch. I drop to my knees in front of her in order to continue the kiss. I pull away only long enough to remove her shirt, immediately resuming my assault on her mouth.

I slowly trace down her arms and up her smooth stomach, smiling to myself when I feel the goose bumps that pebble her skin. I release her mouth when my hands reach the softness of her breasts. The sexiest moan escapes her lips as I gently cup them. She makes no move to touch me and sits perfectly still, watching my hands caress her body. I feel her breathing begin to quicken, but still, she says nothing. Needing to see more than her black bra allows, I reach around to the back, flicking open the clasp. For a moment, I lock my eyes to hers, trying to gauge her reaction. I don't want to push her into something she isn't ready for, but she has made no attempt to stop my wandering hands.

Throwing caution to the wind, I decide to keep moving. I glide the straps off her shoulders, making sure to drag the tips of my fingers across her skin as I pull her bra down her arms, dropping it to the floor beside us. I continue my stare as a slow grin creeps across her face.

"Is this okay?" I finally ask, needing some sort of reassurance.

"No," she says, causing me to immediately remove my hands from her body. "It's not nearly enough," she finishes, reaching forward and replacing my hands on her chest. I shake my head at her ability to crack jokes even while sitting half naked.

I finally have a chance to look down. Her nipples are perfectly hard and pink. I run the rough pads of my thumbs over them as she moans and lets her head fall back against the cushion. I start kissing down her neck and hear her breathing speed. I grab her waist and push her back deeper into the chair, allowing myself more access to her body. My lips move against her smooth skin as I trace my way down to her pert breasts, slowly sucking her hard nipple in my mouth.

She surprises me when I feel her reach down and begin rubbing my dick through my jeans. I can't help the startled noise that comes out, half moan and half gasp. Unfortunately for me, those sounds mingle together, producing a loud whimper. I try to clear my throat to cover the sound, but it's too late. Sarah drops her hand and all but rolls in laughter. I tickle her to cover my embarrassment, but that only causes her to laugh louder.

"So you think that was funny, huh?" I pick her up, tossing her onto the couch.

"Jesus, Brett, did you just come?"

"Not yet. I always make sure the lady gets off first." I reach down between her legs, stroking her through her jeans while sucking her peaked nipple back into my mouth.

"Fuck," she gasps as I move my hands up towards the button on her pants.

Never releasing her breast, I unzip and tug them down. She helps by lifting her hips off the couch while I remove them completely, throwing them over my shoulder and out of the way. A black lace thong greets me, and what a beautiful sight it is. I place small, wet kisses down her stomach, paying special attention to the area just above those sexy panties. She threads her hands in my hair, using it as leverage to push her hips toward my face. Spreading her legs, I kiss the insides of each thigh, her body pleading with me.

"Tell me what you want, Sarah."

"Please, Brett. Please, just..."

Running my nose over her lace-covered core, I can smell her arousal, and I think my dick is about to burst through my pants. Standing up, I toss my shirt over my head and slide my jeans to the floor, leaving only my boxer briefs and a very hard cock for her to see. She moans her approval, and that's all I need as permission. Grasping the sides of her panties, I slowly slide them down her legs, exposing her wet, glistening pussy. I watch as she rolls her nipples between her fingers, pinching and pulling while gazing at me through hooded eyes. The arousal is thick in the air, and I'm physically unable to wait any longer to taste her.

Sliding between her thighs, I pick up her legs and place them, one at a time, over my shoulders. When I flick her swollen bud with my tongue, she lets out a string of breathy profanities. Deciding to take her one step further, I flatten my tongue and slowly drag it up her heat, tasting her sweetness. My eyes roll back in my head. I might just come from her taste alone.

I hear her panting and begging, "Fuck me, baby. Fuck me with your fingers."

Following her orders, I thrust one finger inside. She's so wet and ready for me that I know this isn't going to take long. Adding another finger, I start to match the rhythm of her surging hips. I pause only momentarily when she begins to ride my hand. I can't help but watch her as she unapologetically takes what she needs. Her boobs bounce as her hips roll into my hand. I suck her clit back into my mouth to still her. It only causes her to lose all control. Feeling her inner walls contracting around my fingers, I know she's close.

"Come for me, baby. You taste so sweet. Show me how much you like it."

Her back arches off the couch and her core clamps down on my fingers as she screams out. I feel her body pulsing as she rides the wave of her orgasm.

I remove my fingers as she comes down from her orgasm. Sarah stares at me with a glossed-over look of satisfaction in her eyes. I toss her a wink and a smile when I lift my fingers to my mouth and start to lick her lingering arousal away. She watches, sated, before sitting up and shocking the hell out of me. She grabs my hand and slowly slides my fingers into her own mouth.

"You're not going share?" she asks around my fingers as she sucks herself off my hand.

"Fuck me! That has got to be the hottest fucking thing I have ever seen," I groan out as she continues.

"That is the plan." She releases my fingers with a loud pop.

Dropping her hand to her wet core, she rubs herself the same way I was just doing a few minutes ago. I need to be inside her now or I'm going to come like a horny virgin all over her living room carpet. Making quick work of removing my boxers, I plan to lift her off onto the floor. I'm way too tall for couch sex, and the bedroom is a long way away right now. I don't want to have sex with Sarah for the first time on her living room floor, but I'll settle for anything at this point, as long as it ends with me buried inside her.

As I turn back to the couch, she's already on her feet and moving towards me with a smirk on her face. I can smell the sex in the air, and I know my cock is pointing right at her. She places her hands on my chest and slowly moves them down toward my aching dick, never taking her eyes off mine. She cups my balls with one hand and strokes my cock with the other. I struggle to remain on my feet. Rolling my balls in a circular pattern, she ever so slowly strokes me.

"Baby, you have to stop or I'm going to come, and I really want to be inside you when that happens."

She smiles and gives me a chaste kiss on the lips. "It's my turn to run this show."

I am confused as to what she means, and I start to play the gentleman, telling her that she doesn't have to return the favor. Suddenly, I'm pushed backwards, nearly tripping over the clothes strewn across the floor.

"On your back, Brett," she says, pushing me to the ground.

"Jesus, are you a dominatrix as well as a stripper?"

"Wouldn't you like to know?" She winks.

Sarah is a sight to behold as I lie on the carpet and look up at her. Her body is glowing, still flushed from her orgasm. She lowers herself on top of me, and I feel her wetness sliding over my cock. Pre-cum leaks from my tip, aching to find its way inside. She bends, landing her lips on mine. She doesn't just kiss me. She fucks my mouth with her tongue. Pushing and pulling. Licking and sucking. Our mouths are like starved animals. I'm so caught up in the kiss that I barely feel her reach down and push me inside her tight body, engulfing my cock in her heat in one swift movement. I moan, my toes curling as she takes me in completely.

"Oh my God, you feel amazing," she whispers.

"Fuuucccckkkk," is all I can get out.

She stills for a minute, allowing us both time to adjust.

Placing her hands on my chest, she starts moving her hips up and down, rolling them back and forth as she tries to find her pace. Picking up speed, she searches to find a rhythm she likes. I watch her as she rides me with a supreme confidence. Her breasts bounce and her head falls back, trailing her long blond hair down her back, lightly brushing my thighs. I grab her ass and try to match her thrusts, never taking my eyes off her perfect breasts.

"Holy shit, you are sexy. You need to slow down or there is no way I'm going to last much longer." I finally look up, meeting her eyes.

If I thought staring at her swaying breasts was enough to make me come, it is nothing compared to the way I feel looking into her eyes. I quickly push up into a sitting position, running my fingers into her hair. I grab the back of her head, pulling her down into a rough kiss.

I can feel my balls start to tighten and my dick swell inside her. It's too soon, but I can tell from her pace that she's close too. But not nearly close enough. Not releasing her mouth, I reach between us to rub her clit. This causes her to ride me harder, take me deeper, and grind against my hand on every downstroke. Using one hand to brace herself against my chest, she moves the other back to play with her own nipples. It's obvious this girl knows exactly what she wants and how to get it.

She drops her head down against my forehead, never slowing. I can feel her whole body tightening as she stares intensely into my eyes, never looking away or hiding behind closed lids.

"Brett," she barely whispers as she falls over the edge.

The sensations are too much, and I can't hold back any longer. Arching my back and thrusting into her one last time, I come so hard that I begin to see stars. Slowing her pace, she continues to slide up and down my softening cock as the aftershocks of my release travel through my body. She finally stills, resting her entire weight on my chest.

"You're a dirty girl, Sarah Erickson," I pant out while trying to catch my breath.

"Is that supposed to be a bad thing?"

"No, it's perfect. I have to warn you though. I don't think you are going to be able to get rid of me after that. If you happen to need a new sub for your crazy dominatrix dungeon or just someone to wax your stripper pole, I'm your guy," I try to tease.

"Who says I want to get rid of you? We may have just created a little Danika or Hephzibah!"

My whole body stiffens as it dawns on me that we didn't use a condom.

"Oh shit! Damn. Shit. Fuck!" I scream, jumping to my feet, causing her to crash to the side.

"Hey, is that any way to treat your pregnant girlfriend?"

"Damn, I'm so sorry. Are you okay?" My eyes search her body for any possible injury. As I get to her face, I can see her tight lips forcefully trying to contain a smile.

"Oh God, this is too much!" She flops down on the couch in hysterical laughter, leaving me completely confused.

"What am I missing here?" I ask then notice that I'm standing naked in front of a laughing woman. I pull on my jeans, not bothering to button them before I continue questioning her. "What are you laughing about?" I ask a little too harshly.

If she notices my tone at all, it doesn't seem to affect her. I stand, annoyed, my hands on my hips, staring at this obviously insane woman rolling around naked on the couch in a fit of laughter. Finally able to compose herself, she wipes away her tears and pulls me down to the couch next to her.

"I'm sorry," she says, moving to straddling my lap. "I'm on birth control. No babies." She starts to giggle again, but I level her with an annoyed glare. I breathe out a relieved sigh as she continues. "I didn't mean to forget about the condom. I just got carried away. I'm clean though. You don't have to worry about that either." She rains sweet apologetic kisses all over my face.

"You're evil."

"And dirty," she replies, moving her kissing down to my neck.

"You better show me some more of that dirty to make up for your lame jokes."

"My pleasure," she smiles, sinking to the floor between my knees.

Chapter FOUR

Brett

OVER THE course of the following months, Sarah and I alternated between her house and mine, never sleeping a night apart. We made love, ordered takeout. Sometimes she cooked, sometimes she laughed at me while I attempted to cook, and occasionally, we forgot to eat altogether. Sarah was more than I ever could have expected from the tight red dress I met one random solo night at the club. She was smart, beautiful, sexy, and funny. *God, she was so damn funny.*

We would spend hours making up stupid games just to challenge each other. That nutty woman was the most competitive person I have ever met. We played Jeopardy every night, keeping track of how many answers we each got right. The winner received absolutely nothing but bragging rights, but for us, that was the most coveted prize of all.

"You cheater!" I scream, walking back into the room, carrying her glass of wine. "I told you to pause it."

"No way. You can't pause Jeopardy! You walk out of the room, you forfeit those questions to me. So now I'm up twelve to nine."

"I only got up because you asked for another glass of wine!"

"Well it's not my fault that you lack the ability to say no to a sexy woman." She bats her eyelashes at me.

"Oh, well in that case..." I turn the glass, pouring two drops onto the wood floor.

"Don't you dare, Brett Sharp! You know that's my last glass of wine." She jumps up from the couch, trying to snatch it from me.

"What's the score, Sarah?"

"Twelve to nine."

"Wrong answer." I pour out two more drops.

"Brett! Stop being an ass. I'm serious. Don't pour out my wine!" She stands up on the chair next to me, trying to jump high enough to reach it. She is by no means short, but I've got her by at least six inches.

"What's the score?"

"You know what, just forget it. You can pour out the wine." She walks back to the couch, sitting down and propping her feet up on the ottoman.

Shit. This means trouble.

Sarah never gives up this easily. Last week, we had almost the exact same fight over a "friendly" game of Uno. It ended with my balls being so blue that they were registering on the purple side of the color spectrum. She pretended to give up, walking away just like she did tonight. However, last week, when I got close enough to her, she dropped to her knees, giving me the most amazing blowjob ever to be performed. She kept me on edge for over an hour, working me with her mouth as only Sarah could. When I finally couldn't take it anymore, desperate with the need to come, she kissed the tip and whispered to my throbbing cock, "Sorry, but I definitely said Uno first." Then she walked out of the room.

Trying to shake off the horrible memory, I say, "I'm not letting you near my dick this time."

"Okay." She continues to stare at the TV screen.

"I'm serious."

"Oh, I have no doubt that you are, Brett," she says with an evil smile on her face as she reaches down, pulling her shirt over her head.

"Shit," I say as I watch her lick her fingers and circle her nipples.

"It's really a shame you won't be letting me anywhere near that big dick of yours tonight. You looked insanely hot when you came home all sweaty from the gym tonight. It took everything I had to actually cook dinner and not touch myself, knowing you were naked in my shower." She continues to stroke her breasts while one hand drifts down her stomach, stopping at the waistband of her shorts.

"Jesus." I reach down and start rubbing my growing erection as she continues to torture me.

"If I'm being honest, I've been waiting all night to show you a few new toys I bought online. They arrived today, and while it isn't nearly as big as you are, I'm sure it will help dull the ache on a night like this." She finishes on a groan as her hand finally makes its way into her shorts.

In times like these, you have to let go of your pride. Alone and proud, or balls-deep and coming. So I relent to her sexual terrorism.

"Twelve to nine, and I'll buy you a new bottle of wine tomorrow." I move over to her and crush my mouth to hers, shoving my hand down her pants to join her moving fingers.

"Oh thank God. I wasn't sure how much longer I could keep that up. I loved watching you get hard through your pants like that. I almost got off on that alone."

"You are going to kill me one of these days with all of your crazy games."

"I hope not. I'd miss you."

"Right, because then who would you play Jeopardy with?" I ask, causing her to laugh before she pulls her shorts off and climbs into my lap.

"I love you," she says, sinking down onto my waiting erection. "And thank you for the big bottle of wine."

"Who said anything about it being a big bottle?" I run my hands over her ass, trying to push her down a little faster, but she freezes at my words with only the tip nestled inside. "Okay, okay. Fine. A big bottle. I'll buy you a whole damn vineyard if you stop teasing and fuck me right now."

"Now that I can do." She slams herself down, causing us both to shout out a curse.

That was Sarah, and I loved the entire quirky package. She was everything I wanted and needed in my life. She kept me in line when it was time to study for exams. Including her personal version of oral exams, one lick for every question I answered correctly. Unfortunately for my grades, her licks were entirely too effective and we never made it past question three. She also helped me fill out my application for the academy by straddling my lap naked while feeding me leftover lo mein. She was more than my everything—Sarah was my forever.

Eight months, two days, and twelve hours after I first laid eyes on Sarah Erickson, I asked her to marry me. It wasn't the over-the-top romantic display most women brag about, but it was us. I cooked her a disgusting dinner and made her a tragically ugly cake. I gave her a five-by-seven photo of Alex Trebek with this clue scrawled on the back:

Approximately 2,063,000 men ask this question every year. Only about fifty-four percent never ask it again.

It took her a few minutes to answer. I'm not sure she even truly understood what was happening. When I got down on one knee, holding out the tiniest diamond coal has ever produced, she squealed out in true Jeopardy form, "What is: Will you marry me!" Tears were streaming down her face.

Laughing, I teased, "Yes. You don't have to yell. Of course I'll marry you."

This comment earned me a punch to the stomach, one that didn't even register in the midst of my elation over the fact that this beautiful woman was going to be my wife. I never once let her forget that she'd actually proposed to me.

Sarah and I lived a happy life. It wasn't perfect. We fought like any young couple, but that gave us even more opportunities for make-up sex—a personal favorite of ours. I finished college and entered the police academy, eventually graduating at the top of my class. Sarah put hours of work into writing, yet she never finished a single book. She always said that she just had too many ideas.

Sarah's two best friends, Manda and Casey, were fixtures in our lives. Once we got married, we didn't go to the clubs as often, but occasionally the girls would drag me out. One particular night, we ran into a fellow rookie detective, Caleb Jones. He took an immediate interest in "Regina." He even laughed when I pulled him aside and informed him that her name was actually Manda.

Those two did the on-again-off-again thing for years before Caleb told her he was done with the bullshit and wanted to get married. It was mainly Manda who was playing games, so she was a hard sell, but apparently Caleb can be very persuasive when he wants to be. It was Manda who got the last laugh, accepting his proposal but refusing to actually tie the knot.

The four of us became extremely close. It was nice to have another couple to hang out with on the weekends. Sarah and Manda planned Friday evenings full of drunken board games. If Casey happened to be dating someone, they came too. Caleb and I later ended up being partnered together at work, and eventually, he became my best friend. Even when he and Manda were in an "off phase," Caleb would still meet me at the hole-in-the-wall bar down the street to watch whatever sport was in season.

April 18, 2009, was the day the world came crashing down on our picture perfect little group. The four of us decided to go out for dinner at our favorite pizza joint. Westies has the most delicious deep-dish Chicago pizza you have ever tasted, and the cheap beer didn't hurt either. We went there almost weekly for years, but I've never been back since that night. Caleb and I got called away on a case, and Sarah and Manda decided to stay and finish dinner.

"Got to go, babe," I said to Sarah while nodding to Caleb across the table. "Seems they found Mrs. Reynolds alive and well, shacked up with her pool boy."

"Oh my God, Brett. Isn't she like seventy-five years old?" Manda asked in disgust from across the table.

"Seventy-eight, actually. But we need to go close this one out. It shouldn't take long. We just need to see her wrinkly face and take a statement that she was never really missing. Seven million pages of paperwork all because Granny got horny."

The girls let out loud "ewws" in unison while Caleb and I stood to leave.

"I'll meet you back at the house, sweetheart." I leaned forward, kissing Sarah's forehead while tucking a stray blond hair behind her ear.

"Okay. Y'all be careful. Love you, babe."

"I love you too."

We both kissed the girls one last time, clueless to the fact that, in less than two hours, one of them would be dead and the other would be lost forever.

WE WERE talking to Mrs. Reynolds when our pagers started going off. I excused myself to the other room while Caleb continued to take her statement. The words scrolling across the screen marked the end of what I knew to be my life and would haunt my dreams for years to come.

Single car accident on I290 near Damen Ave. One fatality and one seriously injured. Silver Honda, 2 women mid 20's. Det's Jones and Sharp required on scene immediately.

"Caleb!" I cry, bolting toward the car as the words *one fatality* flash behind my eyelids with each blink.

I jump into the car, dialing Sarah's number, hoping for a miracle. I am desperate to hear her sleepy voice pick up the phone while she lies tucked safely in our bed. Her voicemail picks up and my heart drops to my stomach.

"Oh shit! This is not happening," I whisper to myself. Taking a deep breath and scrubbing my hands across my face, I try to pull myself together enough to drive.

My head starts to swirl with scenarios that would leave them both completely unharmed. Maybe they just got carried away talking and are still hanging at Westies. Maybe they went to see a movie after dinner. There's a bar just two doors down from the restaurant—maybe they went there. I pick up my phone to call her one more time, praying that this time she will answer. In my gut, I know it's just wishful thinking. *One fatality and one injury.* I start the car, barely slowing down as Caleb jumps inside.

"It's not them, Brett."

"Did Manda answer her phone?"

"No, but I just know it. It's not them."

"It's them. I can feel it," I say, staring straight ahead and weaving through oncoming traffic.

"Shut the fuck up. It's not them, God damn it!"

"Silver Honda, two women in their mid-twenties, on the exact route they would take home?" I say with an eerie calm to my voice.

"It's not fucking them!" Caleb screams at the top of his lungs while punching the dashboard. He then grabs his phone, frantically trying to call every patrol cop he has on speed dial. But no one answers his calls.

We drive the rest of the way in silence. *One fatality and one injury.* A few miles out from the accident, I stop hoping that it isn't them in that car. Instead, I do the most horribly selfish thing I will ever do in this lifetime. *One fatality and one injury.* Looking over at Caleb sitting with his head in his hands, I don't feel one bit of guilt as I start praying that it's Manda who is dead.

When Caleb and I arrive at the scene, there are ambulances everywhere. I can see Sarah's car folded in half around a tree. It takes everything I have not to throw up at the very sight. I'm not sure how either one of them could have survived a wreck this severe.

My car barely slows before Caleb is out running toward the mangled heap of metal. I'm not but five steps behind him. Off in the wood line, I can see the sheet covering what I know to be a body.

"Oh God, please. Please don't let that be her," I chant to myself as I make my way to the wood line.

As I squeeze between police cars and ambulances, I'm suddenly shoved from the side and fall into an open ambulance. Dave Young, a street cop I knew from the academy and the only man on the force bigger than I am, shoves me the rest of the way into the empty ambulance. He quickly shuts the door and yells for the driver to go.

"What the fuck are you doing?" I say, lunging towards the back of the ambulance, ready to claw my way out if I have to. I look out the window just in time to see Caleb drop to his knees on the side of the road before I feel the ambulance start to speed away.

"You don't need to be there for that, Brett," Dave says as the familiar siren screams into my ears.

"Where's Sarah?"

"She's probably at the hospital by now. Left a few minutes before you got there. She had a heartbeat and was breathing, but they couldn't get her to wake up. They worked on her for a while. She's got some pretty deep cuts on her arms and legs. She was thrown from the car. She's banged up, but I heard from Dan that she started mumbling something just before they loaded her up. That's a good sign, Brett."

"Holy fuck." The relief I feel at his words leaves me lightheaded. I lean back trying to catch my swirling head and steady my racing pulse. As the adrenalin leaves my body, my hands and legs begin to shake and tears pool in my eyes.

"All right, man. Get it together. We're only a few minutes from your woman, and now would be a shitty time to show her what a pussy you really are," he tries to joke.

I let out a relieved laugh, forgetting all about the heartbreak that is taking place just a few miles behind us.

Chapter
FIVE

Brett

WHEN THE ambulance pulls into the emergency entrance to the hospital, I jump out and run, Dave hot on my heels.

"Slow down, Sharp. You know they aren't going to let you see her yet."

"I just need to know what's going on," I say just as I step up to the desk, pulling out my badge and flashing it to the nurse. "Sarah Sharp. She was brought in a few minutes ago after a car accident. Where is she?" I bark, more anxious than angry. I pinch the bridge of my nose impatiently as she starts typing on the computer.

"Sir, she doesn't have a room assigned yet. Give me a minute and I'll ask the doctor where she is."

"Forget it," I snap, motioning for her to buzz me through the doors into the emergency area.

She pauses, seemingly unsure if she should let such an obviously unstable man into the back. She looks over my shoulder at Dave for some sort of answer. He reluctantly motions for her to let us in.

Dave darts in front, stopping me by shoving his hand into my chest. "You have to calm down! I know you're upset, but no one is going to tell you where she is when you're acting like this. You're scaring the nurses. Even if you do find her, do you think her seeing you this crazy is going to help her? Take a deep breath and chill the hell out!"

He's right. I know he is. But a few minutes ago, I thought my wife was dead. I just need to lay my eyes on her to truly convince myself that she's okay. I take a deep breath and allow Dave to take the lead in asking doctors and nurses for Sarah's whereabouts.

Finally, a doctor informs us that she is awake and they are running a CT scan. He leads us into her room while we wait for her to return. In the corner, draped across a chair, is a plastic bag where they placed all her belongings. I reach inside and pull out her jewelry, trying to find something that will make me feel close to her right now. I just need something of hers to hold, something tangible to ground me. I decide on her wedding rings, but the first thing I pull out is a silly half of a heart that says, "Be Fri." I know that Manda has the other half, and when joined together, they say, "Best Friends." The girls wore these silly necklaces everywhere. While I would love to tell you they have had them since their middle school years, the truth is that they bought them last year while away on vacation together.

"Oh God, Manda." Suddenly, it hits me that she's gone. I fall back into the chair, tears springing from my eyes. "This isn't happening."

Dave leans against the doorjamb, allowing me just enough privacy without actually leaving me alone.

"Where's Caleb?" I manage to choke out.

"He's with the body. They got here a few minutes ago."

"I need to find him."

"No, you don't. You need to be here for Sarah when she gets back. There is nothing you can do for Jones right now."

Again, I know he is right, but that doesn't stop the stabbing pain in my heart at the very thought of what Caleb is feeling right now. I sink deeper into my chair, trying to calm my nerves by reminding myself that Sarah is alive and well. I'm the lucky one in this situation. That's a joke though. This hurts too damn bad to feel lucky about anything.

An hour later, they wheel in a battered woman who barely resembles my wife. I jump out of the chair, and the moment our eyes lock Sarah bursts into tears. I rush over, needing to hold her (although, by the way she looks, it's going to hurt like hell). As gently as I can, I lean over her bed, drawing her face into my neck.

"What happened, Brett? No one will tell me anything. They just keep telling me I was in a wreck, but I don't even remember being in a car. Everyone keeps staring at me, and I can't help but feel like I'm missing something here."

"Shhhh, it's okay, baby. I've got you now," I whisper into her blood-streaked hair. I realize this is the only comfort she has before I have to tell her all about the accident.

"SARAH, CALM down."

"Who was driving the fucking car, Brett? I swear to God, if you don't tell me, I'm going to get out of this bed and ask Caleb myself."

"You have to calm down or the doctors are going to kick me out."

"Who was driving the fucking car?" she screams with a guttural intensity that makes me know she will make good on her threat of asking Caleb. The last thing in the world she needs to do is talk to Manda's grieving fiancé.

"We don't know, beautiful. Witnesses at the restaurant said you were driving, but the first on scene said it was a redhead behind the wheel. You were both thrown from the car. We honestly don't know." I try to explain as gently as I can.

"Oh my God, I killed her. I killed Manda!" she yells, slapping her hand over her mouth and dropping her chin to her chest.

"Hey, stop! You didn't kill her. Even if you were driving, you did not kill Manda." I move closer, trying to find a part of her body to rub that isn't covered in a bruise. I fail miserably, instead deciding to just lean my forehead to hers.

"Get out," she whispers from behind her hands.

"I'm not going anywhere, baby."

"Get the fuck out of my room. I don't want to look at your face right now." Her tone is filled with hate, a strain in her voice that, in all of our seven years together, I have never heard her use.

I look around the room, clueless as to what to say or why her rage is aimed at me. Just as I decide that maybe leaving is the best option if she is going to be this upset, she starts hitting the nurse call button and screaming for help. I stand rooted to the ground as she unravels in front of me.

Kicking and screaming, she tries to get on her feet. She hysterically starts to remove her IV and other monitoring wires but only succeeds in reopening the gash on her arm. I watch, frozen, as blood drips down to the floor. Finally, I snap out of my stupor and grab her battered body to restrain her movements.

"Jesus, Sarah, what are you doing? Stop it. You're going to hurt yourself."

"Get your fucking hands off me. Get out!" She starts flailing her legs and banging her head against the back of the bed when I manage to pin the rest of her body down.

The nurses run in, pushing me out while they try to sedate her. I stand outside her room in a fog, replaying the last few minutes over and over in my head. Despite how long I stand there, I can't figure out what set her off like that. Did I say something, or is this just survivor's guilt running its course? I can't imagine what I could have said. She didn't even react that wildly when we told her Manda didn't make it.

A few minutes later, Dr. Lee walks out and stands directly in front of me. "She's asleep," he says, shoving his hands into the pockets of his scrubs.

"What the hell happened in there?"

"Mr. Sharp, I have no idea. You have to understand Sarah's body and brain have gone through a lot. She is grieving the loss of her friend while trying to heal herself. Sometimes the heart takes a little longer than the brain to heal."

I swear to God, the doctor is standing here giving me his own version of *Chicken Soup for the Soul* while talking about my wife, who just lost her goddamn mind because she didn't want to even look at my face.

"I'm sorry, but I'm going to need to request a second opinion from a doctor who actually attended medical school instead of the Kumbaya Academy of America. What the fuck just happened in there?" I yell, frustrated beyond all reason.

"I don't have any answers for you tonight, Mr. Sharp. Let's let Sarah sleep for a while, and we will reevaluate her physical and mental state when she wakes up. You can go back in now. She has been sedated and should be asleep for at least six hours. I'm sure, when she wakes up, she would like it if you were by her side. These kinds of things happen after traumatic events. Don't read too much into it."

"Right." I nod in absolute disbelief.

I have no idea what happened inside that room, but it's nothing that six hours of drug-induced sleep is going to fix. I saw the look in her eyes when she told me to leave. Those weren't the eyes of my loving wife, even if she was grief stricken. Those were the eyes of my worst enemy, and I have no idea how to even begin processing that.

Instead of going back into her room, I walk down the hall to see Caleb still sitting in the waiting room.

"Hey," I say as I stop in front of him.

"How is she?" he asks but never looks up at me.

Running my hands through my hair, I let out a loud sigh. "I don't know, man. Something's not right, but she'll live."

"Well, that must be nice."

"God, I'm so sorry. I wasn't thinking. I—"

"I can't leave," he interrupts, dropping his head into his hands and ignoring my apology.

"Come on, man. You need to go home. You want me to call one of the guys to give you a ride?"

"I can't leave. Not while Manda's still here."

"Caleb, Manda's not here anymore," I say as my voice catches at the admission.

"Yeah, she is. The body that I held in my arms every night is just downstairs. I know every single inch of that body. The tiny freckle on her chest. The birthmark on her hip. There is even a bruise on her left leg where she ran into the nightstand last night." He pauses, taking a deep breath, trying to fight back the inevitable tears. "The worst part is, I've been in that morgue so many times while investigating. I know it like the back of my hand, and I can't close my fucking eyes without imagining someone pulling Manda out of a drawer. I can't go home and leave her in there—alone." With that last word, he breaks down into gut-wrenching sobs.

I have no idea what to do in this situation. Since I'm a detective, you would think I would be used to the sadness that comes when someone experiences an unexpected loss. I've informed dozens of people that their loved ones were gone. I've witnessed death paralyze far bigger men than Caleb, yet I'm at a loss for what to do now. This just hits too close to home. It hurts to think that Manda is gone. When I think back to a few hours ago to when I thought it was my wife who lost her life, the panic nearly cripples me. I can't even begin to imagine how shattered he must be feeling. So I do the only thing that makes sense. I squat down in front of my heartbroken best friend and wrap him into a hug, holding him while he cries over the loss of his one love.

I'm glad I did, because seven months later, Caleb would return the favor.

Chapter Six

Brett

Four years later...

"WELL HELLO, officer."

"Hey, Jesse."

"The usual?" she asks, reaching over to grab the fruit and granola I eat every morning.

"You know it."

"Did you see the Packers won last night?" she asks over her shoulder while making my coffee.

"Yes," I reply, giving her nothing. I know she's just prodding me for a reaction.

"Remind me again which team you bet twenty dollars was going to win?" She saunters over, handing me my coffee, not releasing her hand even after I grab the cup. "Because as I recall, it wasn't the Packers." She smiles a stunning, white smile.

"All right, all right. You win! Here's your damn money," I say jokingly, slapping a twenty-dollar bill down on the counter, but walk away without paying for my coffee. "The least you can do is buy me breakfast if you are going to steal all my money," I say as I sit down at the table closest to the counter.

"Hey, you're the one who keeps betting against Green Bay. Seriously, Brett, they are six-and-oh. When are you going to learn? Though in light of my newly padded pockets, I will happily buy you breakfast."

"Gee, thanks. You are just too kind." My voice drips with sarcasm. Damn, I hate losing, but Jess walks away giggling, and I can't help but smile.

"What was that all about?" Caleb asks as he pulls up a chair across from me.

"Nothing. Just losing my life savings to the football shark posing as a barista," I say loud enough for Jesse to hear, earning me yet another laugh from behind the bar.

"So when are you going to get off your ass and ask her out?"

"Who? Jesse?"

"Yes, Jesse, you dumbass."

"Newsflash: I'm married!"

"You might still be married on paper, but you and I both know you haven't been married in a long time."

"I'm not talking about this right now." I wave my hand, trying to dismiss the topic.

"It's been four years."

"Wow. Thanks for the reminder, asshole. What would I ever do without your mathematical genius?"

"Whatever. You can be a dick all you want, but it only further proves my point that you need to get laid."

"Christ, Jones. Can you lower your voice?" I whisper-yell, annoyed that he just announced my sexual status, or lack thereof, to the entire coffee shop.

"Oh come on. Jesse is hot in that girl-next-door, sexy-librarian kind of way."

"Oh, Jesus." I shake my head while looking around to make sure no one is listening to our conversation. "Well guess what, Jones. You're not married. Feel free to ask her out yourself."

"Nah. I'm still seeing Lisa. She would lose her crazy monkey shit if she thought I was even looking at Jesse."

"You need to cut that one loose. Preferably before you end up chopped into tiny pieces, buried under her floorboards."

"She isn't that bad. Besides, when she isn't using it to bitch at me about not taking her out in public, her mouth is spectacular! Seriously, she does this thing with her hand and her mouth..." He pauses, making a hand motion and kissing sound like an Italian chef before saying, "Benissimo."

I groan at this ridiculous conversation.

I know, better than anyone that Caleb is still hung up on Manda. In the four years since the accident, he has never been in another relationship. Don't get me wrong. He's had plenty of women to warm his bed, but never anything more. Last weekend, I drove past the cemetery and saw him lying on her grave playing with a little black box. I have no idea what's inside, and no desire to ask him about it either. I just know that box meant something to him and Manda, because he never goes to visit her without it. I ran into his sister the other day, and she told me he still goes to "talk" to Manda three to four times a week. I worry about him, but I understand how he feels. I can't seem to move on either.

"Come on. We have a meeting in fifteen minutes, and I know you didn't finish your paperwork from last night." I slap him on the arm before heading to the door. "Thanks for breakfast, Jess," I say holding up my coffee.

"No prob. See ya tomorrow."

Jesse

UGH, WHY does he have to be so hot? I watch him stride out the door, and I can't help but check out his butt as he goes. I'm sorry, but the man has a good-looking rear end. I love when he wears his suit and tie for work, but my favorite is when he comes in on the weekend on his way home from the gym—all sexy and sweaty, with his shorts and tight T-shirt pulled across his perfectly muscled chest. I have got to stop checking him out every time he comes in here. One day, he is going to catch me, and I won't be able to control the eleven shades of red my face will turn.

Detective Brett Sharp is my idea of the perfect man. Tall, dark, handsome, nice dresser, employed, and since he is a cop, I'm assuming he doesn't have a criminal record. On second thought, he's *every woman's* perfect man. Which could be precisely why he doesn't seem to notice that I'm single, available, and very interested. I'm sure he probably exclusively dates six-foot-tall, blond runway models. He's never brought anyone in with him before or even ordered an extra coffee for someone possibly waiting at home.

I don't just sit around staring at him though. I'm going to make this dream a reality. I have been devising a plan for months to ask him out. Women can ask men out these days...right? Girl power or something like that. Well, one day, I overheard him talking to Caleb about how excited he was for the upcoming Bears season. So I called my brother and asked if he could get me tickets. His company has a big box they use to impress clients. The only problem is, I know absolutely nothing about football. If you want to know the honest truth, when I asked my brother for Bears tickets, I thought they were for a hockey game.

My plan is to pretend I just happen to have an extra ticket and ask Brett if he would like to go with me. The game is this weekend, so I'm really cutting it close. I would have asked him sooner, but I needed to make it believable that I would actually attend a game. I've spent weeks of studying nothing but football in order to pull off this ruse.

Two weeks ago, I asked my brother his prediction on the game so I could make a flirty little bet. Luckily my brother isn't as stupid as I thought he was when we were growing up, and I've won both bets I've made with Brett. The forty bucks I've won only proves that this is an awesome plan. Tomorrow is the day I'm going to launch my stealth operation. I'm so nervous that I may need to come to work drunk in order to actually follow through, but regardless, I'm doing it.

"That is one fine piece of man," I hear from behind me as I try to stop thinking about his butt.

"Yeah he is," I say a little too dreamy.

"So when is the big day?" Kara asks.

Kara Reed is my best friend. She got me this job at Nell's Coffee House six months ago when the family I was a nanny for moved from Chicago to Colorado. We first met in college three years ago when she was forced to attend the same "picking your major" seminar given by our advisor. We were surrounded by ten high school seniors. Kara and I were not new to college, but we had been in school for five years and kept changing our major, thus never actually earning a degree. Apparently his seminar wasn't very effective because, after eight years in college, neither one of us has settled on a major. Unlike Kara, I did actually collect enough credits in one area to apply towards a diploma. I just didn't see a future for myself utilizing a bowling alley management degree, so the very next day I reenrolled.

"Tomorrow," I reply to Kara's question.

"I can't believe you are actually going on a date with that man!" she yells, jumping up and down.

"Well he hasn't said yes yet, but what man could turn down box seats to the Bears game? He'll probably be so excited by the invitation that he snatches me up and kisses me on the spot," I joke while picking up a rag to wipe down the counter.

"Can you imagine? Oh my God, I'm so jealous I actually want to punch you right now!"

"Well, if you are going to get violent, make sure you aim below the waist. I don't want to look like Rocky Balboa for our date on Sunday!" I wink, walking over to refill the chocolate muffins.

"You don't think he will see you below the waist?" She raises a questioning eyebrow.

"Jesus, Kara, I'm not a slut!"

"Okay, so if Detective Nice Ass tries to get you into bed on Sunday, you would turn him down?

"Yes!" I lie, knowing there isn't much I would turn down from Brett.

Smiling to myself at the very idea of feeling his hard body, I let out a little laugh.

"Liar!" Kara screams, causing the three customers we have in the shop to pause and look.

"Would you shut up?" I whisper, trying to get her to calm down.

"Jess is going to get some. Jess is going to get some," she quietly taunts.

"It's official. My best friend is twelve." I pretend to be exasperated, but inside, I'm screaming like a twelve-year-old too.

THE NEXT morning, I got to work thirty minutes early. I couldn't sleep last night, so I took the extra time this morning to actually iron my white button-down work shirt. I wish I could have worn something a little more flattering today. Instead, I'm stuck in this horrible uniform, waiting for God's gift to women to walk in so I can ask him out.

I must have cleaned the tables by the windows a hundred times, hoping to catch a glimpse of Brett before he arrives. I'm a nervous wreck, knowing that in only a few minutes, I will have to go against every rule my mother ever taught me about being a girl. I have to ask a guy out on a date. Before I can obsess about it any longer, he comes sexily strolling in, walking directly to my register.

"Well hello, officer," I tease the same way I always do. Only today, I am so nervous that I have to fight to keep my voice from cracking.

"Hey, Jess." He smiles, revealing his perfectly straight white teeth. Seriously, this man is beautiful.

What the heck am I doing thinking he would want to go out with a short girl who has far too many curves? I do have good boobs though. Darn it! I should have worn a push-up bra today, attracting his attention to the good curves and away from the bad. Ugh, this outfit is bad enough, but a push-up bra totally would have helped.

"Um...Jess?" he asks, snapping me out of my thoughts.

"Oh sorry...what can I get you today?"

"Same old, same old," he replies in a bored voice.

Oh God. Here we go! Come on, Jesse. The worst he can do is say no, effectively stomping on your heart and crushing your dreams. Okay, that might be a little dramatic. You can always quit your job, move to Oklahoma, and marry a rodeo cowboy. Those still exist, right? Crap! Just take a deep breath and spit it out. He's only the hottest guy you have ever met. No biggy. Do it, Jesse! Just ask him to the game!

"So, Brett, my, um, brother gave me two tickets to the Bears game this Sunday. I was wondering if maybe you would, uh, want to go?" I finally stumble out.

"Oh, um, this Sunday?" He stands with his hand frozen behind him reaching for his wallet.

"Yeah, I know it's short notice, but he just gave them to me last night. His company has some sort of box or something. But it's no big deal if you can't go. I'm sure you already have plans or have to work or something..."

"He can go," I hear Caleb say as he walks up behind Brett. "I'd be happy to cover for him at work, ya know...or something," he finishes, winking at Brett and grabbing one of the free apples off the counter before walking over to a table.

Chapter
SEVEN

Brett

OH. MY. Damn. It's official. I am going to kill Caleb Jones. I hear being a cop in jail is tough, but for the stunt he just pulled, the satisfaction of killing him with my bare hands would be completely worth it.

"Oh, okay, great. Thanks, Caleb!" she shouts to my ex-best friend.

He smiles, taking a bite of his apple and waving his hand in a way that signals 'no problem.'

I silently hope he chokes.

"Well, the game starts at noon, so we should probably just meet at the stadium around eleven? I've heard they have food in the box, but maybe we can stop and grab an early dinner after the game. I don't know. Whatever you want to do is fine." She rambles on faster than I have ever heard anyone talk.

"Sure. Sounds good."

"Okay then. See you Sunday," she says then disappears into the back office.

I crack my neck before walking over and sitting in the chair across from Caleb.

"What the fuck was that?" I ask, leaning closer with every word.

"That was me helping you out."

"What exactly were you helping me out with? Because it looks like you just set me up on a date. With Jess. Shit, man." I lean back in my chair, trying to figure a way out of this mess.

"You've got to move on, Sharp."

"Oh, because you have done such a fabulous job of moving on from Manda? You're telling me to move on when you go sit on her grave every other night. Well guess what, Jones? You need to move on too. Manda is gone. Where's your date?" I know it's a low blow, but I keep talking. "Christ,

I'm married. I can't go on a date."

"You know what? Fuck you, Brett. Yeah, I go see Manda, but that's because I'm the only one who visits her. When was the last time you went to her grave? Or what about Casey or even Sarah." He spits her name out of his mouth like it burns on his tongue.

"Don't make this about Sarah." I momentarily calm, knowing this is about to go downhill, and fast.

"But isn't this about Sarah? Isn't it always about fucking Sarah?

"Shut up, Caleb."

"It was supposed to be Sarah."

"God damn it! Shut up!" I scream, jumping to my feet, causing everyone to stare over at us. But their curious looks are far better than the physical and emotional war that is about to take place between Caleb and me...again.

Four years earlier...

THREE DAYS after the accident, Amanda Baker was laid to rest. Sarah was still in the hospital, but I left her with her parents so I could be with my best friend as he buried the love of his life. Because Caleb and Manda were not married, her parents made all of the funeral arrangements. They buried her in some dreadful frilly outfit that she would have despised. But then again, what do you bury someone as extraordinary as Regina Phalange in? Caleb just couldn't accept these details.

"What is she wearing? Oh God, she's going to kill me if I let her parents bury her in that shit." Leaning forward, he rubs his hands quickly across his face. "Seriously, do you think I can destroy those clothes before they close the casket?" He tries to joke but instead falls to his ass on the cold concrete outside the church. "Why is she in a casket? I need to wake up from this because I can't do it anymore."

The loss in his voice is alarming. I knew he would be devastated by Manda's death. I wasn't expecting this level of sheer hollowness in his voice though.

"Come on. We need to get back inside." I try to offer a distraction from his quickly approaching breakdown.

"I miss her," he says into his hands, offering nothing else.

"I know, man. I know."

"Oh, you think you know? You think you know how this feels?" He stands up, wiping his tears on the back of his sleeve. "Last I checked, Sarah is breathing right now."

"You know I didn't mean it like that. We all miss Manda."

"You think you know how I feel, huh?" he asks again, this time accompanied with a manic laugh. "You have no idea what I'm feeling. Sarah lived, and Manda gets to be forgotten—six feet under."

"No one is going to forget her," I say quietly, not wanting to match his level of intensity.

"Have you told Sarah that she killed her yet?"

"We don't know for sure who was driving."

"Oh yeah? Your wife is almost six feet tall. My...fiancée," he spits out the poisonous word, "was only five foot two. Unless Manda was wearing eight-inch stilts, the position of the driver's seat proves it was Sarah driving that car!" Caleb steps up into my face, issuing some sort of challenge.

I stand stock-still, refusing to take his bait. He's broken, pissed off, and looking for a fight.

"You need to back up. I am not your enemy, and I'm not going to fight you today. If you just need someone to punch, have at it." I toss my hands out to the side, opening myself up to the physical blows of the man I would do anything for. "Do your worst. But if you are looking for someone to hit you back so you can forget all this shit for a few minutes, you are barking up the wrong tree."

He then deals a verbal assault that makes me change my mind.

"It should be Sarah lying in that casket."

"Excuse me?"

"It should be fucking Sarah lying in there! How much did she have to drink that night?"

"She wasn't drunk. Don't take this there."

"Her blood alcohol may have showed she was sober, but how long did they wait to run that? She was a cop's wife!" he screams, stepping up, bumping his chest with mine. "You know the only reason they didn't check her blood for alcohol the minute she was brought in is because she was yours."

"She wasn't drunk, Caleb. The witnesses on the scene said it was a redhead driving. So maybe Manda didn't adjust the seat or maybe it shifted on impact—I don't know. But this conversation is over."

But Caleb was just getting started. "She killed Manda and she killed me. I don't know what happened that night, but Sarah may as well have pulled a trigger aimed directly at my head, because she has destroyed my fucking life. I've heard all about her little freak-outs every day, but it still sounds like that crazy-ass bitch got nowhere near the punishment she deserves after killing Manda."

I didn't pause or even think twice. I threw everything I had into punching my grieving best friend. He only staggered backwards a few steps before releasing his own fists on me.

It took five grown men to pull us apart. I left a few minutes later, not bothering to stay for the rest of the funeral. In the end, I knocked out two of his teeth and he blackened my left eye, shattering my cheek bone. We didn't speak after that day for six and a half months. And if it meant forgetting the day he came back into my life, I'd be willing to go another six hundred years without seeing Caleb Jones.

Chapter
EIGHT

Jesse

OH MY God, I'm going to hyperventilate. Deep breaths, Jesse. Deep breaths. That was quite possibly the most embarrassing moment of my life. What the heck was I thinking? Of course Brett isn't interested in me. Crap. Why didn't I realize this sooner? No, instead, I stood there looking like a fool, asking him out in front of the whole coffee shop. I somehow convinced myself that he actually wanted to be with me. First, the football game, but then we'd eventually fall madly in love and make ridiculously tall, green-eyed babies together. Jesus, how could I be so stupid? The look on his face when I asked him to the game was mortifying. It was only made worse when Caleb so obviously threw him under the bus. Oh my God, I'm the proverbial bus! Deep breaths. Deep breaths.

"Stop freaking out, Jess," I hear Kara say as she walks into the back office, leaving the register completely unmanned.

"Did you see his face? How am I ever going to face him again? This was such a mistake. Why didn't you talk me out of that?"

"You just surprised him. That's all. He probably didn't even know you were interested." She tries to reassure me, but it's doing nothing to stop the growing knot in my stomach.

"I've been flirting with him for weeks. How the heck could he not know I was interested?" I whisper-yell, very aware that the object of my embarrassment is just around the corner. The last thing I need to do is make myself look like even more of an idiot in front of him.

"He's a man. Men are stupid," she says as if it should explain all of life's great mysteries.

"How am I going to get out of this? He obviously doesn't want to go.

Crap!" I start pacing the small office, nibbling on my thumbnail and trying to devise yet another plan. Probably not the greatest idea considering my first plan is what got me into this mess in the first place.

"You just need to pull up your big girl panties, meet him at the game, and knock him off his feet with how awesome you are. He may be a little hesitant about going now, but after he gets one look at you at the game on Sunday, you won't be able to get rid of him."

"Crap, crap, crap! This is bad. Oh, this is so bad," I say, pacing. "Wait, what do you mean after he gets one look at me? This isn't exactly a blind date."

"Yeah, but that man has only ever seen you in a white button-down shirt, black pants, and a God-awful apron. Not exactly the outfit that men fantasize about," she says as she runs her eyes down my body.

Trying to cut her off before she gets any crazy ideas, I blurt, "I'm not raiding your closet. You dress like a hooker." I barely finish my sentence when I hear a loud commotion out front.

"What the hell was that?" Kara asks as we both take off to investigate.

When we get out front, I see Brett standing with a finger pointed at Caleb and his chair tipped over behind him. His face is so distorted in anger that I almost didn't recognize him. He's usually so laid back, but this man towering over the table is anything but mellow.

"Shut up, Jones. Shut. Up."

Caleb sits in silence, fearlessly staring him directly in the eye.

I'm trying to figure out what the heck is going on when suddenly it hits me. This has to be about our date. Great. As if I weren't embarrassed enough. Now I have to talk him off the edge of killing someone at the very idea of going out with me.

"This should be fun," I say to myself before rushing over to the guys. "You don't have to go on Sunday. I shouldn't have asked. I'm sorry," I hurry out when I get to the table.

"Not now, Jess!" Brett snaps, never taking his eyes off his partner.

"No, really. It's okay. I'll ask Kara to go to the game or something. Actually, why don't I just give you the tickets and you can take whoever you want. It doesn't have to be me."

The stare down continues, neither man moving a muscle.

"Not. Fucking. Now. Jess," Brett repeats very slowly, pausing between each word.

In order for me to explain to you why this one sentence caused me to lose my mind, you should probably know something about me first. I don't cuss. Cussing is for ignorant people with a limited vocabulary. I think it's rude, crass, and pointless. My mom doesn't cuss, and with the way my brother babies me, it's scandalous when he says "darn it" in front of me. I don't hate people who cuss though. Kara says the F-word sometimes, but it's never aimed at me. It's usually when she drops something or sees a hot guy walk by the coffee shop window. She certainly never snaps it at me in an angry tone while having a hot-guy staring competition. So, being that this is the first time anyone has ever talked to me like that, I believe I should be given a free pass on the freak-out that follows.

"Excuse me? Did you just say the F-word to me?" I say in disbelief and anger. "What the heck did I do that was so wrong? I thought it would be fun to go to the game together, but I'm sorry I even asked you now. So you can just calm down and wipe the crazy ogre look off your face. I officially withdraw my offer. I'm sure you have better things to do and other people to swear at. You are a jerk, Brett Sharp. No, you are more than a jerk. You're a...whatever. You're something worse than a jerk!" I finish on a shout, only pausing to catch my breath. Then I turn very matter-of-factly and look at Caleb. "Caleb, any chance you are free on Sunday? I happen to have two tickets to the Bears game."

Why I asked him, I have no idea. It just came out of my mouth. Maybe it was some hopeful plan to make Brett so jealous that he realizes he can't live without me, thus sweeping me off my feet and heading straight to the wedding chapel. I've seen that work a few times in the movies. It could totally happen here.

"He'd love to," Brett says before slamming his coffee down on the table and walking out the door.

Well, okay then. I assume since Brett just fixed me up on a date with his best friend that I should officially accept that he doesn't want to go out with me. Which reminds me—I need to Google the quickest route to Oklahoma.

"I'm sorry about that," I hear Caleb say as he slumps in his chair. "Damn it," he grits through his teeth while grabbing the back of his neck.

"No need to apologize. I shouldn't have asked him out. It's obvious he isn't interested. I-I um… I don't know." I lean down, picking up the chair Brett knocked over. I sit down, feeling defeated.

"That wasn't about you, Jess." I look up and see Caleb's pale face. He looks like a lost child.

"Are you okay?" I know I probably shouldn't have asked. It's really none of my business, but seeing this man so torn up makes me need to help him though. It's not my fault I was born a nurturer.

"Yeah. No. Shit!" He sighs, obviously overwhelmed by the simple question.

"What was that all about?"

"That was me being a dick. Ugh, he should have punched me."

"What? No he shouldn't have! I'm sorry. There is nothing you could have said that would have warranted being hit by your best friend."

"I told him his wife was supposed to die."

"Oh, well in that case, you deserve to be kicked too. Wait." His words suddenly hit me. "Brett's married?"

"No, no. He's not married," he says, shaking his head.

"You just said 'his wife.' Is he divorced?"

"No. Look, I shouldn't have said anything. He doesn't…" He pauses, looking off to the side. "I mean, he's not...um… Well, he's not currently in a relationship." He slides his eyes back over to mine.

Something's not right with this answer. So I squint my eyes questioningly, letting him know that I don't believe him. But my glare doesn't seem to faze him in the least. He just stares back, and I think I may even detect a twitch at corner of his mouth as if he is trying to force back a smile.

"All right, I need to go apologize to him. He'll meet you at the game on Sunday."

"No way! I am not volunteering to embarrass myself again. Just tell him I said to forget all about it, and I'll see you guys next time you come in."

"He's interested, Jess."

"Yeah, okay, sure. I'm not buying it." I roll my eyes.

"It's been a while since Brett has been out with anyone. You have to be patient with him."

"How is that even possible? The man is hot." I slap my hands over my mouth as my face turns red at my slip-up. But if Caleb notices my embarrassment, he doesn't mention it. I'm starting to think I'm obsessing over the wrong cop.

"Let's just say he's had a lot on his plate recently."

"Well, after the way he reacted today, I'm pretty sure he doesn't want to add me to that plate."

"Brett insists that we meet at Nell's tiny coffee shop, which is several miles out of our way, every Monday through Thursday. He might be a shit cook, but I'm pretty sure he could manage to make his own fruit and granola every morning. Or at the very least, buy it from a shop closer to the station."

"Um, okay," I say, confused by his change in conversation.

"Do you want to know why we only come in Monday through Thursday, Jesse?"

I nod, sucking in a deep breath through my nose, suddenly aware of where he is going with this.

He smiles at me, motions me to lean closer as if he is going to tell me a secret, and whispers into my ear, "Because you don't work Fridays." I sit frozen as he stands and heads to the door. "We may not be here tomorrow or

Thursday, but he will definitely be at the game on Sunday. He's interested, Jess. He just doesn't know what to do with that yet."

And with that, he strides out the door.

Chapter NINE

Brett

I CAN'T believe that I let Caleb talk me into this. After I showed my ass at the coffee shop on Tuesday, I've been avoiding Jesse all together. The vending machine at the station has been my only source of breakfast for the last two days. I polished off my supply of protein bars early, leaving me starving in the mornings. I tried to send Caleb to get me my usual fruit and granola from Nell's, but he refused. He then proceeded to lecture me for forty-five minutes about how I needed to "man up and face Jesse." For a best friend, he is completely worthless. It's all his fault I'm even in this situation to begin with.

I just need to tell Jesse that I'm married, let her down easy, and try to pretend this whole thing never happened. She's a sweet girl, but I am in no position to be dating right now. Besides, Jesse seems a bit young and naïve. She is, after all, twenty-six years old and still working in a coffee house. Don't get me wrong. I'm not one to judge anyone based on their career choices as long as it's what you want to be doing and not just what you have gotten stuck doing. Jesse doesn't strike me as the type of girl who wants to serve muffins for the rest of her life though, so her working at Nell's is confusing.

Above and beyond all of that—I'm still married. That alone is like the blinking neon sign of reasons why I shouldn't be on a date with another woman. I've been broken for a long time now. I don't have anything to offer someone else. *Shit.*

Why did I show today? It would have been easier if I'd just stayed home and apologized for standing her up after the fact.

I wait in front of the stadium, scrolling through Facebook on my cell phone. I swear, if one more of my high school friends posts pictures of their lunch, kids, or dogs, I'm going on a spree reporting everyone as spam. I can't even turn on my phone anymore without being reminded about exactly what my life is lacking. Good food, kids, and a dog!

Just as I end my internal rant, I hear a loud whistle behind me. Turning to look, I see a smoking-hot brunette headed my way. My eyes start on her high-heeled knee-high boots before sliding up her sculpted legs and over her perfectly curved waist. I freeze as I watch her full breasts bounce with each step. My dick instantly gets hard, and I quickly shove my hands in my pockets, trying to rearrange myself before anyone notices. Just what I don't need is for Jesse to show up right now, forcing me to explain why I'm playing pocket pool while staring at some woman walking down the street. That would probably go over about as well as when I cussed at her the other day.

"Hey." I hear as I tear my eyes away from the woman's breasts just in time to see her stop in front of me. I glance up and into a pair of familiar golden-brown eyes.

"Jesse? Jesus, what are you wearing?

"A dress," she answers shortly.

"Are you sure? Because it looks like you left half of it at home," I respond as my eyes rake over the short black sweater dress with a plunging V in the front, revealing most of her tits.

"Don't you dare start with me about this outfit. It took me six hours to convince Kara that I didn't need to wear a red corset and black leather miniskirt here today. So this"—she motions her hands over her luscious body—"was our compromise." Did she just say red corset and black leather miniskirt? Oh yeah, my dick heard her loud and clear.

I try to clear my throat and shake my head to stop myself from staring at her chest again, but damn, she is showing a ton of skin. Until today, I didn't even know Jess had cleavage. I bet I could hook the tip of my finger into her top and stroke her nipple without anyone even noticing. I groan at the thought as she stands looking at me questionably.

"Are you okay? You're making weird noises. Do you want me to go?"

And just like that, my shit life comes crashing back down. I remember that I won't be stroking anyone's nipples tonight unless my left hand happens to wander to my own during a much-needed solo cold shower.

"Yeah, I'm fine. Sorry. No, I don't want you to go."

"Well, can we go inside then? It's getting cold, and Kara said it would be an insult to cover this dress up with a coat so I had to freeze my butt off the whole way here."

"Lead the way." I give her my best uncomfortable smile and motion for her to walk ahead.

I follow her into the stadium as my gaze once again travels down her body. This time, it meets a perfectly round ass that causes my cock to stir back to life. Shit! Caleb's right. I have got to get laid.

We walk into the stadium and up to the VIP box. Normally, I would have been stoked to have such amazing seats, but I know the conversation we are about to have will probably leave me watching the second half from the sports bar around the corner. As we are settling into our seats, our personal waitress stops by to take our drink order.

"I'll take whatever lager you have on draft, please."

"Just make that two," she says as I turn my head in shock.

"Beer, huh? And not even a light beer?"

"Are you saying I need a light beer? Brett, are you calling me fat?"

"No, not at all! It's just that most women drink light beer. I just assumed..." As I trail off, she lets out the most adorable giggle while smiling at my discomfort.

"I was just kidding. Guys always get so squirmy about a woman's weight. But to answer your question, yeah, I'm a beer girl. I'm sad to report that I'm a lightweight. I blame it on my size. Kara says I haven't ever built up a proper tolerance. She once created a daily drinking schedule for me, requiring me to drink an increasing number of shots every night. I did it for the first day and puked on her bed. After that, she deemed me a lost cause, and the schedule was gone the next morning."

We both laugh, falling into our normal casual comfort with each other.

The waitress returns with our drinks a few minutes later, and when I try to pay her, she tells us that all the drinks are free. Damn, I'm really going to hate leaving here after we have this conversation.

"I'm sorry," I start, wanting to get this over with as quickly as possible.

"For what?"

"The other day at Nell's. I was out of line. I had no right to talk to you like that."

"You're right. You didn't, but I accept your apology. Thank you."

She takes a sip of her beer, turning back to the game just in time to see kickoff. Wow, that was easy. Sarah would have given me absolute hell for hours before finally accepting my apology. Jesse, however, just sits there sipping her beer, peering out of the box's glass windows as the Bears move the ball down the field. No sign of residual anger—whatsoever. Interesting. Okay, I guess that part is over. Now on to the hard stuff.

"Jesse." I touch her arm to catch her attention.

When she smiles over at me, clearly enjoying the game, I'm floored by how breathtaking she looks. I'm not going to lie—I've noticed that Jesse is attractive. I am a man after all. She's actually really cute. So tiny and innocent. That's not usually the type I go for, but since I met her a few months ago at Nell's, I've felt some sort of draw to her. It wasn't a sexual attraction though. The way I feel about her is a lot like the way you would feel for your best friend's little sister. You know, the one who makes you laugh and you enjoy spending time with, but you tend to think of her as one of the guys more than a woman you would like to see naked. Right now, though, in this tight-ass dress with her long chestnut-brown hair draped across her shoulders, her legs crossed and showing off those incredible boots and faintly tan thighs, there is no way anyone could describe her as anything but sexy. So before I have a chance to do something stupid, like bending her over the seat and fucking her through the second quarter, I spit out the words that are sure to drive her away.

"I'm married."

Jesse

DAMN! I KNOW I said that I don't curse, but if the moment your date tells you he's actually married isn't the perfect moment to start, I'm not sure when is.

I stare at him for a second before gathering the courage to respond. "Can you excuse me for a minute? I need to use the ladies' room." *So I can burst into tears in private.* Thankfully, I don't say the last part out loud.

"No. Wait, please."

"I'll be right back. I just drank that beer too fast," I lie as I quickly rise to my feet, ready to all but run out of the box.

"Jess, wait!" Brett shouts as he follows me.

I don't slow down. I have to get away for a few minutes to collect my thoughts—and more importantly, my emotions.

How did I not see this coming? Caleb said something the other day about Brett's wife, but I just assumed he was talking about an ex-wife. He specifically told me that Brett was not in a relationship. Last I checked, a marriage definitely counts as a relationship.

"Wait!" I hear as Brett grabs my arm and turns me to face him. I know I'm on the verge of tears, so I avoid his eyes by digging through my purse.

"That's really sweet, but I'll be right back. You don't have walk me to the bathroom." I laugh unconvincingly, even to my own ears.

"Just give me a chance to explain."

"You don't have to explain anything to me," I say quietly, dropping my hands to my side, abandoning the imaginary mission in my purse. Not sure I can look him in the eyes without opening the flood gates, I just stare down at my shoes.

"Yes, I do. I feel like I did something that accidentally led you on. That wasn't my intention at all. I think you're a great girl. It's just that my life is such a mess."

"Don't apologize. You didn't do anything wrong." I take a deep breath, finally raising my gaze to meet his.

I have no reason to be hurt right now, but that doesn't change the fact that I am. I need to remind myself that he didn't ask me out on this so-called date. There is no one to blame for this fiasco except myself—and maybe Kara for forcing me out of the house in this ridiculous dress. Fantastic! I'm dressed like a slut and out on a date with a married man. This just keeps getting better and better. I can't even aim my frustration at Brett. He got sucked into this the same way I did. I asked him to the game, and his best friend made him come. His stupid, lying best friend.

"I'm going to kill Caleb Jones," I mumble under my breath.

"Huh?" He looks confused as I start to get mad.

"Nothing. I just hope you aren't overly attached to Caleb, because I plan to strangle him next time I see him."

"I know that feeling all too well. What did good ole' Detective Jones do to you?" he laughs.

"He told me you weren't in a relationship," I sigh. "Look, I'm really sorry about all this. This was supposed to be fun, and now it's weird. Can we just forget all this happened? Maybe go back in time to last week before I made a total fool of myself? I had no idea you were married. You don't wear a ring, so I just assumed. Anyway...you can go if you want. I'm sure your wife isn't happy about you being out with another woman right now."

"What else did Caleb tell you?" Brett says in a tone so harsh it could wound, causing me to take a step backwards.

"Nothing. Nothing at all!" I backtrack, trying to figure out the reason behind his sudden mood swing.

Replaying the conversation in my head, I come up empty-handed. I have no idea what has set him off this time. It's probably best if I just cut my losses and leave now. He is already going to think I'm a fool, but the least I can do is not confirm it.

"Okay, well thanks for meeting me here today to explain things. I'm going to head out, but feel free to go back to the box and finish the rest of the game. Please apologize to your wife for me. I really am sorry." I turn to walk away, only to feel him grab my arm, pulling me to a stop again.

"Stop running away and just let me talk for a minute. Okay?"

Sweet Brett is back, so rather than open my mouth again, I just nod, fearful of the angry ogre's return.

"I lost my wife in car accident four years ago."

"Oh God, Brett, that's horrible." I gasp, stunned by his announcement. He doesn't even pause to acknowledge my comment.

"I've never tried to move on from Sarah. I honestly don't even know where to start. So yes, I'm married, but Caleb didn't lie to you. I'm not in a relationship." He finishes and simply shrugs as if he didn't just tell me something so heartbreakingly tragic.

"I'm so sorry." I'm not sure why I'm apologizing, but that's what people do when faced with a death.

"It's okay. You should know that the accident is a really sensitive subject for me and Caleb. Hence the fight last week at Nell's. His fiancée was killed in the car that night."

I suck in a breath and throw my hands up to cover my mouth. Tears spring to my eyes. I can't stop myself from reaching forward and wrapping my arms around Brett's waist. He doesn't immediately respond to my unexpected show of affection.

"Are you crying?" he asks uncomfortably. I don't care though. This man needs a hug.

"That's really sad. You both lost your wives in the same accident. It makes my heart hurt. I can't imagine how that must have felt. God, I am so sorry."

He finally wraps his thick arms around me. One hand grabs the back of my head, pulling it to rest on his chest. As the tears run down my face, I feel him ever-so-slightly chuckle.

I crane my head all the way back to see his face filled with humor. "Are you laughing at me?"

"Well, when I imagined how this conversation would go, it sure didn't end with you crying over my broken heart. So yes, I am," he says, looking down but not releasing me.

I rest my head back against his hard chest, sniffling and trying to stop my tears. "We should call Caleb. I need to give him a hug too," I say, causing him to burst into loud laughter.

"I think it's in Caleb's best interest not to see you dressed like this while trying to hug him. So how about you just give him his tomorrow?"

Not completely understanding but not ready to step out of his warm arms, I stay silent.

Chapter
TEN

Brett

OF ALL the ways this conversation could have gone, I never once expected Jesse to cry over Sarah. Yet here she stands, curled into my chest, trying to dry her eyes. I wasn't entirely sure I was going to tell her about the accident at all. But she kept trying to run away from me, and I couldn't stand the idea of her being so upset. This tiny woman brings out something in me that makes me need to protect her. It killed me that she might be hurting. The fact that I was the reason for her pain just magnified the guilt tenfold. This whole screwed-up situation is my fault anyway.

There is no way she could have known about Sarah. I haven't worn a ring in years.

Three years earlier...

COVERED IN my wife's blood, I pace the hospital's hallways. I've become entirely too familiar with these halls over the last seven months. Between all of Sarah's doctor appointments and her two—now three—attempts to end her life, I know every inch of this hospital. I wish I felt lost here. I wish I didn't belong. But here I stand, staring at the same cheesy picture of a laughing couple captioned with a lame message about getting health screenings to extend your future. I've seen this picture a million times before. However, today, it cuts me to the quick.

I could get every test this hospital has to offer and it wouldn't extend my future with Sarah. No. That was stolen from me. As I try to imagine a future without her, my body physically responds to the panic I feel in my heart. I *break into a sweat and I'm forced to prop one hand against the wall to keep my legs under me. I'm not ready to let her go. After today's gruesome show, I'm not sure I have a choice anymore.*

"Detective Sharp?" I hear the nurse say from beside me as I try to calm myself.

"Hey, Debra." I look over at the middle-aged woman I've met several times over the last few months.

"I brought you these scrubs. I figured you would want to get out of those clothes. I also put some soap and shampoo into the shower in room 228 so you can clean up a bit."

"Thanks, but I'm going to wait a few minutes. I need to get an update on Sarah first."

"She's going to be okay. I overheard the doctors talking about admitting her for a psych evaluation again, but for the most part, they have closed up all of her wounds. I think they are just wanting to talk to her for a minute before they allow you in to see her."

"Well, that's good news." I breathe out a sigh of relief before going back to my selfish pity party.

"Just go take a shower. I'll come get you as soon as the doctors will let you see her."

"Okay. I'll be quick," I say as she looks at me sadly, her eyes filled with sympathy.

I walk into room 228 to find it decorated the exact same way as the room the day of the accident. I felt so hopeful that day, knowing that Sarah was alive. We had cheated death. Literally. Today, only seven months later, I feel nothing but defeat.

I make my way over to the shower and turn it to the hottest setting. I need to feel something. The burn of hot water might be enough to help me wash away this day along with the blood of the love of my life. I look down at my hands, dried blood still settled deep into my knuckles. I did my best to clean up with the rag the paramedic gave me, but I wasn't worried about my appearance as I watched them load Sarah into an ambulance—yet again.

While staring at my hands, I notice my wedding ring caked in dried blood. The symbolism of this moment is overwhelming, even for a simple man like myself. Spinning it around a few times, I try to scratch off the chipping brown with my fingernail. I'm too afraid to take it off. Even just for a minute to clean it. In a lot of ways, this ring is the only thing left of my marriage.

Sarah never put her rings back on after the accident. The nurses had been forced to cut them off when she was brought in that night. I took them the very next day to have them repaired. I even went so far as to pay the rush fee to ensure that they would be ready before she was released from the hos-

pital. However, when I handed them back to her, excited to see her reaction, she just gave me a weak smile and placed them on her nightstand. The next day, she moved them to her jewelry box—the very same place they still sit today.

Reaching down, I slide the platinum band off my finger. I hold it up, looking closely at every bump and blemish. I never take my ring off, and it shows in its tattered condition. Inside, it is still shiny silver. Clean and unscratched. My breath catches and my chest tightens when I see the inscription.

No take backs. Love always, Danika.

"FUCK!" I scream, throwing the ring across the tiny bathroom. I step back against the wall, sliding down until my ass finds the cold hospital tile. I know I need to get up, but I don't have the strength to face this God-awful situation anymore. Sitting with my legs bent, elbows touching my knees, I drop my head only to see that silver blood-covered reminder resting directly between my feet. After begrudgingly picking it back up, I move to the sink. Using a damp washcloth, I begin to scrub away the stains. Once it has been returned to its normal worn state, I tuck it into a small pocket in my wallet. Wearing it would just feel like a lie.

SNAPPING BACK to the present, I realize that I've been standing here holding Jess for several minutes now. She hasn't tried to move away either, and if it's even possible, I think she snuggled closer. Her hands are wrapped around my waist, my left hand holding her head to my chest and my right wrapped around her shoulders. Despite my mind screaming at me to let her go for fear of leading her on again, I can't seem to convince my body to release her. It's been a really long time since I've been physically connected to another person like this. I have to admit that it feels amazing. And even more confusing, it feels right.

I step back and reluctantly let my arms fall away. "Did you mean it?" I ask.

"Mean what?"

"About starting over and pretending none of this ever happened?"

"Yeah. I'd love to forget all about today."

"Done," I say before turning and walking away.

She stands stunned by my sudden departure. Looping around a beer cart, I head back in her direction.

"Jesse? What are you doing here? Wow, you look fantastic."

"Um, just watching the game." She timidly smiles, deciding to play along.

"I'm glad I ran into you, I could use a friend to watch the game with. I hate coming to these things alone."

"Really? I happen to have an extra seat in my brother's corporate box if you'd like to join me?"

"A box! Hell yeah, I'd like to join you. I hear they have free beer," I say, causing the small smile to spread across her face.

"Well, then why are we still standing here when there is free alcohol to be consumed just around the corner?" she asks as she starts back toward our seats.

Before we get more than a few steps away, I lean over and whisper, "Friends?" in her ear.

"Friends. Thank you," she whispers back.

I reply with nothing but a wink.

AFTER LEAVING the game, Jesse and I decided to walk around for a bit. Neither one of us was quite ready to go home. Jesse is incredible. She is nothing like the person I thought she would be. Sure, she was a little timid and shy sometimes, but in other moments, she would put me in my place without a second thought. It's an extraordinary combination of innocent and sassy. I love a woman who can challenge me, and it wasn't until today that I started to see that quality in her. She absolutely fascinated me. We talked about everything. She told hilarious stories about her morning spent shooting down Kara's "whore-riffic" clothing choices, and I told her about my crazy sisters and all my nieces and nephews. We had the perfect afternoon. As the game came to an end, I suggested a walk as an excuse to keep her close for a few minutes longer.

"Can we go in here?" Jesse asks, stopping in front of a random bowling alley.

"You want to go bowling?" I ask, surprised by her choice. I figured we would grab an early dinner at a quiet restaurant, but it seems everything about Jesse is surprising today.

"Yeah, why not?"

"You're wearing a dress."

"So?"

"I don't know. I didn't think a dress was ideal bowling attire, but if you want to bowl, then I'm game."

"Do you play?"

"Of course! Care to make a little wager?" I reach out and grab the door but pause before opening it.

"Sure! What do you have in mind? I could stand a little extra spending cash this week," she answers with a smirk.

"Not this time, little lady." I make a show of tipping my pretend cowboy hat. "How about we bet one favor, to be decided upon later."

"What kind of favor?" she asks skeptically.

"Anything. Who knows? This time next week, you could be doing my laundry."

"Oh, those kind of favors! Okay! I'm in!" She actually squeals in excitement, making me a little fearful of her enthusiasm.

But as she jumps around clapping her hands, I can't help but laugh too. *God, she's beautiful!* And that thought had nothing to do with the boob that almost popped out of her dress. Before I can stop myself, I place a hand on her lower back to guide her inside and lean over to breathe in her scent.

"Let's do this, gorgeous."

We walk into the bowling alley to see it packed for a Sunday evening. Dozens of eyes seem to breeze over me, landing directly on Jesse, sweeping her from head to toe. A few of the men openly stare at her chest as she walks. I swear one of them even has the balls to adjust his pants when we passed by his lane! I have to fight the urge not to rip off whatever pencil dick he was grabbing while drooling over my woman…I mean, a woman half his age. I know right now that this is going to be a short excursion.

I'm not about to sit and watch men ogle Jesse as she bowls in this dress. Because of my stupid "just friends" conversation earlier, I can't even wrap an arm around her waist, claiming her for everyone to see. One game—then we are out of here. We'll go to a nice restaurant or maybe find a nice empty bar where we can hang out.

As we reach the counter, I pull out my wallet to pay, but Jesse stops me first.

"I'll pay for myself. Friends, remember?" She looks up at me with a smile on her face.

"Right. Friends." I remind myself again. "Don't worry. I've got this. You get to buy the first pitcher."

"Deal." She heads off towards the bar, followed by the eyes of every man in the building.

"Wait, what size shoe do you wear?"

"Five and a half."

"Holy shit. Is that even an adult size?"

"Laugh it up now, big boy," she says, glancing around at the crowd and then tugging her dress down an inch.

I can't help but mumble, "That's what she said," under my breath as I watch her tight little ass head towards the bar.

I pick out a ball with great attention to detail. I have big plans for this bet with Jesse. I haven't bowled in several years, so I'm going to need all the help I can get tonight. I find the perfect twelve-pound ball and move to lane three. While she is still stuck at the bar, I assign our names, Tiny and Hulk. It seems fitting. When she sees our new nicknames on the monitors, she laughs. It makes it worth every penny of the twenty bucks I tipped the lane attendant to get us set up. It has been years since I last played. I didn't want to still be stumbling with the video scoreboard when she came back.

"This must be a fancy bowling alley. They have a ton of beer on tap. Here, take this. I need to grab some balls."

I groan at the endless number of jokes I could make from that last statement.

"Are you all right?" she asks for the third time today.

I bite my lip and nod, enjoying the view of her walking away again.

I sit down and try to squeeze my feet into the rented shoes. No one ever carries a men's size fifteen, so I have to squeeze into a fourteen. I'll have a million blisters tomorrow. I stand up, looking down at Jesse's shoes lined up with mine, and shake my head at the enormous size difference. It's ridiculous. When she walks up carrying twelve- and fourteen-pound balls, all that ridiculousness is forgotten.

"Oh my God, those balls are huge!"

"Thanks. I'm quite fond of them." She winks in my direction.

"No, I mean, seriously. They're huge! You do know you have to repeatedly throw them down the lane?"

"Golly gee, Brett. Is that how bowling works?" She feigns ignorance.

"Yeah, smartass. It is! Are you sure you don't want me to ask for one of the special kiddie balls?"

"All right, keep it up! When you're washing my car with a toothbrush tomorrow, I hope you remember this moment."

"What moment?" I ask as she bends over, picking up a ball that is nearly half her size.

"This one." She turns and throws it down the lane with a skilled ease.

I watch, my mouth gaping open, as I see Jesse's ball spin to the left, teetering on the edge of the gutter before veering back to the right and slamming into the center. Pins go flying on impact and not a single one is left standing. I close my eyes, shaking my head in utter disbelief that this woman has managed to hustle me yet again.

Luckily, I open them just in time to catch Jesse doing the world's worst 1980's robot dance in celebration. Okay, so maybe losing to Jesse won't be so bad after all.

Chapter
ELEVEN

Brett

"HOW DID I get so drunk?" Jesse slurs as we finish up the fifth and final game of bowling.

Despite my earlier plans to leave as quickly as possible, we've been here for hours. I got over my jealousy issues with guys staring at Jesse. Okay maybe "getting over it" is a bit of a stretch, but I did find a solution. I couldn't let Jesse know I was trying to publicly claim her, but I sure as hell could let these disgusting men know who she was leaving with. Just call me Captain Loophole.

For the first two games, I picked a random gawking man and stared him down while Jesse took her turn. The more beer I drank, the more aggressive my glare became. Eventually, I'm sure they all got the idea. They also probably thought I was insane, but the obvious drooling stopped.

"Well, it could have been the pitcher of beer that you drank by yourself during game four," I answer, watching her flop down onto one of the hard plastic chairs.

"I did not! You drank some too."

"Yes. I drank two sips. Then you stole my beer and chugged it after getting your billionth strike of the day. Are you going to tell me where you learned to play like that?"

"No, it's embarrassing. I'm pretty sure I'm maxed out on humiliation for the year after today."

"Oh, come on. It can't be that bad," I sweetly plead.

"Yes, it can. Don't you try it! Even with those sad puppy-dog eyes, I'm still not telling you where I learned my crazy bowling skills." She laughs, throwing a balled-up napkin at me.

"Shall we make a little bet?" I ask, twirling my thumbs like an evil madman.

"Aren't you sick of losing yet?" She laughs so hard at her own joke that she almost rolls out of the chair. Her reaction alone is enough to make me laugh right along with her.

This girl is drunk...and beautiful. And drunk. And sexy as hell. And drunk. And so very fuckable. Did I mention drunk? She isn't in the danger zone where she is going to be hating her very existence tomorrow. She's in that loose-lipped, say-things-that-will-make-you-cringe-the-next-day stage. I would be lying if I said I'm not enjoying the hell out of seeing her in this state.

Jesse always seems to have a filter when she talks to me. It's as if she analyzes every word in her mind twelve times before actually spitting out a sentence. Since she started drinking, she hasn't stopped talking. She has officially made the leap from best friend's little sister to woman I want to fuck. Jesus, what the hell am I saying? Am I drunk too?

"So is that a yes or no to the bet?" I smile, glancing down and catch a glimpse of her peaked, chilled nipples. "You cold, Jess?" I ask, nodding down at her nipples noticeably showing thorough her skimpy excuse for a dress.

I watch her eyes travel down her own body and her cheeks immediately redden. Oh shit! I really am drunk! Why the fuck would I say that to her? Better yet, when the hell did I lose my filter tonight? Oh God, what else have I said to her without thinking? I frantically try to think of a way to moonwalk out of this conversation. She's uncomfortable, and I'm mortified. We both know it too. It's written all over our faces, but in our drunken states, neither one of us can think of anything to say.

Jesse

OH MY goodness, he just noticed my nipples. Crap. Crap. Crap! What do I even say to that? Brett has been flirting all night. I've caught him checking out my backside on more than one occasion. It took me two full games to learn to stop jumping up and down after every strike. I swear, he literally growled one time after I got back-to-back strikes. We agreed to be friends. At least, I thought we had. The eyes that have been watching me all night are not those of a friend. They are the eyes of a man who wants to rip your clothes off and have his dirty way with you. It may be the abundance of alcohol I've consumed talking, but I'd probably let Brett Sharp do anything he wanted to me right now.

Thankfully, he assumes my hardened nipples are from a chill, but the truth is, I'm turned on like nobody's business. For five games, I have watched his biceps flex every time he picks up the ball. I've watched his firm butt as he saunters up to the lane. Then, I've watched his back muscles ripple through his tight black t-shirt as he hurls the ball towards the pins. It's been a spectacular show of hotness and completely worth the unchallenging game.

Finally, after staring at his pecks for a few more seconds, I am able to form a coherent thought.

"One frame. Winner gets to ask one question. Loser is required to answer."

"Deal!" he answers a little too quickly. Especially for a man who has thrown over half his balls in the gutter tonight.

"Ladies first." He motions for me to start.

I walk forward, blowing on my fingers. I need to sober up. I don't think he would be willing to wait a few hours for that to happen though. Unfortunately, it seems the alcohol wins out. In my first turn, I overshoot to the left and only knock over two pins. I try to clear my head as I ready myself for my next turn. I look back and see him leaning back with his legs spread open, one hand thrown around the back of the empty seat next to him, the other resting on his muscular thigh. I lose any sense of focus that the beer hadn't already stolen. Darn his tight jeans! They leave nothing to the imagination. I do mean *absolutely nothing*. I can very obviously see something in the outline in his pants. I know exactly which side he has tucked his privates tonight. That is more than enough to cause me to throw my next ball directly into the gutter.

Slowly clapping his hands, he rises from his seat and stops a few feet in front of me.

"That wasn't very good." He shakes his head and pouts his delicious lips the way a toddler would. It's a good look for him, and if it weren't for the fact that he's making fun of me, I would have enjoyed the heck out of it.

"Shut up. I'm almost certain my two pins can hold up against your gutter balls."

"Oh, ye of little faith. Watch and learn, Jess. Watch and learn," he taunts, throwing the only decent ball he has bowled all day.

"Noooooo!" I scream—probably a little too dramatically—as he turns with a smile bigger than I thought humanly possible. I stand stunned as I watch his ball slam into four pins on the right side.

"Well, that was fun." He winks. "So, pretty lady, tell me where you learned how to bowl?"

"College," I answer shortly, twirling one of my long brown locks around my finger.

"Oh no! You have to give me more than that. I just destroyed you in that frame. You owe me."

"Seriously? That was the only frame of the entire day you beat me. And honestly, I'm not sure you should be bragging about four pins. I saw the five-year-old in lane twelve knock down at least six," I snap at him.

"Oh my God! You're a sore loser. You have to know how adorable that is." He steps forward, now standing only inches away from me.

"I'm not adorable."

"Sweet Jess, you are definitely adorable." He reaches out and grabs my hips, pulling me into his perfectly muscled body.

"You're drunk?" I ask.

"I'm a little buzzed." Leaning down to reach my ear, he whispers, "Tell me where you learned to bowl, gorgeous."

I have no idea what he's doing, but it's messing with my head. A few hours ago, he was preaching to me about being friends, but now he's holding my body and whispering sexy words into my ear. If my nipples weren't already hard before, they are now. When I'm finally able to catch my breath, I look up into his twinkling green eyes, searching for some sort of answer. I need to know what's going on before I do something stupid to embarrass myself again.

"What are you doing, Brett?"

"I'm trying to find out where you learned to bowl," he repeats as he rakes his teeth over my earlobe, sending a shiver down my entire body. I drop my forehead to his chest and mumble the words I've tried to avoid today.

"You're so hot," I blurt.

"Funny, I was thinking the same thing about you," he chuckles. Reaching around my hips, he places a hand just above my butt then a gentle kiss on my collarbone.

"What are you doing?" I ask one last time before losing all resolve to question this any longer. I reach around his waist and return his embrace.

"I have no idea, but I don't want to stop."

"You don't have to."

We stand holding each other in the middle of a busy bowling alley, oblivious to all the noise surrounding us. Here in his arms, there is nothing but silence. My drunken mind is swirling at this turn of events. I'm not about to stop this though. It feels right. It might be my only chance to enjoy something like this with Brett. Tomorrow, I can blame it on all on the beer. Hey, he can't think I'm any crazier than he probably already does.

Without another thought, I rise to my tiptoes and place a gentle kiss to his lips. Just as I'm about to pull away, he grabs the back of my head and thrusts his tongue into my mouth. I instantly match his movements. This kiss is even better than I ever imagined. And sad as it may sound, I have imagined kissing Brett Sharp since the first moment I laid eyes on him.

Our tongues dance together in a perfect, smooth rhythm. His hands are in my hair, and mine are wrapped around his waist. I boldly pull him tighter against my body, forcing my chest against his, causing him to groan in appreciation. Suddenly, I snap out of my Brett trance, becoming very aware that we are making out in the middle of a bowling alley. I reluctantly pull away, taking a step back out of his reach and looking down at the ground.

"Babe, don't do that. I need to see your beautiful eyes," he says, lifting my chin, forcing me to look back up.

"Sorry."

"What are you apologizing for?"

"For kissing you. For looking down. For kicking your butt in bowling today. I don't know. Everything?"

"First of all, stop apologizing. I believe I kissed you just now, and for your information, it was amazing." I blush at his words. "Secondly, you didn't kick my butt in bowling today. You wiped the floor with me. Is there anything else you are good at that I should steer clear from? I would really like to avoid this kind of humiliation again." Reaching out, he places one hand on my face and rubs his thumb back and forth over my pink cheek.

"You're gorgeous, Jess. I'm not just talking about this sexy dress either. Even in that hideous apron Nell makes you wear, you're beautiful." With his words, my cheeks flash bright red. I know because I feel them warm up. It's confirmed when Brett leans down, kissing where his thumb was just stroking me. "And the fact that you respond like this, babe, I have to warn you, only makes you hotter."

I stare at him, blinking rapidly, not sure how to respond.

"You want to get out of here?"

"No," I answer, pulling my head out of the sexual fog.

"No?"

"I'm not ready to go home yet," I respond a little too honestly, sounding probably a little too needy.

"Okay, what if we head back to my place? I'll cook you some dinner."

"Oh, okay. Sure," I say, shocked by his offer and my immediate excitement about going back to his house.

"When I say, 'cook you some dinner,' I really mean I'll use my phone to order takeout." He smirks.

"I don't like pizza," I respond awkwardly. Darn alcohol. This comment lightens our serious mood and causes Brett to laugh.

"Okay, beautiful. I have a whole drawer filled with menus. You can pick out whatever you want."

"Perfect."

Chapter
TWELVE

Brett

IT'S OFFICIAL. I've lost my fucking mind. I'm honestly clueless as to why I would ask Jesse back to my apartment. What did I expect? For her to fall into my bed naked, legs open, waiting for me to ravage her body? No. She panicked when I kissed her. I can't even begin to fathom how she would react if she knew all the ways I have imagined having sex with her today. I couldn't seem to help myself though. This girl makes my heart swell almost as much as my dick. I know I gave her the whole 'just friends' talk earlier. I really tried, but I couldn't keep my hands off her any longer.

Jesse does things to me. She makes me feel like myself again for the first time since I lost Sarah. I had no idea how good it could feel to not be consumed in self-pity. For those three hours at the bowling alley, I forgot that I was supposed to be miserable. I forgot that my life had been ripped out from under my feet. I didn't think about anything except getting hustled by a petite brunette who says darn, heck, and crap. I forgot it all. And that alone is a magical feat.

The most shocking of it all was that I didn't worry about Sarah once. I should probably feel guilty about that, but honestly, I don't. I obsess over Sarah daily. Is she taking her medications correctly? Is she happy? What will she want for dinner on Thursday? Did she remember to pay her power bill? The list goes on and on. Sarah isn't helpless by any means, but I worry that she'll need me and I won't be there for her. It's not like she would ever call me if she needed something though. Sarah has called me exactly one time since the accident. She wanted to know if I knew of a good divorce attorney.

Four years earlier...

"DAMN IT, Sarah. You are not making these decisions four weeks after almost dying!" I scream at her over the phone while leaving work.

"I'm not doing this anymore. I want to go home."

"Sarah, you are home."

"No, I'm not. This is your house. I don't belong here anymore."

"Fine. You want to move back to Savannah? Let's go. I'm sure I can find a job down there."

"I'm not going anywhere with you, Brett. Let me go!" She starts crying—like she does so often these days.

"Baby, please. Let's go back to that counselor. I'll do whatever you want. Tell me how to fix this."

"There is no fixing this! I don't love you. I haven't loved you in a long time. Even before the accident. Things just weren't right."

"What the fuck are you talking about?" This is the first time she has ever mentioned us falling apart before the accident.

"I asked Manda about a divorce attorney weeks before the wreck."

"Oh really? Because last month you were talking about saving up money for a trip to renew our vows in a silly Las Vegas drive-thru chapel. Now you're trying to tell me you actually wanted a divorce?"

I know she's lying. Sarah never would have asked for a divorce without my feeling it coming months in advance. She was never able to hide her emotions inside. I would have known if things weren't right in our relationship.

"Damn it. Fuck you! I want a divorce. I want to move out. You can't hold me captive in this house. I'm not your fucking prisoner. Get it through your head. I don't want to be with you anymore!"

"Yeah, I think I gathered that when you started this conversation by asking about a divorce attorney."

"See! This is why I hate you. You're a prick. You talk down to me and treat me like a child."

I just sigh, at a loss for words. "How about tomorrow we go visit Manda's grave? I think it would do you some good to finally go say goodbye. You're harboring a lot of guilt and taking it out on me."

"What the fuck! Did you just go all Dr. Phil on me? I'm not going to a grave to visit my best friend. She isn't there!" She shrieks so loudly that, I have to pull the phone away from my ear.

"Jesus. Can you please just calm down? I'm on my way home. We can talk when I get there."

"I'm leaving, and you can't stop me."

This time I'm the one yelling. "I love you! I'm going to do everything in my fucking power to stop you. Damn it. You're my wife!"

"No, I'm not," she whispers, ending the call.

It's not like her to give up so quickly. She's been different since the accident. She's always withdrawn and moody these days, but deep inside, she is still the same Sarah. Never in her life has she given up without a fight. We can argue for hours over pizza toppings, so her just hanging up worries me. I flip on my lights and speed home, grossly abusing my resources as an officer of the law, but something isn't right.

I arrive at the house five minutes later. After parking my car in the driveway, I rush inside to find her tucked into the couch crying. I'm relieved that she's okay. Then I'm saddened when I realize this is what "okay" looks like for Sarah these days. She's curled into a ball, knees pulled to her chest with her arms wrapped around them. She looks so lost, and it kills me that I can't help her. I want to be her rock and help her recover from this, but she won't let me. I need to be able to fix this for her. For me. I miss my wife, even though she is sitting directly in front of me. I can't reach out and hold her like I so badly long to. She won't even let me touch her anymore.

Before the accident, Sarah used to hate being alone. Now, she stays locked away in her own head for days at a time. By the look on her face, I can tell that's where she's at right now. Instead of trying to force a conversation that I know will lead nowhere, I decide to give her some space. Maybe, in a little while, she'll have calmed down enough to talk. I won't hold my breath though.

Disheartened, I walk past her, heading to the bathroom for a shower. As I enter the bathroom door, I freeze at the scene I find in front of me. Littered across the floor is every pill bottle we had in the house. Each one open. Lids thrown haphazardly across the room. All empty.

"SARAH!" I scream, running from the bathroom to find her no longer sitting on the couch.

The front door is wide open, warm air blowing in. I frantically rush outside, expecting to have to chase her down. When I jump off the front porch, not even bothering with the steps, I catch sight of her lying facedown in the grass.

"Sarah!" I scream, hoping for a response.

My legs won't carry me fast enough to what I fear is her lifeless body. It feels like it's taken me an hour just to travel the ten steps over to her. I quickly scoop her into my arms and sink down onto the grass with her limp body in my lap.

"Sweetheart, wake up. I need you to talk to me. Please, Sarah!" I shake her, trying to rouse her back to consciousness.

"Let me go," she softly mumbles.

I breathe out a sigh of relief that it's not too late. I still have a chance to fight to save her life, even if she won't do it for herself.

"Did you take them all?" I ask, pulling my phone out of my inside jacket pocket.

"I don't want to feel like this anymore. Let me go, Brett," she murmurs before closing her eyes and dropping her head to my chest.

"Never, baby. Never," I whisper, kissing her on the forehead. "Yes, this is Detective Brett Sharp, I need an ambulance at my house immediately. 1921 Hunters Court. My wife just overdosed."

"GOT IT!" I hear Jesse say while digging through my drawer-o-menus.

I walk over, wrapping her in my arms, needing her to help me forget all over again.

"Your hair smells good." I breathe in a rich floral scent and rest my chin on the top of her head. The image of innocent Jesse Addison bathing in flowers pops into my head—although my mental picture is more *American Beauty* than a G-rated fabric softener commercial.

"I bet it smells more like a stinky bowling alley right now."

"Yeah, you're right. You should really try a shower sometime," I joke as she pinches my stomach. "Did you decide on a place?"

"Mmmhmm," she nods.

"Good. Just order me whatever and I'll grab some beers out of the fridge."

"I can't order your food!" she shouts.

"Um, why not?" I ask, confused by her sudden freak-out.

"I don't even know what you like to eat."

"Jess, you make me breakfast almost every morning."

"Yes, but I doubt the Chinese restaurant carries fruit and granola."

"I eat at that restaurant three times a week. There is not a dish on that menu that I won't eat."

"You eat takeout three times a week?" she asks my back as I walk into the kitchen to grab our drinks.

"No. I eat takeout seven nights a week. I don't cook."

"Wow. That's just sad. Maybe I can cook you dinner one night this week—" She abruptly stops and her cheeks heat to pink when she realizes that she just asked me on another date.

"I'd love that." I smile, twisting off the top and handing her a beer.

She rushes a relieved sigh as she lifts the bottle to her mouth, taking a large sip.

I'm not sure if it's still the alcohol, but the idea of a date with Jesse doesn't scare me anymore. That's unusual because the very idea of dating usually sends me into some sort of panic mode. But after having spent the day with her, I like the idea of seeing her again. I'm nowhere near ready to jump into a relationship, so I need to be very careful here. Jesse doesn't strike me as the type of girl who can stand casually dating. The last thing I want to do is lead her on, and eventually break her heart when I can't be what she needs.

"Can we talk for a minute?" I grab her hand, pulling her over to the couch.

When she tries to sit beside me, I surprise her by dragging her up into my lap. She sits stiffly for a few seconds before relaxing into me.

"So, as you can tell, the whole 'just friends' thing didn't work out very well." She quietly giggles as I continue. "I'm sorry about everything earlier today. I haven't been on a date in years, and I'm sure I behaved like an ass."

"I understand," she says quietly, staring down at her beer.

"Hey, look at me." I gently coax her eyes back to mine. "Why do you always do that?"

"Do what?" she asks, looking up.

"One minute, you're laughing and giving me shit about my lack of bowling skills. The next, you're staring at your feet and acting like a neglected puppy."

"I don't know. This is just weird..." She trails off without finishing the thought.

"Come on. Talk to me."

"I don't know what to say."

"Tell me what's going on inside that gorgeous head of yours."

"I have no idea what's going on here. A few days ago, I asked you to the game and you obviously didn't want to go. I can only guess Caleb forced you to show up today. Then you tell me you're married, only to later tell me that you lost your wife. Then"—her voice rises a little more with each sentence—"you spend the entire afternoon flirting and staring at my boobs, eventually kissing me and inviting me back to your apartment for dinner. I have no idea when your next mood swing is going to hit. I'll be honest—if you weren't so darn sexy, I would not still be sitting here right now." She pauses before jumping off my lap and screaming, "Crap, I have got to stop drinking and telling you how hot you are!" She finishes by chugging the rest of her beer.

I can't stop the roar of laughter that escapes my mouth.

"Great! Now you're laughing at me. I need to go." She puts the empty bottle down and turns to the door.

"Whoa. Hang on there. Not so fast." I grab her from behind, pulling her back down onto my lap. "I'm sorry. I know I've been a jerk over the last few days. You're not the only one getting whiplash from my sudden changes. I don't know what's going on either. So, what if I tell you a few things I do know?

"I know that I had a blast with you today. I can't remember the last time I've laughed this much. And before you try to cut me off, I'm not laughing at you. I will *never* laugh at you. I think you're cute"—she tries to interrupt me, but I just keep going—"and sexy. I like you. When I'm with you, I feel alive again. I'm not sure what to do with that though. I am in no position to jump into a relationship. Jess, I haven't been with any woman but my wife in twelve years. I don't even know how to start something like this. All I can tell you is that I want to spend more time with you."

"You know, that's what Caleb told me. He told me you were interested, but you just didn't know what to do with that yet."

"Well, finally Caleb was right about something."

"Are you going to go back to the angry ogre tomorrow?" she asks shyly.

"Since I have absolutely no clue what you are talking about, I'm going to say no. But! I reserve the right to change my answer when you explain to me what exactly the angry ogre is." I smile to make sure she knows that I'm kidding. I think she gets my sense of humor, but I can't afford for her to take a joke the wrong way after the way I've acted recently.

"I'll point him out if he ever shows back up. Can we order some food now? I just chugged that beer, and it's going straight to my head."

"Absolutely! But only if you promise to never stop calling me hot." I wink and stand. Still holding her around the waist, I slide her down my body until her feet touch the ground.

"Not laughing at me, huh?" she asks, raising one eyebrow.

"Oh, I'm not laughing at all. I'm thinking about bringing you beer to work every day. You do great things for my self-confidence when you're drinking." This comment earns me a light slap on the arm.

"Just what you need is a bigger ego."

"Jess, you wound me! I bet if you reach up here and give me another one of those kisses, I'd be willing to forgive you."

"In your dreams, big boy. And don't you dare say, 'That's what she said,' again. You are not nearly as quiet as you think you are."

This time, we both bust out laughing. Seconds later, I silence her with my lips.

AFTER ORDERING Chinese food, we spend the rest of night curled up on the couch, pretending to be watching old movies but really making out like teenagers. We were able to keep things on a very PG level. Jesse apparently isn't the type of girl to go any further on a first date. She didn't say this to me, but when I trailed kisses down her chest toward her exposed cleavage, she literally jumped off the couch, making an excuse about using the restroom. After that, I kept my hands and mouth focused above the neck. There is tons of stuff above the neck. I licked her neck and sucked on her ears. She made the cutest moans and sighs when I would let my teeth graze across her skin. I laughed once because I swear she almost got off.

Jesse gave just as well as she took. She did amazing things with her tongue that only served to get me excited to see what else she could do with that mouth.

At almost midnight, she announces that it's time for her to leave.

"Brett, I've got to go home," she says, pulling away from our heated kiss.

"Why?" I follow her forward trying to continue the kiss.

I'm not ready for her to leave yet. After our rough start earlier, this day has been perfect. It's not very often that I feel this way, so I'm reluctant to let her go, leaving me to face my shitty life again. I want to ask her to stay the night, but I remind myself that this is only our first date. Besides, I have been hard for almost ten hours straight. Asking her to stay is not in anyone's best interest. She seems to have loosened up around me over the last few hours, but I'm relatively sure that waking up to me unconsciously dry humping her in the middle of the night would not go over well.

"It's late, and we both have to work in the morning," she says, squirming out of my arms and picking up her boots.

"All right. If you insist. You're still cooking me dinner this week, right?"

"Of course. How about Thursday? I have class Tuesday and Wednesday afternoon, so it won't give me enough time to prepare the food."

"Oh, um…Thursdays are bad for me." Of course she would pick the one night that I see Sarah every week.

And just like that, all of the guilt and responsibilities come crashing back down on my shoulders. It was one night of freedom, but it was just long enough to remind me how great it is to feel like myself again. All good things must come to an end, right? The universe has never been kind to me. I should have predicted that Jesse's only free night would be a Thursday.

"Okay, how about Friday?" She smiles.

"Yeah, that works," I say in somber tone.

"What's going on? You just flipped on me again. You went from funny and sweet to sad and distant."

I let out a loud breath, feeling bad that I keep doing this to her. "No, I'm fine. I just don't want to wait until Friday to see you again." It's the truth, but not the answer to her question. "Can I take you out to dinner tomorrow night?"

"Are you sure you don't want to wait the mandatory three days between dates?" she asks. I have no idea if she is kidding or not, because she looks worried about my answer.

"Yes, I'm positive I don't want to wait three days. If you decide to avoid me for three days, just to play hard to get, I will remind you that I'm a detective and I know where you work," I joke, trying to lighten the mood again.

"Brett, I've asked you out twice now. It's safe to assume that I don't understand the concept of playing hard to get."

"Good. Then it's decided. Dinner tomorrow night. I'll pick you up at seven. Oh and, Jess, please don't let Kara dress you this time. I won't be able to handle seeing you dressed like that again without being able to touch every inch of that sexy body."

And just like that, my mission is accomplished. Her eyes go wide and her cheeks turn pink as she sucks in a shocked breath. She looks so damn adorable that it causes my dick to get hard all over again.

Chapter
THIRTEEN

Jesse

AFTER BRETT dropped me off last night, I stayed awake for hours, replaying every moment of our date to Kara. I ran directly into her room, jumping on her bed to wake her up. I needed someone to help me analyze this whole situation. Kara isn't exactly the best person at giving advice about guys though. It usually ends with her saying, "Then just buy crotch-less panties, and he will be eating out of your hand in no time." Although, at midnight on a Sunday, I didn't have any other options.

"Holy shizzle, Jesse, you twisted tongues with half of the Sexy Detective Duo!" she shrieks when I get to the kiss at the bowling alley.

"*I know!* It was such a good kiss too! His lips were so soft, but still in command. He didn't drool on me at all either. He even had good breath after drinking a zillion beers. God, it was amazing. Then, we lay on the couch for hours, just making out. He does this thing with his teeth on my neck—"

She interrupts hopping to her feet and jumping on the bed, mimicking me a few minutes earlier. "Oh my God, Officer Hot Ass is a freak in the bed!"

"No he's not!"

"Wait! Do you have firsthand knowledge of his bedroom behavior?" she asks, raising her eyebrows questioningly.

"No!"

"Damn it! Why not? I'm dying to know what that man is hiding under those slacks."

"Jesus, Kara. Even if I did sleep with him, you will never know what he is hiding in his pants."

"What? I thought we were best friends? Best friends tell each everything."

"We are, but that's a bit much, don't you think?"

"Fine. I don't need details, but you have to at least compare it to a vegetable it resembles. I bet it's a large zucchini." She smiles, staring off into space, lost in her imagination. "If it will make you more comfortable, I'll start. That guy Jason I was seeing last week was a small carrot. I'm talking the baby ones you dip in ranch dressing." She winks as I stare at her with my lips curled in disgust.

"That's terrible, Kara."

"You're telling me. I wasn't even sure they made condoms that tiny."

"Oh God, this conversation is over. I need to go to bed. We have to be up in five hours."

"You didn't finish telling me about the rest of the date," she whines as I walk out of her room.

"I'm guessing it went really well since he's taking me to dinner tomorrow night," I say, walking down the hall in to my own room.

Just as I start to close my door, I hear her scream, "Shut. Up."

THE NEXT morning, I can't contain the huge smile on my face as the guys walk into Nell's. However, Brett looks anything but happy. If it weren't for Caleb behind him with the world's biggest grin, I would have immediately run to hide in the back office. My mind comes up blank as I try to figure out what could have ticked him off in the eight hours since he dropped me off. So instead, I go straight to the point.

"What's wrong?" I ask as my heart begins to race. Maybe he regrets last night? We had been drinking, but by the time he drove me home and he gave me that toe-curling kiss outside my door, we were both very sober.

"Nothing," he answers shortly as Caleb slaps him on the back of the head.

"Stop being a dick. You're scaring the poor girl," Caleb scolds before looking back at me and saying, "Jesse, you little minx," and flashing me his million-watt smile.

"What are you talking about?" I ask, completely confused, but nonetheless embarrassed.

"Just ignore him," Brett jumps in, looking only slightly less furious than he did a few minutes before.

"Um, okay. What can I get you guys today?"

"You serving up any hickies today?" Caleb asks, laughing as Brett punches him hard in the arm.

Obviously something is going on, and I'm the only one in the dark. "What the heck are you guys talking about?" I ask irritated.

"Oh man, Brett. Jesse said heck! She must be serious," Caleb mocks me.

Before I can even respond to his rude comment, I look over at Brett to see that the angry ogre has returned.

"Make fun of her again, asshole, and I will punch you in the face."

"Whoa, calm down there, buddy!" Caleb laughs, surrendering with his hands in the air. "Although, I have to say, I am digging this caveman thing you have going on right now."

"I am too. It's hot," Kara chimes in from behind me, her eyes glued to Brett.

By this point, I'm beyond annoyed. Nothing is making sense, and no one is stopping to fill me in. I don't know why Brett could possibly be mad at me. He was kissing me breathless only a few hours ago. Now, his best friend is making fun of me, Brett is threatening physical violence in my honor, and my best friend is staring at him like she wants to throw him down to service his vegetable right here in the middle of the shop. It's a madhouse!

"I'll be right back," I say, quickly escaping into the back office. I shut the door and flop down in the chair to gather my thoughts. It only lasts for about thirty seconds before I hear Brett around the corner.

"Jesse?"

"Crap," I say to myself as footsteps approach the office door.

"Jess?"

"Come in. It's open."

"You okay?" he asks, locking his incredible green eyes on mine.

"Yeah," I answer simply.

"Why are you hiding back here then?"

"I'm not hiding."

"Yeah, you are. Don't lie. Your eyes got big and you sprinted back here like a cat with its tail on fire." He crooks a smile.

"Oh my God, don't say that! I love cats. I don't need that visual in my head."

"You like cats?" he asks surprised.

"Of course I like cats! Well, not all cats. The black ones kind of scare me. When I was a kid, I watched this scary movie made by Disney, and it had the scariest black cat in it. So I only really like the white ones." I ramble, not exactly clear why we are having this conversation.

"The Watcher in the Woods!" he shouts.

"Yes! You saw that movie too?"

"Scared the shit out of me. I slept with the lights on for... Well I still sleep with the lights on." He smiles a brilliant, white toothy grin before getting serious again. "Now, why are you hiding?"

"Fine. I'm hiding. You guys were all talking out there. You were noticeably mad at me. Caleb was making fun of me. And Kara was drooling over you. I had no idea what the heck was going on. So I came back here to see if I could catch my breath and sort things out."

"I'm not mad at you, babe. I was annoyed with Caleb. He has been giving me shit all morning. We were at the gym working out and he noticed this." He loosens his tie and pulls his collar over to the side, revealing a quarter-sized bright red hickey.

"Oh my God! Did I do that?" I ask in horror, covering my gaping mouth with my hands.

"Well, you were the only animal attacking my neck last night, so I'm assuming this little beauty is your handiwork."

"I am *so* sorry. I had no idea I was leaving a mark—"

"It's no big deal. If I'm being honest, when I saw it in the mirror this morning, it made me hot remembering last night." He winks and uses my hands to pull me to my feet. "I had a lot of fun, Jess, so I don't want to hear any apologies out of that sexy little mouth of yours."

I try to change the topic, slightly embarrassed by his dirty compliment. "You were really mad at Caleb out there. I know I told you I'd point out when he returned, and that was definitely an appearance from the angry ogre."

"I promised you last night that I would never laugh at you. I'll be damned if I'm going to stand by and listen to anyone else ever do it either. You're already too skittish around me. I want you to feel comfortable and safe with me, gorgeous. If Caleb said or did anything to make you feel otherwise, I would be more than happy to remind him to watch his manners."

"You threatened to punch him in the face. That is hardly a friendly reminder."

"If he made fun of you again, I would have done it, too."

"Um, please don't punch him in the face because he picks on me."

"No promises, but I'll try to restrain myself for you." He gives a small chuckle before pulling me tight into a hug. "So where do you want to go tonight?" he asks after a few moments of holding me in silence.

"Oh, I don't care. Anything is fine."

"As I recall, you don't like pizza?"

"No, I don't."

"Then don't tell me 'anything is fine,'" he half-scolds while pulling me even tighter into his arms.

"I'm okay with pizza...if that's what you want," I stutter out.

"What time is it?" he asks randomly.

"Nine twenty. why?"

"Shit. It's too early to get you drunk."

I rear my head back, shocked at his statement.

"It seems the only time you actually speak your mind with me is when you're drunk."

"That's not true!" I scream at a decibel only a howler monkey could match.

"Really? Do you like pizza, Jess?"

"No."

"Well, thank Christ. At least you're honest."

"You're a jerk."

"And you're hiding," he states, meaning it in more ways than one. "Don't hide from me—ever. Last night, you didn't take my crap. You were this tiny drunk woman who I had no doubt could conquer the world. You gave me a hickey!" he says firmly, as if that one sentence is the answer to all the world's problems. "You made bets, which you lost and still have not paid up on by the way. I didn't forget about that. You still owe me the truth about where you learned to bowl. Don't worry. I'm a patient man."

"I said I was sorry about the hickey."

It's my generic answer. I have no idea how to react to the rest of his comments. He just said that he wanted to get me drunk at nine a.m.! Regardless, if I'm sober or drunk, I can't conquer the world. No matter what he thought he saw in me last night, I'm just little Jesse Addison. I go with the flow and try not to make any waves. But I'm no one's doormat. I might not be a fighter, but I have no problems walking away.

"What do you say you come back out front and I'll try to figure out a pizza-free restaurant for us tonight?" He folds his hands together, pretending to beg. "Please don't make me go back out there alone. I'm a little afraid of Kara."

"You should be more than a little afraid of Kara," I say, pecking him on the lips and heading back out front.

Chapter
FOURTEEN

Jesse

"HOLY SMOKES!" I gasp as Kara turns me around to face the mirror.

I told Brett that I wouldn't let her dress me, but she wore me down after begging for three hours straight. She was relentless. I mainly gave in because I didn't have anything to wear anyway. I'm a jeans-and-T-shirt kind of girl. Nothing about a date with sex-on-legs Brett Sharp says jeans and T-shirt. He didn't tell me where we were going, so I had to straddle that fine line between dressy and casual. If he takes me to a sports bar, I don't want to look like the prom queen. But if he takes me to a nice place, I don't want to look like a homeless woman either. So I allowed Kara to dress me again.

This time, she picked a simple black strapless dress that accentuates my best attributes—my boobs and red slingback wedge heels. All of the real drama is in my eye makeup. She gave me the most brilliant smoky eyes I have ever seen. My usual unruly, long brown hair has been flatironed into submission, leaving shiny, flowing locks in its place. Despite my best efforts, she forced me into a red lace strapless bra and matching thong that she found pushed to the very back of my panty drawer. Even I'm willing to admit I look kind of amazing tonight.

"I know! Right? You look hot! When are you going to learn to trust my expertise?" Kara says beside me.

"From now on, I vow to wear anything you put in front of me."

"Score! If you think I'm going to forget that, you are sadly mistaken. I have some dirty lingerie you can use next time."

"Eww, I'm not wearing your lingerie."

"Okay, fine, but promise I get to go shopping with you when Hottie McHottersen turns you into a sex fiend."

"Since that is never going to happen, I promise. Cross my heart and hope to die."

"Yes!" she squeals, grabbing her jacket and getting ready to leave.

I made her promise she wouldn't be here when Brett shows up. The last thing I need is for her to be here drooling over him and embarrassing me more than she already has.

"I need every single detail when you get home tonight. Or better yet, when you get home tomorrow morning."

I just roll my eyes at her. She's so excited that you would think *she* was going to sleep with Brett tonight. Wait, no one is sleeping with him. Not even me—well, at least not tonight.

After pacing my apartment for twenty minutes, I finally hear a knock on the door. I do one last boob lift and smooth out the front of my dress, trying to calm my nerves. I take a deep breath and pull open the door to see the most beautiful man I have ever seen standing in the hall. He is wearing dark jeans that are perfectly washed out around his thighs and a black long-sleeved button-up that fits his hard muscular body like a glove. His sleeves are rolled up, exposing his defined forearms. I had no idea a man's forearms could turn me on like this. He's wearing black shoes and a belt that so closely match I swear they were made specifically to be worn together. The entire package causes my mouth to go dry. This man could grace the pages of GQ, yet he is here to pick me up. At least I remembered the push-up bra this time. Maybe that will help me rise to his level.

When I finally make it to his face, I see a knowing smile creep across Brett's mouth. He's caught me checking him out. Great! I'll never hear the end of this.

"Jesus, Jess, you look gorgeous!" he says, leaning over to brush a kiss across my lips. "So we're staying in tonight?"

"Oh, um. Sure."

"You're doing it again."

"Doing what?"

"Settling. I know you didn't spend that much time getting dressed in that sexy-as-hell dress, making sure every hair is in place, and putting on enough makeup to guarantee there isn't a man in the world who will be able to take his eyes off of you just to sit on your couch and watch TV. So I'll repeat. Are we staying in tonight?"

He's right. After the time I spent getting ready, there is no way I'd want to waste looking this good—and being on the arm of a man who looks that good—on just staying in.

"Nope, you're taking me out. To somewhere that doesn't have pizza. And just because you are giving me a hard time, I'm ordering the most expensive item on the menu. I hope you brought your life savings with you."

"There she is! No alcohol needed this time either," he says, pulling me into a hug, running his hands across my bare shoulders. "You really do look incredible tonight. I'm not sure I want to take you out in public. You might cause a few men to spontaneously combust, and I'm terrified one of them might be me."

I giggle at his silly compliment. "You look pretty handsome yourself."

"Apparently, I do. I think I saw you froth at the mouth when you opened the door."

"Not my fault. You were the one who rolled up your sleeves like that."

"What? Jesse Addison, do you have an arm fetish? It's not quite as kinky as I was hoping for, but I can work with that," he says while crossing his arms over his chest and using one hand to slowly stroke his exposed skin. We both start laughing, and it feels awesome to be able to joke with him like this. It's a welcome change from the nervousness I usually feel. I guess giving a man a hickey can really loosen a girl up.

"Oh God, you're ridiculous. Can we please go before you start molesting your poor arms in the middle of my living room? You owe me dinner, remember?"

"Lead the way."

When we get outside, he leads me over to a shiny silver BMW sports car. I freeze as he pulls open my door.

"You have a BMW?" I ask in a voice a little higher pitched than I meant.

"Yes, is that a problem? Do you hate Germans?" he tries to joke, but he looks confused.

"Brett, this is a really nice car."

He stands waiting for me to get in, but I'm still frozen in place. "She is, isn't she?" He lovingly runs his hands over the convertible hardtop. The very, very expensive convertible hardtop.

"Where's your Jeep?" I ask, because when he drove me home last night, it was in an older-model Jeep Wrangler. I surely was not expecting him to show up in a nice sports car today.

"It's at home. This is my other car. I'm not taking you out on our first date in a beat-up Jeep I've had since college."

Any comfort I felt with Brett inside has now vanished. It doesn't take a genius to realize that this is a successful man. He's gorgeous, drives a nice car, wears fancy clothes, and probably won't even bat an eye when I order the twenty-three-dollar steak at dinner. He is like...a real adult. Here I am, a too-curvy, twenty-six-year-old college student who works in a coffee shop. I share an apartment to keep costs down, and I'm currently wearing my roommate's clothes because I didn't want to spend the money on a new outfit tonight. It isn't until this moment that I realize just exactly how far out of my league I am tonight.

"What's going on, Jesse?"

"Nothing. It's the Germans thing. Yeah, I hate them." I become unstuck and walk forward, sitting in my seat as he closes the door behind me.

Once he folds his huge body into the tiny car, he turns to look at me. "You do not. Let's try this again. What's wrong, Jesse?"

"I just wasn't expecting you to have such a nice car. That's all."

He chuckles. "I've wanted a BMW since I was a pimple-faced kid. I finally saved up enough money over the years, put down a hefty down payment, and bought it about six months ago. Now, I know it was more than that back there, but I'm really hungry so I'm going to let you work it out on your own. If you want to talk, I'm right here, okay?"

"Okay." I smile back at him as he starts the car and speeds out of my apartment complex.

On the ride to the restaurant, we make small talk and I start to relax again. He's just a regular guy. It's not like he's loaded or anything. He's a detective—they don't make millions. I just have to remind myself of that. Well, that is until he pulls up in front of Langley's Restaurant.

"Oh my God, we are not eating at Langley's!" I screech.

"Why not?" he asks startled.

"This place is crazy expensive!" I continue to scream at a decibel that should have dogs running in my direction.

"All right. Spill it, Jess. First you freak about my car, and now about the restaurant. You have some sort of hang-up on money?"

"No." I stare down into my lap, embarrassed by my outburst. "I'm sorry. That was really rude of me."

"Don't stop there. Tell me what has you all worked up."

"I...um, I... Can we just go eat?"

"Absolutely. As soon as you talk to me. I mean, it will take a few minutes for me to unload all the briefcases of cash I have in the trunk, but as soon as I do that, we can go inside." He winks at me.

I know he is just trying to lighten the mood. That's what Brett does—he makes jokes. Most of the time, I like that about him, but tonight, his humor isn't helping.

"When you make fun of me, it really makes me want to open up to you all the more," I say sarcastically, causing his smile to quickly fade.

"I wasn't making fun of you. I threatened to punch my best friend in the face for picking on you. I told you I would never make fun of you, and I meant it. I was just teasing to get you to talk to me. I meant nothing by it, and I'm sorry if you took it that way."

Aly Martinez

Crap. We are fifteen minutes into our first date and I'm already acting like a fool. I either tell him the truth or allow him to think that I'm a wacko. I'm not sure which is worse.

"Money and expensive things make me uncomfortable. I didn't grow up with money. We weren't destitute or anything, but we definitely didn't have much. My dad took off when I was a kid. My mom raised me and my brother, Eric, all on her own. She was a paralegal at a law firm, so she made enough money to keep the bills paid, but it didn't leave a whole lot left over for fun things or luxuries. I went to public school in a very rich area of Chicago. If you weren't wearing expensive name brands or driving a brand-new car, you were looked down on. My mom always felt the need to spend money she didn't have to make sure we had things, yet she wore the same shoes to work for years. I always felt guilty about that, and I guess it stuck with me over the years."

I take a deep breath, feeling more awkward now that I've poured my heart out to him than I did when he just thought I was weird. He reaches over, soothing my worries by lifting my hand and planting a brief kiss on my palm before setting it down on his thigh and covering it with his own.

"Okay. Completely understandable. Now, let me tell you a few things about myself. Both my parents are teachers, so I didn't exactly grow up in Beverly Hills. It sounds like we probably had it a little better than you did since they both worked, but I have two older sisters who weren't like you. They didn't feel one bit of guilt asking for nice things. My dad would pick up extra jobs coaching soccer after school to make extra money. He taught me that if you want something, you bust your ass to get it.

"I started cutting grass at thirteen to make my own spending money. By the time I was eighteen, I had a small empire. Okay, maybe that's a bit of an exaggeration, but that's the way it felt back in those days. I hired two kids to work with me so we could get more done. We stayed busy because we were cheap and worked hard. Eventually, we were cutting every yard in our neighborhood.

"My junior year in high school, I took an economics class where they gave us fake money to invest in the stock market. I became a bit addicted. What can I say? I'm a little competitive. With my father's help, I started actually investing my yard money and did pretty well for myself. I put myself through college that way. I didn't live lavishly, but I didn't have to work except for when I went home during the summers.

"What I'm saying, Jess, is I get it. I understand that the way you grow up can affect your views on things today. But I need you to understand that is precisely why we are sitting here right now. I'm on a date with a sexy woman, so I'm going to drive my nice car and take her to a delicious restaurant

82

where she is going to order the most expensive thing on the menu. And I'm okay with that, because I work hard so I can afford these moments. Trust me, gorgeous. This moment is totally worth it." He stops talking and rubs his thumb ever so slightly across my cheek. "Now, come over here and give me a kiss so we can go eat."

I breathe a sigh of relief over how Brett laid it all out for me. That could have been a really uncomfortable conversation for me, but he made it easy. He made it something light and moved on quickly. So I lean into him, showing my gratitude with a passionate kiss. Which leads to another kiss. Which leads to us making out in his car like teenagers for a full fifteen minutes.

"Jesus, woman, we're going to miss our reservation." He smiles against my lips when my hands make their way under his shirt.

His words cause me to laugh and I hear him suck in a breath. I look up and find him watching me with a look on his face that I don't completely understand. It's one of adoration, longing, and most of all, peace. If I thought he was sexy before, the look on his face now is enough to set my body on fire. It takes every ounce of my willpower not to launch myself into his lap and rip his clothes off in such a way that would make Kara proud. Instead, I pull down the visor mirror, dabbing my makeup and correcting my smeared lipstick.

"I'm ready when you are."

"Oh, gorgeous, I'll never be ready, but I should probably feed you before I ravage you." His words hold a certain amount of promise that makes me wish I'd brought a spare pair of panties.

Before I can overthink things or ask him to skip dinner, he gets out of the car, walking around to open my door. Tightly taking hold of my hand, he guides me into the overpriced restaurant.

DINNER WAS amazing. Despite Brett's encouragement, I didn't order the most expensive thing on the menu. I settled for a small fifty-dollar steak and thirty dollars' worth of baked potato and side salad. He was the perfect gentleman. When I told him I didn't drink red wine, he ordered us a bottle of white even though the waiter informed him that it wasn't a good pairing for our dinners. Brett very kindly ignored his suggestions and finally told him to bring us beers instead.

As dinner is nearing an end, he asks the one question I have been expecting since he picked me up.

"Tell me where you learned to bowl?" He pushes his empty plate away, reclining back in his chair.

"Ugh, you're not seriously going to make me tell you this story, are you?"

"Of course I am. The fact that you don't want to tell me only makes me that much more curious."

"Fine. One of the bowling professors was, um...very attractive. Kara and I took every class he offered until, one day, his equally attractive boy-friend showed up to take him to lunch."

Just as I expected, Brett throws his head back in laughter. "Wait, let me get this straight. You paid to take bowling classes just because the instructor was good-looking?"

"Pretty much. Well, I didn't pay for them. I was on a scholarship. So technically, the college paid for them."

"Scholarship?" His eyes perk in surprise.

"Yeah. I had an academic scholarship until I got my first degree."

"Wait, you already have a degree?"

"Yep, I have a bachelor's and two associates' degrees."

"Wow! What are you still doing in school then?"

"I didn't exactly think my bowling alley management degree was going to take me very far in life. Honestly, I'm a little creeped out by all the sweaty shoes. I learned to enjoy the sport from my cute professor, but I'm not cracked up to spend forty hours a week in a bowling alley."

"Oh my God, you really did hustle me yesterday." His loud accusation makes me playfully bite my lip and look away. "Shit, that's even hotter than the dress," I barely hear him mumble to himself.

"Yeah, sorry about that."

"No, please don't apologize. Who else knows about this little skill of yours? I believe Caleb needs to join us next time for a bowling excursion. You can win back some of my money he stole in poker last month. You'll be like my own secret weapon."

I barely contain my excitement as he talks about future plans together. Just the idea of a second date brings an instant smile to my face.

"Judging by that smile, I think you like the idea of hustling Caleb too. I've got to tell you, babe. I like that a lot," he flirts, and we both start laughing.

When the check arrives, Brett doesn't even look at the total. He just hands his credit card to the waiter. My eyes must have grown wide, because he shakes his head and says, "Not one word, gorgeous. This has been completely worth whatever is on that total line." He essentially hushes me before I even have a chance to comment.

Chapter
FIFTEEN

Brett

AS WE leave Langley's, I slide my hand down Jesse's back, stopping just above the curve of her ass. God, she looks incredible tonight. I've been wanting to peel off that dress from the first second I laid eyes on her. I never noticed it before, but I think I might have a slight obsession with heels now. For such a short woman, Jesse has the most amazing legs I have ever seen. But then again, the whole Jesse package is sexy.

I was shocked at dinner when she told me that she already has a couple of college degrees. I mean, seriously—I pegged her all wrong. This isn't a girl stuck in a job at a coffee shop. Jesse is a woman with so many dreams that she doesn't even know how to focus them in one place. I dig smart girls, and listening to her talk tonight only reinforced that. She might be quiet and shy at first, but once you break her out of that invisible shell, she's unbelievable.

When she opened herself up to me tonight about her childhood, it killed me. The last thing I was trying to do was intimidate her with my car or restaurant choice. I just wanted to take her someplace nice and do it in style. She deserves that. I hate that my attempts to impress her actually brought out some painful feelings for her. I wish she didn't feel like that, but I loved the way she fearlessly opened up to me. I hope a little insight into my background brought her some semblance of comfort. She has nothing to be ashamed of. We all have a past. Especially me.

"It's still early. You want to go for a drive?" I ask as we leisurely stroll towards my car.

"Yeah, sure." She innocently lifts her big brown eyes in my direction.

It's all I can do to wait the last three steps before pinning her against my car. I catch her off guard, because she stumbles forward, but I won't let her fall. I gently lift her off her feet, spinning her to face me. One hand sifts into her hair, the other tracing down her waist.

"What if we go back to my place instead? I've got some beer and we can pretend to watch another movie." I don't wait for her to answer. I lean down and begin to trail kisses over her exposed shoulder.

"Mmm, that sounds like a much better plan." She turns her head, exposing her neck, inviting me in for another taste of her skin. Who am I to turn down a beautiful lady?

But before I can kiss her again, she buries herself in my chest. Her arms are curled between us as she snuggles into me.

"I had fun tonight," I say while enjoying the moment of closeness. It's been a long time since I've been able to share something so simple with someone.

"Mmmhmm," is her only response.

I think she has taken this moment from hot and sexy and downshifted it to sweet and innocent. But then she loops her hands under my arms, grabbing my shoulders, and pulls me down to kiss the red mark she left last night. She ends the lingering kiss with a wet dart of her tongue, licking up my neck.

I let out a growl. "I need to get you home."

"I agree," she moans.

"In you go." I pull open the door, jokingly shoving her inside as quickly as possible.

Luckily, she gets my joke and starts giggling. Unfortunately for me, it causes my dick to go ridged, and I have to ride home uncomfortably trapped in my pants.

WHEN WE arrive at my apartment, I waste no time grabbing two beers out of the fridge. I walk over to see her sitting on the couch with her jacket still wrapped tightly around her. I place the beers on the table in front of her and remember my manners.

"Here, let me take your jacket."

"No, it's okay. I shouldn't stay long," she says, retreating back into herself.

Jesse is unlike any woman I have ever met. She is either shy and reserved or feisty and hilarious. It's like dating two different women. I thought we made such progress at dinner. She opened up to me about her past, but it seems the drive home has set us right back into insecure territory. It's going to be my personal mission to shatter the shell she uses as a shield.

"What do you mean you can't stay long? You promised me beer and another taste of those delicious lips." I reach forward, tucking her hair behind her ear. "You can't promise a starving man sustenance then take it all away." I glide my hands down the back of her head to cup her neck. Gently, I tilt her head back and place a series of kisses on her mouth. On the last kiss, I gently touch my tongue to her soft bottom lip. "Say you're not going to take it away," I whisper against her lips.

She can't stay stuck inside her head forever, and if I have learned anything with Jesse in the last few days, it's that I affect her just as much as she does me. I'll use whatever means I have to make her go back to the flirty woman who was eager to come home with me outside the restaurant.

When she doesn't immediately respond to my words, I break out the big guns. Literally. I step back pulling off my own jacket. Laying it across the chair beside me, I raise an eyebrow at her.

"Gorgeous, I'm not ashamed to admit that this cute, sweet, shy-girl thing you have going on right now is a real turn-on. However, I miss the woman had dinner with tonight. You might remember her. She was laughing at me and making fun of my lackluster bowling abilities. If I recall correctly, she was even making out with me in the parking lot of a five-star restaurant. She was a firecracker.

"I happen to know she has some sort of fetish with my arms, so this is strictly an effort to lure her back." I reach down, making a showing of rolling up my sleeves even farther. My silly play does exactly as intended. Jesse starts shaking her head and laughing at me.

"You are so full of yourself," she says, rolling her eyes.

"It worked though. She's back! I'd recognize that eye roll anywhere. Care to explain to me where you went?"

She lets out a groan. "I'm just a little nervous. It feels like scheduled hook-up time. When we were in the moment, it was easy, but now…I don't know."

"I didn't schedule this! If this works out, maybe I'll schedule you for next week, but tonight was just pure luck," I tease, trying to ease her nerves.

"Are you always this big of a jerk when a girl doesn't want to kiss you?" Her serious tone makes my head snap up. She walks away, picking up the beer that was sitting on the coffee table. Tipping it up, she completely drains it before turning back to face me.

"Hey, you know I was kidding, right? I wasn't trying to be a dick. I was just trying to make you laugh. That's all. There is no pressure tonight, Jess. I just wanted to spend more time with you. I like having you around."

"You know, for such a big tough guy, you really are a sucker." She winks at me.

"You little..." I don't complete my thought before racing across the room, sweeping her petite body up, and softly dropping her onto the couch.

She lets out a squeal the minute her feet leave the ground. I watch her writhe under me while I pin her to the couch, tickling her. As much as I like to think of myself as the gentleman I portrayed tonight, I can't help but wish she were writhing in ecstasy while I was buried inside her. Just the thought makes my pants stir. I'm lying on top of her, and the way she's moving has caused her dress to ride up. I realize that my denim zipper is directly against her panties. And damn if that doesn't almost finish me off.

I lock my eyes to hers and stop moving. She's staring at me with flushed cheeks as if she just realized our position as well. Just as I begin to move away, I see her tongue peek out, wetting her lips. Oh yeah, this is happening.

Jesse

OH MY God, oh my God. This cannot be happening...can it? Brett has this hooded look like he wants to devour me, and my panties are soaked. I am surprised I'm not leaving a wet spot on his jeans. Oh please, don't let it be leaving a wet spot. That would be humiliating.

Okay, Jesse. It's time to woman up! You can do this. Deep breath! This is what you have been dreaming about for months.

"Jess?" Brett asks with slight hesitation in his voice.

Before I give myself any more time to chicken out, I lift up, cup the back of his neck, and pull him into a deep kiss. Proving to myself that I'm okay with this...whatever this may be. Pushing up on my elbows, careful not to break the kiss, I reach down to unzip my dress.

"Let me do that, gorgeous," he breathes into my mouth.

His hands glide down over my breasts to the zipper on the side of my dress. My skin is on fire, and he can probably see the blush from my head to my toes. Brett slowly peels the top down and exposes my red lace. He traces around my hard nipples with his fingertips before reaching around to unclasp my bra. With one flick, I feel it loosen and begin to fall away.

Just before it completely exposes me, Brett pulls each side tight against my body, leaning down to catch my eyes with a questioning look. He has skills and he radiates confidence, but he's still searching for permission. Which is something so sweet that it immediately makes me throw all caution to the wind. I lie back down, pulling my bra from his hands and tossing it off to the side of the couch, where we are still lying entwined.

Lying half naked before this jaw-dropping man should be terrifying, but the look on his face makes me feel confident, even sexy. Brett makes quick work of removing his shirt, discarding it into the rapidly growing pile of clothes on the floor. I die a little when I get my first glance at his hard body. He couldn't be any more perfect. He's trim but well defined. Every muscle in his shoulders ripples as he moves himself back into place over me. I can't stop myself from reaching forward and tracing a finger over the ridges on his stomach. His skin is tan, and a small amount of hair dusts across his chest. He's the masculine ideal, nothing like the boys I've been with in the past. This is a man in every sense of the word.

Brett captures my lips in a heated kiss but doesn't deepen it. Instead, he moves to my neck, trailing wet kisses down to my chest. His descent is too slow for me. Reaching forward, I thread my fingers in his hair and arch my back, thrusting myself closer to his mouth. Surprised by my boldness, he looks up at me with a lust-filled gaze, silently begging for permission to continue. All I can do is bite my lip and nod my enthusiastic approval. He wastes no time sucking a nipple into his mouth and lightly tugging on it with his teeth. I can't stop the moan that comes out of my mouth.

Fire immediately pools between my legs. I squeeze them together under his weight, trying to alleviate some of the tension.

He chuckles against my heated flesh. "Soon, gorgeous. I'm going to taste that sweetness soon, but I'm not done with these yet," he says as he continues his gentle exploration of my breasts.

Every so often, he surprises me with a rough nip or tug before returning to his soft caresses. I realize that my panties began to ride down my hips at some point. I am far too filled with desire to try and remember when that happened.

I feel a rough hand slide between my legs as he lets out a low, approving moan. As he runs his first two fingers over my lace panties, I know he can feel how wet I am for him. I am tempted to be embarrassed by this, but the look on his face once again brings me back to comfort from knowing that I make him feel the exact same way.

Finally, he sits back, removing my dress, which has become twisted around my waist. His fingers trail all the way down my legs, never breaking contact, even when he has to momentarily kneel before dropping the dress to the floor. I assumed he would return to what he was doing before, but he remains on his knees, staring down at me. I can feel the heat rise to my cheeks as his eyes slide over my entire body. It embarrasses me a bit to see this sexy man looking at me this way. I'm not muscular and hard the way he is. Unable to take his surveying eyes any longer, I move to cover myself with a soft blanket he keeps draped across the back of the couch. Before I'm able to drag it over me, he pulls my hands away.

"Don't. You're so fucking beautiful. I want to see all of you." He hooks his fingers in my panties, pulling them slowly down my legs. "These are hot," he says, shoving them in his pocket and smirking at me.

"You're not keeping my panties," I say a little too breathily, excited about the very idea of him wanting something so personal.

"These are mine now." His eyes sparkle with mischief, and my voice chooses this moment to not work any longer.

Still kneeling over me, Brett leans forward and places a warm, soft kiss on each breast then pushes my legs apart, settling between them. He runs his nose up the inside of my thigh, leaving goose bumps in his wake.

Suddenly, his tongue runs up my heat, causing me to almost come completely undone. He groans and runs his tongue over me again. "Jesus, Jess, you taste so fucking good. I knew you would be sweet, but I'm never going to get enough of this." His words make me shiver.

Never has a man talked to me the way Brett does. He makes me feel comfortable and special. And, if I'm being honest, a little dirty at the same time.

He wraps his lips around my swollen bud and gently sucks it into his mouth. The sensation is too much, causing me to moan and arch into him. "Brett..." I reach down and grab his shoulders, desperately searching for something to keep me grounded.

He begins sucking and licking, pushing me closer and closer to the edge. I inadvertently rake my fingernails across his back, trying to grab hold of something before I lose myself completely.

He lets out a growl, murmuring, "So fucking sexy," against my opening. He pushes a finger inside, causing me to make a noise I don't think any human has ever made before. His hand and mouth work me in a smooth, synchronized rhythm.

"I'm close. Please don't stop."

Bright lights from behind my eyelids nearly blind me as the orgasm begins to course through my body. I lift my hips off the couch, panting his name. It seems like I'm floating forever. As I come down, I feel him kissing the insides of my thighs.

"That was amazing," is all I can get out.

"You have no idea, gorgeous." Brett's deep voice rumbles against my skin.

Somehow finding strength, I push up on my arms. "No really, that was... wow. Thank you."

"You don't have to thank me! That was my pleasure." His face is heated, and I wonder if he is as worked up as I felt just a few minutes ago. I may not be very experienced in the oral department, but I can't leave him hanging like this.

"Good. Then you won't mind if I return the favor?" I ask shyly.

"No, babe. This is not a tit-for-tat type deal. I wanted to do that. I don't expect anything in return."

"Well," I start, trying to dredge up some courage, "maybe I want to do this."

I quickly move on top of him. I can see the bulge under his zipper. I swallow nervously while giving myself a mental pep talk. I'm scared I'm not going to do this right, but I would be stupid to pass up this chance with Brett.

I begin to sink between his legs, but he stops me by pulling me to my feet. "I don't want you on your knees, babe. Come on. Let's go to my room."

He grabs the blanket off his couch and pulls it around me. He scoops up my discarded clothes and leads me to his room. As soon as we reach his bed, he plucks the blanket away from my naked body.

"Now where were we?" He winks at me and pulls me onto the bed on top of him.

I, once again, slide down his body and settle between his legs. I take my time to really study him. He's an undeniably beautiful man, but I can see a few faint scars across his chest that remind me that he's no more perfect that I am.

I snap out of my thoughts as I hear him chuckle. "See something you like?"

Actually, I see a lot I like, but I'm not about to tell him that. I just blush and awkwardly look away.

"Don't do that, babe. Don't get embarrassed and hide your pretty face," he says quietly.

That's easy for him to say. What does he have to be insecure about? A few scars on his chest? He's so sexy that women probably throw themselves at him daily. What the heck does he want with a girl like me?

I have no idea what I'm doing here. Sure, I've gone down on a guy a few times before, but only *one* other guy. I'm definitely not as skilled as Brett. Here I am, talking myself out of being with him. He wants me, and he just showed me how much. It's time for me to step it up and show him how much I want him as well. No more stalling—I'm doing this.

I lean forward and begin kissing down his stomach. I can only hope what I'm about to do for him will make him feel even half of the way he made me feel. When my mouth reaches the button of his jeans, I peek up at him through my lashes.

"Go ahead, Jess. You don't have to ask for permission. Don't do any-thing you're not comfortable with. I enjoyed making you come. No payback is needed."

GAH! The things this man says to me. Suddenly, I can feel the heat between my legs again. I undo the button of his jeans and slide the zipper down. Lifting his hips, he makes it easier for me to pull them down his toned legs. I toss them aside, but I can't take my eyes off the tight boxer briefs. They hug his sculpted body and his very large, very obvious arousal. I swallow but hesitate for only a moment. I don't want him to think I am doing this out of obligation. I'm doing this for the best reason of all—because I want to.

I slide his boxers down his legs and his hard-on bobs, lightly slapping his stomach when I release it. Oh my God, is it possible for a man to have a beautiful penis? Because I can find no other words to describe it. I never really thought about a man in that way before, but Brett is no ordinary man.

I bend down and pepper light kisses over his abdomen. I can't help but smile when his muscles tense beneath me. With a quick breath, he relaxes back on the bed, placing his hands under his head so he can see me. Slowly moving down towards his hard-on and mimicking Brett's earlier move, I kiss the insides of this thighs. I'm rewarded with a softly whispered curse word.

Letting the saliva pool in my mouth, I run my tongue up his length and wrap my lips around the tip. He lets out a groan, and it gives me all the encouragement I need. I wrap my other hand around the base of his shaft and slowly take him inside my mouth. When I feel him hit the back of my throat, I pull back slowly. Adjusting my hand so it's wrapped where my mouth stops, I bob my head up and down a few times to get him nice and wet.

"Fuck, Jess. You feel so good." Hearing his words gives me even more confidence.

I start sucking him into my mouth faster and work my slick hand up and down his shaft. The moans I hear coming from Brett must mean that I'm doing something right. I decide to press my luck and try a little trick Kara has told me about a million times. Tentatively, I reach down and stroke his balls, never slowing my relentless rhythm up top.

"Fuck...Jess." His voice is deep and gritty. "Gorgeous, if you do that one more time, I'm going to come in that hot little mouth of yours, and I'm really trying to be a gentleman here."

Of course, I continue. If anything, I quicken my pace, sliding him in and out of my mouth faster. I don't stop my hand. He made me go wild under his touch. I want to do the same for him.

I feel his muscles go taut before he says, "Damn it, Jess. I'm going to come..."

Suddenly, he pulls himself out of my mouth with a loud pop and grips himself. Running his hand up and down his shaft, come spurts onto his stomach. I can't help but feel disappointed as I watch him finish himself off.

Feeling vulnerable, I back away just a bit.

I have no idea why he did that. He got to feel me come against his mouth, and as worried as I was when I started this, I was looking forward to giving him that too. Did I do something wrong? Was I not doing it right? The sounds he made were definitely those of a man enjoying himself. Oh, God. It sucked and he was just trying to make me feel better by saying those things to me.

Feeling like a failure, I subtly try to cover myself, but it's no use. I sit between this handsome man's legs, humiliated, watching as the last of his orgasm leaves him sated and smiling. Too bad there's no smile on my face.

Brett

I COME down from the most amazing high I've ever felt. I never expected anything so bold and sexy from Jesse. She is always so timid and nervous. Even when she started, I thought I was going to have to coach her though how to give a proper blowjob. But the moment her lips wrapped around my dick, I knew she had it under control. I've never come harder, or quicker, in my life. I could blame it on my years without a woman, but I think it has more to do with Jess than I'm even willing to admit right now. I didn't think she would be so enthusiastic—or possibly even willing to do it at all—but I'm quickly learning to never underestimate this woman.

I feel her move from between my legs, but I'm nowhere near done with her. I reach out to grab her. I need to clean up, so this party is officially moving to the shower. I grab her hips before she can roll off the bed.

"Oh, I'm not finished with you. Where are you going?"

"It's really late," she says quietly, all the confidence gone from her voice.

Shit. I'm hoping she's just a little awkward after the fact, so I go with what I know best—flirty humor.

"Did you use me for my body?" I tease.

When her head snaps up to my eyes, I can tell that was the wrong move. The hurt and embarrassment are written all over her face, which makes my heart sink and, honestly, thoroughly baffles me.

"Jesus, Jess. Are you all right? What's going on in that beautiful head of yours?" Even before she can answer, my mind flies to all the possible answers. Did I push her too far? I wasn't expecting anything from her tonight. She was more than a willing participant in that. Or at least that's what it felt like.

"It's just... I'm just... I don't know."

"No way. We just spent the last hour getting to know each other intimately. You're not locking up on me now. Talk to me."

She lets out a resigned breath before answering. At least she's rational. "Why did you stop me?"

"Stop you? I didn't stop you?"

"You pulled away from me just before you, um...finished," she says, glancing down to my stomach, reminding me that I'm chatting while still covered in come. *Wonderful.*

I stand up and head into the bathroom. I grab a washcloth and quickly clean myself off. When I walk back into the room, she's already half dressed.

"What are you doing?" I knew she was bothered by something, but I didn't expect her to be bolting out the door already. "You aren't going anywhere until you sit and talk to me. This is crazy, Jess. You aren't running out of here after what we just did."

"You're you, Brett. And I'm just inexperienced little Jesse Addison." She stops talking as if she just explained it all.

"What does that even mean? I'm sorry, but you are going have to stop talking in code and just tell me what's going on here. I'm obviously not following the bouncing ball." I can see the gears turning in her mind. She has some sort of internal debate going on, and it almost worries me.

"I didn't realize I was doing a bad job when I was, um, doing that to you. It's just that I've not done that a whole lot, and I just... You made some noises, so I thought I was doing a good job. Maybe next time you could tell me what you like. I mean, if there is a next time. I understand if there isn't though. I'm sorry you had to, you know, finish it yourself. I could probably get better," she rambles out as fast as she can.

It may make me an asshole, but when I see this beautiful woman standing in a bra and panties and acting self-conscious after giving the best head I've ever had, it causes my eyes to go wide and a smile to spread across my face. I mean, she's *upset* that I didn't come in her mouth. This might be the best conversation I have ever had in my life.

"No," I answer shortly. I know I must be grinning like a madman, because I can see her eyes narrow at me.

I love the way she goes from shy to pissed with only one smirk from me. If I ever do break this conservative woman out of her shell, she is going to be quite the handful. That thought only makes my smile widen. Cause and effect, pissing her off more. We stand staring at each other. Arguing with no words. It's an evil stare down, my humor versus her insecurities, but I need to wave the white flag before lightning bolts shoot from her eyes.

"You are absolutely, one hundred percent not allowed to get any better at sucking my dick."

Her cheeks flash pink and her eyes widen at my dirty words. I purposely try to poke the beast a little more. I love seeing her mad. It's adorable and a little terrifying too. But most importantly, it's sexy as hell.

"Gorgeous, you've had me in your mouth once. I'm already half tempted to quit my job and lock us both in this apartment for the rest of our lives. We can survive solely on protein shakes, beer, and Chinese takeout. So no, you are not allowed to get any better. If you do, it might convince the other half of my brain to follow through with that ridiculous plan."

I walk over and pull the dress she's holding in front of her out of her hand. "I'm honestly a little afraid for you, Jess. If your mouth was any preview of how it's going to be when I get inside you, there is a very good chance you may never see the light of day again."

I reach down, dipping my finger into the top of her bra, brushing against her nipple. "Did you want me to come in your mouth?" I look down to find, just as I hoped, all anger and embarrassment erased from her face. All that's left is pure heated desire.

When she doesn't answer me, I take it one step further by pushing a hand into her panties. "Did you, babe?" I ask again and push the tip of my finger inside her.

She lets out a loud gasp, reaching forward, using my biceps to balance. Leaning her head against my chest, she nods.

"Jesse, you have to stop worrying so much. I like you, and I enjoyed the hell out of everything you did tonight." I wrap my free hand around, cupping her perfect ass. "I loved everything about what happened in that bed. Have a little faith that I'll be honest with you. If I don't like something, you'll know right away. However, I want you to be comfortable enough to try. Okay?"

Again she only nods.

"Now, I want to get you naked and try all of that again, just to make sure we both enjoyed it as much as we think we did. Purely for research purposes. For the betterment of science."

She lets out the most amazing giggle. I swear I can feel it in my soul.

It really should terrify me. If I were a smarter man, this would be the moment I realize that things are moving entirely too fast. I would put some space between us, back up, and recognize that I am getting in too deep. It's been two dates. My soul isn't supposed to be anywhere near this yet. However, I'm not a smart man, so I suck in a deep breath and revel in feeling something again for the first time in over four years.

Chapter
SIXTEEN

Brett

WHEN THURSDAY night rolls around, I am in no mood to go visit Sarah. Things have been getting worse with her recently. She's hated me for a long time. I like to think that I have gotten used to that over the years, but every time I see her, it still burns. When I look into her eyes, I can still see the wild and crazy woman hiding underneath her sad, broken exterior. She is only a shadow of the woman I used to love. She's lost too much weight over the years, and for a woman who used to love shopping, she is almost always wearing yoga pants and T-shirts these days.

Two years ago, Sarah cut off all her beautiful blond hair and dyed it red. I'm not talking just any color red either. She dyed it a shade of red that is not found naturally...anywhere. It's definitely not like Manda's deep, vibrant shade of wine. Sarah's hair is the color of a fire engine. Ronald McDonald would probably sue for trademark infringement.

The first time I saw her new hair, I picked up a vase that was sitting on her kitchen counter and shattered it against her living room wall. I turned and immediately walked out, slamming the front door and causing a nearby picture frames to fall to the floor. I had already lost her mentally, but that was the first time I didn't recognize her physically.

I mourned her loss all over again that night. I stayed up for hours alternating between drinking beer, breaking things, and punching holes in my walls. It killed me, and not because I'm one of those superficial assholes who cares when my woman cuts or colors her hair. It was just one more thing about Sarah that was lost to me.

"Wow, is it Thursday again already?" Sarah asks, pulling the door open.

"Yep." I walk in carrying takeout gyros. Her favorite.

"Did you get extra Z sauce and feta?"

"Don't I always?"

"Whatever." She walks to the kitchen, pulling two beers out of the fridge. "What have you been up to since the last time I was graced with your presence?" she asks, but I know she doesn't care. It's a common courtesy she offers every week. She tunes out the moment I open my mouth to respond.

"We need to talk," I say while moving to sit down on the couch.

"This should be good. What did I do wrong this time?"

"Don't start with the attitude, Sarah."

"If you don't want my attitude, don't come over anymore."

"Do you ever get sick of being pissy all the time?"

"Nope! Do you ever get sick of hanging out where you're not wanted?"

I shake my head and sigh. I'm exhausted from this back-and-forth we do all the time. It used to be something I just accepted, but after hanging out with Jesse for a few days, I don't have the patience for Sarah's verbal abuse anymore.

"Look, I'm not doing this tonight."

"Oh, yippee!" she says sarcastically. "You know where the door is. You don't have to do anything tonight."

"I met someone," I rush out before she has a chance to unleash anymore of her bitchiness. I've become the master of ignoring her snarky comments, but that doesn't mean I'm immune. It still hurts like hell when she treats me like shit under her shoes.

"What the fuck!" she yells, shocking me with her reaction. I was expecting her to throw a freaking party, but judging by her tone, I have definitely pissed her off again. "You met someone?" She jumps from her seat and leans into my face aggressively.

"What is your problem?"

"You are my problem, Brett! I have been asking for a divorce for years. YEARS!" she screams only inches from my face.

I slide over far enough to get up without having to touch her. She has that crazy look in her eye, and I know if I sit there, even a minute longer, she will slap me. New Sarah has zero issues with getting physical during an argument. Sometimes, I think she hits me just because she knows I'll leave as soon as she does.

"So this should make you ecstatic then!"

"You are such a dumbfuck!"

"Wow, thanks! Got any other cuss words you want to try out on me?" I know I'm not making this any better, but damn it gets under my skin when she starts acting like this. I try to reel it in though. Hopefully we can have this conversation before shit *completely* hits the fan. "Look, can you please calm down?"

"So…let me get this straight. I have been begging for a divorce and you fought me at every turn. I hired a divorce attorney. You and Caleb pulled some strings and had him drop me as a client. So I very kindly asked you for a divorce and you gave me some bullshit reason why we needed to stay married."

"Sarah, you have no job. You need my health insurance for all your… care."

"I have money! I can pay my own damn medical bills."

"That settlement from the wreck isn't going to last forever. Why would you waste it on expensive doctors' bills?"

"So us staying married was only so I could use your health insurance?"

I can't answer her without lying, so I stay silent.

"I didn't think so. You are a selfish son of a bitch, Brett Sharp. You have made me fight to get rid of you, yet you still show up week after week like a lost little puppy dog who can't find a home. I only let you in on Thursdays because I feel sorry for you. It's pathetic! Now you stand here and tell me that you're in love with someone else, so I guess I'm finally allowed to move on with my life, huh?"

"I didn't say that I'm in love with Jesse."

"Oh goodie, your soul mate has a name. Jesse—how perfect."

"Are you jealous?" I ask almost humorously.

"Hell no! I'm pissed. You have been smothering me for years. Now some little tramp comes along spreading her legs and suddenly I'm allowed to move on with my life?" she says, and her slam about Jesse makes me lose all my calm and rational thoughts.

"I'm not going to say this again, Sarah, so I want you to listen very closely. Don't you dare talk about Jesse like that. You can call me whatever you want, but you will watch your damn mouth when it comes to her."

"Oh my God. You are such a tool!" She busts out laughing as if I'd told a joke. "She must be really dirty in the sack to have turned you into such a pussy already. If I recall correctly, that's how you like it. Dirty, right?" She continues laughing, pausing to bite her lip and questioningly lift an eyebrow.

"Screw you. Send me whatever divorce papers you want. I'll happily sign so that you can finally be rid of me once and for all."

"Yeah, that's not going to happen. You're going to have to work for it—the same way I have for the last four fucking years."

"Okay, this conversation is over. When you are done acting like an ass, send me the papers." I'm turning to walk away when I see her rear back, surprising me as she slams her fist into the side of my mouth.

"You bastard! You don't get to make all the decisions. You don't get to decide when this is over."

I've never in my life hit a woman. I sure as hell would never lay my hands on Sarah. But this woman standing in front of me is really testing the limits of my self-control. I dab the blood from my lip, snatch my jacket off the back of the chair, and stride out the door before I can say or do something I will forever regret.

Standing in front of my car, I pat down my pockets, trying to locate my keys. "Fuck," I mutter when I remember putting them on her table, along with my cell phone, when I first arrived. It sucks that I forgot my keys, but without my cell phone, I can't even call Caleb for a ride. I have no choice but to go face that crazy woman again.

I wait a few minutes, giving us both time to calm down after our heated argument before walking back up to her front door knocking quietly.

"Who is it?" I hear her singsong from the other side.

"It's me. I left my keys and phone. Can you just hand them to me and I'll leave you alone?"

"Oh, no problem, sweetheart," she says, cracking open the door. Sarah is standing in the doorway with a shit-eating grin on her face and holding my phone to her ear when she drops the bomb on me. "I was just chatting with Jesse."

Chapter
SEVENTEEN

Jesse

"WELL, *HELLO*, officer," I say when Brett's number pops up on my phone.

"Jesse?" I hear a woman's voice on the other end of the line.

I pull my phone away from my ear, checking the caller ID again. Yep, it definitely says Brett. "Yes."

"Hi. This is going to sound strange, but I found your phone number in my husband's phone. I know this is crazy, but we have had some infidelity issues in the past, and I had such a bad feeling when I ran across your number."

"Um, okay?" I stumble out.

"Do you know Brett Sharp?"

"Yes," I whisper as my heart drops to my stomach. Brett's words from the Bears game flash into my mind. *"I'm married."*

This must be some type of mistake though. He specifically told me that he'd lost his wife in a car accident. Crap. What if he lied to me? I don't know him outside of the coffee shop. Who knows what he has going on at home. Feeling sick, I walk towards the barstool to sit down before my suddenly flimsy legs give out underneath me.

"Well, my name is Sarah Sharp. I'm Brett's wife." And with that one sentence, all of my fears are confirmed. "I just wanted to speak to you myself, make sure he wasn't cheating on me again. I'm sorry. I know how awkward this must be for you. Trust me—I'm embarrassed myself. It's just that I love him so much, but sadly, he has a bit of a wandering eye if you know what I mean. I just can't seem to convince myself to leave him though. Jeez, now I'm just rambling. Anyway, I'm sure there is some explanation for all of this and I'm just overreacting. Do you work with Brett?"

"No." I say nothing else, trying to keep the tears that start to pool in my eyes out of my voice.

"Do you know him from the gym then?" she asks in a weird jovial tone.

"No." The tears start to flow down my cheeks and into my lap.

It's ridiculous to feel this upset over a man I have been seeing for five days, but I stupidly thought Brett and I had something special. After hearing that he has been unfaithful in the past, I know those were just my own misguided feelings. I'm nothing special to him at all.

"Well, can you tell me where you *did* meet?" she snaps. I can't even be mad at her attitude. She is just as much a victim here as I am.

"He...um, comes into Nell's coffee shop for breakfast every morning. I work there, so we met a few months ago but only started seeing each other, uhh, romantically a few days ago."

"Oh gosh, I can't believe he is doing this to me again! Are you sleeping with him?" she asks a little too calmly for a woman who just found out her husband is seeing someone else. Jeez, he really must do this a lot for her to be taking it so well. I'm more of mess than she is right now.

"Um..." I drone out, trying to buy myself some time to figure out how to answer this question. I don't know this woman, and I surely don't want to explain to her that, yes, I've been naked with her husband but haven't actually had sex with him.

Crap! Brett is someone's husband! I'm assuming she would consider what Brett and I did on Monday night to be cheating, so I decide to just give her the abridged version, sparing us both the pain of the details.

"Yes, but just once. It was on Monday night. He took me out to Langley's. Then we went back to his place... Oh God, did I do it in your bed?" I ask, and I swear I hear a muffled laugh. I can't imagine what she could find humorous in this situation. But before I have a chance to wonder about her strange reaction, she responds.

"No. He has a place he stays in Chicago when he has to work late. The kids and I live about thirty miles outside the city. It's hard for him to commute sometimes. Gosh, I thought that apartment was such a good idea when he suggested it, but now it seems like he takes every woman he meets there! I just assumed he was working late. I'm such a silly woman." She sniffles into the phone.

"You...you have kids?" I cry harder, imagining beautiful green-eyed babies who look just like their father.

"Yes. Two girls. They are the ones hurt most by his...extracurricular activities. They miss him so much when he stays in the city."

My heart breaks for those innocent children. I can't believe he would do this. He seems so genuine and sincere, yet he's out cheating on his wife every opportunity he gets. Great, he's cheating on his wife and children with me!

As I dry my eyes, I decide I no longer want to be a victim here. She needs to know the man she is married to so she can finally get free of his lies.

"He told me you were dead," I tell her quickly and quietly before I lose my nerve.

"Oh, no, sweetheart. I am very much alive." She begins to loudly laugh into the phone. It confuses the heck out of me because she doesn't even attempt to cover it this time.

For the life of me, I can't figure out what could be funny right now. Whatever. I guess we all react differently in stressful situations. I just need to fill her in so I get off this phone and forget all about this conversation and Brett "Cheating" Sharp.

"He said he lost you in a car accident." I pause as something dawns on me. "Crap, did he lie about Caleb's fiancée too?" I hear a loud bump then nothing but cold silence. "Hello? Are you still there?"

"I'm...here," she says, and for the first time since I answered my phone, I hear real tears in her voice. It's all probably sinking in for her now. Maybe her shock has worn off. Mine certainly hasn't though. I listen to her sniffle for a second, knowing that, in a way, I am responsible for this.

"God, I'm sorry. I had no idea he was married. You should probably know he doesn't wear a wedding ring either."

"Yeah, um... I should go," she answers as I hear a knock at her door over the phone. "Hold on just one second, Jesse."

I can hear her go to the door. Her voice clears up as she completely transforms from the sad woman she was only few seconds ago.

"Oh, no problem, sweetheart. I was just chatting with Jesse."

"Sarah, what the fuck!" Brett's voice roars over the line.

"She needed to know."

"Really? What did she *need* to know?"

"That you're my husband."

"Jesse, hang up the phone!" I hear him shout over the phone as they exchange a few muffled words.

"You are such a dick, Brett! Is that any way to talk to the love of your life?"

And that is all I need to hear in order to close this screwed-up chapter in my life. I hang up the phone, leaving Brett and "the love of his life" to hash it out between themselves.

I turn off my phone, fall into bed, and cry over a man who doesn't deserve my tears. I try to forget, but I can't take my mind off of him. I think back over the time we have spent together, racking my brain for all the signs I should have seen. I wonder what he told his wife while we were together. Would he sneak away from his family to call me every night? How long would he have strung me along before getting bored and moving on?

I must have fallen asleep at some point, because I'm awakened by an angry knock at my door. Half asleep and forgetting the craziness from earlier, I wander down the hall to see who is causing such a racket at...jeez. It's only nine p.m. I must have crashed out. I peek out to see Brett standing outside. Lord, he's sexy even with his face contorted through the oval glass of the peephole. Suddenly, everything about the last few hours comes back into focus, causing me to slide down the door just to keep myself from opening it.

"Jesse, open the door," he says quietly. I have no idea how he knows I'm here, but the fact that he doesn't shout at the closed door lets me know that he does. "I can see where you're blocking the light at the bottom of the door. It wasn't there a minute ago." He answers my unspoken question.

Knowing I've been caught, I quickly flip off the hall light, sending the room into darkness.

"And now I know I was right because you just turned off the light completely. I'm a detective, remember?"

I drop my head back against the door, causing a loud thump. Wonderful, now I've confirmed his suspicions.

"Please, gorgeous. I have no idea what Sarah said to you, but let's talk about it."

"Go away." The sharp pain in my chest is too much.

"That's not going to happen. Let me in."

"I can't... I want you to leave me alone. Go back to your wife and kids. It's not right for you to be here." I begin to choke back the tears all over again. This is just ridiculous. I can't believe he even has the audacity to stand outside my door after his wife called me. "Go home!"

"I can't go home, Jesse. Not knowing that you are in there, hurt and upset," he says, and the pain in his voice is almost enough to make me want to reach out to hug him. *Almost.*

With his wife's words ringing in my ears, I remind myself that I am no one's dirty little secret. As much as I like Brett, he's a lie. It's better that I found this out now, before I had a chance to fall in love with the façade. I rise to my feet, squaring my shoulders, ready to fight for the only person I can really trust—me.

I yank open the front door to see him instantly meet my gaze. His assessing eyes glide over my tear-stained cheeks. Rushing forward, he pulls me hard into his chest. He holds me, caressing my back, but I don't reciprocate. As I'm tucked tightly into this man's arms, my anger begins to fade from my body, but I refuse let it go completely. I stand limp, feet anchored to the ground, the rest of my body swaying, barely balanced enough to stand. He won't let me fall, and that realization hits me like a hard punch to the stomach. I mentally allow myself one minute to melt into his safe and comfortable arms, smelling his scent and feeling his strength as he kisses the top of my head. I enjoy this feeling for one last second before snapping out of the trance.

Shoving him as hard as I can, I push myself out of his grasp. I must have caught him off guard because he stumbles backwards a few steps.

"Get out, go home, and never speak to me again. Find a new place to eat breakfast, too. You may think I'm a naïve, easy play, but I'm not falling for your crap anymore. I know who you are Brett."

"Oh really? Who am I, Jess?" He roughly runs his hand through his hair. Tousling it in the sexiest way. *Crap!*

"You're a liar and a cheat. You played me, which is bad enough, but for God's sake, you played your own family, too."

"What did she say?" he asks, and I can almost see the flames shooting from his ears.

"Go home."

He sucks in a deep breath, trying to collect himself. "Jess, when I'm angry, I cuss...a lot. Last time I cussed at you, you freaked out. So let me prepare you, because I'm about to say a lot of words that you may not like. Please, don't take this personally, but I won't be able to watch my mouth." His calm voice rises to a shout as he obviously loses whatever control he collected just second ago. "Especially when you are telling me to go home to my wife and fucking kids. Now, before my head explodes, what the fuck did she tell you?" he screams.

"It doesn't matter what she told me. None of this is her fault, so don't you dare try to blame it on her. You're the one who lied to me. Why don't you try telling the truth for once? You would be amazed how liberating it feels. Jesus, Brett, you told me your wife was dead. How do you sleep at night?"

"I never told you my wife was dead," he says, clearly befuddled.

I throw my hands up in the air and walk away, leaving him standing in the doorway. I grab a beer from the fridge, not even bothering to offer him one. "You told me you lost her in a car accident. You said Caleb lost his fiancée too. Do you two work together? Lying about your dead wives to gain sympathy from unsuspecting women, just to get them into bed?" I ask, taking a much needed sip of the beer.

He's still standing in the foyer, his biceps bulging when he crosses his arms across his chest. Seriously, I have to stop checking him out. No wonder he got me into bed so quickly. This man is good. Even knowing he's a big fat liar, I can't stop myself from lusting after him. *Damn it!*

"I told you I lost my wife in a car accident, and that is the truth. I didn't realize that you thought she was dead. I see now how you would have assumed that though. I truly apologize for not being more clear. I never meant to imply that she was dead, but you have to know, that is the way I feel about her. She died years ago."

He sucks in another deep breath, ready to continue. "Caleb and I are not working some big play to get women into bed. You are the first, and only, woman I have gotten into bed in over four years. Caleb's fiancée, Manda, actually died in the car that night. She was Sarah's best friend, and her death is a large part of the reason why Sarah is the way she is today. "

"Sure. Are you done yet? Because, you really need to leave." I can't listen to his lies. He is explaining away the fact that he has a living, breathing wife. I'm not buying it.

"Sarah and I are still married." He finally tells the truth, and even though I already knew, it still hurts to hear him actually admit it. "But she is not my wife anymore."

"That's not what it sounded like on the phone tonight."

"Jess, I have no idea what she said to you, but I'm starting to piece some of it together. She is the one who lied to you. We don't have any kids. We haven't lived together in over three years. I did lose her in a car accident that night. She didn't die, but I lost her all the same," he says in such a sincere voice that I almost want to believe him.

Then I remember the heartbreak in his wife's voice when all of his deception hit her tonight. That alone is enough for me to never speak to him again.

"You must think I'm a complete idiot. I spoke to her!" I shout to prove to him, and myself, that there is no getting past this.

"Where's your computer?" he asks oddly.

"I don't have one."

"You're a college student and you don't have a computer?"

"Are you here to make fun of me now? Add insult to injury? No, I don't have a computer. My old one broke, and I didn't have the money to replace it. I work in a coffee shop, and I figured rent was a little more important than a new computer," I say sharply.

"I'm not making fun of you. Stop getting so defensive. I told you I would never laugh at you. I meant it."

"Yeah, well you told me a lot of things that weren't true, so please excuse me for not believing you now."

"Jess, I want to show you something. Where is your phone? Sarah wouldn't give me mine back, and I didn't have the time to fight with her about it. I wanted to get over here and make sure you were okay. Which you obviously are not."

"You need to leave."

"Where is your phone?" he repeats, not at all fazed by my stern command.

"On the table." I give in, punctuating it with a huff as he walks across the room to retrieve my phone. He hands it to me and steps away, careful not to invade my personal space.

"Type this into Google: 'Sarah Sharp Manda Baker April 2009,'" he instructs.

Willing to momentarily humor him, I open the Internet browser on my phone and do a quick search. I'm floored by the number of articles that pop up. First about Manda's death and the investigation into who was driving the car. Then there are several articles about Sarah's attempted suicide covered by the local news. There's even a picture of Brett covered head to toe in blood, wrapped in Caleb's arms, while standing on the front porch of a small white house.

"Brett," I whisper. I'm not sure what any of this proves about our current situation, but I feel horrible for the tragedy these two men experienced. A single tear escapes my eye, and for the first time in hours, it's not for myself.

"Are you ready to listen now, gorgeous?" He steps back towards me. He barely drags his fingertips over my neck while gently brushing my hair off my shoulder. The graze of his gentle fingers sends chills all the way down my spine. It's something so common, but the way he does it makes it intimate.

"I'll listen, but I can't promise I'll believe you."

"You'll believe me. I won't accept it any other way."

"Then tell me about Sarah before I lose my nerve."

"Sarah and I met when we were twenty-one, and I was lucky enough to keep her for seven years before I lost her one tragic night in a car accident on 290. She and her best friend, Manda, wrapped their car around a tree on the way home from dinner. To this day, no one is sure who was driving. Sarah can't remember anything about the accident. They were both thrown from the car, but Manda was killed on impact. Sarah was unconscious afterward but eventually escaped with just some pretty serious cuts and bruises. Or at least that was the way it looked at the time.

"It wasn't more than a few hours after the accident that I noticed something wasn't right with her. She hated me as if I had done something to cause the wreck. See, Caleb and I got called away from dinner to close up a case. They were laughing and eating pizza when we left. So full of life. I never would have left if I had known it was the last time I'd ever see my wife. I'm not talking about Sarah. I've seen her a lot since that night. But I never saw my wife again.

"At first, I felt like maybe she was harboring some bitterness towards me for leaving them that night, but within days of coming home from the hospital, it was obvious that something more was going on with her. She wouldn't even sleep in our bed. I had to go out and buy a whole new bedroom set for our guest room just to keep her under the same roof with me. A month later, she tried to kill herself."

I take in a deep breath as his voice painfully cracks. I'm not sure I want to hear the rest of this story after seeing Brett covered in blood in the picture online.

The pain of his memories is etched on his face as he continues. "She took every pill we had in the house. If I hadn't found her when I did that night, she would have been successful.

"She thankfully made it to the hospital in time to avoid any permanent damage to her body. Even knowing the way she had become after the accident, I was unwilling to accept that my Sarah would have done that to herself. I became a madman on a mission, demanding answers from everyone who even walked into the room. The doctors, for the longest time, said that it was guilt eating her away, but she just refused to talk to anyone. I knew it was more than that though. Even her taste in food changed. She just became a different person.

"I beat down the door of every doctor in town, trying to get someone to help me get my wife back. In the end, one doctor finally diagnosed her with Post-Concussion Syndrome as a result of her head injury after being thrown from the car. There is no cure or treatment for PCS, so he just sent us along on our merry little dysfunctional way. But at least we had something. After that, all of her doctors started taking her issues a little more seriously.

"Over the seven months after the accident, she tried to kill herself a total of three times. Each time, the method she used became more drastic. The last time, she sliced open what seemed like every inch of her body with a kitchen knife." He looks down at the ground, intertwining his fingers and resting them on top of his head.

I can see the effort it is taking him to keep it together during this story. It is heartbreaking to hear this level of devastation, but it's worse to watch him relive it.

"After that, I let her move out, and it actually helped a lot. I think not being forced to deal with her issues with me calmed her down a good bit. I basically just let her live in denial. She doesn't face any of her issues, but she doesn't try to kill herself either."

It isn't until Brett pauses that I realize I have been holding my breath while he was speaking. My heart actually hurts for him, but I don't know what I could possibly do to help. It sounds like Sarah isn't the only one not dealing with their issues.

"So listen to me, Jess. I am an idiot for phrasing it the way I did when I told you I lost Sarah. But you have to understand, I never lied to you. Never. Not once. That is not the way I'm wired. I tell the truth even when you don't want to hear it, and you probably aren't going to want to hear what I have to say next."

He leans into me, forcing my eyes to lock with his. "I go to Sarah's apartment every Thursday night. I take her favorite dinner and spend time with the evil woman who now inhabits her body. I've been doing this for years. She doesn't like it when I show up. I've never quite been able to figure out why she hates me the way she does, because before she changed, we were more than happy together. We were perfect."

He's right. I don't want to hear this. My mind is spinning. I can't figure out if I should believe him. What's worse is that I no longer *want* to believe him. What he is telling me now is almost more disastrous than the things Sarah told me earlier. If he is a liar and a cheat, I can walk away with no guilt of my own. But I have no idea how to deal with the idea that he might still be in love with the living, breathing ghost of his wife.

"Is she still in love with you?" It surprises me that this is the first question that pops out of my mouth. I'm too scared to ask what I really want to know—if he still is in love with her.

"No. Tonight, I told her I met someone. She deserved to know, and honestly, I thought she would throw a party in celebration. She has been asking for a divorce since she first came home from the hospital. However, when I told her about you, she flipped her lid. The phone call tonight had way more to do with me not giving her a divorce, which she has so desperately wanted for years, than it did about her feelings for me.

"I've fought her every step of the way about the divorce. I feel like I have a responsibility to take care of her. I owe it to my old Sarah not to turn my back on her, regardless that this new person has turned her back on me.

"She doesn't work, and she lives off the settlement from the auto insurance company. She's completely alone. Slowly over the years, she has closed herself off to everyone. She doesn't speak to any of her friends or family. Every week, she lets me in, and it's silly, but even just that simple act makes me believe that somewhere, deep inside, is my wife. She spends the entire night abusing me, reinforcing that my Sarah really is gone. Yet week after week, I return. I think, after tonight, I'm done though." He stops talking, and I can almost see a decision being made and a weight lifting from his shoulders.

"Did she do that to your lip?"

"Yes. She was pretty pissed. After she hit me, I took off before things could escalate. That's how she ended up with my phone. I left it sitting on the counter. Jesus, I'm so sorry you had to put up with all of this tonight. Please,

Jess, I don't want to stand here for another minute without kissing you. I've had a shit night and I'd love to forget it with you. When I'm with you, the world goes silent." His last words make my heart stop. I feel the silence, too, but I'm nowhere near ready to forget.

"Brett, I'm really confused right now. I don't know what or who I should believe. I need some time alone to think."

"Can you please tell me what poison she injected into your brain? I can't be your anti-venom if I don't know what she bit you with tonight."

Crap. He's right. I don't know if I believe him or if I will ever be able to trust him again. But I have just enough belief in his words and hope in my heart to make me tell him everything.

"She told me she was your wife, and she loves you, but you have a wandering eye. Your apartment is just to save you the commute home when you work late. You have two children, and they suffer the most from your infidelities. Oh, and she asked me if we had slept together." I can't help but look down at my feet, partially embarrassed but predominately terrified of how he is going to respond. Which parts are true? Which parts are lies?

Out of the corner of my eye, I see him reach up and grab the bridge of his nose. He takes in a quick breath before closing his eyes for a second then snatching up my beer bottle and hurling it across the room. I've seen Brett mad before, and I've seen the angry ogre, but I just witnessed this man go nuclear.

Stunned by his violent outburst, I instinctively take a step away from him and push my hands up between us to keep him from following my retreat.

"You're scaring me," I choke out before my throat closes, blocking any further words.

This seems to snap him out of it, and his face flashes with shame before he starts to apologize. "Shit! Come here, gorgeous. I'm sorry."

But I can't move. I stand, staring at him as his mood drastically changes directions yet again. "Can we talk about this tomorrow? Please, just let me have some time."

"Okay," he answers, resigned. "Let me explain something first. Jess, I have been living in a fog. I can't tell you that this will work out between us. Hell, after tonight, I'm not sure if this isn't already ruined. I'm a mess. I'm angry half the time and a miserable bastard the other half. You're a good girl who deserves someone who can open themselves up and actually offer *you* something. You deserve more than I can probably ever give you. I don't know if I can handle even saying the word forever again.

"So with all of that said, I'm sorry for scaring you tonight. I'm just so frustrated. I think I have used every cuss word I know at least fifteen times tonight." He tries to crack a joke, but it only sounds sad. "I feel like Sarah is determined to completely ruin me, even more than she already has.

"I'm broken, Jess, but I need you to hear these words before I go. Trust me, I know saying this makes me a selfish bastard, because I've seen you cry three times in the five days we have been together. But for me, these last few days have been an awakening. I now see the sun behind the fog, and it's a damn good feeling.

"I'm sorry about all of this. I truly am. Please believe me and think about what I've said. I can't promise you anything more than tomorrow, but maybe one day, the fog will disappear, leaving only sunny days ahead." He doesn't stall even a minute longer. He simply walks to the corner, cleans up the broken glass, and then walks out the front door.

Just as the door clicks, I hear a breathy, "Whoa!" come from behind me. I turn to see Kara standing in the hall. "Are you okay?" she asks, walking a few steps in my direction before checking the door to make sure Brett really left.

"No."

"Come here, girl." She walks over and slings an arm around my shoulders, trying to comfort me. "You understand you're the sun in that scenario, right?"

"What if I don't want to be the sun?"

"I don't think you have a choice. Do you think a man like that is going to let go of his only way out of the fog?"

"How much did you hear?" I ask needing advice.

"All of it."

"Do you believe him?"

"He's telling the truth, Jesse," she answers with absolute certainty in her voice.

"How can you be so sure? You should have heard his wife on the phone tonight. She was so weird. She kept quietly laughing then suddenly crying. Though, after hearing him describe her, a lot more of the conversation makes sense. Kara, I'm not sure what to believe anymore. I'm so confused about everything. Even if I do believe him, do I want to get mixed up with all of this drama?"

"I can't answer that part for you, but I can tell you why I believe him. I grew up with Casey Black. I never knew Sarah or Manda, but I knew the three of them were tight. I remember when the accident happened. Everyone says it destroyed Casey, losing her two best friends like that. She just kind of fell off the map after that. Anyway, I've heard people talking about Sarah and how she has basically lost her mind. She tried to kill herself then became a recluse. I heard she virtually never leaves her apartment. I didn't realize she was Brett's wife until tonight though. I believe him. His story matches up with everything I have ever heard. And I'm not just siding with him because he's hot." She finishes with an exaggerated wink.

"He's going to break my heart. You know that, right? He still has some serious issues with her. I think I'll always feel like the other woman. He has a wife. Regardless that she is a different person, he is still very much married to her. And if she is as terrible as he says, why would anyone stand by her?"

"He loved her. I actually respect the hell out of him for standing by her for as long as he has. What you need to figure out is if he still loves her or if he's ready to move on."

"What if he can't ever move on? You heard him. She was perfect."

"You're missing the keyword—was," she says as I sigh, knowing that I have no choice but to hear Brett out. Get some answers so I can make an informed decision. "Maybe you just have to wait out the fog."

"What the heck happened to you? You're getting all poetic on me. Where did your 'crotch-less panties solve everything' speech go?"

"You didn't let me finish! I was getting to that part," she jokes.

"Do you think he'll come in for breakfast tomorrow?"

"Tomorrow's Friday, so I doubt it," Kara answers, reminding me that it's my day off.

"Ugh! I'll call him and see if he wants to meet for breakfast in the morning."

"Good, because did you see his ass in those jeans tonight? Seriously, I would gladly go to jail just to hump his leg." She starts thrusting her hips in the air and we both start giggling like teenage girls.

Chapter
EIGHTEEN

Brett

I ARRIVE back at my apartment feeling utterly lost. It seems like every time I get comfortable in life, someone flips over the life raft I've been so desperately clinging to. I haven't been happy in a long time, but the last few days, I haven't been drowning. As much as it makes me a pussy to admit, Jesse was only the reason for that. Knowing that she is potentially gone too, I feel worse than I did a week ago. Now I remember what it feels like to be alive again.

In the middle of my pity party, my house phone begins to ring in the kitchen. I called the station earlier to make sure they forward all my calls to my home number. There is no way I am going back to Sarah's to get my phone. I'll scrap it and buy a new one. I'm not sure if I'll ever go back over there.

"Detective Sharp," I answer, assuming it's a work call.

"Hey." I hear the soft voice that makes my chest hurt. First in relief that she is reaching out to me, but then I panic that something's wrong.

"Jesse, are you okay? Did Sarah call you again?"

"No, no. I'm fine."

"Phew, okay. I didn't expect to hear from you tonight. I'm glad you called though." I smile to myself.

"Do you think we could, um...maybe meet up for breakfast at Nell's in the morning? You know, to talk about things. I have something I want to ask you," she questions timidly. I hate to hear her nervous. We made great strides over the last few days, but we are right back where we started after the clusterfuck tonight.

"Of course, Jess. Anything. I'll answer any questions you want to ask. Please don't be nervous okay."

"I'm sorry," is all she says.

"Please don't apologize to me. I'm sorry for all of this. I can't say that enough."

"Okay, well, tomorrow then?"

"I wouldn't miss it for the world, gorgeous. Sleep tight. I promise I'll do my best to dry those beautiful eyes in the morning."

"Goodnight, Brett."

"Night, Jesse." I hang up the phone and throw an excited fist pump into the air. I'm down, but I'm not out yet. Now I just have to figure out what the hell I'm going to say to her to make this right.

I WAKE up the next morning, calling out of work by taking a personal day. I haven't taken a day off in years. I had no reason to. I didn't have anyone to take vacations with or play hooky while spending the day under a blanket on a cold, snowy morning. I have plenty of days stored up, and this feels like the perfect time to use one. I know Jesse doesn't work on Fridays, so I want to spend the entire day making up for last night. Maybe I'll take her some-place nice where we can snuggle close and I can apologize to her properly. Preferably by using my body.

I walk into Nell's to see Jesse in jeans that perfectly hug her curvy ass and a tight long-sleeved purple shirt. Her thick brown hair falls around her shoulders, barely curling under at the ends. She doesn't look like the sex kit-ten she has the last few times we have been out, but she still looks amazing. She looks relaxed and carefree compared to the slightly nervous and uneasy woman I figured would show up this morning. And let me tell you, this looks so damn good on her. Maybe something I said to her actually penetrated last night.

She stands at the counter laughing with Kara while the two guys waiting in line smile in her direction. Her laugh is infectious. I can't blame them for staring. I was staring too. However, I can stop them before they get any ideas about making a move. Even though I'm not quite sure where we stand this morning, it doesn't stop me from walking up behind her, brushing her hair away from her neck, and planting a lingering kiss just below her ear. Thank-fully, she doesn't slap me, but I can feel her tense. I pretend not to notice it. She may not want it, but I need to touch her.

"Come on. Let's go sit down and talk." I drape an arm over her shoul-der, giving the two guys watching a knowing nod as we walk past. We sit down at my usual table, the one closest to the counter. "You okay?" I ask as

Jesse starts chewing on the edge of her thumb nail like she so often does. I reach forward, grabbing her hand, and pull it way from her mouth.

She drops it to the table and tries to slide it away, but I refuse to let go. I hear the bell over the door, but I'm too focused on this little hand-holding war that I'm having with Jesse to even give it a second thought.

"Well, isn't this cozy."

I see Sarah standing beside our table. I'm not talking present-day Sarah either. I'm talking Sarah from seven years ago. Tight red dress, black fuck-me heels, blond hair. It's slightly shorter than it was back in those days, but it's definitely blond again. The flash from the past causes me to spring to my feet, releasing Jesse's hand.

"Sarah?" I ask genuinely confused. I haven't seen this woman in years, and I would be lying if I said my stomach didn't jump at the very thought of her standing in front of me.

She lets out a distantly familiar laugh, and I'm stunned, shocked, and—worst of all—hopeful. She pushes up to her tiptoes to kiss me chastely on the lips before leveling her glare on Jesse.

"Hey, honey. Care to introduce me to your little friend?" She grins an evil smile.

I look down at Jesse, who is still sitting and now chewing on her bottom lip. Her eyes are wide with amazement and maybe even a little fear. I look between Jesse and Sarah for a second while I try to figure out what dimension I'm currently in.

Jesse finally drops her eyes to her lap when Sarah wraps an arm around my waist. Her touch is cold and calculated, not at all like the woman who appears to be standing in front of me. I quickly jump out of her reach.

"What the fuck?" I bat her hands away when she tries to grab me again.

"Brett, stop being so silly. Introduce me to your friend."

I stand still, blinking and knowing that any second the world is going to stop spinning. There is no other explanation for this absurdity.

"Hi, I'm Jesse," she says, standing to her feet and looking up at all six foot one of Sarah in heels.

"Well, aren't you cute?" Sarah pauses to look at me. "Very interesting choice. She isn't at all who I expected when I found out you were cheating on me."

"Cheating on you?" I have to clarify because I know I couldn't have heard her correctly.

"I believe we spoke last night, Jesse. Remember, you admitted to being the slut who is sleeping with my husband?"

Jesse leans back, trying to dodge the verbal slap, but it lands exactly where Sarah planned. And Sarah doesn't let it sit long before she throws another blow.

"The kids have been missing you."

"Wow, that's interesting! I wasn't aware we even had kids."

She ignores me completely and continues to follow her carefully crafted script. "Samantha got her class photo back yesterday. She cried herself to sleep last night when you didn't come home for her to show it to you." She pulls a school picture of a little girl I know looks exactly like me out of her purse.

She has green eyes and long, dark pigtails, and she towers over all of her classmates. I can actually feel the breath get sucked out of the room as I glance to Jesse, who is standing with her eyes glued to the picture lying on the table. Just as I start to lose it, I see the one thing that causes me to go speechless. On Sarah's left ring finger, I catch the sparkle of a diamond. I know it's the one I placed there all those years ago. The one that has been sitting in her jewelry box for over four years. I've wanted nothing more than to see those rings adorn her finger again, but it enrages me to see them on the hand of this fraud.

"You have got to be shitting me! Sarah, what are you doing?"

"You need to come home, Brett. Last Tuesday night, I felt like everything was finally right again. When we made love, it was amazing. Honey, I'm hoping that will give us the little boy we have been trying for."

"Umm, I should probably go," Jesse whispers while backing away on unsteady feet.

"Wait!" I say to Jesse, but a table and Sarah stand between us. I have no way to stop her.

"I was wrong. I can't do this." She glances between me and Sarah.

"Yeah, that's right. Go poach someone else's husband. You're nothing but a whore," Sarah hisses as Jesse retreats behind the counter.

"Go home, Sarah. We'll talk about this later." I rush after Jesse. I reach her just before she makes it behind the counter, but she squirms out of my grasp.

"Don't touch me!" Jesse shouts.

"Don't touch her!" I hear from behind me as Sarah quickly moves towards us.

"Go home, Sarah."

This situation is quickly spiraling out of control. Jesse is running, Sarah is chasing, and I'm caught in the middle, trying to make one stay and one leave.

The next few seconds move in slow motion. I have no idea what I did in a past life to deserve these things to happen to me. I know I'm being punished for something though, because I swear, the universe has it out for me.

Jesse finally makes it to the office just as the waterworks start. She tries to slam the door behind her, but I'm successful in throwing one hand against the top, blocking it from closing. *Score one point for Sharp!*

Sarah storms up behind me, ducking under my arm and sliding into the room with Jesse, effectively shutting and locking the door behind her. *Score one point for the unfair bitch of a universe!*

I pound on the door. "Sarah, open this God damn door." My stomach begins to churn. I know what Sarah is capable of, and the idea of her unleashing that on innocent Jesse is literally enough to make me sick. I press my ear against the door to hear Sarah shouting but nothing from Jesse.

I back up, prepared to kick open the door, just as Kara rushes in front of me, shoving a key into the lock. With the flick of her wrist, the office door pops open. I see Jesse sitting on the couch, leaning forward with her face in her hands. Sarah stands over her, one finger pointed in Jesse's face yelling, "He fucks me so hard, I see stars. I bet he couldn't even keep it up with you."

With one swift movement, I reach from behind Sarah, one hand landing over her mouth and the other across her waist. I lift her off her feet and carry her into the hallway. She is kicking and flailing the whole way, but I don't put her down until we are completely clear of the room. I place her on her feet but keep one hand pinning her against the wall as I look around the corner to check on Jesse. She's still sitting on the couch with tears running down her face, but Kara is squatting down, quietly comforting her. I return my attention to the woman who's responsible for all of this.

"Don't say another fucking word, Sarah. I have no idea what you are doing, but I swear to God, if Jesse wants to press charges for your little stunt in there, I will do the paperwork myself."

"I really thought you had better taste. That woman is a joke. You should have seen how easy it was to make her cry. Honestly, Brett, that was more fun than I have had in years." She begins to laugh at herself.

The universe makes its final play when Kara chooses this moment to guide Jesse out of the office. Unfortunately, it's Sarah who sees them first. She reaches around me with both hands, grabbing my ass and pulling us hip to hip.

"Jesus, right here in the middle of the hall, Brett? I love that you can't keep your hands off me."

I jerk back, ready to lay into Sarah. I'm done with the bullshit. I have seen daytime soap operas that were less dramatic than the crap that has gone down here. But I'm not the one who gets to her first.

As Jesse scrambles to get away from this crazy, messed-up situation, Caleb rounds the corner and she runs directly into his chest. His eyes quickly rake over everyone, finally landing on Sarah. She immediately stops laughing and cowers behind me. Caleb's face fills with rage as his scrutinizing eyes take in the situation. This has just gone from terrible to damn near explosive.

Caleb and Sarah have seen each other once in the four years since the accident. I wasn't there, but by all accounts, it was bad. Sarah showed up at his door one night about three months after Manda passed away. She was drunk, sobbing and begging for Manda's half of the best friend's necklace. Caleb has always blamed Sarah for the wreck. So when she showed up that night, apparently drinking and driving, he lost his mind completely. I never got the full story from either one of them. I just know that Sarah is now terrified of him and Caleb loathes her.

"Get out," he says to Sarah with a scary calm as he tucks Jesse under his arm.

The tone of his voice is enough to cause Sarah to let out a small whimper, and she slides farther behind me, attempting to disappear completely. My eyes are stuck to his arm around Jesse. She has her hands covering her face and her entire body pressed against his side. It's the wrong time to care. I should be grateful that she has someone to comfort and protect her right now, but it pisses me off that it's him and not me. I hate that he is even touching her right now. With any other friend in the world, I would ask them to take Sarah home so I could hold Jesse myself. But there is not a chance in hell I could leave Sarah alone with Caleb.

"Caleb, calm down for a minute. You're freaking her out," I say while trying to figure out the best plan to get everyone into their separate corners.

"Are you fucking kidding me, Brett?" he snaps. "I have no idea what just happened here, but I can promise you that crazy bitch hiding behind you is at the center of this problem."

I feel Sarah start trembling behind me. He's right. She has proven herself to be crazy today. But feeling this woman who used to own my heart shaking in fear is more than I can take. I reach behind me and pull her into my arms. Our position almost exactly mirrors the way Caleb is holding Jesse. He stands staring and shaking his head in disbelief while wrapping his other arm around a still-hidden Jesse.

"You have issues, Brett. I thought you were moving on from this, but I think we can all see now that you are still stuck, rooted in a past that you will never be able to reclaim. You need to take a good, long look at this situation for what it really is. You're walking out of here holding the wrong woman, and everyone knows it but you." He bends over, lifting a still-emotional Jesse into his arms, and carries her out the back door.

I know he's right, but I can't see what other options I have right now. I look up just in time to see Jesse peeking at me over Caleb's shoulder as I hold Sarah. The pain on her face shatters the few remaining broken shards of a heart I have left.

Kara walks back toward the front, pausing only long enough to finish me off. "You know, I had you pegged all wrong. You talked such a big game last night. That whole bullshit about sunshine and fog. I even believed you." She lets out a humorless laugh. "Get her the hell out of here, and stay away from Jesse. I'm not going to stand by and watch you destroy her the same way you did that one." She nods toward Sarah, who is still nestled in my arms, before walking away.

Chapter
NINETEEN

Jesse

THE FIRST thing I clearly remember is sitting in Caleb's truck. He's talking to me, but I can't think of anything except the image of Brett holding Sarah. Protecting her. It's burned into my memory. I may never be able to see anything else again.

"Are you okay?" Caleb asks, causing my eyes to snap up to his.

"Umm..." I say as my lip begins to quiver. I can't continue without crying again, and to be honest, my head hurts. I need to be in my bed. Alone, except for the seven hundred beers I'm going to need to forget the last twenty-four hours. "Can you take me home?"

"Absolutely." It's only one word, and I've never been so thankful for brevity in my life.

I'm not in the mood to talk. Not when I can still hear Sarah telling me all about the night she had with Brett on Tuesday. The night after he and I were together. The idea of him touching her within hours of leaving me is enough to make me ill. She told me every sickening detail of their night together. Her mouth was a knife, verbally gutting me open. There are a lot of things she could have told me that would have done less damage, but somehow she knew that giving me the play-by-play of their sexual escapades was more than enough to send me over the edge. She knew my insecurities and she played right into them.

"She's so pretty," I whisper as Caleb drives us towards my apartment.

"Yeah, she is on the outside. But she's ugly on the inside."

"No, I mean his daughter."

"Whose daughter?" he asks, obviously confused.

"Brett's."

"He doesn't have any kids."

"But she had a picture of a little girl who looked just like him. Big green eyes. Dark brown pigtails. Said her name was Samantha or something."

"Oh shit. This is a whole new level of crazy, even for Sarah. Samantha is his niece. Brett's whole gigantic family looks exactly the same. Must be good genes, because his sisters are hot."

"Oh."

"What else did she hit you with back there?"

No way am I repeating the things she told me about their sex life to Caleb. I want to get as far away from that particular topic as possible.

"That was really horrible." I hiccup a breath, remembering.

"I'm so sorry, baby girl. No one deserves to be on the opposite end of Sarah Sharp's wrath. Least of all, you."

"So, they really are married?" I know the answer, but after meeting her today, I can't imagine Brett ever falling for a woman like that. She's beautiful, so I can definitely see why he was attracted to her initially, but her personality couldn't have been more different than the sweet and funny guy Brett is.

"Yeah, they are." He glances over at me while driving.

I find myself wanting to know more about this mystery woman. It's plain to see from her reaction tonight that she and Caleb don't get along. I think it would help to hear their story from someone who isn't in love with her.

Apparently, that shows in my face because he shakes his head and says, "Listen, I'm really the wrong person to talk to about Sarah. Kara should be getting off work soon. You two can talk and do whatever the hell girls do in this type of situation. Shit, you want me to stop and buy you some wine?"

"It's nine in the morning."

"And?"

"Tell me about Sarah." I finally say the words.

"No," he says simply. The pain in his voice leads me to believe that he doesn't just want to avoid talking about Sarah. He doesn't want it to lead into a conversation about Manda.

"I won't ask about...*her*," I plead, putting emphasis on her so he knows exactly who I'm talking about.

"Damn it, you just did!" He slams the heel of his hand against the steering wheel. Apparently, anger issues are not isolated to Brett. "Jesse, you're a good girl," he says, exasperated.

"And?" I throw his earlier words back at him, determined to get some answers.

"I'm not doing this with you. Not here, not now, not ever."

"Please. I don't know who or what to believe. She tells me one thing, but Brett tells me another. I deserve to know! Can someone just tell me the darn truth?" My words cause Caleb to crack a smile, and it infuriates me!

"Darn? Really?" he asks, still smiling.

"Shut up. As much as I hate him right now, I wish Brett were here to make good on his threat to punch you in the face."

"I'm not making fun of you. I think it's cute that you don't cuss."

"Great. Someone else who thinks I'm cute."

"I think you're sexy as hell too if that helps," he says, winking at me.

I bite my lip and look out the window to keep him from seeing the color that fills my cheeks. I don't respond to his flirty comment. When we pull into my apartment complex, it's Caleb who finally breaks the silence.

"Everyone is so sympathetic towards her. She's always been wild, but at least before, it was entertaining. Now, her craziness is disgusting. She doesn't give a damn about anyone but herself. She is a selfish bitch, and I make sure she knows I'm not falling for her bullshit."

"Does she care about Brett?" I find myself once again inquiring about how she feels about him. Why is this question so important to me? Shouldn't I be worried about how he feels? Heck, after today, I shouldn't care about that either.

"Yes." Shifting the truck into park, he sighs. "She hates him. That counts for caring, right?" I feel guilty for the relief his answer causes me. "Why are you still asking about Brett and Sarah after that little spectacle back there?" He raises his eyebrows knowingly. "You should still be crying and freaking out, but here you sit, interrogating me. What's your end game, Jess?"

I don't immediately respond. It's not that I don't understand his question. I just don't know the answer. Why the hell am I still asking about them?

"Something just isn't right about all of this. I'm confused, and if I've learned anything by spending the last eight years in college, it's that if you ask enough people, someone will eventually know the answer."

"You want me to give it to you straight? Okay, fine. Here it is—Sarah is batshit crazy. She was nutty before the accident, but she is off her fucking rocker now. It scares me that she even knows you exist. Brett's an idiot for telling her your name. She hates him, but she takes great pleasure in knowing he still loves her. She has done her damnedest to drive those who loved her away, and that includes me. Everyone has given up on her. Everyone but Brett.

"If your next question is how you fit into that equation, let me tell you now that I have no fucking idea. As someone who has come to call you a friend, I want to tell you to run as far away from them as you can get. After today, I would suggest you pick up and move to Canada. However, as Brett's best friend, I can honestly say that I have never seen him even notice a woman in four years. If I didn't know better, I would assume his dick has rotted off from lack of use by now. But judging by the blush in your cheeks last Tuesday morning, it's apparently still in working condition."

My face heats to red, but he doesn't even slow down to take a breath. The man is on a roll.

"He looks at you subconsciously. His eyes track your every move in the mornings. He's been trapped in the past for too long, and it's like he knows you are the one person who can save him. His problem is that he can't let go of her.

"He doesn't love Sarah anymore, just in case you are wondering. But he can't seem to walk away from her either. By the time he actually does, it's going to be too late. That's what frustrates me the most with him. He has gotten through the hardest part—he's stopped loving her. The walking away should be easy."

Staring deep into my eyes to make sure I'm really listening, he continues. "So, Jesse, if you are hoping for me to tell you what to do here, you are asking the wrong person."

I'm overcome by emotions at everything he just said, but I don't have any tears left to cry.

"He watches me?" I squeak out.

"Jesus, is that all you heard in that?"

"No, I heard you. I just always thought I was the one staring at him."

"You have no idea the effect you have on Brett." His words only leave me more confused.

"Then why was he holding her?" Suddenly, all of my bitterness from earlier returns.

"Because he's a good guy. She's broken, and Brett always feels the need to fix things. I don't like it, but he knew I would take care of you. If he left with you, Sarah would have been alone. If you are still crazy enough to want any type of relationship with him after today, you're going to have to accept that he will never let her be completely alone. He's just not that type of guy. It sucks, but he's a package deal."

"Do you think I could maybe talk to Sarah without her going ballistic on me? I'm not very fond of her, but if what everyone says is true, it's really sad that she doesn't have anyone to lean on. She needs a friend or something. I think I could have handled her a little better if she hadn't surprised me the way she did. Maybe I could try to talk to her one on one, you know, when Brett isn't around."

"She's not like you, Jess, so don't try to figure her out. She isn't a stray puppy you can rescue. Trust me. Brett has tried for years. Please hear me when I say this—stay away from Sarah. If you see her again, you call me immediately. Not Brett. You call me. I'll have some words with her tonight. She shouldn't bother you anymore. Okay? Promise me you'll stay away from her."

"Fine, I promise."

I realize we are just sitting in his truck, parked in front of my apartment. I'm no longer excited about the prospect of spending the day alone. Kara works all day on Fridays then usually goes out with whatever guy she is sleeping with this week. I need a distraction or I'm going to obsess about Brett and Sarah all day.

"So, umm...do you want to come in for a little while? I can cook you some breakfast. You kind of saved me from the beast today. The least I can do is make you some pancakes."

"Eggs, too?"

"Of course!"

"All right, baby girl. I'll hang for a bit," he says, seeing right through my lame excuse.

"Thank you."

"Thank me with breakfast. I'm starving." He exits the truck and guides me inside.

Chapter TWENTY

Brett

IT'S TAKEN me four hours to get Sarah settled. For the first hour, she was shaking and crying, randomly talking about Manda. I managed to get her to take a few of the sedatives the doctor prescribed for when she gets overexcited like this. After that, she fell asleep, and I spent the next two hours taking all the pills and knives out of her house. Then it took forever to find a home health nurse to come sit with her. She's cussed out almost everyone I have ever hired, so I end up paying two times the normal wage just to get someone to come over and make sure she doesn't do anything stupid. It's worth it though. After seeing her in action with Jesse today, then her reaction to Caleb, I'm not about to take any chances leaving her alone.

I pull up to Jesse's house just after one. I park next to her car and head straight for her door. I have a lot of explaining, apologizing, and probably groveling to do. I looked like a dick earlier, no denying that. I saw it in her eyes when she left with Caleb. I knock on her door, not giving myself any time to prepare what I'm going to say. I'll wing it, even though that hasn't been working out so well for me recently. I have to talk to her, explain everything. Jesse is very levelheaded. She'll understand. *God, please let her understand.*

No one immediately comes to the door, and it makes me wonder if she is trying to avoid me. I can't blame her if she is, but I sure as hell can make sure she isn't successful. I turn, looking back at the parking lot just to be positive it was her car I parked beside. In my scan, my eyes run across an all-too-familiar truck. What the hell is he still doing here? They aren't close. I can only think of one reason why he would still be here.

Women love Caleb. He's six foot two and blond, and he has that bad-boy thing going on that women swoon over. I know exactly how much Caleb loves the ladies. He doesn't have a type. He appreciates them all. I swear, if he is appreciating Jess right now, I'll kill him.

"Caleb! Open the fucking door!" I pound my fists against her door, all the while contemplating if I could kick it down. Just as I step back to give it my best attempt, Caleb yanks open her door.

"What's up, big man?"

Seeing him standing in Jesse's apartment is enough to rock me back on my heels.

"What the hell are you doing here?"

"Oh you know, just cleaning up your mess. Better question is what are *you* doing here?"

"Is this your little idea of payback for having to see Sarah today? I swear to Christ, if you touched Jess—"

"Exactly what are you going to do Brett? If I recall correctly, you watched me pick her up and carry her out this morning. You didn't try to stop me then. Now you suddenly care that we are spending time together? God forbid I touch the woman you threw to the wolves. It only took you, what"—he stops to check his watch—"four hours to get here. If Jesse means so much to you, what the hell took you so long?"

"She is not one of your conquests to make you forget about Manda! She's not yours!" I yell words that I have no control over.

"Oh, but she's yours? Because that is not the way it looked today while you were holding your wife."

"Fuck you! Yes, she's mine! You, of all people, know that!" I step up, ready to once again go toe-to-toe with my best friend. Only this time, he doesn't respond to my challenge. He begins to laugh instead.

"Just checking." He pats me on the chest, doing nothing to calm my rage.

"Caleb, stop," I hear Jesse say as she walks under his arm, stopping in the door way in front of me. "Hey," she says in that shy way I'm getting used to.

"Did he touch you?" I swear it just spews from my mouth. I had no plans for those to be the first words I say to her, but apparently my testosterone had other ideas.

"What? No!"

"Then why is he still here?" I ask accusingly.

"I asked him to stay. I didn't want to be alone. While you were off doing whatever you were doing with Sarah, he was nice enough to hang out."

"Jesse, I know Caleb. He doesn't just hang out with women. Don't bullshit me right now. Is something going on with you two?"

"You know what. I'm not doing this. You need to leave," she answers, rightfully annoyed.

"Not happening. We need to talk." I look up at Caleb, who is still protectively standing behind her. "You, however, can leave. I've got it from here."

"The hell you do! Besides, I'm not going anywhere. Jesse is cooking me lunch. You should have tasted her pancakes this morning." He pauses to wink and lick his lips before finishing with, "Benissimo!" That one word is all it takes for me to lose it. But for reasons known only to my dick, I lose it on the wrong person.

"You blew him? Jesus Christ, Jess, what the hell?"

"And here we go," Caleb says at the same time I see Jesse's eyes widen as she morphs into a madwoman.

"You did not just say that to me!" she screams as Caleb lifts her off her feet, dragging her away. His touching her only pisses me off more. "Put me down! Put me down now!" She kicks her legs trying to break free of his hold.

If I were an outsider looking in, I would think this tiny woman was comical. I'm not an outsider though, and it's my tiny woman he's manhandling.

"Get your hands off her!" I snap.

"Oh, now I know you're kidding, asspuck! She is about to claw your eyes out, and if you keep this up, I'm going to let her. You're being a dick. Both of you just need to calm down."

"You couldn't keep your hands to yourself for a few hours? I've felt something for the first time in years with her, yet you swoop in and steal it away just to get your rocks off. Shit!" I finally realize what's going on. "Oh my God, you're jealous that I'm moving on! Why did I not see this coming?"

"First off, you sound like an idiot right now. I didn't do shit to steal anything from you. You're doing a bang-up job of ruining this all on your own. Secondly, I'm jealous that you're moving on? Where can I preorder tickets to your new comedy show? Because you should take this shit on the road. Moving on? If you really think you're moving on after what went down this morning, apparently Sarah isn't the only delusional one. Nothing happened between me and Jesse, so the next words out of your mouth better be a fucking apology."

"Right, because you two clearly look like two people who were barely even friends last week." I look down to where he is still tightly holding her against his body.

"Stop talking about me like I'm not here! Get out, both of you!" she yells, still trying to fight out of Caleb's grip.

This is too much. All of it. Maybe I'm just delaying the inevitable by holding on to Jesse. If I were a better man, I would turn and walk out the door right now. Fortunately for me, I'm an asshole, so I'm going to fight for her only to disappoint her later down the line. *Outstanding!*

"I'm not leaving until we talk. I have a lot to say."

"Well, I don't feel like listening anymore. You think just because we made out once that I'm going to hook up with every guy who looks at me?" she yells, fighting Caleb's grasp around her waist.

I have no idea what has come over me. I know nothing has happened between these two. Jesse isn't that type of girl, even if Caleb is that type of guy. Still, I somehow can't keep myself from being a prick.

"Oh we did far more than 'make out.' I have the claw marks on my back to prove it."

She immediately goes quiet and I know I've said too much. She's such a private person, and here I am, airing her bedroom behaviors in front of other people.

"Claw marks? Really?" Caleb raises an eyebrow with a smirk lifting the corner of his mouth.

"Shit, I'm sorry. I have no idea why I said that. I'm just pissed... I—"

She finally breaks free from Caleb and crosses the room, stopping inches in front from me. Standing on her toes to make herself as tall as possible, she screams into my face, "What the hell, Brett? I'm the one who's supposed to be mad. You didn't just walk in on me hugging and defending my husband. Oh wait, that's because I don't have one!"

Shit. I'm doing a really bad job at apologizing right now. None of this is going to win me any points. This is precisely why I should have had a plan when I got here. This is the shit that happens to me when I try to wing it.

"You're right, you're right. I'm sorry."

"Damn right you're sorry," Caleb pipes in from behind her, still smirking.

I can't take this back-and-forth anymore. It's ridiculous, and I'm exhausted from all of the drama over the last few days.

"Stop. Just...stop!" I let out a loud breath. "I can't take this. I know ninety percent of this has been brought on myself, but I need it to stop. Damn it, Jess, I'm sorry! Please don't make me let you go. This has been chaos from the first day. Just give me a chance to show you it won't always be that way. I'm a good guy. At least I think I am. I'm trying and failing, but mainly, I'm trying to make something work between us. It just seems like every step of the way something or someone keeps tripping me up. I feel like I'm losing my mind.

"Caleb...I wish I had something positive to say to you, but I really want to beat your ass right now. So please just go, and let me handle this. I'll buy you a beer or something when I'm in a better mood."

"You okay with that, baby girl?"

I swear, as soon as I get Caleb alone, he and I are going to have a serious conversation about boundaries. It sets my blood on fire to hear him call her *baby girl*.

Jesse nods with her eyes glued to mine. She's mad and she has every right to be. Time to pull out some charm and see if I can get back in her good graces.

Jesse

"YOU WANT something to drink?" I ask Brett as Caleb collects his coat and shoes preparing to leave.

"No thanks." He flashes me one of his beautiful smiles.

"You hungry? I was just about to make lunch." I try to be polite, but the last thing I want to do right now is eat.

"Don't you dare make him my panini!" Caleb says as he finishes putting on his shoes.

"For the love of God, get out!" Brett shouts at Caleb.

"Fine, but you owe me, Jess. I was really looking forward to that bacon avocado thingy you mentioned."

I giggle because I know he's lying. He almost threw up when I mentioned avocado earlier. Caleb apparently is not a fan of the green superfood. He walks over, pulling me in for a quick hug, then kisses me on the forehead. This would have been weird yesterday, but Caleb and I have bonded over the last few hours. Now, it just feels nice.

He leans over and whispers, "Remember that you promised to call me if you see Sarah? I mean it. I put my number in your phone. Day or night, you call me if you need anything."

"Thank you," I respond as my heart warms at how gentle and caring he can be. He really is a good guy.

I look up to see Brett watching us with an infuriated look on his face. Call me mean, but I decide to give him a little dose of his own medicine. I reach out, giving Caleb a tight, lingering squeeze of my own. He chuckles, seemingly onto my game.

"I may have underestimated you, little Miss Addison," Caleb says before lowering his voice to a whisper again. "I like it. Give him hell." He releases me, turning to face Brett. "All right. I'm out. Brett, I'll expect that beer soon. Be good, ladies and gentlemen," he says, strutting out the door.

Brett releases a breath, running his hands through his hair. "He is such an ass."

"Oh yes, Caleb is the jerk. Not the crazy man who just showed up beating down my door and accusing me of sucking off his best friend." I throw my hand up, covering my mouth. I can't believe I just said that. I really have to stop hanging out with these foul-mouthed guys.

"I've done a crap job of handling things with you recently. Can we just sit down and talk for a minute. I have a lot of explaining to do. Why don't you let me order in some food? I don't want you to have to cook right now."

"I'm not hungry anymore. Just talk."

"I'm sorry about last night. And this morning. And for pounding on your door. And for insinuating you were 'sucking him off.' I'm appalled with your dirty language, by the way." He tries to tease me, and to some degree, it works. I can feel the corner of my lips twitch. "Damn, I really do have a lot of apologizing to do," he says, shaking his head. "Where do you want me to start?" He walks over to the couch, sitting down on the edge. He doesn't bother to lean back or get comfortable.

"Where's Sarah now?" My question must surprise him, because it takes him a second to answer.

"At her apartment."

"You should go be with her."

"What? Jess, no!" he says, flying back to his feet.

"No, I don't mean it like that. I just mean she isn't exactly stable. I would hate for you to be over here and her do something to hurt herself. We can talk on the phone later. Or maybe one day next week."

"God, I'm such an asshole. After everything that's happened, here you are worried about Sarah." He walks over, knocking me off balance and pulling me hard into his chest.

I have no choice but to let him hold me. It only takes a few seconds for me to melt into him. No matter how much I want to fight it, being in Brett's arms just feels right. He holds me, whispering heartfelt apologies into my hair. I'd pull away on pure principle alone, but I can tell by his slight rocking and content breathing that he needs this. It's strictly for him though. I don't love every single second of it. A tear definitely does not slide down my face at how perfect this feels. I absolutely don't send up a prayer for this to never end. That would be stupid after all the crap we have been through. Yet I do it all anyway.

"Ask me anything," he says as I reach between us to wipe away my stray tear. "Jess, I don't know what she said to you, but I do know the truth. I'm an open book. Don't let anything fester in that beautiful mind of yours. Please just ask it. No matter how small it is, I want to give you the answer."

"Okay," I say, not yet releasing him. I'm needy for this connection too.

I've been in an emotional upheaval for days now. I just want someone to lean on, even if it isn't real.

Caleb was great company, but with the exception of the hug when he left, he didn't touch me at all. Besides, there is just something special about the way Brett holds me. It makes me believe he would never let me struggle. It makes me feel safe. Too bad it's a load of crap. He made me feel anything *but* safe today. He abandoned me...for his mentally injured wife. *Great.* When I think about it like that, maybe I'm the jerk in this situation.

"Is Sarah alone right now?" I ask.

"No. I hired a nurse to sit with her. I gave her some meds, so she's most likely still asleep. The sitter has my number. She'll call if she needs anything."

"Oh, um...okay."

"Don't let it stew, Jess. Ask it. I can see in your eyes that you have a million questions for me."

"Did you sleep with her on Tuesday?"

"No!" he shouts, notably curious why I asked this question. "Damn it, what did she tell you?"

I just shake my head, not wanting to rehash the morning. I've already gotten most of these answers from Caleb, but I have to hear the important ones come from his mouth.

"When was the last time you were...uh, with her?"

"The wreck was in April of 2009. That was the last time I was with anyone," he answers frankly, shocking me.

The idea of sexy detective Brett Sharp remaining untouched for over four years is unbelievable to me. I don't want to pry or make him uncomfortable, but I need to make sure I heard him correctly.

"No one?"

"No one but you, babe," he confirms. He pulls away and walks back to the couch. I start to sit in the chair, but he catches me first. "No, babe, sit with me. I need you to feel that I'm telling the truth. I don't want there to be any doubts about this stuff."

He drags me into his lap but doesn't wrap me in his strong arms like he usually does. Instead, he throws both arms out to the side and over the back of the couch, physically and emotionally opening himself up to me. He's giving me my space to think but still keeping us connected.

"How do you feel about Sarah?" I can't bring myself to come right out and ask him if he still loves her.

"Responsible," he answers with one word, and I stay quiet, waiting for him to elaborate. "Jesse, I don't know. I didn't cause the wreck, but I feel like I have to fix it. I have an obligation to her. I married her once. I vowed for better or worse, but I didn't just get worse. I got nonexistent.

"My Sarah is gone, but that doesn't release me from my responsibilities to her. She doesn't have anyone else. Her parents are both dead. She didn't even go to their funerals. Her sister has written her off completely. They had a big blowout a few weeks after she first tried to kill herself. Her only real friend, Casey, just disappeared. I guess Manda's death was too much for her to handle. She moved down to Ohio and hasn't been back since. I'm all Sarah has left, and she hates me, so I don't know how much help I really am."

"I'm so sorry."

"Stop apologizing. Did you cause the accident that night?"

"Of course not."

"Then I don't want to hear a single 'I'm sorry' ever escape your lips again." When he says this, he leans in close, and I know he's about to kiss me. I'm still upset, but I'd pay good money to get one of those toe-curling Brett Sharp kisses right now. He looks down at my lips as if he can read my mind, but he just shakes his head and leans back against the couch. "Now, gorgeous, what else do you want to know."

"No kids?"

"None. The picture was my niece. She looks a lot like me. I didn't even know Sarah still had any pictures of my family. When she moved out, she didn't take anything with her. Everything she has now is new, with the exception of her jewelry box. That's it. I have all of her other stuff in storage near our old house. She used to be a writer. You couldn't pry her laptop out of her hands on most days. She's never even asked for it again."

"I'm..." I stop myself from apologizing. I finish with, "That's sad," instead.

"It is sad, but it's also reality."

"What do you want from me?" I move to the core of this entire conversation. Today, I have learned the full story of Sarah and Brett. But I have no idea where that leaves Brett and Jesse.

"I don't know."

"Well that was fun." I jump off his lap, embarrassed, ready to sprint to my bedroom.

I don't know was not at all the answer I wanted or expected. He's obviously come here for a reason. I thought it was to win me back, make things right, fight for me. Apparently, my assumptions were all wrong.

"Slow down. You're not going anywhere until you let me finish." He pulls me back down, although this time, he doesn't give me the same space he did before. He cradles me in his arms, half restraining, half tenderly holding me. "I don't know what I can give you." He leans forward, placing a soft kiss to my temple. "I want to be with you. I want to spend time with you. I want to get to know you. And if I'm being honest, I want to touch every inch of your body with every inch of mine."

Even though I'm hurt and upset, his words still make me heat. I shift in his lap, trying to cover my breathy reaction when I feel his hard-on grow underneath me.

"Jesus, even as fucked up as things are, I can still turn you on with just one sentence." He finishes by placing a wet kiss on my exposed collarbone, sending chills down my body.

"Stop. We need to talk." I try to shake him off.

"Then talk." He continues kissing up my neck. It feels so good that I'm almost willing to end this conversation now. Almost willing to start a new one in the bedroom. *Almost.*

"Brett. Please. I need answers. I can't think with you touching me like that. It's too much."

He finally stops, reluctantly removing his arms and throwing them back over the couch. "You're right. I got carried away. Keep talking," he relents.

"I don't know what to do with you. I think you are just as messed up as Sarah."

His head snaps back as if I'd slapped him. "Wow, um…Wow," he says, stunned. "That is quite an insult after today."

"I just mean you have baggage. A lot of it. I'm not just talking about Sarah either. I'm talking about your guilt and self-imposed punishment for the way she is now."

"Caleb really got into your head today, didn't he?" he asks.

"Yes. He told me a lot about you and Sarah."

"Did he mention that he hates her? Blames her for the wreck? Wishes she were the one dead instead of Manda? Did he mention any of that while he was giving you a little history lesson?" He begins to get angry.

"Yes, he actually mentioned all of that."

This isn't what he expected me to say. I know he thought Caleb filled my head with horrible ideas about Sarah. He didn't do that at all though.

"He told me she used to be funny. Always the girl dancing on the stage or talking your ear off. He said everyone who ever met her loved her. Most of all, you. He told me she was beautiful back then." I can see his eyes fill with unwelcome tears as I talk about her. He bites his bottom lip, nodding while trying to get his emotions back in check.

"I don't want you to know about her, Jesse. Sarah is a part of a past that I don't want to share with you. And that's not because I don't want to tell you about it. I'm happy to tell you everything you want to know since the wreck, but it kills me to think about back then. The fact that you even know this much about my old life hurts like hell. Despite everything that has gone down, I had hopes of keeping you and Sarah in separate parts of my life. No crossing lines. She's my past, and I'm sick of living there.

"I am who I am today as a result of the all years I spent with her. That goes for both the happy and broken parts of me. I want to start over without this cloud of Sarah hanging over my head. I want to escape this pressure I feel to finally fix things. When I'm with you, Jess, everything else is silent. It's magical. I can't change anything that's happened. I can, however, try to move forward with my life.

"So, to answer your question earlier, that's what I want from you—to move forward. Jesse, I worry that I can't be who you need me to be. I'm hesitant to make you any promises or commitments because I'm not sure I can back them up. I'm willing to try though. Something beyond my control draws me to you. You make me feel alive again, and as selfish as it sounds, I will do absolutely anything to hold on to that. But I'm terrified that it will mean breaking you in the process."

"I'm not made of glass," I answer him, equally touched and frustrated by his words. "You can't break me. I'm not her. I may be naïve when it comes to relationships, but I'm stronger than I look. I just need to know what I'm getting myself into first. This isn't something I can walk into blind.

"You're not the only one confused here, Brett. You have a lot of cons, but I'm still standing here, aren't I? Let me watch out for myself and decide what I can and can't handle," I answer with resolve. I'm going to try to make something work with him. He may not have anything to give me, but that's a bridge I'll cross when it crumbles under my feet.

"Jesse—"

"No. Don't 'Jesse' me. I'm a big girl. I can make my own decisions. I don't need a keeper, and you don't need any more jobs."

"You're not a big girl. You're actually a very, very tiny woman." He smiles up at me. "Don't get me wrong. I like it."

"I'm serious, Brett."

"Okay, so where does this leave us?" he asks.

I have been thinking about this question all day, and finally, I feel like I have the right answer.

"We date. We slow down this crazy, drama-filled relationship we have had for the last few days. Who the heck knows? We may not even like each other this time next week. We don't have to jump into anything serious. Let's just go with the flow.

"I don't need any promises from you right now, so you don't have to stress yourself out over not being able to fulfill them. Brett, it's been six days now! Do you usually have this type of conversation with every girl you date for less than a week?"

The grin that creeps across his face is spectacular. It renders me completely unable to move my eyes from his mouth.

"I don't date, remember?" He pulls me over to straddle his lap. "With this new arrangement, can I still kiss you? And maybe touch you a little too?" he asks, ever so lightly pushing his hips up until they connect with mine.

I let out a soft moan. He must have seen my lips part, because he instantly reacts, crushing his mouth into mine. Our warm tongues tangle in a kiss I've so desperately wanted all day. I crawl even deeper into his lap, needing to be closer. He must feel the same way, because he stands, lifting me as he goes.

"Which one's your room?" he asks, holding me with both hands on my butt.

"End of the hall," I respond, thrusting my hands into his hair while kissing the underside of his chin.

"I don't think we can consider this slowing down," he says with a smirk.

"Well, no. But then again, we didn't do the whole just-friends thing very well either. Perhaps, I should rephrase and say 'no rush' instead of 'slow down.'"

"Same thing, babe," he says, but he continues to carry me down the short hallway. Pausing just outside my room, he asks, "How far tonight, gorgeous? It's completely up to you, but I want to know before we go in here. I want whatever you are willing to give, even if it's just standing here in the hall all night. But I've messed up enough recently. I don't want to push you into something you aren't ready for."

"I want to be with you," I say against his neck.

"You have to be more specific. Tell me what you want?"

"I want to make your world go silent."

He doesn't hesitate any longer. He walks into the room, kicking the door closed behind us. Striding to my bed, he lays me down more gently than I thought possible. As he stands over me, I can tell he's beginning to rethink this. I'm done thinking though. Done caring about the what-ifs and fighting over things we can't change. I'm ready to feel.

"Touch me." I cross my arms, pulling my shirt over my head. The room is lit by the bright midday sun, but I can't bring myself to care about how much he can see right now. He reaches out, rubbing the back of his finger against my hardened nipples.

"I'm going to tell you that you're beautiful, but it won't be enough." He bends over, pulling the fabric of my bra down just enough for my nipple to peek out. His tongue darts out and dampens his lips, but he doesn't move any farther.

I can feel the wetness seeping into my panties. I wish he would touch me already. Lying here exposed while Brett towers above me fully dressed is unnerving. We need this though, so I lie still and allow him to make his own decision.

"Are you sure about this?"

"Please," I say, reaching back and unclasping my bra, slowly pulling it away from my body.

"Fuck, you have the best tits, Jess." He finally reaches down and palms my breasts in his large hands.

He plants gentle kisses to my chest and his breath breezes over my flushed skin. His hot, wet tongue begins to tease my nipple. I need more though. Running my fingers up his back, I tangle them in his hair, pulling him closer.

He chuckles against my breast. "Calm down, babe. We have all night. And if I have anything to say about it, this is going to happen more than once."

Heat floods my veins. I'm on fire for this man and he has barely even touched me. It's the promise in his words that causes me to release a small moan. Brett is drop-dead gorgeous, yet he talks to me like I'm the sexiest woman alive. It all just feels too good to be true. He continues to tease and suck my nipples, grazing his teeth as he pulls away, reminding me that this is definitely real.

I slide my hands down his back and pull the bottom of his shirt up and over his head. I hope I never get used to the way I feel when I see his naked body. Every muscle on his stomach is tense, showing off the muscular curves where his jeans rest on his hips. The one arm he is using to balance on the bed is flexed under his weight, and before I can stop myself, I lean over and lick up the bulge of his bicep.

"Christ, you really do have an arm fetish."

I bite down at his joke, but it only causes him to shudder. Apparently, Brett likes it a little rough. I reach up and run my nails up and down his back. Goose bumps pebble his skin, and I smile to myself.

"I can't wait to have you clawing my back while I'm fucking you."

My cheeks flame red. I know I'm lying naked in front of him, about to take him inside me, but his dirty talk still makes me blush.

He trails hot kisses down my stomach and plays with the top of my pants, running his fingers back and forth and dipping fingers below the seam. He looks up and cocks one brow, silently asking for permission.

"Take them off," I say with far more confidence than I feel.

He slowly unbuttons my pants and pulls down the zipper. He reaches one hand back up to knead my breast one more time. I feel like I'm going to come out of my skin if he doesn't get inside me soon. Lifting my hips off the bed, I urge him to remove my pants, which he all too quickly complies. Lying in just my panties, I once again feel a wave of vulnerability. It's still so hard to believe this man wants me—plain old Jesse. My eyes connect with Brett's, and he bites his lip, giving me a crooked smile. I immediately blush from head to toe and try to cover myself while looking away.

"Baby, look at me," he whispers.

Turning back, I expect to find Brett's eyes dancing with amusement. Instead, they are filled with so much emotion that it puzzles me. It's hard for me to tell what he's thinking, but I know he's feeling something serious.

"Don't hide yourself from me. Please. I think you're beautiful. I wish I could spend all day looking at your sexy body." His voice is rough and deep, mixed with lust and some other emotion I can't put my finger on. It's the same one showing bright from his eyes. "Promise me, Jess. Keep your eyes open and on me. Watch me so you will have no doubts how you make me feel." He slides his fingers over my wet folds. I moan and arch into his hand. "Eyes up here," he reminds me. "Does that feel good?"

"Oh God..." I breathe as he pushes a finger inside.

"I don't see anyone named God here, baby. I want you screaming my name when I make you come, not God."

"Brett."

"There we go. Much better."

At some point, Brett must have unbuttoned his jeans and pulled down his zipper. I can see the tip of his erection peeking out the opening. I want to see the rest of it. It's only fair that we both are naked.

"Brett, take off your jeans," I command.

"My pleasure, gorgeous."

He makes quick work of taking off his jeans and tossing them somewhere in the room. My suspicions are correct. Brett Sharp is going commando. *Jesus, that's hot!*

He's painfully hard, and the tip is swollen and pink. I ache with anticipation of having him inside me. I lick my lips and drag my gaze away from his length. His eyes are hooded, and his chest is rising and falling faster.

"If you don't stop looking at me like that while licking those luscious lips of yours, I might embarrass myself and come all over those fucking perfect tits. I would really like to come inside you tonight."

I shiver, but not because I'm cold. I feel like I am going to spontaneously combust with lust. He pushes my panties to the side and returns his hand to the teasing strokes.

"Fuck me, Jess. You're so wet for me."

All I can do at this point is nod and bite my lips. I want to yell and beg for him to put it in, but I also don't want him to stop the amazing things he is doing with his hand.

He pulls my panties down my legs and tosses them over his shoulder. He then runs his tongue up my leg and over my clit for one torturous lick. "Fucking hell. You taste like heaven."

It's going to happen. I know it is. As soon as he pushes inside me, I'm going to come. He won't even have to move. With all of this buildup, one thrust is all it's going to take. Then he is going to realize how inexperienced I really am. Attempting to buy myself some time, I take in a deep breath of my own, reach down, grab his hard-on, and slowly stroke him. His chin drops to his chest as he watches my hand gliding over him.

"Stop. Please stop," Brett pants, causing me to immediately jerk my hand away and turn my head away in embarrassment. Crap. I can't believe he just shot me down.

I gasp as I feel an unexpected finger enter my wet heat. A strangled moan escapes, and I snap my eyes back to his.

"What did I tell you, Jess? Don't fucking turn away from me. You're sexy as hell, and I want to see those big brown eyes."

"I just... I thought maybe you didn't like—" I stumble over my words. Brett's hand never stops moving inside me.

"Stop thinking and trust me. I needed you to stop because, if you kept that up, I was going to come like a fucking sixteen-year-old virgin," he all but growls at me, "I need to be inside you now. Tell me you want this, Jess. Tell me you want me to fuck you as bad as I want to do it."

"Yes, Brett, please..." I'm reduced to begging.

"Shit. I need a condom, babe."

"I'm on the pill," I rush out, hoping to speed this up. Probably not my most responsible idea, but I physically can't wait any longer.

"No, gorgeous. We need to be smart about this. I've got one in my wallet...in the car." He lets out a string of expletives and withdraws his hand.

"Condoms. Top drawer of the nightstand." I groan at the absence of his fingers.

"We are going to have a conversation about why you have condoms in your nightstand later." He opens the drawer, pulling out a foil packet.

"Kara," I explain as he rips it with his teeth and rolls it down his length.

He nods in understanding, and I thank God for my best friend and her ridiculous hopes that I would one day get laid. I really love that girl right now. Then I squeak when he grabs my legs and pulls me towards him.

"Last chance, gorgeous. Are you sure you want to do this?"

"Please, Brett..."

In one swift move, he fills me. I cry out in both pain and pleasure, and Brett moans into my neck. He gives me a much-needed minute to adjust to his size. I cling to his back and my legs start to shake.

"Shit, I'm sorry. You're so fucking tight. I should have done that a little slower."

Yes, he should have done it a little slower, but it felt amazing, so I'm glad he didn't. Now is not the time for explanations. "Brett...move...please."

He slowly starts to move his hips in small, gentle thrusts. Easing his way in and out of me. He's trying to be gentle now, but I need more.

"Harder."

"No," he says, taking my mouth into a deep, apologetic kiss.

"Brett, I'm fine. Please...I need you to move." I roll my hips roughly into his.

"Fuck, Jess, you feel so damn good. This is going to be quick, baby, so keep up. I'll make it up to you, repeatedly, tonight."

He begins to move over me, every muscle in his body strained as I drag my nails across his back. I can feel my release building, and I know I'm going to fall over the edge at any minute. Brett groans and kisses my neck as he pick up his pace. I feel him grow inside me as he pushes deeper than I knew possible.

"I need you to come first. I hope you're close because I don't know how much longer I can last." When he slides his hand between us, I feel his finger rub at my swollen clit while he keeps up his relentless rhythm inside me. "Come, Jesse. Let me feel you." His words send me stepping off the edge as I arch off the bed.

I can barely hear myself screaming his name, but the fireworks going off in my body make it impossible to focus on anything else. He stills, but I can feel him pulsing inside me, repeating my name into my neck.

As I come down from my orgasm, he begins pressing light kisses over my neck and shoulders. Sated and feeling like jelly, I smile to myself.

"What are you grinning about?" Brett asks with a smile matching my own.

"I can't feel my body," I giggle.

"Oh yeah? Is that a good thing?"

"No, it's the best thing," I answer, absolutely silly on a sexual high. That was amazing. The horrible day has been completely washed away.

He throws his head back, laughing. "Jess, have I told you lately how amazing you are?"

I shake my head.

"Well, I guess I'll just have to show you. Let me get rid of this condom while you get ready for round two." He winks and walks into the bathroom.

I watch as his perfect butt disappears around the corner. My grin immediately stretches across my face into a full-blown smile, and I have to bite my lip to keep the schoolgirl scream from escaping.

Chapter
TWENTY-ONE

Jesse

"G'MORNING, BABE," I hear Brett whisper as he kisses up my chest.

He pauses only momentarily to drag his warm tongue over each nipple. I grab the blankets, pulling them tight across my body, remembering that I'm naked. Very, very naked. All the memories from last night—and again earlier this morning—flood my mind. I had sex with Brett freaking Sharp last night. Just to be sure it wasn't just a dream, I squeeze my legs together, feeling the tenderness that lingers after a night of unbelievable lovemaking. Oh, who am I kidding? That was the first night of good sex I've ever had. God, it was—

"Brett!" My eyes pop open as I feel his finger thrust inside me.

"What?" he asks, pretending to have no idea what I'm talking about. "I just wanted to make sure you're awake. Don't you have to work today?"

"Crap!" I fly out of bed, careful to drag the sheet with me. I can't believe I forgot this is my weekend to work. Kara and I swap working every other weekend. Nell used to schedule us each for one day every weekend, but Kara got sick of not being able to party one night each weekend. We agreed that, every other weekend, one of us would work both Saturday and Sunday. It's great because Nell gets coverage without having to hire a third person, and we each get two whole weekends off each month.

"It's only seven, gorgeous. Slow down."

"CRAP!" I scream. "I'm supposed to be there at seven! I'm late! I'm never late."

"I'm already a bad influence on you," he laughs, throwing his hands behind his head and crossing his ankles.

He's lounging on my bed fully nude, and I've see never seen anything sexier in my life. I want to pull a Leonardo DiCaprio and whip out my sketch pad to draw this Adonis—Titanic style. Although, with my artistic abilities, he would end up as a stick man with an overgrown mushroom between his legs. I may not be able to draw, but I can still take mental snapshots of him relaxing in *my* bed. *God, he is hot!* My mouth goes completely dry at how confident he is. Here I am, tugging a sheet tightly around my body, while he's all but showing off.

My eyes must be glued to him, because he has to snap me out of it. "Babe, go get in the shower. I'll make you some coffee."

"Make it breakfast. I can get coffee at work," I shout over my shoulder, rushing into my bathroom to unfortunately wash him off my oversexed body.

"Shit," he says to himself, reminding me that he can't cook.

I want to tell him not to worry about it. I've eaten breakfast more than once at Nell's. But I'm really interested to see what he comes up with, so I keep my mouth shut and head for the bathroom.

One minute into the world's fastest shower, I'm adding the conditioner to my hair when I hear Brett on the other side of the shower curtain. "Um, Jess? What's a vegetable report?"

"What?" I ask, confused.

"Kara left a note. You can calm down. She went in for you today. She said a bunch of stuff then ended it by saying she earned a vegetable report for working for your Saturday."

Noooo! I scream in my head while trying to play it cool on the outside.

I never was any good at acting. I know Brett immediately catches on to my little cover. Willing to momentarily forget about my nakedness in order to forgo any further embarrassment, I rip back the shower curtain and snatch the handwritten note out of his hand. I feel his eyes accessing my soapy body, but I'm too focused on the note in my hand to care.

Jesse,

You dirty girl! I hope you know what you are doing and not just falling prey to Tightass McCrazyson. Either way, I'm jealous. I just heard a few unbelievably hot noises come out of your room, so I'm sleeping with earphones on so I don't feel the need to physically assault you...or my vibrator :) Anyway, I saw Brett's hot guy car out front, so I assume that is where the noises are coming from and you guys are patching things up. I'm working for you tomorrow. You can pay me back when I land a stud of my own. However, I do have one requirement for working your Saturday! I expect a full vegetable report. You have denied me for entirely too long. It's been like four days now. No more holding back. Best friends, remember? XOXO (Although I'm betting you have been doing enough of that tonight, hooch!)

Love,
Your horny and jealous roommate.

I quickly ball up the note and search the shower for some way to dispose of it. You have no idea how tempted I am to shove it in my mouth and eat it. When I glance up at Brett to find him smirking, I know that isn't an option. He read it, and he's read me too. He knows I'm hiding something, so I have no other option than to pull out every woman's secret weapon—boobs. Men get confused so easily when they come face to face with boobs. I can definitely use this to my advantage.

"You okay?" he asks as I stare up into his eyes.

My goal was lust-filled bedroom eyes, but I think it's coming off as bug eyes with a slight twitch.

"What are you talking about?" I ask, dropping Kara's note into the shower, successfully ruining the physical evidence.

"You're acting weird."

"What? No, I'm not," I say, shoving my hands into my hair and pushing my breasts into his face.

His eyes automatically move to my chest as I unnecessarily scrub the conditioner into my hair. My boobs are swaying with my motions, and I quickly stretch to my tiptoes under the water to make them bounce just a tad too. I'm willing to do anything to keep from having to explain Kara's note. I have nothing to feel guilty about. I didn't kiss and tell. But darn it, she really said too much this time. I'm going to kill her, but first, I have to deal with Brett.

After last night, he must be partially immune, because even while watching my boobs bounce, he still asks questions.

"Is Kara a vegetarian or something?"

He's just offered me the out I was mentally searching for.

"Yes!" I jump at his explanation. "She is strictly a vegetarian. Although, I have it on good authority that she doesn't like baby carrots."

I start to ramble. The more details I give, the more he will believe me, right? So I begin a five minute soliloquy about all the vegetables Kara likes. By the time I'm finished, the water is beginning to run cold and Brett hasn't moved his eyes from my naked body once.

"So there you have it. She doesn't eat anything but vegetables, and I give her a report every week about what's in season."

"What's in season this week?"

Eek! How did I not anticipate this question?

"Umm..."

"What's wrong, Jess?" He smiles knowingly.

He then reaches down and pops open the button on his jeans, muddling my already frazzled mind even further. As he begins to push his jeans to the floor, I can see a thin trail of hair running down his body. I swallow deeply, very aware of where this is going.

"Gorgeous, I have no idea what you are trying to hide here, but it's pretty cute listening to you talk about seasonal vegetables while trying to distract me with these beautiful tits." He reaches one hand forward, cupping my entire breast and stepping into the shower. "I know we haven't been together long, but I have a feeling we are going to be together quite a bit from now on, so there is something you need to remember about me. I'm a detective. My job is to figure things out and recognize when someone is lying to me. I'm good at my job because I see the little details others miss. Like just a minute ago, when you tossed that note down into the water so I wouldn't read it again." He raises one eyebrow at me before continuing. "I'm also not a quitter. I'll search for answers long after everyone else has given up. So it would probably save us both a lot of time if you just come out with it." He rubs his thumb across my nipple.

"However, you are so fucking hot right now that I'm willing to let this slide long enough for us to christen your shower properly. I'll just talk to Kara when she gets home." He leans over, placing a very promising kiss on my shoulder.

I jerk away from him, slipping and sliding in the shower. Thankfully, he grabs my hips, keeping me from toppling out onto the bathroom floor.

"You can't ask Kara!" And I'm serious. He can't. She will make it sound way worse than it really is. She would probably even hit on him and stare at his pants while she tells him.

"Then why don't you let me in on your little secret. I probably wouldn't care if you weren't so desperate to hide it from me."

Crap. I'm going to have to do this. I let out a frustrated groan and stare at the ceiling to avoid his eyes. "She wants me to tell her what vegetable your penis most closely resembles." I sigh and wait for his reaction.

Brett has a great sense of humor. I'm sure he'll laugh about this. But I hate being laughed at, even when it's obviously something as silly as this. I feel his hands grip my hips a little tighter. My eyes slide back to his, and I find him standing with a blank look on his face. No humor dancing in his eyes. Nothing.

"Well?" he asks, void of all emotions.

"Well, what?"

"I have no idea how to feel about this until I know what vegetable you picked," he says seriously.

"Oh, um...I don't know. I didn't exactly plan on answering her." I stumble over my words.

"Okay, well let's discuss this." He backs up, gliding his hands through the air, showcasing his privates like a Price is Right model. "See, if you said green bean, I'd be very upset. However, if you told her an eggplant, I'd probably never wear pants again. So what's it going to be, Jess?"

This conversation has just crossed over into crazy town. Brett is always funny, but this ludicrous conversation is a bit odd, even for him. Just as I'm about to mentally inventory the produce department, I catch a small glimmer in his otherwise serious eyes. Oh my God! He's messing with me. Again. Hopefully I'm not wrong about this, because I'm about to turn the tables on this jokester.

I slide my eyes down his body. Swaying my head side to side, I pretend to weigh my options. "Well," I answer quietly, "I guess I would have to say a kosher dill pickle."

"What?" he asks incredulously.

"Yeah, definitely a dill pickle spear." I look down at his feet, pretending to be embarrassed but really trying to keep him from the seeing the smile I'm desperately attempting to hide.

"What?" he yells. "A spear?! Not even the whole pickle? Jesse, you need glasses!" he screams, trying to defend his deflating manhood.

I can't hold back the laugh that's building inside any longer. I burst out laughing, causing the disbelief to fade from his face.

"Oh, I get it. You're a funny girl today, huh? Ha. Ha. Hilarious, smartass." He pretends to be annoyed as I continue to laugh. "Yeah, laugh it up now, because I'm about to pickle you." He leans forward, so close I can feel his breath against my ear as he whispers, "Hard."

I abruptly go quiet, as I feel myself getting wet, and it has nothing to do with the chilly water coming from the showerhead. Who knew such ridiculous words could have this kind of effect on me, but the way Brett says them instantly turns me into a wanton woman.

When he lifts me off my feet, I wrap my legs around his waist as he pushes me against the wall. He uses one hand to turn the water as hot as it will go. It only warms a fraction of a degree, but it's just enough to keep us in the shower for another twenty minutes. Brett utilizes those minutes and makes good on his promise. We properly christen my shower. *Hard.*

Chapter
TWENTY-TWO

Brett

IT'S BEEN seven weeks since Sarah showed up at Nell's. I have to say that I thought I would never have another shot with Jesse after those first few days. Everything went so wrong so fast, but I never should have underestimated her. She hasn't asked about Sarah again, which really surprises me. I keep waiting for her to sit me down to have "the talk" one day, but she never does.

After the first two weeks, I realized how weird she gets when I drop her off on Wednesday nights. She always hugs me extra tight and repeats over and over again what a good time she had. She talks a million words a minute and chews on her thumbnail. I've learned that both are telltale signs that Jesse's nervous. At first, I couldn't figure it out, but when she made zero attempts to reach me on Thursdays, it didn't take me long to figure out why.

Jess and I text all day. She sends me sweet notes, and I send her dirty ones. On Thursdays, though, she goes quiet. I realized that she must remember that I visit Sarah on Thursdays. So I go out of my way to call her every night as soon as I get home. We talk for hours, and those are the best hours of my entire day.

Jesse may dread Thursdays, but I've grown to loathe them. I went to Sarah's every day after her freak-out at Nell's. For the first two days, she stayed locked in her bedroom. She wouldn't eat anything, and if it weren't for the fact that I could occasionally hear her TV changing channels and the shower going on and off, I would have worried. On day three, I ducked out of work a little early to check on her, and when I got there, she was standing in her kitchen with a huge smile on her face.

Seven Weeks Earlier...

"HEY, SEXY! I was wondering when you were going to show up," she says, tossing her blond hair over her shoulder. As she moves her hands back down, I catch the sparkle off her left hand.

"How you doing, Sarah?" I ask, trying to figure out what the hell she's doing still wearing her rings.

"I'm good. Are you just going to stand in the doorway and stare at me all night, or are you coming inside?" Her candor is nothing unusual, but I'm still suspicious as hell. "I made dinner," she says, pulling a casserole dish out of the fridge.

Sarah always made the weirdest food. I guess they aren't weird to everyone, but I was never a fan. She made Southern dishes like potato soup made with more butter than milk or fried macaroni and cheese bites. I'm sorry, but does mac 'n' cheese need to be deep fried? Her family raved about her cooking, but I never could get on board with soggy bread-like noodles in chicken soup. She called it chicken and dumplings. I called it gross. However, when she would branch out into different types of food, it was always delicious.

My favorite of all her meals was her seven-layer Mexican dip. She always made it for my birthday or any time we were celebrating something special. God, it was good. So when I see her unwrap a dish topped with lettuce and decorated with dollops of sour cream, my eyes jump to hers.

"What is that?" I ask skeptically.

"Seven-layer dip." She acts like it's nothing more than ingredients tossed in a bowl. We both know it's more. It's a memory. It's happiness. It's our past.

I have to restrain myself from reaching out and slapping that stupid-ass dish across the room. I want to see it shatter into a million pieces, just like our future. Fucking seven-layer dip!

I try to compose myself enough to speak. "I'm glad you're feeling better. I need to get back to work."

"Baby, you haven't eaten yet."

"Don't call me that!" I shout.

"Jesus, it's just fucking dinner. Stop freaking out," she responds, rolling her eyes at my outburst. "You're acting like a douche right now." Yep, still the same new Sarah.

"Dinner. Right." I nod, knowing that she's flat-out lying, but I can't figure out why. "What are you doing? You haven't cooked for me in years. Now, two days after showing up and freaking out on the woman I'm seeing, you make my favorite meal? For what?" I begin to get angrier as I talk. It's

one head trip after another with this woman. "Please, just tell me why!" I scream across her room.

"Because you are the only one who hasn't turned their back on me," she rushes out, stepping towards me. "Because I know I messed things up for you a few days ago with that girl. And...and because I miss you," she says in a voice unlike any version of Sarah I've ever seen.

I take a step forward, trying to get a better read on the situation. She's done nothing but push me away. Now she misses me? Stunned by her admission, I can't even stop to evaluate my feelings, but that doesn't stop a knot from forming in my throat.

She closes the distance between us, resting her hands on my chest. "I miss you, baby," she repeats, staring down at the ground. "Maybe we could try to work something out, get to know each other again." Using her foot to draw patterns in the carpet, she leans into me.

I don't recognize this woman. She is so timid and shy. She's so...Jesse. Shit! Jess. I quickly take a step backwards out of her reach, and thankfully, she doesn't follow.

"Start talking," I demand.

I have an unexplainable need to hear her out. My mind is racing, but I'm not excited like I thought I would be at finally hearing those words come out of her mouth. A few weeks ago, I would have been at her mercy, ecstatic to have another shot at a life together. Only now, I feel apprehensive.

"Um, I just thought..." she trails off.

Any hope that started to fill my heart quickly deflates when I see the humor twitch in her cheek. This is yet another one of her games.

"Fuck, Sarah!" I explode, unable to can't catch my breath.

This woman stands before me joking about missing me after the hell I have been through. Years spent holding on to hope that, one day, I would get my wife back, yet it's all one big joke to her. The only thing stopping me from unleashing the brunt of my anger is that I know it's not her fault. I lost my wife, but she lost herself.

These games are a different story altogether. I have every right to be pissed about this. She may not have been able to control who she became after the wreck, but she made the decision to wage emotional war on me over the past few days. First with Jesse, and now with this bullshit. It's drama upon drama where Sarah is involved. I have nothing left to say. I've already tried every possible combination of words to move past this. It's time to suck it up and admit that there is no fixing us. At some point, you have to cut your losses and walk away, but I can't seem to convince myself that the fiery woman who used to own my heart is a complete loss.

I turn to walk out the door. I won't give her the satisfaction of seeing me react again.

"Brett, wait!" she says, softly laughing. "I meant it. Maybe not the way you want me to mean it, but I do miss you. You won't believe me, but I remember being happy with you. I remember the day you proposed. Jesus, that was corny. That whole Jeopardy thing." She laughs a little louder. "Seriously, that was cheese dick."

I put my hands on my hips, assuming the position for her to sling hate-filled words at me.

"But I do remember the way I felt when you asked." She reaches down, spinning her rings around her finger. "I loved you," she says, completely devoid of emotion. "I want to feel like that again." She finally looks into my eyes, and I see a flash of something genuine before they go blank again.

I can barely breathe. My chest feels like it's going to collapse at any second. I know what I'm about to say, and it is scares the hell out of me. I can't do this emotional roller coaster anymore. I don't want the drama, the longing, the feeling that I'm constantly waiting for something to change. I may not be able to give up on her as a person, but I can finally let my Sarah go.

"I loved you too." I suck in a breath. The past tense of those words is enough to bring me to my knees, but I have to finish. "Sarah, I'll always be here for you. Every single Thursday for the rest of your life, I'll be knocking on your door. You can act like a bitch, you can call me names, you can try to lock me out, but I'll always come back. You would have done that for me. But there will never be another Brett and Sarah Sharp.

"You moved on four years ago, and tonight..." I pause, terrified to finish the sentence. It needs to be said though—for both of us. "Well, tonight I'm moving on too." I wait for my words to sink in. Surely this will have some emotional effect on her, but she stands stock-still, seemingly unfazed.

Just as I'm about to repeat myself, a small, mischievous smile creeps across her face. "Okay," she says, walking out of the kitchen and into her bedroom, locking the door behind her.

Oh shit. This isn't good.

"Sarah!" I knock on her bedroom door. I just unknowingly issued some sort of challenge and she was all too happy to accept it. "Open the door." I continue to knock.

She never answers, and after a few minutes, I have no choice but to leave it alone for now. I decide to head home and deal with this tomorrow. Awesome. More drama to look forward to.

When I get outside to my car, I have an overwhelming urge to drive directly to Jess's apartment. It's been a week since we started dating, but I've already become addicted. She always makes me forget everything else. It's more than just a distraction though. My life has been on autopilot, nothing in my control. I have no choice but to go along for the ride. For a man, it's a damn near crippling feeling. Jesse grounds me. She looks at me like I'm the prize, but she has no idea that I'm the winner every time we are together. I want to rush to her right now and fall asleep buried inside her. But that's not fair to her. We agreed to take this slow and not rush into something I can't give her when my life explodes again. The same way it always does.

I walk into my apartment, wasting no time before heading directly to the phone. If I can't see her, I damn sure am going to talk to her. As soon as I hear her pick up, my whole load is lightened.

"Hang on, Brett!" she shouts distantly. "Okay, I'm back...hello."

"Well, you sound busy."

"No, I was just trying to catch Paprika."

"Um, I'm not exactly a chef, but does paprika run away often?"

My words cause her to giggle, and it's as if that small sound makes the world tilt back onto its axis.

"No, Paprika is a cat that Kara adopted from the shelter."

"You got a cat?"

"Well, no, Kara got a cat, but we can't keep him. Our landlord has a strict 'no pets' policy, but Kara thought she could get him to cave. He lets the girl downstairs with the big boobs have a Chihuahua. Apparently, Kara is not well-endowed enough for his tastes."

"What the hell! He said that?"

She starts laughing again. "No, he didn't say that exactly, but you know how Kara is. She flirted him up hardcore and still got the door slammed in her face. She told me I should give it a try next. She thinks I'm more his type."

"Jesse, you are not going anywhere near your landlord."

"Oh I know. That guy gives me the creeps. He's, like, thirty-five and always staring at my boobs."

"Gorgeous, I'm thirty-two and always staring at your boobs."

"I never said you weren't creepy too."

"That is a title I will gladly accept, because unlike your pervert landlord, I get to actually touch those boobs."

She laughs again. I would do anything to hear that sound.

"Well anyway, we have to give the cat back tomorrow, so we are just hanging out, playing with all the kitty toys we bought earlier. You should see him. He is so cute. He's white with a few orange speckles. Kara said she was going to call Nell and see if she wants him."

She continues rambling about the cat for a few more minutes. I grab a beer and collapse onto the couch, closing my eyes and listening as her words free me from the stress that keeps me weighted down. It's funny to hear her get like this. A few days ago, she would have been saying nothing but 'uh' and 'um,' but now she has barely stopped talking long enough to breathe.

"Jeez, I'm talking a lot," she says. "What have you been doing tonight?"

"Not much. Just lying on the couch, wishing you were here with me." The words come out before I really think them through, but it's the truth. Damn it, I should have gone to her place.

"You want some company?" she asks, reading my mind.

"No, it's okay, babe. I know you have Paprika there tonight. Today was just a little crazy. I'm fine now though."

"Chocolate or vanilla?" she randomly asks.

"Huh?"

"I'm bringing ice cream and beer. Oh, and a movie. You sound like you need to watch a movie."

"Jesse, we never actually watch movies... Oh, um...okay. I could definitely watch a movie right now." We both start laughing when I realize she isn't talking about a movie at all.

"Okay, give me about thirty minutes and I'll be there."

"Gorgeous, you don't have to do that. You're already cooking me dinner tomorrow night. Don't think I'm going to let you off the hook for that one."

"I'm not trying to get off the hook for anything. I like cooking for you. If I called and said I had a crap day and wanted you to come over, would you?"

"Of course, but—"

"Okay. See you in a few." She hangs up before I can say anything else.

I guess I'll be seeing Jesse tonight after all, and that thought propels me off the couch and into the shower. This day just got a hell of a lot better.

Chapter
TWENTY-THREE

Jesse

OVER THE next few weeks, Brett and I fall into an easy groove. We see each other every morning at Nell's and hang out about three to four times a week. I make a point to cook him as many meals as I can, including preparing his favorite fruit and granola for him to keep at home on the weekends. Last week, he asked me to put together a grocery list for him, and now he keeps his fridge stocked with ingredients for me to cook dinner at his place. When he first asked about it, my heart stopped at the idea of how serious that sounded—my making his weekly grocery list. I talked myself out of reading too much into it. I have to remind myself daily that we are just dating. Nothing serious...yet.

I haven't heard from or seen Sarah again since that day at the coffee shop. She all but disappeared. I have no idea if Caleb spoke with her or not. I can't imagine that would have gone over well with Brett. He was so protective of her after the way she reacted to Caleb. I don't think he would be very pleased if he caught wind that Caleb showed up to have a "talk" with her.

Brett doesn't talk about Sarah or even acknowledge that she exists. That doesn't mean it escapes me when he disappears on Thursdays. I don't ask questions, and he doesn't offer any answers. I've grown to dread Thursdays. Always worrying about what's going to happen. Is she going to assault him? I can't help but feel like one day she is going to realize what she is letting go and want Brett back. I can't compete with her. He spent years loving her. Maybe he still does. I can't think like that though. I promised myself to give him the benefit of the doubt, but it's a struggle.

My mind goes wild with ideas. I understand what he is doing by spending time with her and why he does it. It still hurts like hell when he disappears every week though. Like clockwork, he calls me every Thursday night at eight. And even though we only live three miles from each other, we spend two hours talking on the phone.

I'd love to see him every night, but with as wild as things got in those first few days we were together, I know it's best if we take this slow. By slow, I mean having sex every time we are in a fifty-yard radius of each other. Brett is always in the mood, and trust me, one look at Brett "in the mood" would put you in the mood too.

One day last week, he had an early meeting at work, so he came for breakfast around ten. Nell's was empty. The breakfast rush had come and gone. I was excited, thinking it would give us time to talk and hang out. Brett had other plans. He flipped the sign on the door to 'closed' and dragged me into the back office for a mid-morning quickie. It was better than his usual middle-of-the-night quickies we have on the weekends when I sleep over at his apartment. Brett may have made me a little more adventurous, but that doesn't mean I've completely escaped my shy ways.

For days after the office make-out session, I wondered if there were cameras in the office. I went so far as to freak out when I realized that I'd probably just made a porn that, one day, my mother and brother would stumble across on the internet. I don't know why my mother would be looking at porn on the internet, but that doesn't make the thought any less consuming.

I was so nervous that, one night, I woke up Kara to ask if there were any cameras. Of course she knew the answer to this question and assured me that Nell isn't that high tech. She then told me all about her sexcapades in that office, thus ensuring that it was a one-time deal for Brett and me. I'll never be able to look at that office desk the same way again.

By early November, Brett and I are floating right along in our non-relationship relationship. We pretend that what we are doing isn't serious, but we both know it's pretending. One Friday night, when we get home from the most amazing greasy dinner at a hole-in-a-wall restaurant twenty miles outside of town, he surprises me by asking me about my holiday plans.

"So, gorgeous, tell me what you do for the holidays?" he asks when he pulls up to his apartment.

"Well, Thanksgiving, I usually spend the day at my mom's house. I help her cook while my brother sits on his lazy butt watching football. Then Christmas, I usually just hang with Kara. My mom goes to visit her sister down in Florida for a week, and Eric goes to his college fraternity Christmas party in Boston." I stop talking when an annoyed look crosses his face. "What's wrong?"

"Your brother goes to a fraternity party and leaves his little sister alone on Christmas Day?"

"It's no big deal. Kara's family lives in Washington, and tickets are too expensive that time of year. For the last few years, we've had Christmas Eve spa nights. Then we spend Christmas Day watching movies and spiking our hot chocolate with peppermint schnapps. If I were with Eric, then Kara would be alone. Really, it works out best for everyone."

"Bullshit!"

"Um, excuse me?" I ask, startled by his reaction.

"Bull. Shit," he repeats slowly so there is no confusion about his opinion on the situation. "There is no way I would leave my sisters alone on Christmas. That's a special day that is meant to be spent surrounded by family. So I have a big problem that he would think his douchebag fraternity brothers are more family than his own blood," he finishes, blatantly upset.

"Okay, I agree that my brother is a...douche, but I disagree about everything else. I do spend Christmas with my family. Kara. You think her being alone is better than us having a fantastic day laughing and watching *A Christmas Story* and getting drunk? Seriously, that movie only gets funnier when you've been drinking. I love my brother, he's great, and he would do anything for me, but it would be a miserable day spent staring at each other. We still fight like we are twelve. I'm not even joking. Last time I saw him, he tied my shoelaces together. He may be a fancy bigwig attorney now, but he's still my annoying older brother deep down. Before you judge me, what exactly do you do during the holidays?" I ask, throwing some sass in his direction.

"For the last four years, I've worked every Thanksgiving. I volunteer so none of the guys with families have to work. My sisters both go to their in-laws. So it's not like I'm missing anything. Christmas, on the other hand, is kind of a big deal with my family. Every year, we get together at my parents' house. Everyone, including all five of my nieces and nephews, spends the night and we wake up the next morning to my mom's homemade monkey bread and breakfast casserole. Santa comes for the little kids in the early morning. Then, while they are playing with their toys or sleeping from a sugar crash after eating the entire contents of their stockings, the adults swap presents."

He shrugs likes it's no big deal, but it makes me pale. Jeez, after hearing about Kara's and my Christmas drink-a-thon, it really is sad.

"Let's go in, Jess. I don't want you getting cold, and that shirt isn't going to do much to keep you warm," he says, glancing down at my pink scoop neck sweater, which reveals a good bit of cleavage. This is yet another item from the Kara Reed collection.

"Are you working this year? On Thanksgiving, I mean."

"Nah. The guys caught on that I've worked the past few years, so Smith signed up to work before I could. He gave me some speech about being happy to avoid his in-laws, but I know it's a load of shit."

Before I give myself a chance to really think it through, I rush out an invitation that I know is going to freak him out. "Spend Thanksgiving with me and my family."

"No, babe. That wasn't the point of this conversation. You go spend time with your family. Maybe afterward, you can come spend the night and give me all the thanksgiving I need," he jokes, but his smile doesn't quite reach his deep green eyes.

I know this isn't going to be an easy fight to win. He doesn't even know it's a fight yet. But he's already lost this battle. No way am I leaving him home alone on his first Thanksgiving off in years.

"Please come, Brett! You can watch football with my brother while mom and I cook. We always make so much food. You can help keep it all from going to waste. Please! I can introduce you as a friend. It doesn't have to be a 'meet the parents' situation. I know we are taking this slow, but I'm not going to let you spend Thanksgiving alone. Please!" I whine, begging like a child.

He rolls his eyes and lets out a loud sigh. "All right, babe. No need to start batting your eyelashes. I'll come. What kind of beer does your brother drink?"

I squeal, launching myself over the small center console and into his lap. He really needs a bigger car. I'm not a big girl, but this thing is tiny. I only manage to get my upper body over it before getting stuck, so I work with what I've got. I smash my chest against his then give him a deep, passionate kiss.

He laughs against my lips. "I vote we start Thanksgiving tonight. You don't happen to have an Indian costume, do you?" he asks, reaching behind my awkwardly positioned body. He shoves both hands into my jeans and squeezes my butt.

"Brett, your hands are freezing!" I try to jump away, but he's holding me too tight and there isn't anywhere to go in this sardine-can-sized car anyway.

"I know. I told you we should get inside. Just give me a minute. I'm warming up my hands." He laughs while I squirm to get out of his icy grip.

It's no use though. He is so much bigger and stronger than I am. I can, however, hit him where it really hurts, and I'm not talking about actually laying a finger on him.

"If you don't stop now, I'm not, um...having sex with you tonight." For some reason, this only makes him laugh louder.

"Oh, sweet Jesse. Don't make threats you can't follow through with."

"I could totally withhold sex for one night," I say, feigning confidence.

"Well how about this, gorgeous. We don't waste time trying to figure it out. Trust me. No one wins in that situation."

He's so right. I might be annoyed with him, but I am so looking forward to a night spent naked with Brett.

"Can we just go inside? The beer in your fridge is calling my name."

"Why, Jesse Addison, are you becoming a lush on me?"

"Probably," I answer truthfully. I have been drinking more since I met Brett, but there is just something about curling up on the couch together and drinking a few beers.

"Well, I like it! You always get a little kinkier when I'm fucking you after a few beers." He opens his door, and heads around the car to open mine.

If there is one thing I will never get used to about Brett, it's that he's always a gentleman. Yes, I do realize I called him a gentleman after he said something about f-ing me. That's just Brett though. He drops the F-word like it's a comma. If he's drinking, it spans all parts of speech: noun, verb, pronoun, adjective. At first, it shocked me, but now I kind of like it. I hate to say it, but I've accepted his colorful vocabulary as part of the sexy Sharp package. It might make me a naïve fool, but hearing him refer to our nightly bedroom activities like that makes me a little hot. Okay, I'll admit it—a lot hot.

"So, Thanksgiving at my house?" I question one last time before stepping out of the car. I want to make certain we're on the same page.

"I already said yes. Thanksgiving at your house. I'll bake a pie or something."

"No!" I shout, startling him.

"Jesus! What is wrong with you?" He stops in the middle of the sidewalk.

"Brett, I've tasted your cooking. The last thing I need is my mother and brother keeling over from food poisoning. Just bring beer, and don't get any ideas about brewing it yourself."

"Damn, that was harsh! Just for that, I'm taking it nice and slow tonight." He continues to my door.

"Is that a bad thing? Because it sounds pretty, um...stimulating to me."

"Oh, babe, you have no idea what you are saying right now." He drags me into his apartment.

A few hours later, he proves that nice and slow isn't always good. It's torturous—and my absolute new favorite.

Chapter
TWENTY-FOUR

Jesse

ON SATURDAY night, I arrive at the bar to meet Caleb and Brett. The guys spent the evening smoking cigars and having drinks for one of the detectives' retirement party. Brett called earlier asking if I wanted to meet them out or if I would rather stay in for the night. As appealing as staying in on a cold and windy Chicago night sounded, we do that all the time. Going out sounded like fun, especially when Brett told me it was a dance club and not our normal sports bar. Since we were doing something out of our norm, it gave me the opportunity to wear something special too.

After shopping for three hours this afternoon, I found a super short navy-blue dress. I wanted to wow Brett. That's what keeps relationships alive, right? This little dress should have no problem spicing things up. The top crisscrosses in the front, doing a great lift-and-push-together trick on my boobs. I paired it with the same knee boots of Kara's that I wore on our first date at the Bears game. Brett spent the whole night staring at my legs, so I know he liked them.

I must have been lost in my thoughts because I didn't see Eric until I slammed into his chest.

"What are you wearing?"

Rubbing my cheek where I face-planted into my brother's chest, I look up to see a furious look on his face. "Jeez, Eric. What the heck is your problem?"

"Are you aware you just walked into a bar...in your underwear?" he asks like I have lost my mind. Apparently that's what he thinks I have on, because he quickly takes off his suit jacket and throws it over me.

"Stop it. You're going to mess up my hair," I say, swatting his stupid jacket away.

"Jesse, what are you doing here?" He leans into my face, trying to intimidate me. He is such a jerk sometimes. I swear, he still treats me like his seven-year-old baby sister.

Eric is three years older and he's always been hard on me. While I may be short, Eric is definitely not. I look like my mom, and Eric is the spitting image of my dad. Sandy-blond, perfectly styled hair and toffee-colored eyes. He isn't huge like Brett, but he isn't anything to sneeze at either. When we were in high school, he ran off every guy who even looked in my direction. When he went away to college, he left half of the football team behind to look after me. I blame him for the fact that I didn't have a real boyfriend until college. So listening to him question me about my clothes and why I'm here annoys the crap out of me.

"Get out of my face, dog breath," I say, reverting back to our teenage years. I try to walk past him but he grabs my arm, spinning me in a full circle before pushing me up against the wall.

"Let's go. I'm taking you home. I have no idea what you think you are doing here, especially dressed like that, but I can promise you aren't staying."

"Are you kidding me here? Get your hands off me! Guess what, loser! I'm a grown woman. You can't make me do anything. Now let me go before I knee you in the jewels."

"All right. Up you go." He bends down, planting a shoulder into my stomach and lifting me up onto his shoulder.

"Put me down! I'm wearing a thong and you are flashing everyone my butt!" I yell, trying to grab my skirt.

I am going to kill him for this. I swing my legs, hoping at least one of them lands a kick to the stomach. I must have accomplished my goal because I hear him grunt. Then I feel hands around my waist lifting me to my feet. Instead of being released, though, I'm crushed into a man's chest. When I struggle to free my head enough to look up and see who's holding me so tight, Caleb's irate eyes meet mine.

"It's all right, baby girl. I've got you." He tries to comfort me then whispers again to himself, "I've got you."

"Jones, cuffs!" I hear Brett yell from behind me.

I turn, confused to see my brother lying facedown on the ground. Brett has one knee in his back and both of Eric's arms pulled behind him. For the first time in my life, I hear my brother cussing. And not just your average run-of-the-mill bad words. He is saying things that would give Brett's mouth a run for its money. Caleb releases me only long enough to flash his badge to the police officer and bouncer rushing over to us. The officer pulls out his cuffs and tosses them to Caleb, who pulls me back into his body, tucking my head into his chest. I hear the click of metal and Brett reading Eric his rights.

"Caleb, let me go."

"Shhh...you're okay. Brett's coming," he responds so lovingly that it makes me melt. See, now this is how a big brother should act.

I feel Brett's hand touch the back of my shoulders just before I hear him ask, "Is she okay?" I don't even have a chance to answer before I feel him reach under my legs and pick me up.

I have no idea what it is about men thinking that, just because I'm small, they always need pick me up. My legs work just fine. I don't need to be carried around like a toddler everywhere I go.

I finally find my voice. "Put me down!"

"I've got you, gorgeous."

"I'm well aware you have me, honey. The only problem is you also have my big brother cuffed and laying on the floor." He stops moving and looks back at my brother, who is now sitting up and talking to the uniformed officer.

I prepare to explain this whole mishap to him when he turns back to look at me. "You're not bailing him out, so get that look off your face."

"What do you mean I'm not bailing him out? Of course I'm not—" I can't even finish my thought before he interrupts me.

"Good. That asshole is sleeping in a cell tonight."

"No, he isn't. I'm not bailing him out because you aren't taking him to jail."

"Well, not personally I'm not, but he is definitely going."

"No, he isn't!" I scream at how ludicrous the entire situation has become.

My mind is spinning. Everything has happened so fast. Thirty seconds ago, I was having a little-worse-than-normal argument with my brother. Now, I'm arguing with Brett about whether or not Eric is going to jail. My mind can't keep up.

"Gorgeous, I saw him put his hands on you. He's lucky he still has both arms connected to his body. If there weren't a hundred witnesses, I would have laid him out—and I'm not just talking about restraining him on the ground. So I'll repeat, that asshole is sleeping in a cell." He leans in close, and it ticks me off.

"Have you lost your mind? That's my brother!" I poke his chest. Nothing proves you are seriously mad like poking someone in the chest.

"And?"

"Oh my God, you really have lost it!" I scream, walking over to Eric, who is sitting on the floor.

I turn in a circle trying to locate Caleb. Hopefully he is a little more rational about this crazy mess. I give up and shout his name to find him in the crowd that has now surrounded us.

"Over here, baby girl!" I hear him yell from behind me while talking to the bouncer.

"You know these jerk-offs?" I hear Eric ask, but I ignore his stupid question and return my attention to Caleb. The sooner I can get him to un-cuff Eric, the sooner we can put this all behind us.

"Un-cuff him. That's my brother."

His eyes go wide as he looks over at Brett, who is standing where I left him with his hands on his hips. He is clearly not pleased with this turn of events.

"Your brother?" Caleb asks.

"Yes, my brother. Am I speaking a foreign language? Get over here and freaking let him go!"

"Watch your mouth!" My brother tries to correct me from the floor, but he looks ridiculous telling me to watch my mouth while sitting in handcuffs.

"Freaking is not a bad word, and you should know after the filth that just came out of your mouth!" I yell at Eric.

"Well if your friends here hadn't brutally assaulted me while hiding behind a badge, I imagine I'd be able to keep my language locked up a lit-tle tighter," he answers sarcastically. "Just go home, Jesse. You look like a hooker."

I start to get mad. Really, I do. My brother is a real butt sometimes, but this isn't new information. He loves me and tries to protect me. It just doesn't always seem that way. I feel a cool breeze beside me, and I swear I'm in the middle of a Twilight movie because Brett just appears in front of me.

"You son of a bitch." He grabs my brother by the collar, pulling him close. "I don't give two shits who you are to her. You are going to watch your fucking mouth," Brett says calmly even though the look on his face is murderous. "Apologize. Now."

"Who the hell do you think you are telling me how to talk to my sister?" Eric, still handcuffed, steps up to Brett, bumping him with his chest.

This is not exactly the way I hoped Brett and Eric would meet. It's actu-ally the worst-case scenario, but seeing Brett stand up for me like this is hot, and it makes me feel all warm and fuzzy inside.

"I'm her fucking man, so you better start apologizing before you be-come her dead brother."

Yep, definitely hot. His words make my heart swell and my panties wet. Does that make me his woman? *Oh my God, I'm Brett Sharp's woman!*

Forgetting about the crap show that is going down in front of me, I feel a huge smile spread across my face. I mentally begin a victory dance and vow to myself to give it to Brett any way he wants it tonight. *Her man.* Eek!

I see Caleb move between the two angry guys, which breaks me out of my inner celebration. "You sit down," he says to Eric, "and you back the fuck up before you do something stupid. For Christ's sake, he's her brother. You just cuffed him. Somehow I don't think brawling with him is going to win you any promotions. So back it up. Both of you." Who knew Caleb would be the rational one in this testosterone trio?

"You're dating this asshole? What the fuck, Jesse?" Eric leans around Brett, looking at me with crazed eyes. "Is this the dumbass who has you dressing like that and coming into bars alone?" Brett doesn't even let his words hit me before shoving Caleb out of the way and gripping Eric around the throat, pushing him hard against the wall.

"Are you dumb or just a prick? What the fuck did I just tell you? Watch you're fucking mouth when speaking to her."

I surge forward to where he has Eric pinned. Brett must know the security here somehow, because they are all just standing back watching this play out in front of them.

"Stop, you're choking him!" I yell, smacking Brett's hand, trying to get him to release my brother, who is slowly turning blue.

He drags his eyes away from Eric long enough to glance at me for a beat. Then, one finger at a time, he removes his hand. I squeeze between them and feel Brett wrap a protective arm around my waist from behind. I'll deal with him in a minute, but right now, my jerk-face of a brother deserves my attention. Repeating Brett's words from earlier, I lay into him.

"You are going to watch you're freaking mouth when you talk about him. I'm not going to listen to you say one bad thing about him." Okay, so maybe I cleaned it up a little bit. I didn't want to break every rule I have just seconds before doing the one thing I have wanted to do for years.

Pulling my knee back, I slam it directly into Eric's crotch. I didn't want Brett to hurt him, but that didn't mean I wasn't going to do it myself. It wasn't as hard as I would have liked for it to be, but I would like to have nieces and nephews one day, so I guess it will have to do.

I love Eric, and tomorrow I'll feel horrible for doing it, but I've had enough of his crap. There is never going to be a better opportunity either. He was standing helplessly handcuffed against a wall. I'm sure he will run home and tell Mom, but I don't give a rat's tail about the repercussions tonight.

Brett sucks in a breath behind me, lifting me off my feet and spinning me around so I can't reach Eric again. I'm not going to do anything else though. I figure one knee to the groin is enough retaliation towards my overprotective brother for one night. Suddenly, I remember that, even though I'm ridiculously turned on by Brett's little macho showdown, I'm still annoyed at him for trying to arrest my brother.

"You!" I lean forward, poking him again. It worked so well the first time that I figured I'd give it another shot. "You are not arresting him. He didn't do anything wrong. Well, maybe he did, but it was nothing more than a sibling argument. His heart was in the right place even if he was being a butthead about it. So un-cuff him and let him go. Be quick about it too, because we are going home."

"Gorgeous—" he starts, but I wave my hand to silence him. I'm done listening tonight. I just want to get him home and rip his clothes off piece by piece. Crap, Kara was right. He has turned me into a sex fiend.

"That's my brother and he's a lawyer, Brett. You are not arresting him. I'm annoyed and ready to leave. I spent two hours getting dressed up tonight. Now I'm wasting it all by going home, so you better make it worth my while when we get there."

His eyebrows pop up as an amazing white smile slowly spreads across his face.

I turn and head towards the door, catching Caleb out of the corner of my eye. He's shocked, standing with his mouth hanging open. I hear him whisper, "Fuck. Me," as I pass. Clearly my behavior shocked him, and it makes me bust out giggling as I walk outside.

I find Brett's BMW parked out back and lean against the door, waiting for him. I'm not left waiting for more than a minute when I feel a coat drape around my shoulders.

"You're going to freeze out here without a jacket." I smile to myself as he wraps his arms around my neck, leaning his cheek on my head. "I'm sorry about all that. Jesse, I saw him grab you, and I saw red. I wanted to murder him. The idea of someone trying to hurt you..." He fades off, shaking his head like it hurts just to think about it.

"Hey, I'm okay. He was being stupid, and now he'll have to sleep with an ice pack between his legs." I shrug.

"That was sexy, by the way. Watching you take charge like that. Stand up for yourself. God, Jesse, I was so pissed off. Then you kneed him and I swear I've never gotten hard so fast." He rubs his growing hard-on against my butt to prove his point.

"Take me home. That whole badass thing you had going on in there really turned me on too. I need to appropriately thank you for defending my honor."

"That's my favorite way to be thanked." He leans forward, kissing me breathless.

We make the short drive back to his apartment. Once we get there, I thank Brett twice. He thanks me four times.

Chapter
TWENTY-FIVE

Jesse

"WE'RE LATE!" I yell at my oven. I told my mom that Brett and I would be there at noon to help her cook dinner. I also told her that I'd show up with an apple pie. *Dang it!*

"Calm down, gorgeous. I don't think screaming is going to make it cook any faster." Brett sneaks up behind me, wrapping his arms around my waist and nuzzling into my hair. "You look beautiful," he whispers against my skin, trailing kisses down my neck. All thoughts about the pie are forgotten. Heck, it's Thanksgiving, but I'd be lucky to tell you what month it is when he's touching me like this.

"You can't be sure of that. You've only seen my back. I could be wearing an 'I'm with stupid' T-shirt and KISS makeup right now," I tease, and he works his way down to my shoulder, pulling my T-shirt aside to gain better access.

"You'd still be beautiful, but I'm not a KISS fan, so you'll have to let me fuck you from behind," he says, grinding against me.

"Brett!" Great, we're going to be even later because I need a cold shower and dry panties now. I feel his body begin to shake as he starts laughing and steps in front of me.

"Hey, babe." He stares down at me with a sexy smirk.

"Hi."

"No KISS makeup, huh? I'm not going to lie, I'm a little disappointed. I had such high hopes for taking you from behind tonight." He rubs his thumbs across my cheeks, knowing they are about to flame red. I can tell they don't disappoint him when his smile widens.

"Is the makeup a requirement to make that, um...happen?" I have no idea why I still get nervous with Brett. There isn't an inch of my body that he hasn't touched. It may have something to do with his lack of commitment.

It's been almost two months, and since that first night in the beginning, we have never had a single conversation about our relationship. It weighs on my mind, and as the weeks go by, it's starting to invade my dreams too. Last week, I woke up twice in a cold sweat. They start off hot enough—it's always Brett making love to me—but then it all goes wrong. Every time, Sarah swings open the door at the most inopportune time and starts screaming at me to get off her husband. Okay, maybe I have a few issues with Brett still being married, even if it isn't a real marriage.

"Why, gorgeous, what are you trying to suggest? Would you like it if we tried a little something new tonight? Don't be shy with me. Tell me what you want, babe. I'm open to anything with you. Well, almost anything. You're not a closet kinkster, are you? I'm not sure I can get down with whips and chains. Although, now that I'm thinking about it, the idea of you in a leather getup is doing wicked things to my imagination. Perhaps we should try something new right now? You know, save us both the torture of having to wait until tonight." He lifts a sexy eyebrow questioningly.

Just when I'm tempted to take him up on his offer, the oven timer goes off, reminding me that we need to get to my mom's ASAP.

"Sorry, big boy. You're just going to have to wait." In a random moment of boldness, I spin around in his arms, leaning over to pull the pie out of the oven, and rub my butt against the zipper of his pants. I hear him groan as I step out of his grasp. "Don't just stand there. Let's go," I say, heading to the door.

"Fuck." He adjusts his pants and follows behind me. Steps before we hit the door, he pulls the pie from my hands and pushes me into the wall. Using his long arms to hold my famous apple pie away from us, he says, "Gorgeous, I hope you know what that little stunt back there bought you. It's going to be a long night for you, so I suggest you drink a few beers after dinner. You know, loosen up a bit." He winks before pulling open the door and guiding me out.

It's a miracle I can even walk after that.

WHEN WE arrive at my mom's, I'm thrilled to see that Eric isn't there yet. After the incident between him and Brett at the bar, I know today is going to be a little tense. The day after Brett tried to have Eric arrested, I got a call from my mom asking a million questions. Apparently Eric really is a twelve-year-old, because he called my mom first thing the next morning to tattle. Mom was more concerned with who I was dating than anything that happened at the bar. When I told her Brett would be coming to Thanksgiving, she got all excited and rushed off the phone to order a bigger turkey.

I've never brought anyone home before, so telling my mom makes this is a really big deal. I need to get to her though and make sure she understands that Brett and I are not all that serious yet before she starts asking him about kids and picking out china patterns. That is a conversation that would be much easier without Eric adding his stupid two cents.

When we get to the front door, I don't bother knocking and just head inside.

"Mom?"

"In here, JJ!" I hear my mom call from the kitchen. I peek around the corner to see her holding a huge turkey in the sink, stuffing it with spices. "Little help here?"

"Holy crap, Mom! That turkey is huge."

"I know. We need to hurry and get this thing in the oven or it won't be ready until Christmas."

I leave Brett standing by the counter and rush over to help before my mom drops the giant bird on the kitchen floor. "Why did you buy one this big?" I grunt while trying to pull the slippery turkey into the roasting pan.

"I heard your man was a big one, so I figured I needed a big turkey to feed him," she says, washing her hands and wiping them dry on her old-school apron.

I roll my eyes and glance over my shoulder to see Brett chuckling to himself.

"Mom, this is Brett Sharp. Brett, this is my mom, Rachel Clay."

"Ms. Clay." Brett steps forward, offering a hand, but I know my mom, and a handshake isn't going to cut it.

"Brett, please call me Rachel, and get that hand out of my way. I'm a hugger." She reaches up on her tiptoes and slings an arm around his neck.

This time, I'm the one laughing as Brett's eyes go wide in surprise. I might be shy, but that was one of the few things I didn't get from my mother. She has no problem speaking her mind and hugging anything that happens to walk past her.

"Now, I've heard a few things about you from Eric. Most of them are not so great. So tell me about yourself. Prove to me that what my arrogant son said was all wrong."

"Mom!" I scream, embarrassed. This is worse than when I thought Eric would be here. She didn't beat around the bush at all.

"Did you just call me arrogant?" I hear Eric walk into the kitchen. *Fan-*

tastic!

Brett wastes no time closing the distance between us and sliding a possessive arm around my hips.

"I like it," my mom whispers, smiling approvingly at Brett's protective gesture. "Oh, Eric, everyone here knows you're arrogant, including you. So give up the surprised act and get over here and show your old mom some love."

Never taking his eyes off Brett, he walks over to my mom, giving her the same kiss on the top of her head that he has since he was twelve and had grown taller than her.

"Go ahead, Brett. Tell us about yourself," she asks, curling an arm around Eric's hips.

"Well, I'm thirty-two. My family lives here in town. I have two older sisters, three nieces, two nephews. I make a living as a detective and spend my free time either with your daughter or watching football...and if I'm lucky, both."

"I think you forgot to include the little part about you being married—and not to Jesse," Eric sneers, dropping the bomb.

I feel the temperature drop in the room as the ice rolls off Brett. Besides a single flinch in his hand against my waist at the initial blow, he doesn't move a muscle.

"What the hell, Eric!" I scream across the room. I'm going to have to knee him again for pulling this crap.

"Language, Jesse," my mom scolds.

"What is wrong with you?" I ignore her, and Brett remains frozen at my side.

"Sorry, JJ. I know this must be a shock for you. I had a buddy do a little background research on the good Detective Sharp," my brother says, smiling with pride. "He finally got back to me last night. Brett has been married since 2002. Where's Mrs. Sharp today? You should have brought her with you. We could have had one big party."

I have no idea how Brett is controlling himself, because my brother is acting like a grade-A jerk right now.

"You are an idiot, Eric. Yes, I know he's—"

Brett interrupts me before I have the chance to finish. "I'll handle this, gorgeous," he says calmly, taking a single step forward. "I appreciate what you were trying to do. I like that you are man enough to look out for your little sister. However, this show is a classless low. If you have something to say to me, be a man and speak with me in private. There is no reason to make an ignorant, snide comment, upsetting your mother and sister on Thanksgiving. You are doing nothing but stirring up drama, and I assure you, Jesse and I have enough of that in our life without you pulling bullshit like this.

"Eric, if your *buddy*," he says with an overstated sarcasm, "had done more research, you would have learned that I have been living separately from my wife for over four years. I'm not hiding anything from your sister. Jesse has had the unfortunate experience of meeting Sarah in person. It wasn't pleasant, and it's not something we like to discuss. However, you have made this little accusation in front of your mother, and I do respect her enough to give her a full explanation. For the record, I don't respect you or give a damn what you think about me or my relationship with Jesse. But then again, you probably figured that out last week when I had you cuffed, laying on a dirty bar floor." He pauses long enough to aim one last murderous glare at Eric before turning to face my mom.

"Ms. Clay, please excuse my language. As you can imagine, this is not my favorite topic to discuss. Sarah has issues as the result of a car accident she was involved in years ago. She left me shortly after the accident. It's been a difficult road for everyone involved. She isn't stable and requires a good bit of care. We are still legally married for a myriad of reasons. One being that she still uses my health insurance to help cover her medical bills. I know this is not the ideal situation for a man to be in when dating your daughter, but I assure you, while there may be a legal document still binding me to Sarah, I am not a married man." He leans down, kissing me on the top of my head, reading my tight body at how uncomfortable this conversation is for me.

There is a good chance that I just fell in love with this man. The way he handled my brother firmly but never raised his voice then turning to kindly explain this awkward situation to my mom. He somehow managed to keep his calm even when recounting such a painful and personal story to virtual strangers. That's more than I would have been able to do. The fact that he took even a second to think about me causes me to feel things I knew were possible but nonetheless unexpected.

"I appreciate you inviting me over today, but I think it's best if I leave now. I'm sorry for any trouble I caused you today, Ms. Clay. Jesse, call me when you're ready to go. I'll come pick you up. Have a great day with your family, babe."

"Now, wait just a second. I have a twenty-two-pound turkey that will be ready in approximately three hours. No one is going anywhere until that bird has been eaten," my mom announces before Brett even has a chance to release his hold on me. "Eric, apologize," she says, shocking me.

I figured that, if they found out about Brett's marital status, it would earn him a permanent spot on the "no way" list. Apparently, I underestimated my mom.

"Um, do you need a hearing aid? He is married. I'm not apologizing to him," Eric responds, dumbfounded that she would even suggest it.

"Yes, you are. He just explained his situation to us, and he didn't have to do that. He obviously didn't lie to Jesse, and that means more than anything you could have dug up on him. So apologize or head out the door. I hear the Chinese Palace is open today."

"Mom, it's Thanksgiving. I'm not eating Chinese."

"Exactly! So start apologizing!"

"This is ridiculous! I didn't do anything wrong." Eric tries to defend himself but just comes off sounding like a whiney child.

"Let me see if I've got this right. You put your hands on your sister at a bar, and her boyfriend defended her—like a man should. Oh, then you got cranky, checked up on him, and aired his private business in public, essentially embarrassing everyone involved. And the icing on the cake is you think you didn't do anything wrong. Please tell me I did not raise such a selfish and ignorant man," my mom says as Eric rolls his eyes.

"I'm sorry," Eric begrudgingly says to Brett, who just nods in his direction. It's going to take way more than a forced apology for these two to get along.

"Okay, now that's settled. Eric, here's a list. I need you to find a store open and pick up a few things I forgot."

"All right. I had to park at the end of the street. One of your neighbors parked a sweet Beemer in front of the house. It's like that one we looked at a few months ago. Same convertible top and color too. You didn't happen to win the lottery and buy me an early Christmas present, did you?" He laughs, switching gears back to the sweet mama's boy he's always been.

"That's mine," Brett speaks up, breaking some of the awkward tension that's still lingering in the air.

"Really? I was looking at one a few months ago, but I was torn between that and a Benz. You like it?" Eric surprisingly asks without even a hint of attitude in his voice.

"When did you become such a snob?" I respond before Brett has a chance. "I remember scouring the classifieds for your first car. It was almost impossible to find one that would actually start for less than five hundred bucks. We must have looked at a million pieces of crap before we found that hunk-of-junk Honda."

"Hey! Cecilia was beautiful. Don't knock her. She drove you to and from school for two whole years before she went to junkyard heaven. May she rest in peace." He attempts the Catholic crossing, but since we have never been to mass a single day in our lives, it looks more like he's giving himself a cooties shot. "All right, I'm headed to the store. I'll be back in a few. We have plenty of beer, right?" Eric asks.

"Yes. Brett brought more than enough," I say, making sure he knows who paid for his drinks.

"Cool. I'll be back soon."

"Here." Brett throws his keys only slightly harder than he needed to. "Take my car. It's closer, and you can see why the Benz is absolutely zero competition."

"Oh, okay," Eric says, surprised by the gesture.

"You are some hotshot criminal attorney who can afford to replace her, right?" Brett says humorously, but I know he's serious. Eric's eyes slide to me. "Don't worry. Jesse didn't say anything. You aren't the only one who did their research." Brett smiles a sugary-sweet and menacing grin. I won't lie—it's incredibly hot.

Eric leaves but doesn't bother giving Brett back his keys. I'm assuming the prospect of driving his BMW is more appealing than the shot to his pride.

"All right, I wouldn't be a good mom if I didn't ask this question," my mom says, walking to stand directly in front of Brett. "We have established you have some private things going on in your life. I won't pry. Jesse is smart and way too cautious, so if she is dating you, I'm going to assume she already knows this answer. But, honey, I need to know if you are romantically seeing anyone other than my daughter?"

"No, ma'am."

"Okay," she pats him on the chest. "Grab yourself a beer and make yourself at home."

"Here, Brett. I'll show you to the TV room." I drag him out of the room, needing to speak with him in private after that little showdown. I immediately start apologizing. "I'm so sorry!"

"It's okay, gorgeous."

"No, it's not. I know that was awkward for you. Just so you know, as soon as Eric gets back, I'm going to let him have it."

"Your brother is an ass, Jess. But I know he's just trying to look out for you. If one of my sisters brought home a married man, I would have reacted the same way. Maybe a little more privately, but still the same. The last thing I want is for you to get into it with him again. I know he's your brother, but I'm not going to be able to listen to him calling you names. Please, let's just try to have a quiet, uneventful day. I could really use one of those." He pulls me into a tight hug.

"I'm glad you came," I say into his chest.

"I'm glad I came too. I can only imagine how that whole conversation would have gone down without me there to clarify."

"No, I mean I'm glad you're here spending the day with me and my family."

"Come here, babe." He tilts my head back and presses a long, deep kiss to my lips. There's no tongue. Nothing to make it sexual. It's just pure, heated emotion and by far the best kiss I've ever had.

"I LIKE him," my mom says as I walk back into the kitchen.

"I do too," I sigh.

"He's a good man, JJ."

"Oh, Mom, you don't even know him." I start rinsing the potatoes.

"Do you have doubts about him?"

"No. Well, maybe a little. I can't wrap my mind around why he would stand by Sarah if he isn't still in love with her," I answer—a little too honestly if I'm trying to get my mom to like him. I need some advice though. I feel things for Brett, and it scares me to know he may never return those feelings.

"Let me explain something to you. I didn't have the best luck with men, so I might be an old lady wearing rose-colored glasses. The way that man kissed you? Even I felt it. Not all men are like that, sweetheart. Your father left me when I had no job and two small kids. It's been twenty-three years, and I've never even gotten as much as a phone call. But that man sitting in there has been through hell and still won't let her be alone. He takes care of a woman even when she isn't his wife anymore. Now that is one you want to hold on to. One day, when he gets his head and heart together, he could be your husband. Who wouldn't want a man that loves so deeply?"

"I don't know. It's just so hard for me to put myself out there. What if he doesn't feel the same way about me?"

"I saw him with you tonight, Jesse. He cares about you. There is no doubt about that. Did you notice how, as soon as Eric walked in, he slid up on you like the devil himself had just walked through the door? Jesse, you're so guarded. Live a little. Put your heart out there and see what happens. Who knows? He might grab hold and never let go."

"He also might walk away," I interrupt.

"But if he does, you don't have to second-guess yourself. You can honestly say you gave it a real chance. He would be lucky to have you, sweetheart, and if he doesn't realize that, then walk away with your head held high, knowing he isn't the only good man alive."

God, I love my mom. She's right. I know Brett has issues about committing again, but from here on out, I'm moving this relationship forward. He can either get on board or get off completely, but this train is moving.

Chapter
TWENTY-SIX

Brett

Two Weeks Later...

"JESSE!" KARA yells down the hall. "There is a fine-ass gentleman here to pick you up. He's wearing a fancy uniform and everything. You better get out here before I throw him down on the couch and hump his brains out."

How the hell Jesse and Kara ever became friends, I will never know. Ying and Yang is my only explanation, and it seems to work for them.

Tonight is the police station's Christmas ball. They always do this big formal affair at a nearby hotel. I've only been once since losing Sarah. It was horrible to watch all the happy couples, so I vowed to never go back. This year, I feel like I actually have something to celebrate though. It's a huge step for me to ask Jesse to go with me tonight, but something between us has changed since Thanksgiving. I guess I finally broke through her shell.

Jesse has been a new woman over the last few weeks. She's been strong, confident, and insatiable. A far cry from the shy and nervous girl I've always known. Last week, she threw me against the wall at the bowling alley and all but mounted me in the hallway leading to the arcade.

It's not just the sexual changes either—although those are my favorite. She got mad at me the other day when I forgot about a date. I had a bad day at work, and honestly, I just wanted to crawl into bed with her and never leave. When I got to her place, she was all dressed up and I was in sweats expecting to head back to my place for an adult sleepover, hopefully of the dirty variety. I'd forgotten completely that she'd bought us tickets to the Nutcracker Ballet.

Jesse from last month would have dismissed it as no big deal, thrown on PJs. and never said another word. However, this new attitude-filled Jesse read me the riot act and forced me to drive home, put on a suit, skip dinner, and fuck her in the parking lot outside the theater. I'd wondered why she'd insisted on taking the Jeep. Apparently she'd had plans that required the extra space.

"Well, hello there, officer," I hear from behind me as I wait, trying to avoid eye contact with Kara. I spin on my heels and lay eyes on the most beautiful woman to have ever put on a dress. She's wearing a short strapless black dress. It has some silver beading around the bottom that draws my attention to her perfectly sculpted legs then down to her silver heels that give her a full four inches of height. Her hair is pulled back, exposing her flawless chest and neck. She's stunning, and it causes my heart to stop and my mouth to go dry. I don't want to throw her into bed and have my way with her. I want to hide her from the millions of eyes that will no doubt be mentally undressing her tonight. Mainly, I want to lock her in a room and keep her all for myself.

"Fuck." Maybe not the most romantic of words, but definitely the most appropriate for the way she looks.

"Look at you!" she squeals walking over to me.

"I told you the uniform was hot!" Kara says as I remain speechless and silently drooling over the woman who will be on my arm tonight.

I finally find my words. "You sure you want to go to this thing? We could always just stay in, order some takeout…"

"Oh come on. You promised me a night of dinner, drinks, and dancing. I might even drink some liquor, and you know what that means for you when we get home." She winks in my direction. See? Totally new Jesse.

"All right, you kids have fun." Kara pats me on the ass. I'm shocked, but Jesse just laughs. "Be safe, JJ, and if you decide to go streaking later, make sure you call me first," she says, causing me to look down at Jesse questioningly.

"Shut up. Thanks again for the dress." Jesse hugs Kara as we head for the door.

"No problem. Really it's Brett who should be thanking me when he sees what you have under—"

Jesse slams her hand across Kara's mouth and whispers something into her ear.

"Okay, okay," Kara says, muffled by Jesse's hand.

"Let's go," she says calmly, as if the last ten seconds never happened.

"Um, sure." I place my hand just above her ass and guide her out the door. "Later, Kara!" I shout over my shoulder.

"Night, hot stuff. Don't forget you owe me. We can talk about payment later." She bursts into a howling fit of laughter as she closes the door.

"What was that all about?" I ask Jesse when we get outside.

"You'll see later." She tosses me a sexy grin.

"If you aren't giving away any of the fun details, then at least tell me why everyone calls you JJ? I've been meaning to ask you since Thanksgiving."

"My name is Jesse James Addison," she answers, causing me to stop walking. Surely she's joking. Who names their daughter Jesse James?

"No, it's not," I laugh, only to stop when she flashes me some 'Oh yes it is' attitude. "Wait, you're serious?"

"Yep. My dad was a big fan of Westerns. My mom thought I was going to be a boy, so when my dad threw a fit about wanting to name me Jesse James, she gave in. It wasn't an issue until I was born without a penis. Mom says she argued with him, but the other names he chose were so bad she eventually gave in."

"Can I say something about it without you getting pissed?" The look on her face implies that I obviously cannot, but that doesn't stop me from saying it anyway. "That name is fucking hot! Don't ask me why, but it's definitely hot."

"It's a porn star or a stripper's name." A flash of insecure Jesse peeks out.

"No, babe. It's your name. It fits you. If I've learned anything about you over the last few months, it's that you're a dichotomy. You have one side you allow people see. Then you have this ballsy alter ego you only show when someone gets close. I like this Jesse James woman." I pull her into me and roll my hips into hers.

I know her weakness. At some point, Jesse became a sexual beast. While her soft moan ensures that I'm turned on too, a wave of something else passes over me. I feel a sense of contentment with her wrapped in my arms. So I open my mouth and say words I have no business saying.

"I love..." Thank God I stop myself before I get to the most important word of all. But that doesn't stop my brain from firing one last absurdity. *I'm going to marry this woman.*

What. The. Fuck. I have no idea where that ridiculous notion came from. It's absurd at best. First of all, I can't marry her—I'm already married. Secondly, I will never allow myself to get into another relationship like I did with Sarah. I can't lose her again. *Damn it, Jesse isn't Sarah!* I scream to myself. I mean that in all the good ways—and the bad. *Damn it. I hate my life.* This inner dialog is killing me, so I try to focus back on the woman in my arms.

Jess doesn't react, so like an idiot, I breathe a sigh of relief. She must not have heard me. I should have learned by now though—God hates me. Big brown eyes look up at me. Standing on the sidewalk outside her apartment, she asks a question. The one damn question that could change everything.

"What do you love, Brett?"

You. Oh for fuck's sake. What is wrong with me? This is dating. Get your shit together, asshole, and answer the center of your world's question. Jesus Christ. I'm getting all poetic now. I need to shut up and get in the car before my mouth starts spewing Shakespeare.

"I love that your name is Jesse James. I have every intention of chanting it later tonight." Sex. Yes, sex is a safe topic. Let's stick with that.

"Oh...um, yeah. I like the sound of that." She tries to pretend that she isn't disappointed by my answer. I can see it in her eyes. I know she was hoping for more, but I have nothing more.

"Come on, gorgeous. I owe you dinner, drinks, and dancing."

She stays silent, and disappointment paints her face.

Damn it. This was supposed to be a good night, but once again, I've screwed everything up. I need to bring her back to me. So I leave out the questionable parts and tell her the truth.

Backing her into the side of my car, I tell her some things she doesn't know. It's not what she wants to hear, but hopefully it's enough to make the spark flicker back into her eyes.

"Gorgeous, look at me." Her eyes immediately flash up to mine. "I love spending time with you. I love watching you wake up in the morning. You always do this adorable little stretch and roll away from me so I can't smell your morning breath." I laugh, and she just rolls her eyes. "I love watching you cook, because even when there is no music, you always shake your ass to an imaginary beat. I love watching you lie on the couch, pretending to like football." She tries to interrupt me, so I lean forward and place a soft kiss to her lips to keep her quiet. "I've known for weeks that you don't like football, but I love that you pretend for me. I have no idea how you beat me in those bets a few months ago, but it's obvious you aren't really a football shark. I love that too." I look down to see tears pooling in her eyes.

The tears confuse me. I'm giving her the only substitution I have for those three magical words I can't possibly begin to say.

"Brett, all of those things are sweet, and there are a lot of things I love about you too. Most of all, I just love...you."

I suck in a breath, knowing things will never be the same again. "Jesse..." I start to say something, but I have no idea what. Luckily, she stops me first.

"I love you. I'm an idiot, and I know you don't feel the same, but I freaking love you. I promised myself a few weeks ago I was going to give this thing with you my all, and that includes my heart. If it falls apart, so be it, but at least I'll know I tried. I won't say it again, but I needed to say it just once before I had a chance to chicken out. So there you have it. I love you. Do with it what you want. Run, hide, file it away under 'crazy things psycho girlfriends say'—I don't care. But at least now I know it's out there." She pauses to wipe away a single tear.

"Jesse..." I try to think of something to fix this but come up empty-handed.

"Can we please go now? I have a sudden urge to get drunk, and I'm not talking sexy drunk. I'm talking drunk-enough-to-forget-the-last-twenty-four-hours-of-my-life drunk. It's open bar, right?"

I just nod and pull her into a deep, apologizing hug.

I can feel her shoulders shake as she begins to cry into my dress uniform. This is not the way this evening was supposed go. Outside her apartment, standing in the freezing cold, I hold her, giving her all I have to offer: a heartless, warm body.

"I'm done."

My nonexistent heart lurches into my throat at the possible meanings of her words. "Umm..."

"Are we going to be okay?" she timidly asks, not wanting the answer any more than I want to give it. "I mean, can you handle that I'm in love with you? Or is this the end?"

"Can you handle the fact that I can't tell you the same thing?" I ask the bigger question.

"Look, don't mess around with me here. Please. If this is a point you will never get to, let me go now. I don't want to go, but if you know this isn't something you want, then please let me go before I lose myself completely in you."

"Jesse..."

"Stop saying my damn name and talk!" she yells, frustrated by my inability to communicate.

"I don't know what to say! I can't make you any promises, and I'd be setting us both up for failure if I tried. Gorgeous, I want to be with you. I want to see where this goes. I can't tell you those magical words, but I'm not ruling out that one day I will."

"What the heck does that even mean?" She begins to pace.

"It means we could go round and round, but I don't have any answers. The only thing I know is I don't want to lose you. I'm sorry I'm a douche-bag who can't give you what you deserve. Fuck, I want to give it to you. If I didn't care about you, I would look into your eyes and tell you the words that mean everything." I throw my hands up the air. "If and when I know, I will tell you. Jesse, when I say them, you can trust that I will mean it with my entire soul. I want to give you that one day. And if that never happens, I'll be the one who loses. I will be the dumbass."

She finally gives me a small one-sided smile. It's fake, but at least I'm one step closer to holding her again.

"Can we pretend again? Can we do what we did at the game and pretend I didn't say anything."

"Absolutely not." Her head snaps to the side. "Gorgeous, those are the most beautiful words you can say to someone, and I'll be damned if I'm going to forget the sound of them coming from your lips. I'm sealing this into my memory for the rest of my life. I just hope that, one day, I'll be able to give that back to you."

"Do you promise to tell me if you realize you'll never be able to fall in love with me? You know...not string me along."

"I swear on my life."

"Do you promise to tell me the split second that you realize how stupid you are and that you have loved me all along?"

"I look forward to it."

"Do we have time for me to go fix my makeup?" she asks, running her fingers through the black mess under her eyes.

"I'll wait forever if I need to."

She looks down at her sexy shoes and shakes her head, "The sad thing is...so will I."

"Jesse, I won't make you wait forever. Just give me a little more time to get my head straight." I worry that, if I don't touch her now, I might not ever get the chance again.

Reaching out, I circle her into my arms and kiss her head. I don't want this to be sexy. I just want to give her back even an ounce of what she has given me tonight, but she pulls away all too quickly.

"Okay. I'll be right back." She heads up the stairs, leaving me alone, standing in the cold, and feeling like a total jackass. *Very fitting.*

A few minutes later, she returns looking more beautiful than ever. A smile is plastered across her face. I know it isn't real, but it still manages to steal my breath.

I swing open the passenger's side door, and she slides inside without a single word.

"Jesse James, are you ready for some horrible banquet food?" I ask, trying to lighten the mood.

"Brett, promise me something." Her voice is stern and serious. I prepare myself to make her yet another heartfelt promise. Hell, I'll promise her anything at this point. "If dinner sucks, promise me we can order room service."

I laugh, leaning my head back in relief. "I swear. Actually, even if it's not terrible, we should at the very least order dessert."

"Maybe we can get into our pajamas and order one of those chocolate cakes with the melted chocolate inside."

"Absolutely. Well...except for the pajamas part. No pajamas."

She finally gives me a genuine Jesse smile.

Chapter
TWENTY-SEVEN

Jesse

Two weeks later...

THINGS HAVE surprisingly been great since I opened my big mouth, con-
fessing my love to Brett. I figured it would get weird or that it might even
scare him away completely. But if anything, he's started coming around
more often. It's as if showing up almost every day is his way of proving to
me that he does care. I think he might feel guilty for not sharing my feelings.
Just what Brett needs—more guilt.

He and I live in a perfect little world of denial. We don't talk about
Sarah or our feelings. We definitely don't talk about a future together. We
just exist, hanging out and talking about our days, but never our tomorrows.
Somehow it works. I keep telling myself that I should ask about Sarah. Maybe try to help Brett move forward, but I always chicken out at the last minute
and end up having sex with him instead. At least we're good at the sex part.

Last week, Brett shocked the heck out of me by asking me to spend
Christmas with his family. I used every excuse I could think of to get out of
going. It's not that I didn't want to go. Okay, it was completely that I didn't
want to go. I'm not ready to meet Brett's family. What if they look at me like
the other woman? I'm sure they were close with Sarah. What are they going
to think of him seeing someone new now? But Brett pulled out the trump
card and invited Kara first. She of course jumped at the opportunity to spend
the night with the Sharp family. When I informed her later that he doesn't
have any brothers, she was pretty disappointed.

Today, I'm going to the station to meet Caleb on his lunch break so he can help me shop for Brett's Christmas present. I'm buying him size-fifteen bowling shoes. Every time we hit the lanes, he always limps for days afterward. They don't offer rental shoes that big, so he crams his feet in a size too small. Caleb agreed to help me pick them out. At least this way, if he hates them, I can blame it on Caleb.

"Hey, baby girl," I hear Caleb say as I walk into the front of the police station.

He's sitting on the desk, flirting with the sixty-year-old receptionist. I look around, equally trying to avoid and hoping to catch a glimpse of Brett. I'd love to see him in his work element, but I don't want him to know that I'm going shopping with his best friend.

"You can relax. He's not here."

"Oh, um...okay," I say, disappointed. "You ready to go?"

"Yeah. Come on back. I need to grab my jacket." He leads me around a surprisingly quiet police station.

He stops on one side of two desks pushed together. "Give me just a minute. I need to send out this email and close out my computer." He nods to the desk facing his. "That one is Brett's. Have a seat."

I slowly walk over, trying not to look too eager, but inside, I'm dying to see what pictures are inside the two frames propped on his desk. I feel a rush of relief when neither of them is of Sarah. One is a family photo of a herd of beautiful people. Caleb wasn't wrong. That is a good gene pool. The other is a picture of him with his parents at his graduation from the police academy. God, he looks so young, but he's way better-looking now. He's filled out and looks more like a man than the boy in the picture.

I sit in his chair and study his workspace. He's a pretty neat guy. His apartment isn't immaculate, but it's always tidy. His desk is no different. All the papers are in stacked baskets, pens all stored in a Chicago Bears mug, and his paperclips cling to a magnet next to his keyboard. I want to open all of his drawers and get a closer look at this professional side of Brett Sharp, but I'm relatively sure that digging through a detective's desk is frowned upon in the eyes of the law.

Something under his keyboard catches my attention. I can tell it's the edge of a photo, and my heart drops. Ah, this must be where he hides the picture of Sarah I so feared he would have. Unable to stop myself, I reach forward, uncovering it.

My breath hitches at what's revealed. If finding the picture hadn't already stolen my breath, the beautiful image in front of me would have. It's a picture of us at the police ball. I have no idea who took this. It's not posed. It's just us standing and talking. I'm staring up at him, and he must be saying something dirty, because my cheeks are flushed—his thumb caressing the red. He's wearing a sexy smirk, and my face is glowing. I don't remember standing there with him, but I can feel a rush of the million emotions captured with one click of a camera.

The corner of the picture is slightly worn where someone frequently handles it. It may have been hidden, but it's obvious he looks at it often. I get an idea and quickly slide it into my purse.

"You okay, Jess?" Caleb draws my attention away from grand theft photo.

"Yeah, I'm great. Why do you ask?" I try to be smooth.

"Because I just watched you steal Brett's prize possession."

"I-I just..." I stumble over my words.

"It's okay, baby girl. I don't blame you. It's a really good picture. We'll get some copies made while we're out. He'll lose his shit if that thing's missing for more than thirty seconds. I'll put it back for you later."

"Thank you," I rush out in a breath.

"Let's go. We have some ugly, non-scuffing shoes to buy!" He mocks excitement, and I punch him in the shoulder.

CALEB AND I must have gone to every store in town that offers bowling accessories. They either didn't have size-fifteen shoes or the selection was beyond hideous. It got to the point where Caleb would walk into a store and say, "Show me what you have in a size fifteen." They would bring us two or three pairs and we would sneak a peek then move on. Two hours later, we finally hit the last athletic store in a fifty-mile radius.

"That's them!" I scream as the sales girl holds out a kick-butt pair of black-and-blue-checkered shoes. "Please say you like them?" I turn to Caleb, waiting for the final verdict.

"Sold!" He slams his hand down on the counter.

Exhausted from the day, I jump around, thrilled that we have finally found something. I only have five days left until Christmas, so ordering online was out of the question. I should have planned this better, but I was waiting for my most recent paycheck to spend on Brett's big Christmas gift. Fortunately for me, these are way better than any shoes I would have picked out from just a picture online.

I launch myself into Caleb's arms, ecstatic and grateful for his help. "Thank you. Thank you. Thank you."

"Jesse, I didn't make them."

"I know, but I probably would have given up four stores ago if you hadn't been here to help."

"All right, all right. You're welcome. Now let's get out of here. I need to get back to work."

"Wait! We still have to stop and get the pictures."

"I couldn't forget that." He winks.

"Caleb, earlier...you said that picture was Brett's prize possession."

"Yeah, it is," he answers quickly. "He thinks he's being sly and no one can see him sliding it from under his keyboard two hundred times a day, but we're all just so fucking happy for him that we don't call him out on it."

"I told him I love him," I confess. Caleb may be Brett's best friend, but he's safe. He won't share my secrets. But hopefully he will share some of Brett's.

"Really! How did he react to that?" Caleb asks, shocked.

"He doesn't exactly feel the same way." I shrug, pretending that it doesn't break my heart every time I think about it.

"Give him some time. He's a good guy."

"So everyone keeps telling me."

"Do you need a Brett pep talk?" he teases, expecting me to punch him in the arm again.

"Maybe," I squeak out honestly.

"Jesus..." He looks around to make sure no one is listening. Whenever someone does that, you know it's always good information they are about to share. "He hasn't seen Sarah in over three weeks."

"WHAT?!" I shriek. He disappears every Thursday. I just assumed he was with her.

"For the last few weeks, we have been meeting for drinks."

"Why isn't he seeing Sarah?"

"She froze him out. Won't open the door. He's been sending over care-takers, who she surprisingly lets in, so he knows she's okay. She just doesn't want to see *him*."

"Well that's good she is letting someone in," I say, relieved. Why should I care about her? Oh that's right—because Brett loves her. Or loved her. Or... heck, I don't know. I've never bothered to actually ask.

"Baby girl, I don't want to fill your head with false reassurance. Sure, he and I talk, but I'm not in his head. I've seen him through a lot of stuff, but this thing with you two is new territory for us. Did he ever tell you about how we became friends again?"

"Again? I had no idea you two were ever *not* friends."

"We exchanged a few punches at Manda's funeral."

At the very mention of her name, Caleb pauses for a second too long. I don't rush him, but I recognize that this isn't a conversation we should have in the checkout line of Al's Sporting Goods. I hold up my finger, asking for one minute, and hurry to the register to pay.

When we get back to his truck, I turn to him and see sad eyes. I know I'm asking him to relive something tragic, but I need help. Caleb is my only connection to Brett.

"Okay, now keep going."

He lets out a loud breath before he bares it all.

"Blows were thrown at Manda's funeral. It was the hardest day of my life, and I used Brett as my punching bag. Physically and emotionally. The love of my life was gone, while Sarah sat sipping soda in a hospital across town. I lost everything, and fucking Brett escaped with only a few scratches. Sarah caused that wreck. She was drunk and decided to drive my girl home. She killed her because she was too damn lazy to wait for me and Brett or even just call a cab. I'll never in a million years forgive her. I know she's all fucked up now, but part of me thinks she deserves it. Brett doesn't deserve this though, and he's gotten the brunt of her issues.

"Anyway, after words were exchanged at the funeral, we didn't speak for seven months. I took a leave of absence at work and put in for a different partner when I came back. I managed to avoid him completely. I stood by as Sarah tried to kill herself twice. I almost enjoyed watching both of them suffer. God knows I suffered enough. It was time for someone else to have a turn. I'm a dick—you got that part, right?"

I nod quickly, not wanting to slow him down. When Caleb starts talking, you stop and listen. He may not do it often, but it always leads you somewhere.

"I was driving home that night when I heard his address over the radio. Dispatch was asking for immediate assistance. I was only a few blocks away, and as much as I didn't want to go, something inside of me turned the car and headed towards his house.

"I was the first on the scene. The ambulance hadn't even gotten there yet. I rushed inside and found him holding her lifeless body on the bathroom floor. You know what he said to me?" I can't hold back my tears. "He looked directly into my eyes, stood up off the ground with her in his arms, and said the words that have haunted me since they rolled off his tongue. *'Please help me. I won't survive without her.'* I understood that feeling. The desperation in his voice reminded me of how I felt when they told me Manda was gone. I would have done anything to save Manda. While I hated Sarah, Brett's my brother. I'd do anything to save him.

"I immediately went to work trying to put pressure on all the places she was bleeding. She did a job on herself that night. She didn't just slice her wrists. She was determined to end it all. Wrists, ankles, neck—you name it. She was bleeding from everywhere. I didn't think there was any way she could possibly live through wounds like those. Mentally, Sarah is a quitter, but apparently her body is a fighter. The ambulance showed and took her from Brett. He didn't even have it in him to ride along with her." He pauses, only long enough to find my eyes.

"Jesse, that was the night Brett was forced to finally let go of Sarah. He's convinced himself that he's still holding on and that he can't move on. It's a load of shit, and that picture of you two together is proof. He's trapped. Torn between doing the right thing as a man and a husband and making himself happy."

My tears are openly flowing, but I keep my mouth closed because I need to hear the rest of it. I need to finally know why Brett is terrified to commit to me.

"I got to say goodbye," he says, confusing me. "Maybe it wasn't the way I wanted, but I looked at Manda's beautiful face and stroked her silky red hair and told her exactly how our life would have happened. How many kids we would have had, what kind of car I would have bought her, and the size of our house. No detail was too small. She might have been gone by the time I said it all, but I know Manda heard me." A small tear escapes his eye, and I crawl across the truck to curl into his side. He drapes his arm around me, accepting my condolences.

"Brett didn't get that. When the ambulance left with Sarah barely cling-ing to life, he just stood frozen on the front porch. I could see a breakdown coming. All the guys from the station just walked by, patting him on the back. No one knew what to do to help the shattered man covered in his wife's blood standing just a few steps away. I did though. Months earlier, he offered a shoulder to me when I needed it most. It was long past time I returned the favor. No words were spoken. Just a simple bond between two men who lost everything.

"Baby girl, if you really love Brett, give him time. He's already made it further in four months than I ever thought possible. I guess a good woman will do that to you." He squeezes me against his side and flashes me a sad smile.

"You'll find someone like that one day."

"I already found her. And buried her."

"I want to meet Manda," I announce.

"You're about four years too late, sweetheart."

"Take me to her grave. I want to introduce myself. I saw her picture on your desk today. She was really beautiful."

"You have no idea," he says, shaking his head and turning away to stare out the window. After a few minutes of silence, he pulls his arm off my shoulder and scrubs his face. "Fuck it. I'm not going back to work. You want to grab a beer?"

"What about the picture? Won't Brett notice its missing?"

"Yeah. We can get your car and I'll replace the picture. Then we can hit the bar next to Brett's apartment. That way we can call him to drive us home when he gets off work." Caleb starts laughing at his own plan.

Brett's probably going to be pissed when he finds out that Caleb and I are together drinking in middle of the day. More about the me-being-with-Caleb part, less about the drinking in the middle of the day. Oh well. I just dragged this man around all of Chicago. The least I can do is buy him a beer.

Chapter
TWENTY-EIGHT

Brett

I JUST picked up the last of Jesse's Christmas gifts, and it took way longer than expected. It's completely worth it though. I have to say that I'm pretty proud of myself for thinking of this one. She is going to love it. I'm running late, but thankfully I still beat Jesse and Kara to my parents' house. I walk into the house, arms filled with boxes, and I swear my entire family has piled into the hallway to greet me.

"What the hell are you guys doing?" I ask, confused by the mass welcome.

"Is Jesse with you?" I hear my mom ask from behind the crowd. Oh, right! Jesse.

Ever since I told my family I was bringing someone home for Christmas, it's all they've talked about. Knowing my sisters, they probably have a phone tree set up to share little details they find out about Jesse. For the last two weeks, one of them has called daily to interrogate me. What does she like to eat? What's her favorite color? My sister actually asked me her bra size, and after that, I shut down all further conversations about Jesse. It pissed them off, but my family is nuts. I know this is a big deal to them.

Over the last few years, the women in my family have given at least two lectures a month about moving on and finding someone new. When that didn't work, they tried to recruit my dad and brothers-in-laws to help their "Save Brett" mission. Luckily, the men refused.

I'm nervous as hell about introducing Jesse to my family. It's such a big step, and if it weren't for the idea of her spending Christmas alone and getting drunk with Kara, I'm not sure I would have invited her at all. Well, at least that's what I tell myself. I can't remember ever being this excited about Christmas, and I know it's all because of her.

"You people need to take a deep breath and calm the hell down. You're going to scare her if you bombard her like this."

My words don't faze them in the least. My mom walks over to the door and searches outside as if I may have forgotten Jesse on the front porch.

"Jesus. She isn't with me. She and Kara are driving themselves over after they run some last-minute errands." I hand my sister the boxes in my left hand. "Erin, can you wrap these for me? Nothing crazy. I have a one-bow limit with gifts I give people, so keep that in mind."

"You should have Leah do it then. Jesse would think it was sweet if one of the kids wrapped her presents."

"Oh, shut up! Don't be jealous! I give better presents, so no one cares how they are wrapped," my oldest sister Leah snaps over at Erin.

"What time are they supposed to be here?" my mom asks, almost giddy.

"Ma, you have got to calm down. She's not like Sarah. She's quiet, and this family is crazy enough without the added excitement. Don't swarm her when she gets here. Now, Kara is another story. She will fit right into this loony bin. Focus on her."

"Brett Thomas, it is not every day my only son brings home a woman. I'm allowed to be excited. I won't embarrass you, but I can't wait to meet her."

"I promise, son," Dad says, clapping a hand on my shoulder. "I'll keep them in check."

"Right. That's worked so well for you over the years," I say sarcastically. My dad can't control the Sharp women any better than I can. It's a lost cause. I'd be better off just warning Jesse.

As if she heard us talking about her, there is a knock at the door. I hand the last of her gifts to my sister to hide in the back room and head to the door. I take a deep breath and look back at my family all wedged into the tiny hall. Rolling my eyes, I pull open the door.

"Brett!" Kara squeals, launching herself into my arms. She slams into me, causing me to stumble back a few steps. "I can't believe you're introducing me to your family already!" she exclaims.

I'm about to get pissed when I look up to see Jesse softly laughing. She's wearing a clingy white sweater and a light-blue scarf that sets off her brown eyes. *Jesus, she's beautiful.* I pry Kara from my body. Not bothering with introductions, I swipe one arm around Jesse's waist and pull her in for a quick, deep kiss.

I can't help it. I know my family is watching, and she's stiff, but it's worth every second of the shit I'm going to catch for it later. Still holding her, I spin to see eight surprised and confused faces. Giggling, Kara loops her arm through mine. It occurs to me that, while my family is full of nut jobs,

Kara Reed is going to give them all a run for their money.

Judging by the smiles on the men's faces, they are all assuming I'm part of some kinky threesome. I should probably correct this assumption. If Jesse weren't tensing beside me, I'd let this go on the rest of the day. However, I don't want to make her uncomfortable the very first time she meets my family.

"Everyone, this is Jesse Addison." I pull her against my body. "And this"—I roughly snatch my arm away—"is her very affectionate best friend Kara Reed."

"Hello, ridiculously attractive Sharp family!" Kara waves from beside me.

Even with her antics, she may as well be invisible. All eyes are on Jesse. My mom is the first to speak up. Only she doesn't actually say anything at all. Tears spring to her eyes as she shoves my sisters out of the way and rushes forward, dragging Jesse into a hug. *Not awkward at all.*

Releasing her, she steps away and extends a hand. "Hi, Jesse. I'm Evelyn Sharp, Brett's mom."

Jesse takes her hand. "Jesse Addison. It's so nice to meet you."

My whole family is still watching them like the freak show at the circus.

"Ladies, this is my sister Erin and her husband Jack, Leah and her husband Ryan, and the tall guy in the corner is my dad Will. Everyone, this is Jesse and Kara." No sooner than I finish, everyone rushes forward welcoming both women with open arms.

As my loved ones all gather around her, amongst the chaos of a million introductions, I hear the most amazing sound that only Jesse can give me—silence.

THE AFTERNOON flies by. The women drink wine and hang out in the kitchen, and the men lounge around the den, making sure the kids don't destroy the Christmas tree. Kara fits right into my family, and if I'm not mistaken, I overheard her talking to Erin about a date with Jack's younger brother. As expected, Jesse is quiet. I can tell she's overwhelmed by the barrage of questions from my family, but she holds nothing back. She answers everything they throw at her.

"Mom, can we watch the movies yet?" I hear Samantha ask as we finish up dinner.

When Jesse met the kids, she adorably introduced herself with a handshake to each and every one of them, including Erin's eight-month-old little boy. I felt it the moment her eyes landed on my oldest niece Samantha. I knew she was reliving the moment Sarah slapped her picture down on the table at Nell's and claimed Samantha to be mine. I also knew she didn't let it fester long, because she looked up at me grinning.

"She's gorgeous."

"Yeah, she is."

"And tall! She's like eight and taller than I am already. Your family is full of giants."

"Nah, we're just average. You're actually just a snack-sized person," I tried to tease, but I caught an elbow to the stomach instead.

WHEN DINNER is over, we all pile into the den for the annual pajama exchange. I can see the panic in Jesse's eyes as she is handed a gift.

"Brett, you didn't tell me there was a pajama exchange. I didn't bring anything for anyone else!" she whisper-yells into my ear.

"Simmer down, gorgeous. I bought for you and Kara. No reason to get all worked up." She still huffs in my direction. "But you have to promise to take them off tonight." Her eyes go wide and I catch yet another elbow to the ribs. By the end of the night, I'm going to have a bruise or twelve.

Kara is the first to rip open her package. She even beats the kids to tearing off the wrapping paper.

"Shut. Up!" she screams entirely too loudly. "Vegetables!" She cackles, holding up a pair of footed pajamas covered in every vegetable known to man.

"I heard you were a vegetarian." I lift my eyebrows at our little inside joke.

"Exclusively." She winks.

My family continues around the room, one by one, opening gifts. Finally, it makes a full circle and lands on Jesse. *Shit!* I was hoping she could open hers amidst the chaos and blend in. But here she is, the focus of the room. I have to warn her. She'll never speak to me again if I give her sexy panties in front of my entire family.

"Don't remove the bottom layer of tissue paper," I whisper into her ear.

"What?" she tries to whisper back, but it catches Erin's attention.

"Yeah. What, Brett?" Erin shouts across the room.

Jesse acts fast, pulling out only the top half of the box, slamming the top back on, and handing it to me. I sheepishly nod at her unspoken chastise.

"Oh my God."

"You like them?" I ask as she holds up the pajama equivalent of our relationship.

Grey fleece pants covered by cartoon versions of bowling pins, beer bottles, Chinese takeout containers, coffee, pickles, and of course, sunshine. Yeah, okay, I may have stumbled upon a place online where they make custom pajamas. I couldn't resist. It was too fitting, and the smile that lights her face is worth a million-fold more than the money I spent on express shipping.

"I love them. Seriously, Brett, these are perfect." In the most un-Jesse-like fashion, she plants a bold kiss on my lips in front of my whole family. "I promise, I'll wear whatever you're hiding in that box," she whispers, causing me to chuckle against her mouth.

I look up to see smiles glued to the faces of everyone in the room. Jesse never notices everyone's face because her eyes never leave mine.

Jesse

HE MADE me pajamas. Freaking amazing, sweet, and thoughtful pajamas. He didn't just go down to the mall and buy me and Kara any old set of PJs. He took the time, got creative, and had them made. Ever since I poured my heart out to Brett, I've been trying really hard not to read into things. That just went flying out the window though. He made me freaking pajamas that tell the story of our relationship. Seriously, this is huge. No one gets it. I bet they all think I'm a pickle-obsessed alcoholic who is currently laying a wet one their brother/son/uncle, but I don't care one bit. I'm going to enjoy the heck out of this moment.

AFTER WATCHING *A Christmas Story*, *Love Actually*, and *It's A Wonderful Life*, everyone decides to turn in for the evening. I'm not sure where Kara and I are sleeping. Brett took our bags somewhere when we arrived, and I haven't seen them since.

"Where are Kara and I sleeping, handsome?" I smile hugging his muscular stomach.

I haven't had this much fun on Christmas in years. His family is hilarious, and even though they were a bit overbearing at first, I knew they were just curious. I'm just happy they welcomed me the way they did. I was expecting someone to give me the cold shoulder, but they all seem to be thrilled.

"You're sleeping with me, and Kara is in the bedroom in the basement."

"I'm not sleeping with you in your parent's house! They'll think I'm a slut."

"I don't mean we'll be having sex, Jesse. I just mean sleeping in the same bed with me."

"Oh, I know exactly what you meant and the answer is still no way, Jose."

"What? Why the hell not?"

"God, I should have bought you Q-tips for Christmas. Your family will think I'm a slut if I sleep with you!"

He tries to fight it, but fails when he bursts into laughter. It really annoys me, but he doesn't seem to care that I'm shooting daggers at him.

"Jesse, I'm thirty-two. My family is not going to think anything if you sleep in my room. Besides, they love you. If you sleep in the basement, I can't promise they won't hunt you down in the middle of the night with pitch forks and torches."

"They love me?"

"Gorgeous, everyone loves you."

Everyone but you, I sadly think to myself.

"You sure they won't care?" I ask.

"I swear. Mom already took Kara downstairs. You're all mine for the rest of the night."

"I like the way that sounds, but don't get any ideas. I might be willing to let them assume I'm easy, but I'm not going to prove it."

"There is nothing easy about you, Jesse James." He squeezes me tighter than necessary. I know he's trying to convey something to me with this hug, but I've done enough reading into Brett for one day.

"Get a room!" Erin yells from the end of the hallway with a huge grin on her face. She's propped up against the doorway like she's been watching us for a while.

"Excuse me for a minute," Brett says, releasing me and charging down the hallway.

"Shit!" Erin yelps as Brett tackles her. They wrestle around in the hall-way for a few minutes until Erin's husband Jack walks out shirtless in his Christmas pajamas pants.

Unable to maneuver around them, he casually steps over the fighting siblings. This must not be anything shocking to him. He doesn't even ac-knowledge it. He just points to the bathroom and asks, "Is anyone in there?"

When Brett and Erin finish the Christmas Royal Rumble, they both stand and I can't help laughing at them. Eric and I fight, but we aren't playful wrestlers. This funny relationship they have makes me smile.

"Bedtime." He walks over to me like a caveman and slings me over his shoulder.

I wave goodnight to his ecstatic sister as she bounces on the balls of her feet. I guess they really do love me.

Chapter
TWENTY-NINE

Jesse

I'M CURLED UP against Brett when the morning arrives all too soon.

"Merry Christmas, gorgeous," he whispers into my ear, sending chill bumps down my body.

"Merry Christmas, Brett." I place a kiss to his throat.

As if on cue, I hear the patter of feet running up the stairs and a myriad of knocks on the door.

"Uncle Brett, wake up! Santa came. It's present time!" The kids sprint off to wake up the rest of the sleepy adults.

"Come on. You heard them. Santa came." Brett's excitement is infectious, and even though I'm tired and nowhere near ready to crawl out from under the warm blankets, I get excited right along with him.

"Point me to the coffee," I say, dragging myself to my feet.

"Pointing you to a hairbrush might be more useful," he says, smoothing down my sleep-mussed hair.

"Excellent point. I should freshen up. I'll meet you downstairs."

"I'll have the coffee waiting." He kisses my forehead and walks away.

I use the few minutes to dig out the bag of gifts for him and his family. Kara and I weren't sure what to get them, but Brett assured me that they all love coffee. So we utilized our Nell's employee discount. I bought them all nice insulated travel mugs and Kara bought fancy flavored coffees. It's nice and it fit into our budgets, thanks to Nell practically giving them to us at cost.

"Babe, you coming? I'm not going to be able to hold the kids off the presents much longer. There is about to be a riot down here!" Brett shouts from the bottom of the stairs.

After a quick stop at the bathroom, I head down to my first ever Sharp

Family Christmas.

AFTER THE kids finish opening the roomful of presents, Erin and Leah let the older ones go down to the basement to play one of the video games they received. Like a well-oiled machine, Mr. Sharp stands up and starts passing out Christmas gifts to all the adults. By the time he's done, I have an intimidating pile stacked in front of me. Hmm, maybe I should have bought these people more than travel mugs. I look over and catch Kara's eyes as she sits on the floor, clapping at her mountain of gifts like one of the kids.

"Okay, Jess, you go first," Brett says, placing a beautifully wrapped box on my lap.

I'm mortified that everyone is going to watch me as I open presents. I hate being the center of attention. Worse yet, I'm going to have to watch them all, one by one, open my crappy mugs. Instead of immediately ripping open the box, I begin to chew on my thumbnail. Suddenly, I'm very uncomfortable and wishing I could skip this and go downstairs to play video games too.

"Gorgeous, relax," Brett whispers into my ear as his family looks on.

Fantastic, they are going to think I'm crazy for freezing up about a silly gift exchange. I suck in a quick breath and plaster on a smile as I tear through the wrapping paper.

"Oh my God," I say, staring down at the brand-new laptop in my arms. *Crap!* "You bought me a laptop?" I ask.

The horror of his buying me something so extravagant must show on my face, because his smile quickly disappears.

"You said your old one broke."

"You bought me a computer?" I repeat a little louder.

"It's just a present, Jesse. Stop overthinking it. It's Christmas, babe," he tries to reassure me before I hit full freak-out mode.

"Brett, I can't accept this. I, um...I can't. This is too much."

"Gorgeous, take a deep breath. I bought you a computer because I wanted you to have one. Stop thinking about the price tag. This isn't about money. This is about me wanting you to have a computer for school."

"Good job, honey. That's a really nice one," his mom says, trying to defuse an obviously awkward conversation.

I can see that they are all confused by my reaction. I bet most girls would love an expensive gift for Christmas, but I'm not most girls. All I see in front of me is a pile of money Brett spent on me, and I'm about to give him bowling shoes. *Double crap!*

Brett answers his mom with a simple, "Thanks," never moving his eyes from mine. "Jess, stop thinking about the price tag. I know that's what you're doing. Remember what I said? I work hard for moments like this. It's just a computer."

I nod, but I still hate it. As soon as we leave, I'm going to refuse to accept it. It was a sweet thought, but it's too much.

"Me next!" Kara yells, reaching toward her stack of gifts.

"No!" The whole room shouts at once.

Kara looks up puzzled.

"Kara, I have one you have to open first. Babe, there's another one for you too," Brett says, walking out of the room.

Great, he bought me another present. What's next, a new car? Oh God, please don't let it be a new car!

"Close your eyes," he says from around the corner. "Both of you."

I close my eyes, hoping to disappear. His family begins laughing, so I know Kara is making grabby hands and acting silly.

"Okay, open them."

I open my eyes to see Brett, standing in front of us, holding two of the cutest kittens I have ever seen. Kara snatches the white-and-orange one while shrieking. I stare at him for a minute before pulling the fluffy white ball of fur from his hands.

"You got me a cat?" I smile as all of my anxiety from earlier vanishes. "A white cat?"

"I know the black ones freak you out." He smiles, and I can't help but launch myself into his arms. "Now this was the reaction I was hoping for with the laptop." He snuggles me against his chest.

"It's perfect. You remembered I only like white cats," I say, feeling touched that he would remember such a trivial detail from a conversation months ago.

"Of course."

"Wait, we can't have cats, Brett," Kara whines.

"Yes, you can. I had a little chat with your asshole landlord. He was kind enough to waive the pet fee also." Our landlord is anything but kind. Brett either paid the deposit or had more than just a simple discussion with him. "By the way, neither of you are ever allowed to be alone with that scumbag." Yep, more than a chat.

"You talked to our creepy landlord? Seriously, hot stuff, this is the best present ever." Kara begins to buzz around the room again.

"I love it. Thank you so much," I say, grinning from ear to ear.

"Now...will you keep the computer? I know you were planning to give it back later."

"Yeah." I give in. I'm such a jerk for reacting the way I did. He was trying to do something nice, and I clammed up over a price tag.

Realizing that Kara and I have taken over the morning, I sit down, clinging to my kitten, who I decide to name Daisy, and urge his family to continue with gifts.

The next hour passes quickly as all the presents are unwrapped. His family seems to love the mugs, and they even start arguing over the coffee flavors. Brett's family gives me and Kara accessories for the cats. Beds, bowls, toys—we get it all. His father even bought matching rhinestone collars for them. They're perfect.

The time comes for me to give Brett the presents I bought him. I'm nervous, but I'm also confident he will love at least one of them.

"Jesse!" he exclaims as he pulls off the top of his shoes. "These are awesome. Shoes that actually fit! You're in real trouble now. Ill-fitting shoes have been the only thing holding me back from beating you." He laughs, sliding them on and strutting across the room.

Even in pajama pants and bowling shoes, Brett is a sexy man. It warms me in all the wrong places while I'm sitting in a room full of people.

Next up is the picture. I'm not quite as confident about this one. I have no idea how he is going to react. I've talked myself out of giving it to him twenty-seven different times since I picked it up from the shop. Yet somehow, it still managed to get wrapped and make its way under the Christmas tree. The shoes were easy. I knew he'd like them. But this picture... It's a risk. And if he doesn't the feel the same way, I'm putting myself out there for some serious embarrassment.

He opens the cheap cardboard box, and the smile on his face fades, leaving him utterly blank.

I have no idea what to think of his reaction, but I give him the benefit of the doubt and a minute to figure it out.

Caleb and I took the picture from the ball to a design lab. They specialize in artistic imagery, and they took the already amazing picture and turned it into a work of art. Thankfully, my brother used to date the girl who owns the shop, so she cut me a fantastic—free—deal. Caleb made the frame for me. Who knew Caleb was crafty? But when I told him my idea, he told me he could easily make it. Together, it turned out perfect.

The lab took the picture and added a foggy filter over the top. It starts at the bottom left corner of the picture and creeps toward the top right. You can still see Brett and me, but the haze obscures your view. Caleb made the picture frame of natural rustic wood. In the top right corner, he carved a sun with its rays stretching across the top and down the side. When you put them together, it looks like the sun on the frame is pushing back the fog. I may have cried when I saw it. It's stunning, even if you know nothing about our history.

I watch him closely for some sort of reaction, but he doesn't move a muscle.

"What is it?" Leah asks. It's clear to everyone that even more dramatics are happening in our little corner of the family room.

"Jesus." Brett stands up and walks out of the room, leaving the picture frame on the couch beside him.

His family are all looking at each other, and I can hear the guys rumbling questions. I'm not sure what to say. His reaction honestly surprises me. I look to Kara for silent advice. She knows the whole fog-and-sun story, but she offers nothing more than a wide-eyed shrug. I hand her Daisy and decide to follow him. At the very least, I should apologize for my unknown transgression.

When I quietly make my way up the stairs, I hear him pacing in our room.

"Hey." I step into the room, closing the door behind me.

"Where did you get that picture?"

"I saw it under your keyboard when I went to pick up Caleb." He suddenly stops pacing and looks at me questioningly. "He helped me pick out your shoes. It was that night you picked us up from the bar." My answer must satisfy his curiosity because he resumes his pacing and runs a frustrated hand through his hair.

"Fuck."

"I'm sorry." I don't know what else to say. I'm clueless as to why he's acting like this.

Before I can't analyze it any deeper, I'm lifted off my feet and thrown to the bed. Brett's mouth lands harshly on mine. I only struggle for a second. Then it's all hands and lips.

"Jesse, that picture is amazing. It randomly showed up on my desk the day after the ball. I must have looked at it every five minutes since then." He roughly bites down on my nipple through my shirt, causing me to cry out. "Too hard, gorgeous?"

"No." I gasp for breath as he continues.

"I love it." He pins my hands over my head and rolls his hips into mine.

It's around ten on Christmas morning, his entire family is sitting downstairs, yet I still find myself lifting my hips so he can remove my pants. I hear a familiar foil packet rip. Then he swiftly slams himself inside me. I let out an uncontrollable moan, and he presses a hand across my mouth.

"You need to be quiet. This will have to be quick, so don't hold back on me."

He wasn't kidding about it being quick, and I'm not talking about him. Brett puts every trick he has into getting me off. With his mouth on my breast, his thumb on my clit, and his length buried to the hilt inside me, it only takes a few strokes before I unravel underneath him. A few seconds later, he follows with a silent release of his own.

Still fully dressed, with our pants around our ankles, he lies on top of me, catching his breath.

"That...picture."

"You don't have to put it on your desk or anything. I just got the idea in my head—"

"Are you fucking mad? I'm definitely putting that on my desk. Hell, I feel the need to blow it up into poster size and hang it on my living room wall," he teases. "Jones would have to make a huge frame for that though."

"You knew he made it?" I ask, surprised. I thought Caleb was doing me a special favor.

"Yeah, but I have to say, he really outdid himself with that one. Seriously, Jess, it's amazing!"

"You seemed mad when you opened it."

"I was just a little overwhelmed. That's all. Sorry if I bit you too hard."

"It's okay. Thank you for my computer and Daisy."

"Daisy, huh?"

"Yeah. It's my favorite flower."

"Good to know." He winks as he slowly pulls out.

We need to go back downstairs, but what I wouldn't give to spend the day in bed with him. Unfortunately, that isn't an option, so I pull up my pants and watch him head to the bathroom.

All in all, even through our ups and downs, this is unquestionably my best Christmas ever.

Chapter
THIRTY

Jesse

IF I thought our relationship got better after Thanksgiving, Brett and I have come a million miles since Christmas. It's like something happened that day two months ago. A huge, realistic, life-altering rubber band snapped everything into perspective. Considering that we have only been together for four months, I would say our relationship is pretty serious. That is if you don't consider that we still haven't talked about our actual relationship.

Not a single day passes that I don't spend the night with Brett. Well, if you don't count Thursdays. Caleb has reassured me on more than one occasion that Brett isn't with Sarah. He says that they meet up and go drinking at the bar for a few hours. It still burns when Brett disappears though.

Every other night, Brett comes to my apartment or Daisy and I go to his. For someone who claims to be a dog person, he sure does love that cat. I don't have to bring her every time I go to his place, but he usually insists. He once gave me the silent treatment when I showed up alone.

We still don't talk about Sarah. I know what you are thinking. How can you not talk about the crazy, hot, blond elephant in the room? Well, it's easy. Denial is a hell of a tool. I just pretend like she doesn't exist. I know doing that doesn't help us move forward. It also means that I don't have to face the fact that my boyfriend, who I'm in love with but who doesn't reciprocate, is married to another woman. Maybe I'm the crazy one, not her—or at least that is what I think until Sarah comes prancing back into my life.

It is Wednesday afternoon and I am doing Brett's grocery shopping. He gave up on me making the list a few weeks ago and just started giving me his credit card so I could do the shopping myself. At first, I was a little uncomfortable spending his money, but after the third time he brought home cottage cheese instead of cream cheese, I snatched his card and walked out.

Today is a very adventurous trip to the store. I'm focused on the row of spices, trying to figure out the lowest price on garlic powder when someone plows into me.

"Shit! I'm so sorry. I wasn't paying attention. Jesse?"

I see a woman with black hair I vaguely recognize.

"Ummm...yes," I respond questioningly. I should know this woman, but I can't seem to place her face.

"Sarah Sharp, remember?" she says, filling in the blank and making my skin crawl

"Oh, um...hey," I say, turning back to the shelf, hoping she'll walk away.

"Do you live around here?"

"Yeah, just down the street," I clip in her direction.

"Hey, while you're here, let me ask you a question. I'm making Brett a big anniversary dinner tomorrow, and I was wondering if you know a good side dish to go with the steaks I'm making?"

Seriously, I must be confused. There is no way Sarah is standing here asking me for recipes.

"Um...what?"

"Brett loves my cooking, but tomorrow is our anniversary, so I want to do something special. You know, spice things up a little." She laughs a hollow sound that sends chills down my spine.

"Um, baked potatoes?" I mumble then push my cart forward trying, unsuccessfully, to get away from her.

"Jesse, I think we got off on the wrong foot. Let's start over." She sounds sincere, making me pause only long enough to see the sarcastic smile on her face.

Last time I came face to face with her, she ran the show. She pushed my buttons and tortured me with information about her and Brett. I've tried to forget about her, but you can't pretend someone doesn't exist when they are coldly mocking you in the middle of a grocery store. I'm not going to let her pull this crap again.

"Sarah, I have no recipes to share with you, nor do I have any desire to kiss and make up. You can make whatever the heck you want to tomorrow, but just know that, at the end of the night, he will be in my bed."

Was it dirty to say that to her? Heck yes! Did it feel better than winning the lottery? Heck yes! Did it hurt like crazy when she slapped me across the face? Hell yes!

"You fucking whore! You think Brett cares about you? Well, guess what, bitch? He loves me. He always has and always will. The difference between me and you is I have him and you never will."

"Right."

I try to walk away, my face still stinging, but apparently Sarah wasn't finished yet. She yanks my arm, digging her fingernails into my flesh, and snatches me around to once again face her.

"Stay the fuck away from my husband," she says, finding the chink in my armor. *My husband.*

As bad as her words hurt, I know this is a worthless conversation. Sarah isn't just damaged—she's destroyed. I'm not arguing with a sane woman. She's delusional and manipulative. No verbal sparring is going to win this argument. This time, I don't cower though. I'm done with that. We both know Brett is mine. Heck, everyone but Brett knows that. This conversation is about her.

"Sarah Erickson." I purposely use her maiden name. Yeah, that fancy new laptop Brett got me may have Googled her. "I am going to pretend you didn't just put your hands me. I am going to pretend you didn't just call me a whore. Hell, I'm even willing to forget you followed me here today." This little chance meeting is too much of a coincidence for her not to have followed me. I don't have time to really let that sink in though. "I'm not, however, willing to let go of the fact that you think this is somehow a competition between the two of us. Sarah, you need help. You need to talk to a counselor, and you need to visit Manda so you can, once and for all, let go of your guilt."

This time, I see it coming. She slings a closed fist at my face, but I duck, causing her to knock down a spice display. I keep talking because she needs to hear this. I'm probably not the right person to tell her, but she definitely needs to hear it.

"You need to take care of yourself, Sarah. You may not know it, but people love you. I know bad things have happened to you, but for Christ's sake...just let someone in. You are not alone in this. There may have only been one funeral, but four people died in that car. You're not alone." I repeat the last sentence for good measure.

As I walk away, I fully expect to be pegged in the back of the head with canned vegetables. Surprisingly, it never happens. I leave the cart filled with groceries and walk directly to my car. As the adrenalin rush wears off, I begin to shake. I want to call to Brett, but I know this whole situation will only cause him more heartache. I remember words from months earlier.

"If you see her again, you call me immediately. Not Brett. You call me."

I pick up the phone and dial Caleb instead. "Where are you?" I say as soon as he picks up the phone.

"Where are you, baby girl?" he responds flirtatiously.

"I just ran into Sarah at the grocery store."

"Fuck! Where are you, seriously?" he says, scarily concerned.

"Harps on St. Charles."

"Drive across the street and wait for me. Do not go home under any circumstances, got it?"

"Okay."

"Stay on the phone. I'm about five minutes away."

"Caleb, I'm okay. Really. I think she just—"

"What did she say, sweetheart?" His voice returns to the gentle softness I've become familiar with.

"Um...." Crap. He is going to be pissed when I tell him she slapped me. Maybe I can just leave that part out. When I look in the rearview mirror and see my swollen cheek and a small trickle of blood on the corner of my lip, I know it's a lost cause. "She said a bunch of stuff, but the gist of it all was for me to stay away from Brett."

"Are you okay?" He's asking about my emotional state. It's the obvious question after the last time I had the pleasure of talking to Sarah. However, tonight it has a much more superficial answer.

"Um..."

"Fuck!" he screams at my non-answer. "What did she do?"

"Calm down. I'm fine. She slapped me and it busted my lip."

I honestly think I can hear his head explode over the phone. "She did what?" he booms across the line.

"Stop, really. I'm okay. I'm just a little shaken up. That's all."

"Grab your purse. I'm almost there. Park your car. You're coming with me."

"Okay," I say, relieved at the idea of not being alone.

Caleb doesn't say anything else, nor does he hang up. When he parks next to me, he doesn't even give me a chance to get out of car. He snatches open my door and drags me out, using my chin to examine my face.

"Stop. I'm fine." I try to bat his hands away, but he crushes me against his chest. These macho men really treat me like a rag doll sometimes. He doesn't say another word until we pull up in front of a small brick house in a family neighborhood.

"Come on. I need to call Brett."

"No! You can't call him. He'll be so mad."

"Well it's about damn time he got mad, don't you think? He treats her like a china doll. Sarah went too far this time. He should be pissed. Maybe this will cause him to finally get off his ass and do something about her bullshit."

"Caleb, please don't call him," I begin to beg. Things have been so great with Brett and me recently. The last thing I want is him diving back into the guilt-filled pit of Sarah.

"Sweetheart. I'm calling him. A man deserves to know when his woman has been assaulted. How exactly do you think you're going to explain that welt on your face to him?"

Dang it! He's right. Crap. Brett's going to lose his ever-loving mind about this.

"I'll call him," I sigh.

"Nope. Wrong again, baby girl. If you tell him about this over the phone, there is no guarantee he will actually make it over here to pick you up. I don't want to leave you alone, but I have things to do."

"What are you going to do, Caleb?" I ask, scared by the look in his eye.

"Nothing you need to worry about."

I feel the need to remind him. "She a broken, disturbed, and insane *woman.*"

"Jesus, Jess, I'm not going to hurt her. What the fuck kind of asshole do you think I am? I'm just going to have a little conversation with her and make sure it actually sinks into that crazy-ass brain of hers," he says, putting his phone to his ear. "Sharp, get your ass over to my house. Jesse's here. Warning—you're going to be pissed."

I hear Brett shout on the other end of the phone, but Caleb hits the end button.

"Well, that was a little dramatic, don't you think?"

"Probably, but it will get him here faster. Whatever bullshit he is making up in his head right now will probably be worse than what really happened. It should soften the blow for him."

"That's horrible and mean...but also brilliant," I say, walking up to his front door. "Can we please go in now? I'm freezing."

I SIT inside Caleb's surprisingly clean and well-decorated house waiting for Brett. It only takes him about five minutes to get there, but I feel bad knowing he worried the whole way. He doesn't bother knocking when he gets there. He storms in, searching for me.

"Jesse!"

"I'm in here," I cautiously yell from the couch.

"What's going on?"

I've been planning the way I am going to gently and reassuringly tell Brett about today's drama. I want him to know that everything is fine. We just need to sit down and talk about the next step in trying to help Sarah. I'm not quick enough though, because Caleb not so gently rushes out the facts.

"Sarah stalked Jesse down at the grocery store today. Yelling at her to stay away from you then hit her before riding off on the crazy train again. Now, are you going to man the fuck up and finally do something about this?"

Well, okay then. I guess that's one way to break it to him.

"Jesus, are you okay?" Brett's eyes glide over me.

"I'm fine. It really wasn't as bad as it sounds."

"Why didn't you call me?"

"Umm, I didn't want to upset you." It's a statement, but my voice rises at the end, making it sound more like a question.

"You didn't want to upset me? What the fuck, Jesse? You called Caleb instead of me?"

"I just thought—"

"You just thought what? That maybe I wouldn't want to know that my ex-wife hit you?"

I expected Brett to be mad. I just never expected him to be mad at me. It's shocking and confusing, but mainly, it's infuriating.

"Yes, because my calling Caleb is the big issue here, not the fact that your *wife*"—I purposely leave off the ex-part. It makes my blood boil that they are still married. I'm not letting him brush it under the rug either—"followed me to the grocery store, telling me that you were hers and asking for recipes to cook for your anniversary dinner tomorrow. Obviously, I'm focusing on completely the wrong part." I push up my sleeve, revealing the hidden bruises where Sarah grabbed my arm. "I'm sorry. I thought these were somehow the important part."

"What the fuck? You didn't tell me about those!" Caleb yells, and Brett sucks in a deep breath. They must look pretty bad, because the rage on both men's faces is unmistakable.

Whatever. I don't care anymore.

"Brett, I want to go home. Then you two can handle this whole Sarah thing on your own. It's obvious I don't need to be involved." I grab my purse and head to the door, not waiting to see if Brett follows.

We ride to my house in silence. Brett walks me to my door and kisses me on the head. He leaves without a single word spoken. We may not be speaking, but I didn't want him to leave. I'm not willing to put my pride aside and stop him though. He ticked me off with his reaction. This was not at all the way this conversation was supposed to go, but they seldom go as planned for us.

***

I DECIDE to call it a night. Grabbing a beer and a book, I head to the bathtub. I'll feel better after a long soak and some smutty romance. Two hours and an empty hot water heater later, I crawl into bed. I'd be lying if I say my mind doesn't drift to the day as I stare at the ceiling. Sarah doesn't scare me. She just needs help. I'm in no position to give that to her. Maybe I'll break my personal denial rule and talk to Brett about getting her the help she so desperately needs.

I think the best part of the day is the way I felt when Brett left. Or maybe it's the way I didn't feel. I wasn't paralyzed with fear that I'd never see him again. Or that this fight would make him realize he doesn't need any extra drama in his life. Silly as it sounds, those thoughts are always going through my head. Today, when they should have been running rampant, I felt content. Brett and I had a fight. It wasn't earth shattering. It wasn't the end. It was just a fight. It actually makes me smile as I fade off into sleep, feeling like we are—finally—a real couple.

Minutes later, I'm startled awake when a man crawls into my bed. I dart out of the bed, terrified, but he grabs me before I make it far.

"Shhh. It's just me, gorgeous."

Even with the adrenalin coursing thought my body, I melt into his arms.

"Hey," I say, rolling to face him.

He doesn't waste any time before apologizing. "I was an ass...again. It scared the shit out of me that, once again, Sarah hurt you, and this time physically. I took it out on you. I'll try harder next time to place my anger where it really belongs."

"I know," I sigh.

"Fuck, Jesse. Don't let me off the hook so easily. I feel like a jerk. This would be a lot easier if you yelled at me."

I reach out, running my hands through his thick hair, placing a soft kiss on his lips. "You really were a jerk, but I don't want to yell at you."

I kiss him again. He takes charge and glides his warm tongue into my mouth. He grabs my butt and pulls it tighter against his growing erection. His hand snakes up under my shirt, and we both groan when he finds my bare breast. I want this to go further, but I promised myself I'd finally talk to him about Sarah.

"Brett, wait. We need to talk."

"Do we have to?" He rakes his teeth across my ear, just the way he knows I like it.

"Yes," I say firmly, but I immediately regret it when he rolls away.

"Okay, gorgeous. Let's talk."

Crap. I really have to follow through and have this discussion now.

"I know you don't see Sarah on Thursdays anymore. Why do you still disappear?" This is the one question I am dying to know the answer.

"I made a promise that I would always be there for her on Thursdays.

Even though she won't see me these days, I intend to keep that promise. I don't want to treat you like my backup, because you aren't. You're important to me, babe. If I kept you on standby every Thursday just in case she didn't want to see me, what does that say about how I treat you? I would rather just stay gone than know that you might be waiting for me."

Wow. That was a good answer. I close the distance between us and curl into his side.

"Why won't she see you?"

"I have no idea. She's gone off hinges recently. It worries me, and today's little episode only makes it worse."

"What did you say to her today?"

"Nothing. I used my key to her apartment, but she was locked in her room. She did tell me to go fuck myself though, so I think she's okay. I hired someone to stay with her for a few more days. She's actually been nice to the ladies sitting with her. Last week, one of them reported they baked a fucking pie together."

"Maybe not having you hovering around has helped," I say, immediately regretting my choice in words.

"You think I hover? I see her once a week. If she were handicapped physically, I'd be an ass for not visiting her more often." He has a point.

"I didn't mean to upset you. I'm sorry. I shouldn't have said anything."

"I think, after today, you have every right to say something. That doesn't mean I'll agree with you though."

"I know."

"I went about telling you this in the wrong way, but I do want to say, it bothered the hell out of me that you called Caleb instead of me."

"I'm sorry. He told me months ago that, if I ever ran into her, I should call him. I guess it stuck with me. After the way things went down last time, I think I secretly wanted someone who would side with me, without question."

"I'm always on your side, babe." He actually sounds a little hurt.

"I don't doubt that when it comes to anyone except Sarah," I say as he lets out a loud, exasperated sigh.

"Look, I really don't want to talk about her anymore tonight. This moment right now is the highpoint of my day."

I suddenly realize Kara isn't home, and I know I locked the door. "How did you get in here?"

"I used your key. I went and picked up your car. I thought you might need it for work tomorrow."

"Oh, jeez...thanks. I didn't even think about that."

"Well, I'm glad I'm good for something." I giggle as he tickles me. "I love that sound." *I love you.* "Can we finish this conversation tomorrow? I need to make you come then fall asleep inside you," he says, and I instantly go wet.

"Um..."

"Please, Jesse. I need your silence more than anything right now. It doesn't have to be sex, but I need to feel you right now."

"Did you just take sex off the table?"

"Hell no!" he says, appalled that I would even suggest such a thing.

"Good, because I had a rough day too." I smile.

"Shit, I'm sorry about everything. All of it."

"Shhhh. I don't want your apologies. I want the silence too."

That's all it takes for him to roll me over and satisfy his need to make me come. Twice. He really is an overachiever.

Chapter
THIRTY-ONE

Jesse

"WHERE ARE we going?" I ask for the hundredth time since Brett picked me up.

"Jesse, I don't care how many times you ask me. I'm not telling!" he says, amused and frustrated.

"This is torture."

"This is not torture. This is me trying to surprise you by doing something fun. Stop complaining."

"I'm not complaining," I say, shocked that he would even think that. "I'm excited, Brett. You know I don't do well with surprises. I'm sorry if you think I'm complaining."

"Gorgeous, don't get all upset. I was just picking on you. Even if you were complaining, I wouldn't care." He never takes his eyes off the road, but he still manages to flash me a sexy smile.

Brett picked me up at nine this morning. He got called away last night and decided to sleep at his own apartment since he got home so late. I hate when he has to leave in the middle of the night, but I guess it's all part of his job. He showed up, bright and early, with coffee and muffins, so it's not like I could be annoyed. He told me to dress warm and be ready in thirty minutes. I wanted to offer up some attitude, but when he refused to tell me where we were headed, I was so curious that I immediately got ready.

"Where are we going?"

"Still not telling you," he sings beside me. "Seriously, babe. You are going to ruin this. It's not a huge deal, and if you keep asking, I think you are going to be let down."

"Did it cost you a small fortune?" I ask teasingly, but I'm totally serious inside.

"It cost less than dinner last night if that makes you feel any better." It does.

Brett is always paying when we go out. Which I would think is nice if he took me to normal date restaurants. No, Brett insists on taking me to nice places. He's not a fancy guy, so for a while, I couldn't figure out if he just wants to eat at those restaurants or if he had some misplaced need to impress me. He could have taken me to Mickey D's and I would have still been thrilled just to be spending time with him.

When I finally got up the nerve to ask him, he laughed at me. To my face, flat-out laughed at me. My hang-up on money gets under Brett's skin. I can't help it. I hate when he spends more than my meager weekly paycheck on one dinner. He's a freaking detective, not a corporate CEO. I have to give up the fight though. He's a big boy. He can spend his money however he wants.

"Did you bring extra clothes?" he asks as we turn down a dirt road. We are at least an hour outside the city. I can't imagine what we could be doing today.

"Yeah," I absently answer while searching for clues out the window.

Thank God we brought the Jeep today, because I'm not sure the BMW would have made it down this rough road. Suddenly, Brett steers the car to the side and throws it into park.

"We're here."

"Um...what?" I look around at nothing but trees and dirt.

He doesn't acknowledge my confusion. Instead, he gets out and walks around to open my door. "Let's go, gorgeous." He pulls me to my feet, my eyes still searching for a destination. He slings a bag over my shoulder and walks off into the woods.

"Brett! Where are you going? Don't leave me here."

"Then hurry up!" he shouts, not bothering to turn around.

The idea of being left alone in the middle of the woods definitely puts a little pep in my step. I rush after him into the woods. Just after I hit the tree line, I see a clearing, and it's staggering. I look around to see nothing but a frozen pond. The snow on the ground has been cleared into piles lining the perimeter. It looks like something out of a fairytale.

"Do you ice skate?" Brett asks, sitting down on a bench, the only man-made structure in sight.

"Do you?"

"Yeah. I played hockey in high school." He opens his bag, revealing a gigantic pair of skates.

"This is beautiful." I look around, wide-eyed, taking in our surroundings.

"It's my favorite spot. Leah's husband's family owns this land. Every year, when it gets cold enough, they clear the pond and use it for skating."

"Is it safe?"

"Of course, crazy. Wait, you do weigh less than the tractor that cleared it, right?" he jokes, and I shoot him a death glare. "Here." He pulls out a pair of skates from his bag.

"You did not buy me ice skates!" My yell echoes back at me.

"Okay, you sit here and freak out about a pair of cheap skates, but I'm going to take this pond for a spin. Let me know when you get over it, and I'll help you so you don't bust your ass." He steps onto the ice and flies away.

I watch him glide around for a few minutes. I hate it that he's right. The skates probably only cost him fifty bucks, but he needs to learn to talk to me first. I have a perfectly respectable pair hanging in my closet. Sure, these are really awesome—powder blue with white glittery laces—but I didn't *need* them.

"Jesse James, chop chop! You can worry about it later. I'll even give you the receipt so you can be fully informed in your obsessing, but right now, you need to get your sexy ass out here. I'll teach you. Stop procrastinating."

I let out an annoyed sigh. Rising to my feet, I take a few shaky steps toward the ice. Just before the edge, I reach out and grip his hands for balance.

"I've got you. One foot at a time. Just slide forward. I'll keep you balanced."

He holds my arms, skating backwards as he pulls me forward. I slip once and almost fall, but he lifts me off my feet and places me back down in front of him. He wraps an arm around my hips and curls me into his hard body.

"All right. Let's go slow. I don't want you to end up covered in bruises."

Leisurely, we spend the next hour arm in arm, gliding around the frozen pond. True to his word, Brett never lets me fall, but I never let go of him. It felt amazing to spend the day tucked tightly under his arm. I would keep up the ruse all day, but of course, Brett has to open his mouth.

"So what do you want to do tonight?" he asks when we flop down together on the bench.

"Um, maybe stay in. We can go to your place and I'll cook dinner. Something quiet."

"Jesse, you cooked dinner every day last week. Let me take you out this weekend."

"No, your idea of *out* is very different than mine."

"What is that supposed to mean?

"It means you take me to delicious, fancy restaurants that most girls would adore, but really I just want to go to the sports bar and eat wings."

"Gorgeous, you don't eat wings. You loved dinner last night. You squealed when the waitress brought your food out."

Dang it, he's right. The food was amazing.

"Can we please just stay in tonight and let me cook?"

"You're going to be sore tonight. While I don't mind rubbing you down later, I don't want you standing over the stove cooking. You have no idea the muscles you use when skating."

"If I can prove to you that I won't be sore tonight, can we hang out at home?"

"You can't prove you won't be sore, gor—"

Not even waiting for him to finish, I jump up and sprint my way around the ice. I make a full circle, skating with ease.

I've actually been skating since I was a kid. I'm not a figure skater or anything, but I can probably skate as well as Brett. It was fun to watch him baby me though. He took such good care of me and kept me tucked into his body. I was more than happy to play the 'helpless woman in need of rescue' role. He looked like he was really enjoying it.

I slowly glide back in front of Brett, who is sitting with his mouth hanging open, a lip curled in disgust.

"I promise I won't be sore. Can we please stay home tonight?"

"Yes, we can stay in, but you're definitely going be sore, and I'm not talking about from skating." He flies off the bench, throwing me over his shoulder and spinning in circles around the ice. Maybe I don't skate as well as Brett after all.

The rest of the day on the pond is a blast. We act like kids, challenging each other to races and arguing about who wins. Brett is only slightly annoyed that I pretended not to know how to skate, but he is very annoyed that he didn't already know that about me. So we spend the afternoon sharing silly facts about ourselves.

We are frozen, but I think we are both reluctant to leave our little picturesque haven. We drive home, still chattering about anything and everything. It really is perfect.

Chapter
THIRTY-TWO

Brett

I'M AN ass. I know it. You know it. And tonight, Jesse learns it. We just spent the best day together. She hustled me again. I really should start expecting that from her. She told me random facts about the real Jesse Addison. Like how she color coordinates her M&M's before eating them and how she has some weird obsession with new socks. I felt whole today while skating around the pond with her. And it scared the shit out of me.

Jesse has wedged her way deep into my heart. She loves me. I can see it every time she looks at me. It kills me to see such emotion in her eyes, knowing that I can't give her back what she deserves. Do I care about Jesse? Unquestionably. Do I see a future with her? Yes, for as long as she is willing to stick around. Can I be the man she deserves? Absolutely not.

We got back from our day at the pond and jumped directly into the hot shower. We were both still shivering, even after the long drive home with the heat on full blast. I would have been fine with a cup of coffee, but when Jesse suggested the shower, I felt obligated to take advantage of her naked body. I'm a gentleman like that.

I gave her a few orgasms in the shower before carrying her to the bed to retrieve a condom to finish things off. That's one thing I don't play about. We're always safe. Even though she is on the pill, the last thing I need is to bring a baby into this fucked-up life of mine. Maybe one day, but that is so far in the future that it doesn't even register on radar.

The sex is always amazing with Jesse. Her body was made for me. Every curve of her small frame is nothing short of spectacular. For a girl who is so shy in other aspects, Jesse is not afraid to tell me how she wants it in bed. I roll on a condom and she tosses her inhibitions out the window. Fully clothed, she still blushes when I tell her what I want to do, but once she's naked, she gives as well as she takes.

"Stop!" I yell as she straddles my lap, tickling my oversensitive stomach.

"Say it."

"No, I'm not ticklish. I'm a fucking man!"

She continues laughing as I squirm underneath her. "Say it, Brett. I'm not stopping until you say it."

I have no idea who she thinks she is. The only reason all one hundred pounds of her are still sitting on top of me is because I like the way she feels naked, sitting on my stomach, and still wet for me. She reaches back and teasingly drags her nails up my sides, causing me shout.

"Sarah, stop!"

The entire world stops turning. I immediately go still, and I'm not even sure if Jesse is breathing.

"You just called me Sarah," she says so quietly that I can barely decipher the words from breaths.

I know exactly what she said though. I have two ears. I heard the name come out of my mouth. I look up to see her sitting frozen, staring down with the sparkle of tears forming in her eyes.

"What? No I didn't!" I laugh. We both know it's a lie, but I can't help the fact that I say it anyway.

Staring into her eyes, I can see her gears turning as she tries to figure out her next move. I know I need to say something. I don't have an explanation though. I have no idea why Sarah's name flew out of my mouth in that moment. But like the true dumbass that I am, I just lie still and wait for her reaction.

Finally, after a few minutes of silence, she screams, "Shit, I knew it! You still love her!" She jumps out of bed and begins whirling around the room, grabbing random clothing as she goes. Damn, I really should have said something before her mind went there.

"Jesse, get back here."

Her eyes are wild, looking like she just woke from a horrible nightmare. It's hard to tell, though, if she is genuinely hurt or just downright pissed that I said something so off-the-charts stupid.

"Are you kidding me? You just called me your wife's name. In bed. Oh God, that makes it sound even worse. She isn't even your ex-wife." She's talking a mile a minute, working herself into more of a frenzy. "Christ, how is this even happening right now? Damn it, where is my bra?!" She screams the last sentence as if it's the punctuation to her rage.

"Jesse, STOP!" Wrapping the sheet around my waist, I cautiously step in her direction, afraid that, if I move too fast, she'll bolt. I gently grab her wrists as she frantically tries to pull her shirt over her head, apparently giving up on finding the bra altogether.

"I need to go." She pulls away, snatching her hands out of my grasp while backing towards the door. She doesn't get far before I grab her perfectly curved waist, letting my fingers splay across to her back. God, I'd give anything just to get her back in bed.

"Please don't do this, Jess. It just came out. I'm sorry...I..." I trail off, mumbling something about how it means absolutely nothing. But I'm not really sure what it means at all.

"You're still in love with her."

It's not a question. It's a declaration of fact—and just enough to push me over the edge of rational thinking. I should be apologizing to her, but something inside me snaps. Using her to replace Sarah isn't just her worst fear—it's mine as well.

"What do you want me to say? That I've never been with a woman before you? For fuck's sake, you know I can't tell you that!" I yell as she stands perfectly still, startled by my sudden outburst.

She's oblivious to why the verbal shitstick she just poked me with has lit me on fire. I can see the hurt and confusion in her eyes, but I can't find it in myself to care right now.

Still wrapped in a sheet, I start pacing the room, feeling trapped for the very first time since Jesse landed in my bed. Call me crazy, but I don't want to sit here and hash out my feelings like it's a God damned therapy session. I want to walk across the room, wrap her soft body in my arms, and pretend this never happened. Maybe take her back to the room, lay her across the bed, and bury myself to the hilt, losing myself inside her. At the rate I'm going, I'll be impressed if she ever lets me touch her again. But again, like a dumbass, I say nothing else.

"Just tell me you are not still in love with her," she whispers carefully, almost begging.

Seeing her so lost and helpless is my undoing. I stride over to her, losing my anger and the sheet on the way, reaching out to grab her only to have her swat my hands away.

"Please, Brett. Just answer the damn question. Are you still in love with her?"

The threatened tears finally escape the corner of her eyes. I manage to wrap my arms around her shoulders, pulling her to my chest. But she doesn't nestle close. Her arms hang at her side and her eyes are glazed over as she looks anywhere but at me. A steady stream of tears are falling from her face, soaking my arm. She never moves a muscle, not even to wipe her eyes. This might be the worst punishment of all.

I could deal with her being angry. I could deal with her turning into a crazy woman, throwing things around the room. But to look down at this woman, who is usually so vibrant and energetic, and see her so defeated is more than I can take. I just don't have an answer to give her. Especially not the answer she wants to hear. Am I still in love with Sarah? No. Yes. Fuck if I know.

I do know I'm not going to figure this all out right now. Where is the rewind button like in that silly Adam Sandler movie? Christ, just let me go back five minutes and say the right woman's name. A Freudian slip. A Freudian fucking slip is going to cause me to lose the best thing that has happened to me in four years. And I can do nothing but sit here and try to hold on to yet another broken woman.

"I have to go," she repeats.

Maybe I should let her leave. Maybe if she goes home and sleeps on it, she'll forget all about the fact that I called her my wife's name. Shit, I am such a bastard. Who does that? I'll tell you who. Brett fucking Sharp. Asshole extraordinaire.

I could go into hiding and reemerge a few days from now, when she's had a chance to cool off. We can go right back to the crazy, sex-filled, serious-yet-unlabeled relationship we have had for the last few months. Nothing will change. Even my ridiculously hopeful mind knows this is a bullshit plan.

"I really have to go," Jesse finally says, the somber inflection of her words breaking through my thoughts.

"Babe, please. Don't leave like this. Let me grab some beers. We can cook dinner, watch reruns...whatever you want to do. I'm sorry. Just stay tonight. We can figure this out tomorrow." The desperation in my voice does nothing sway her.

"Let me go, Brett."

"No," I childishly reply, hoping that one word is enough to make her stay. *See? I told you. Total dumbass.*

"Let. Me. Go."

I know she isn't talking about physically releasing her anymore. I get the sinking feeling that, somewhere in this huge crap-tastic misunderstanding, she was hoping for some grand gesture or declaration of love. Yet my silence has spoken more words than everything else I've ever said combined.

So I do the only thing I know to do. I hold her tighter than humanly possible. I can hear her breath catch and her grunt in discomfort, but I know that, when I let go, she's walking out my door. And just like Sarah, she will probably never come back. Maybe calling her Sarah wasn't so wrong after all.

A minute later, I lean down, kiss her hair, and finally do what I should have done after our first night together. I let Jesse walk away.

Chapter
THIRTY-THREE

Jesse

THIS IS all my fault. This is what I get for falling in love with an unavailable man. The bridge is officially crumbling under my feet, and instead of holding on like I swore I would do, I walked away. But I don't see Brett rushing after me, begging me to stay. He's probably cracking open a beer and pretending none of this ever happened right about now. He's good at denial. I am too, usually, but I can't stay trapped in that relationship anymore.

I love him. I could have gotten over his calling me Sarah if he'd told me how he really felt about me. About us. Brett fought harder to make me stay months ago when we had only been on one date. This time, he had nothing to say. He looked at me with no more words than he had emotions. No sun and fog romantic speech. Tonight, I got a hug and nothing but bone-chilling silence. He always says I make his world go silent. So I guess it's a fitting end for us.

I tried to do what my mom, Caleb, and Kara had all urged me to do. I tried to give him time. Granted, five months isn't long, but it's all I have to give. It took me half of that to realize I want to spend the rest of my life with him. I knew this was going to be hard. He told me he couldn't commit or make me any promises, but I thought we had moved past that. We've come a long way since that night by his car when I poured my heart out to him. Heck, we might as well be living together. But tonight said it all. All I've ever done is fight for us. In the beginning, I was willing to do that because Brett was fighting too.

Now, as I walk down the cold street, trying to hail a cab, I see it all too clearly. Sarah is the only woman Brett will ever truly fight for.

Brett

THE PAIN in my chest is unbearable. The noises of the world are swirling around my head. I've now officially failed both of the women who have trusted me with their hearts. Sarah might be the broken one, but I'm damaged beyond repair too. I won't be the same after Jesse. There is no way I can put myself out there just to selfishly crush another unsuspecting woman. Why the hell couldn't I just open my mouth and fucking tell her how I feel? I know I feel...something. I just can't figure out what that something is.

I snatch my phone off the table and try to stop myself from dialing her number. Maybe I should call and apologize. And tell her what? That I still can't give her what she wants from me. It's been five fucking minutes. Nothing has changed. Instead, I dial Caleb.

"What's up?" he answers—thankfully. It's Saturday night. There was no guarantee that he wouldn't be in the middle of banging his way through the female population of Chicago.

"I need a drink."

"I'm kind of busy. Can we do it tomorrow?" I hear a woman's voice in the background. Obviously, I was right about his activities tonight.

"Jesse left."

"To go where?"

"I called her Sarah and she bolted. I'm pretty sure we're done. I need to get drunk or I'm going to end up destroying my apartment. You in or not?"

"Shit! I'm about twenty minutes away. Want to meet at the bar?" he says as the woman begins to whine in the background.

"Sounds good."

"Hey, what did you say to her after you called her Sarah?"

I let out a loud sigh. "Nothing. Absolutely nothing."

"Fuck, you're an idiot. I'll be there soon."

"Thanks," I reply, but he's already hung up.

TWENTY MINUTES later, I'm sitting at the bar, relishing in the burn as Jack Daniel's slides down my throat.

"She loves you. What the hell are you doing sitting here with me?" Caleb asks when I finish telling him the whole story. Usually Caleb and I would bullshit about work or football, but as much as it pisses me off, he and Jesse are close.

"She left," I say, annoyed.

"So?" he responds like I'm the biggest dumbass in the entire state of Illinois. He's probably not too far off the mark tonight.

"What was I supposed to do? I can't tell her I love her!" I yell, slapping against the bar for another shot.

"And you think that's the only thing that would make her stay? Not 'I'm crazy about you' or 'I'm fucked up but I don't want to be with anyone else'?" he says, pulling away the new shot in front of me and tossing it back.

"She knows all of that!" I motion to the bartender to keep the drinks coming. If ever there was a night to get rip-roaring drunk, this would be it.

"She's not asking for an engagement ring, asshole. She wants a commitment. She wants reassurance that this isn't temporary to you because it sure as hell isn't to her."

"I have to say that your knowledge about how my girl feels is highly disturbing."

"Well, if you two would get your shit together and stop dragging me into the middle, maybe I wouldn't know any of this."

I rest my head in my hands and stare down at the bar. "You think she'll take that? Just a commitment of some sort?"

"Nope." He takes a sip of his scotch on the rocks. "But I do think she would accept a real commitment. None of that 'some sort' bullshit. Is that something you think you can give her?"

"I don't know," I answer honestly.

"Then take a few days and figure it out."

"I can't go a few days without her."

"Jesus Christ! Open your fucking eyes, Brett! You're so caught up on the semantics of what a commitment means that you're missing the fact that you've already committed. You spend every waking minute with Jesse. You're terrified to move on from Sarah, but you've already done it. It's done! Man up and recognize it!" he says, growing more and more pissed.

"Fuck, Sharp! The hard part is done!" he repeats again, pulling out his wallet and throwing money on the bar. "I need to go. If I knew this was going to be a poor-pitiful-Brett party, I never would have left the blonde who was begging me to fuck her. Get your shit together and say you're sorry. Just don't fuck with Jesse's head. She's a good girl who deserves way more than this bullshit you're spouting right now."

He heads toward the door but only gets a few steps before turning back to ask, "You drive here?"

I shake my head but stay focused on my drink as I hear him walk away.

"You all right?" the bartender asks.

"Hell no, but I need the check."

IT'S ONE in the morning when the cab pulls up in front of Jesse's apartment. She lives on the first floor, and I can see the light still on through the small rectangular window next to her door. I walk up and gently tap, not wanting to wake Kara. The curtain slides, and I see her face peek around the side. Her eyes are puffy and she looks exhausted.

"Go away, Brett."

"Never."

"Fine. It's supposed to be seventeen degrees tonight. Try not to freeze." She flips off the light.

"I'm not going anywhere, so I hope you can deal with my frozen body blocking your doorway in the morning." I try to joke, but I get no response.

I slide down the wall and sit next to her door. The sidewalk is freezing, but I'm not going home without her.

"I know you're still there, gorgeous," I say to the door. "I'm sorry. I know I say that a lot. I'm sorry for that too. Just talk to me."

"I can't do this anymore," she responds.

"Then let me say goodbye to your face," I lie. No way am I saying goodbye tonight.

I'm about to open my mouth again when I hear the click of the deadbolt. The door only swings open a few inches, and I see timid Jesse from months ago shyly standing in the darkness. I try to catch her eye, but she won't look up at me. *Shit, this is bad.*

I can feel my own heart banging around in my chest. What if I'm not able to fix this? I know she doesn't want me to come in, but I'm not having this conversation in the breezeway. Careful not to hurt her, I push open her door wide enough for me to squeeze inside.

"Brett!" she yells as I close the door behind me.

"Sorry, gorgeous. Add it to the list. I've got things to say, and I need you to listen." I'm lying. I still have no idea what the hell I'm going to say. Why do I never plan this shit out? "Come here." I pull her into my arms.

"Have you lost your freaking mind?" She moves out of my reach. "Say what you need to say then leave."

It's now or never. Time to dig deep and figure this out. I need to fix this with Jesse so I can escape this screwed-up existence I call a life. I've learned over the last four years that there is no escaping it, this really is my life. Suck as it might, you either live it or leave it. I glance over at the tiny brunette leaning against her kitchen counter with a glare that should be melting my face. Somehow, it just makes me smile instead. She looks like a tiny, pissed-off fairy—a description that would surely earn me even more of her pixie wrath. As my eyes slide over her, I realize that leaving Jesse isn't an option. Caleb was right. I've committed.

I walk to the kitchen cabinet, grabbing Kara's bottle of Vodka, and pour us both a shot. I'm going to need this if I am possibly going to get through this conversation. I'm about to rock her world, and I know because this revelation just rocked mine.

Tipping back the glass and pushing one towards her, I start. "Jess, I had a wife and I loved her with every fiber of my being. She was my life for seven years. She was my best friend, and I miss her...a lot. Yes, I thought I was going to spend the rest of my life with Sarah, but it didn't work out that way. She's gone forever. You can't hold that against me. I lost her four years ago, but it took meeting you to realize I lost myself on that same damn night."

She starts nibbling on the edge of her thumbnail nervously like she so often does.

"What if one day she changes her mind? I mean...what if she isn't really gone?"

"Yes, she is still breathing, but the woman I loved is dead. Jess, I can't change my past. I was lucky enough to meet a woman at twenty-one, fall in love with her, and spend seven of the best years of my life with her. Did you know we planned to have three kids? We had all these silly names picked out. There was supposed to be a little Danika and Hephzibah running around, tearing shit up right now. God, those names were ridiculous." I smile and laugh to myself.

"She wanted unusual names, something about her name being so plain, and I could not have given two shits what she named them. They were going to be ours, and that was enough for me. We wanted to move to Georgia. Live on the coast. Buy a big house on the water and spend our weekends lounging on the dock, arguing about who won last night's Jeopardy challenge. That is all I have ever known about my future. Those were our plans. Then one day, I woke up, and just like Sarah, everything was gone." I pause to take a breath and Jesse pounces.

"Jesus, Brett, why are you telling me this? This is exactly our problem. You're sitting here reminiscing with a Cheshire cat grin on your face. You have dreams and the perfect little storybook life of you and Sarah in your head. How am I supposed to compete with that? I struggle every single day knowing I have to share you with her. I can't do this. I can't be her replacement." She wipes a tear away from her eyes while scanning the room for an escape. "You need to go."

"Please shut up. It's about to get better, I swear." I take two steps closer, effectively blocking the doorway in case she decides to run.

"No, you need to leave." She crosses her arms over her chest in an adorable display of attitude.

"Christ, Jess, stop running. You are always running from me. Just hear me out. I have a point. I'm not trying to rub anything in your face."

"I don't want to hear you out!" she shrieks in a tone unlike anything I have ever heard before. "Call me a quitter or whatever you want, but I can't live like this. Everything I do, it always flashes through my mind: 'What would Sarah do?' She was your perfection. She was your happily ever after. It's fucking exhausting living in her shadow. I can't do it anymore. I love you. I really do. But damn. At some point, you have to say enough is enough. This"—she frantically waves her finger between us—"is not working."

I run my fingers through my hair as I look around the room, hoping for some sort of divine intervention. "Clearly, we are having some sort of miscommunication, because this"—I wave my finger between the two of us the same way she did—"is very much working."

"No it's not. This relationship is crap. I am the only reason it's even a relationship at all. If it were up to you, we would be nothing more than friends who have sex. I'm sick of pushing you for more. It's not going to happen and I have to accept that. I get that you're scared. You had your life snatched out from under you. I can even see why you would be hesitant to get back into a relationship. If things had slowed down back in September, none of this would be happening right now. You can't honestly think we have been taking this slow.

"I'm not some crazy woman who's in a rush to get married and settle down. I'm definitely not trying to force you into some big serious relationship if you aren't ready. Brett, it kills me that you are the only one who doesn't recognize how you feel. I can see it in your eyes. I'm not stupid. I know you love me. I can feel it when you make love to me. Yep, I said it. It's making love when we do it—not fucking!"

She pauses to take a deep breath, and just as she did earlier, I jump in before she can say anything else.

"Did you just say fuck?" I ask at what I will later learn to be 'completely the wrong time.'

"Oh my God, did you not hear anything else I said?"

"I'm sorry. I've just never heard you say fuck before...and you just said it twice," I reply, laughing, which only serves to piss her off more.

"Yep, that's it! I'm done here. You can sit there laughing it up that you made good girl Jesse Addison say fuck. Congratulations, jackass. You will have plenty of alone time to bask in your triumphant glory, because I quit!"

Finally, her eyes land on her car keys across the room, and I know it's time.

"I want a future with you," I rush out before she can take off on me yet again.

"No, Brett, you want a future with some woman who will fit into Sarah's shoes. But guess what? I don't want to play Jeopardy with you every night or settle on the coast of Georgia. I want to live in the mountains. And I want two kids, not three. And I like plain names like John and Beth. I don't want to spend the rest of my life waiting on a man to finally admit that he's in love with me. Jesus, why am I even still standing here arguing with you? If you won't leave, I will. You know what—"

"Jess, shut up!" I have no choice but to shout. She has worked herself up into such fit that she can't stop talking.

We both stand here staring at each other for a second, her chest heaving as she tries to catch her breath.

"I don't want to play Jeopardy with you either. Honestly, you really suck." I give her my best smile and wink to let her know I'm kidding, but she just continues to glare at me. "However, I do want to eventually kick your ass at the bowling alley." At that, she gives me an eye roll.

Even though nothing has been solved, with that small gesture, I know that, for once in my life, everything really is going to be okay.

"Jesse, you're my perfection. I'm sorry if I've made you feel that way about her. You're right. At one point, she was my everything, but then I met *you*. We could play the 'what if she hadn't been in the accident' game all night, but it's not going to get us anywhere.

"The truth is, for you, Jesse James Addison, I would move to Egypt. So if the mountains are what you want, I'll break my lease tomorrow. You want two kids? I'm fine with that too. John Sharp has a nice ring to it. But you have to promise me that, if we have two girls, we can try for a boy. And if we end up with three girls, you'll let me adopt a bulldog. I'm not sure I can handle that much estrogen in one house without some backup." She finally gives me a small grin that fuels my fire. "Now, gorgeous. If you can just stop freaking out on me for just a minute, I promise this is about to get better." I suck in a deep breath and prepare myself to say the three words I never thought I would say again.

"I love you. I have loved you for months, and to repeat your very crass words"—I jokingly raise my eyebrows in shock—"it isn't just fucking. I have made love to you every single time I have touched your body since the first day we met. Except that one time in the bathroom at Nell's. Just so you know, I won't classify it as anything but fucking if a man has urinated within a three-foot radius of where we are doing it." I pause while she rewards me with a soft giggle and a slight smile that barely curves her lips.

I close my eyes for a second, taking in a deep breath and listening to the magical sound that is Jesse's laughter. Any hesitance I had about my feelings before has all vanished. Yes, I love this woman. I'm not just saying it out of some misplaced obligation or a fear of losing her. I say it because it's a truth that I have no doubt was coded into my DNA the day I was created. It has taken me too long to realize it. I've put her through hell on the journey, but I know I will spend a lifetime making that up to her.

With the absolute need to feel her in my arms, I rush across the room, crushing her to my chest. "Gorgeous, I know you're still pissed at me. I get that. I've been an ass. But, Jesse, I love you. You won't understand this, but I need to be inside you. You are just going to have to trust me that I'm going to make this work with us, no matter what. I'll try to explain in a few minutes, but some serious stuff just happened and I have never needed to feel you more than I do right now. I love you, gorgeous. Can you do that for me? Just let me make love to you and I swear I'll show you everything."

Her eyes slide from surprise to aroused as she gives the tiniest of nods.

That is all it takes for me to pick her up, push her against the wall, and land my mouth roughly on her unprepared lips. I thrust my tongue forward as she tries—and fails—to match my frantic rhythm. I can't slow down. I need to claim her. I continue my assault in her mouth, pausing only briefly to pull her shirt over her head. Finding her nipples already peaked, I rub my thumbs over them, watching as they harden. She takes a deep, gasping breath, leaning forward and latching on to my neck. This time, I'm the one shuddering.

I place her feet back on the ground and growl, "Fuck, Jess, take off your pants." She still hasn't said a word since my declaration of love, and it's completely unnerving. I need to get inside her. I need to say it with more than words to make sure she believes me.

She shimmies out of her jeans and pink boy shorts as I continue to caress her breasts, alternating between gently tugging her nipples and kneading. Once she's fully naked, I step back, taking a moment to appreciate the stunning woman standing before me. My woman. *Mine.* I reach forward with one finger, stroking the junction between her legs, finding her already dripping wet. If at all possible, my cock hardens even further, twitching as it desperately searches for a way out.

"You're beautiful," I say, continuing to stroke her clit. "I love you. I know you've waited entirely too long to hear those words, but I'm saying them now. I hope you realize the door you've opened, because I am never going to stop saying it."

I rub my finger slightly faster, causing her to her throw her head back, banging it into the wall. I quickly reach around her curvy waist to help her balance while she loses herself in the movement of my hand.

"Brett, please," she finally speaks.

I know she is lost in the hunt for her release, but I want to hear her say it. I want to finally be able to respond.

"Say it, baby."

"Please, Brett," she breathes as I pause my hand.

"Jess, say it."

"Say what?"

I smile because she knows exactly what I want to hear. This torture is her small dose of payback for the last few months.

"Jess, I'm about to fu...make love to you against this wall until you are physically unable to walk the three feet to the couch and are forced to sleep on the ground, exhausted from the sheer number of times I have made you come."

I push forward, rolling my hard cock into her stomach. "We have just established how I feel. Combine that with the fact that you are one thrust away from an orgasm and this should really be an easy decision for you." I brush the hair away from her face, licking my way up her neck, pausing by her ear before firmly whispering, "Now. I want to hear you fucking say it."

"I love you," she finally answers just seconds before I push two fingers deep into her dripping pussy, sending her into a full-body climax.

Holding her close, I feel her sway as she rides out her sexual high. I bury my face in the top of her hair, breathing in the sweet floral scent I have memorized to be Jesse. I reply on a long, content sigh. "I love you too, gorgeous. I love you too."

Chapter
THIRTY-FOUR

Jesse

"DON'T GO." I grab Brett's legs, trying to drag him back into bed.

"I have to, babe. It's my Sunday to work."

"Call in sick." I rise to my knees and kiss his naked chest as he stands over the bed.

"God, I wish I could. I'd stay in bed with you all day."

"Please," I beg, knowing it's worthless.

I knew yesterday he had to work, but that doesn't make our long night any shorter. Last night was the most amazing day of my life. Brett Sharp is in love with me. I want to fly to Austria today just to find a field to spin around in like Julie Andrews singing "The Sound of Music." It's probably easier to do a happy dance in the shower. I'll stick with that.

"What time do you get off today?"

"It should be a light day. As long as nothing crazy comes up, I'll be done by six. How about I grab sushi and pick you up around six thirty? Maybe we can finish what we started last night." He shoves a hand into my hair and rakes his teeth across my neck, sending a shiver over my body.

"I'm all for continuing it, but I'm relatively sure we finished."

"My sweet Jesse, you have no idea what you are talking about. Last night was just the beginning."

I blush a little, remembering all the things we did last night.

Brett was a maniac. After he made love to me on the floor in the den, we did it again on the couch and in the shower, and we finished off the night in my bed with his head buried between my legs. There isn't a single muscle in my body that isn't sore this morning, but watching Brett get dressed causes an ache somewhere completely different.

"I'll call you if anything changes, okay?" he says, pressing a deep, closed-mouth kiss to my lips that leaves me lightheaded.

Everything was magical last night. Brett told me he loved me then showed me he loved me. I wasn't nervous about how things would be this morning. I knew he meant it last night. But then again, I also knew he loved me months ago. He told me once a while back that, when he finally said it, he would mean it with his entire soul. After last night, I have no doubt that he does.

I'm still not comfortable with the whole Sarah situation. We have a long road ahead of us as we try to figure out a solution that will work for everyone, including Sarah. Brett promised me in the shower that he was hiring an attorney this morning to help push the divorce forward. I'm glad he brought it up, because even though I feel confident in our relationship now, I don't think I will ever be truly comfortable until the divorce is final. He also promised to tell me if, and when, he goes to see her. No more avoiding the topic.

"Okay. I'll see you this afternoon," I reply, but Brett stands, staring at me expectantly. "What?" I ask when he doesn't leave.

"You don't have anything else to say to me?"

"I don't know. Do *you* have anything else to say to me?" I toss a little attitude his way, making him laugh.

"You're going to make me pay for making you wait, aren't you?"

"Pretty much." I smile, and he shakes his head.

"Fine. I'll make up for two months' worth of I love yous, but then we are even."

"Deal."

"One more kiss, and I really need to go." He leans over, tucking my hair behind my ear. "I"—he kisses my lips—"love"—he moves to my neck—"you." He finishes with a nip on my ear.

"I love you too," I whisper as his hot breath sends chills down my body.

"Go back to sleep, Jess. I want you well rested tonight!" he shouts over his shoulder, closing my door behind him.

I'm exhausted. I really should go back to sleep, but it's a lost cause. I have plans today, but first I need to tidy up the mess Brett and I made last night. Things got a little intense up against the wall. A few of the picture frames fell, and I heard at least one of them break. Kara should be home soon, and the last thing I want to do is answer a million inappropriate questions from her. I also want to hit the mall to buy Brett a little surprise for tonight. I sling back the blankets and get ready for the day.

AROUND NOON, I hear a knock at the door. I pull back the curtain to see a man holding the biggest bouquet of white daisies I have ever seen. I yank open the door and all but snatch them from the delivery man.

Gorgeous,
I figured these would be a good first step. I've never even bought you flowers. I'm sorry for that too.
Last night was amazing. Thank you for waiting.

I love you.
Brett

P.S. Why are you awake and cleaning? I told you to get some sleep.

Even though I know he's busy at work, I immediately dial his number.
"Detective Sharp," he answers.
"Well, hello, officer."
"Hey, babe. What's up?"
"They're beautiful. Seriously, Brett, I love them."
"Really? I was sure you were calling to give me hell about buying you something."
"No, you're allowed to buy me flowers any time you want. I'll just pretend you handpicked them from your garden."
"My garden, huh? Babe, you can pretend anything you would like. Whatever it takes."
"Thank you."
"You are very welcome. Now answer my question. Why are you awake? We had a late night, and it's your day off."
"How did you know I was cleaning? Do you have cameras in my house?"
"Just the one over your bed," he answers nonchalantly.
"What!" I scream into the phone.
"Jesus, I'm only kidding. No cameras. I just saw the mess this morning but didn't have time to clean it up. I knew you wouldn't be able to let it sit."
"Oh, well, okay then."
"Listen, I need to go. My phone is blowing up with blinking lights."
"I love you, Brett."
"I love you too. If flowers were all it took to get that out of you, I really might have to invest in a garden."
I giggle at his silly joke. "I'll see you tonight."
"You couldn't keep me away. Bye, babe."

"Bye." I hang up the phone, knowing nothing would be able to erase this smile from my face.

Three hours later...

"WHY ARE you doing this?" I whisper with my knees pulled tight against my chest as tears stream down my face.

"Because I have to. Because it's been four fucking years, and I can't live like this anymore."

"I'm sorry all of this happened, but you don't have to live like that anymore. Things can change." My words are meant to be encouraging, but I know they fall flat.

"Please stop crying."

"Why? So you don't have to feel anything? If you're really going to do this, you should feel it."

"No, because I can't watch anyone else cry over the shit-fest that is my life."

"I'm not crying for you. What happened to you is sad, but it didn't ruin your life. Altered, yes. But not ruined. So no, I'm not crying for you. I'm crying because this whole situation is so unfair. There isn't a single winner."

"That's not true, Jesse. You and Brett won. You found each other."

"That's not fair."

"It never is."

Brett

"I'M SORRY, Mrs. Kaplan. My hands are tied. I'll let you know as soon as I hear something."

My day has been shit, and if last night hadn't ended with Jesse in my arms, I'm not sure I could handle this. I've been slammed with cases all day. Nothing useful. It's been one dead end after another. I feel like I've been banging my head against the wall for the last six hours. My phone rings yet again, breaking though my frustrations.

"Detective Sharp."

"Detective, this is Sandy with emergency dispatch. We have a 911 caller who is claiming someone broke into her home and she is asking to speak with you. We have units on the way already, but she is insisting to speak with you."

"Did she give her name?"

"Kara Reed."

My heart stops beating and the room begins to spin.

"Put her through!"

"Brett?" I hear Kara on the other end of the line. Her voice is frantic and scared, unlike anything I have ever heard from her before.

"Kara, what the hell is going on?" I jump to my feet, grabbing my jacket off the back of the chair, and head toward my car.

"Where's Jesse?" she asks.

"Cleaning, last I heard. What's going on? Did you say someone is in the apartment?"

She begins to sob into the phone. "She's in the house. She has a gun and I think she has Jesse."

I have no idea what she's talking about, but the fact that she used Jesse and gun in the same sentence has me sprinting the rest of the way to my car.

"Who, Kara? Calm down. Tell me what's going on!" I scream into the phone, anything but calm myself.

"Sarah. I got home a few minutes ago and she snatched open the door and waved a gun in my face. She threatened me, but I took off running. You don't think she would hurt Jesse, do you?"

Oh God. This isn't happening. I'm not losing the woman I love…again. Different woman, different situation, yet another tragedy I can't control. No, fuck that. I'm not losing Jesse. I flip on the lights and speed toward her apartment faster than anyone, cop or not, should drive. I'm not thinking about anything but getting to Jesse.

"Kara, you still there?" I realize I'm still holding my phone to my ear.

"Please answer me. Sarah wouldn't hurt her, right?" The fear in her voice matches the pain in my chest.

I have no idea what Sarah is capable of anymore. She might as well be a stranger to me. I know she isn't afraid to kill herself, but now I'm terrified that she isn't afraid to take Jesse with her either.

"I'm on my way. Do not go back to the door. Are the officers there yet?"

"Yes, they just pulled up. Shit, Brett. Jesse's car is here. I think she's in there."

"Go to the officers, tell them everything, and make sure to tell them Jesse's mine. They'll take care of her if you tell them that. I'll be there in about ten minutes." I flip my phone onto the passenger's seat and slam my hand down on the steering wheel, cussing Chicago traffic. Even with my lights on, I'm still a lifetime away.

Officer Eli Tanner

"HELP!" I hear the small woman yell as she runs my way.

I immediately reach down to my service weapon. She doesn't look dangerous or armed, but she does look scared as hell.

"Freeze! Put your hands in the air!" I yell as she comes to a complete halt.

"Please help me. There is a woman with a gun in my apartment. She has my best friend in there with her."

"Keep your hands in the air and slowly walk towards me."

She complies, and when she gets close, I see the tears dripping off her chin.

"Please. Help her."

"What's your name?"

"Kara Reed."

"Do you know who broke in, Kara?" I question while patting her down.

"Sarah Sharp."

Fuck. I'd recognize that name anywhere. It was the name that changed my life all those years ago. "Excuse me?"

"Sarah Sharp, and she has Jesse Addison, Detective Brett Sharp's girlfriend in there with her."

Son of a bitch! How can one woman fuck up so many lives? "Stay here." I leave her standing next to my patrol car as I head to the door, praying this is some sort of a mistake. My day has been boring as hell, but I'd give anything to be able to dismiss this as one big catfight over a man. I draw my weapon and slide up beside the door. Careful to move out of shooting range in case she really does have a gun of her own, I test the doorknob and find it locked.

"Sarah Sharp!" I shout, using my boot to knock on the door. "Officer Tanner, CPD. Open up. If you have any weapons, I suggest you put them down first."

"Fuck you, Eli! Where's Brett?" she screams from the other side of the door. Obviously, she remembers me too.

"I have no idea where Brett is. Are you alone in there? Where's Jesse?"

"She's not a part of this problem anymore."

Damn it! That's the wrong fucking answer. "Sarah, I'm coming in. Back away from the door." I radio for backup as my partner rounds the corner to watch my six

Before I reach the door, I hear the unmistakable bang of a shot fired. I should back away and follow protocol, but I know this woman. I rush to the door, banging and praying for a miracle.

"Sarah, open the fucking door!"

"Find Brett or I swear it won't just shatter a few picture frames next time."

"I need to talk to Jesse. I need to know she's okay."

"Um, she isn't exactly speaking to me right now," she laughs.

"Is she okay? Does she need any medical care? You have to give me something here. I can't just call Sharp out here without any details."

"Tell him I need him. He'll come running. He loves to play the hero."

Brett

I DRIVE like a maniac the whole way to Jesse's apartment. I keep flipping between pissed off and terrified that Sarah is going to hurt Jesse. I've never in my life wanted to hurt Sarah, even when she physically abused me after the accident. It never crossed my mind. But today, if she so much as lays one finger on Jesse, I can't be held responsible for my actions.

I thought Sarah had gone crazy when she showed up at the coffee shop. And I definitely thought she'd gone too far when she slapped Jesse in the grocery store. But this... This is worse than I ever could have imagined. Today, it ends. I'm getting Jesse back even if Sarah gets hurt in the process. I want her locked up somewhere where she can't hurt anyone, including herself, ever again.

"Nine one one, what is your emergency?"

"This is Detective Brett Sharp, badge number 712. I need to be patched through to the officers on the scene at 12 Daven Court."

"Please hold, Detective."

A few clicks of the line later, I hear, "Officer Tanner."

Oh, thank Christ. Eli's there. He knows what he's doing. I've worked closely with him for years. Best of all, he's familiar with Sarah.

"Eli, it's Sharp. What the fuck is going on? I'm about three minutes out."

"Brett, do not show up here. Sarah is asking for you. I think she's waiting for you to get here before she does something stupid. Do not give her that. Stay the fuck away from here."

"Have you lost your fucking mind? I'm on my way!" I boom into the phone. "Tell me what the hell is going on? Have you gotten Jesse out of there yet?"

"No, and Sarah won't let us talk to her. She's locked up in the apartment and won't let anyone inside. She just keeps asking for you. Shots were fired a few minutes ago. Sharp, I'll be honest here. It doesn't sound good. She keeps making comments about Jesse not being an issue anymore. I really think you need to let us handle this."

I feel like someone took a sledgehammer to my stomach. The wind is knocked out of me completely. The car swerves to the side and I overcorrect, barely missing oncoming traffic. I'm overwhelmed with crippling panic. I can't go through this again. I'll kill her. I can honestly say that. If I have to choose, I will definitely pick Jesse over Sarah. Losing Sarah almost destroyed me, but if I lose Jesse, I won't be able to survive.

"You still there, Sharp?"

I swallow past the knot in my throat. "Call Jones. I have no idea why, but she listens to him. He can talk her down. I'll be there soon. I'll stay out of sight if you really think she's waiting for me."

"Jones isn't answering. Shaun is headed to his house now. Park around back. I don't want her to have any idea you even know this is happening."

I drop the phone and send up one last pleading prayer.

Jesse

"HOW LONG did it take you to realize you were in love with Brett?"

"Ten minutes," I answer honestly. This conversation has been going in circles for hours. The ground is too hard and my butt is killing me from sitting for so long, but I don't dare get up.

"That's bullshit. You can't know in ten minutes that you love someone."

"Yes, you can. How long did it take you to fall in love?"

"A week."

I nod at the admission. Ten minutes or a week, it's all the same thing. We aren't talking months or years. We are talking about recognizing that you would share an eternity with a person within minutes or hours of meeting them. I felt that with Brett. I was too afraid to see it at first, but it was always there. That first day he walked into the coffee shop, I knew I was going to spend the rest of my life with him. Convincing Brett was the hard part. I laugh to myself and wipe a lingering tear from my cheek.

"What's so funny?"

"Nothing," I answer shortly, not wanting to share the details that caused the unlikely smile to creep across my face.

"I'd die to feel like that again. To smile like that and actually feel something. The void is the hardest part sometimes."

"You could find it again someday. You could find someone who reminds you what it feels like to be truly alive. Someone who will give you meaning and hope again."

"I don't want to find someone else. I just want to feel it again."

I drop my head to my knees. I want to say the right words, but I can't seem to find any.

"I know. I'm sorry."

"I know, Jesse. You've said it a million times. Stop fucking apologizing."

I flinch at the outburst. So much for talking.

Brett

I PULL up, throwing the car into park and darting toward the line of uniformed officers huddled at the side of Jesse's apartment. All eyes rise to mine, and the looks of sympathy on their faces do nothing to put out the fire that is currently blazing in my veins.

"Talk to me," I snap at Eli.

"Nothing has happened since we got off the phone. No more shots, but also no sign of Jesse. Sarah isn't talking anymore, but we can still see her pacing through the window next to the door."

"Okay, you're going to have to let me talk to her."

"No way. If we give you to her now, we have nothing to use as leverage later when she gets tired of playing games. You know the way this works. We just need to wait her out for a little while."

"I'm well aware of the way this fucking works. I'm also well aware that my woman could be in there bleeding to death."

"Sharp, Sarah's fine. She—" one of the peanut gallery butts in.

"I don't give a fuck about Sarah, asshole. Jesse's in there!" I roar.

Eli steps up into my line of sight, blocking out the rest of guys. "Just calm down, Sharp. We're clearing some of the tenants out of connecting apartments and informing everyone else to stay inside. Once we get that done, I'll go reevaluate how Sarah's doing. See if I can get her talking again, maybe get some info about Jesse."

I release a loud breath. This is not the time to lose my shit.

"Yeah, okay. Did anyone get in touch with Jones?"

"Not yet."

"Find him. She's terrified of him. He might be able to freeze her up long enough to buy me some time to get in there."

"You're not going in there, Brett. You're too emotionally involved."

"Go fuck yourself, Eli. If it were Casey in there, you'd be tripping over your own dick busting down that door. You're going to have to shoot me to keep me out."

I know I shouldn't have mentioned Casey. It was low, but fuck him. He thinks we don't all know he's still pining over her. Hell, he was dumb enough to think no one knew they were fuck buddies. At least that's the way Casey, Sarah's best friend, classified their relationship. The look on his face right now proves that he was slightly more attached.

"You're a dick. This isn't your call, so stay away from that door or I really will shoot you." He walks back to the huddle of uniforms surrounding a squad car.

"Brett!" Kara yells, running in my direction. She doesn't slow down as she gets closer and crashes into my chest.

I pull her close, and silently hold her for a few seconds. "What's going on? No one is telling me and they keep trying to get rid of me. I'm not leaving. Tell them I can stay."

"Sweetheart, you really should leave. There isn't anything you can do. I'll make sure nothing happens to Jesse." I'm such a fucking liar. I can't control this any more than I could control Sarah's accident.

"No! I'll stay out of the way. I'm not leaving until I know she's all right. You didn't see the look on Sarah's face. It was really scary."

"Okay, just go sit in my car. Turn the heater on and stay out of the way."

"I'll sit on the trunk and stay out of the way. I want to be able to hear if anything happens."

"It's going to be okay, Kara. I'm not leaving here without her. I just got her. I'm not about to let go." I give her one last squeeze before gently pushing her toward my car.

Jesse

"SAY GOODBYE."

"I can't."

"You don't have a choice. None of this was ever up to you. It's time."

Brett

THE SOUND of a gunshot pierces through the otherwise silent afternoon air. No one is sure where it was aimed, but I know for certain where it originated. Ignoring the rush of officers headed to stop me, I take off at a dead sprint to Jesse's front door. Sarah can kill me if she wants. I don't care anymore. But I'm getting Jesse the fuck out of there first. I storm the front door, drawing my gun.

"Sarah, open the God damn door! Sarah—" I don't get another word out before a vase filled with daisies comes flying out the window, slamming into my shoulder.

A guttural scream rips from her throat. "You don't love her! You love me."

"No I don't! Right now, I really fucking hate you! Give her to me. You can do whatever you want with yourself, but I swear to God, Sarah, if you harm one fucking hair on Jesse's head, there will be hell to pay.

"Why would you send her flowers?" She begins to cry.

Obviously the pissed-off route is getting me nowhere, so I decide to change tactics.

"Please just tell me she's okay. Sarah, if you ever loved me, I need you to let Jesse go."

"Why? So you can have your happy ending and I get nothing? You can't leave me!" she shrieks.

"Where is she, Sarah? I'm not going anywhere. I won't leave you, I swear. I just need you to let Jesse go so you and I can have a conversation about us." The word 'us' feels disgusting rolling off my tongue. There is no us. I reach down to re-holster my gun. I won't shoot her, and deep down, I know she won't shoot me either.

"Sarah, I'm coming in." I reach through the shattered window, turning the deadbolt to unlock the door.

Just as I begin to twist the lock from the inside, Sarah screams and does the one thing I never thought possible. She aims at me and pulls the trigger.

Jesse

"THANKS FOR going with me today, baby girl," Caleb says as we finally head back to my apartment.

It's been a rough day, and I'm exhausted, both mentally and physically. My eyes are painfully red from crying, and although I'm sore from sitting on the cold, hard cemetery ground, Caleb needed me today. He needed to say goodbye to Manda once and for all, but he needed the push from an outsider to finally do it.

We sat at her grave for hours and talked. His emotions were all over the place. He slid from despair to longing then somehow ended up pissed off. He said he wanted to let her go, and I think he meant it. I don't think he even realizes how stuck he is. My relationship with Brett has forced him to realize there really is something missing in his life. He wants to move on, but he's still so angry about losing Manda that he can't see past it and into a future. God, it was horrible to watch. He's always so strong, and to see him so lost, sitting while tracing the name on her headstone... It was heartbreaking.

"You're welcome. I'm not sure how much I helped though." I offer him a weak smile.

"You helped." He pats me on the leg and rounds the corner into my apartment complex. "What the fuck?" he yells when we both see numerous cop cars surrounding my apartment. He swings into a parking spot a building over from mine. "Stay in the car. Do not get out under any circumstances. Got it?"

"Yeah, okay," I nervously respond.

Caleb gets out and walks over to a police officer, and out of curiosity, I roll down my window to see if I can hear their conversation. The minute my window cracks barely even an inch, I hear the scary sound of Brett screaming Sarah's name and glass shattering. At that moment, there isn't a lock in the world that could have kept me contained in the truck. I sling the door open and take off running toward my apartment. Towards Brett.

I'm trying to keep it together as I race down the sidewalk with Caleb chasing behind me. I have no idea what's going on or what I'm going to find when I get there, but the strain of fear in Brett's voice is more than enough to keep me moving in his direction. Just as I get close enough see my door, I hear the unmistakable sound of a gunshot. I instinctively freeze, allowing Caleb just enough time to catch up.

As I stand there, the whole world seems to be frozen too. I know there are a million things going on around me, but all I can see is Brett stumble back from my door before falling to the ground. It painfully steals my breath, and for a split second, I'm not completely sure I wasn't the one who caught the bullet. But the pain that rips through my chest as I watch the man I love fall to the ground is far worse than any gun could ever cause.

Brett

"BRETT!" I hear Jesse's strangled scream.

I can't figure out where it came from, but I know I'm going to find out. Hope swells in my chest that she's still alive, and I jump to my feet, ready to climb through that impossibly small side window to get to her.

"Brett!" I hear her terror-filled scream again.

This time, her voice clearly comes from the parking lot. I glance to my left and see Jesse standing on the sidewalk, trying to fight her way out of Caleb's restraining arms.

I'm not too much of a man to admit that tears of relief immediately flood my eyes. My knees go weak as I stand and stumble in her direction. If I didn't need them to get to her, I have no doubt they would buckle completely under my weight. I don't know how she is standing there unharmed, but it is the most spectacularly beautiful sight I have ever seen. Tears may be running down her cheeks and her wide eyes are full of fear, but the way she looks at this moment could never be topped.

My life just began again.

I jog over to her as she launches herself into my arms. "Oh my God, Brett! Are you okay?"

"I'm better than okay, gorgeous." I bury my face in her neck as the last few tears escape my eyes.

"What the hell is going on?" she asks, never releasing me.

"Jesus, I thought you were in there. Jesse, fuck. I thought…" I trail off, trying to get my emotions in check.

"I was with Caleb. We were at Manda's grave."

I pull my head back to see Caleb standing with his arms crossed over his chest, wearing a pissed-off expression, but there is no mistaking the lingering redness in his eyes.

"I've been calling you for hours," I say to him.

"Our phones were in the car. I'm sorry."

"Thank you," I say without hesitation.

"I had no idea, or you know I would have been here."

"I don't care about any of that. Thank you for taking her with you. I owe you for this," I laugh, squeezing Jesse tight enough to make her wince.

"Brett, you're bleeding!" She wiggles out of my grasp and backs up to examine my arm.

"Gorgeous, I'm fine. It's just a cut from the broken glass."

"Are you sure it's not a bullet?" she says as the worry creeps back across her face.

"I'm positive. See?" I roll up my sleeves, showing off a pretty nasty slice across my forearm, "I'm okay. I'll get it looked at tomorrow." I look up to find that Kara has joined us. She's tucked under Caleb's arm and reaching forward, holding one of Jesse's hands.

"Excuse me, Sharp?" Eli walks up behind me. "I'm really happy you found Jesse, but Sarah is still asking for you. The door is open now, but she still has the gun."

"Fuck her," I say without an ounce of guilt. She may not have had Jesse in there with her, but I'm positive that was the point of her breaking in today.

"Brett! You don't mean that," Jesse scolds.

"Yes, I do. I just spent the last few hours thinking you were either dead or dying. Jesse, I can't do this anymore. She broke into your home...with a gun. Who the hell knows what would have happened if you had been there."

"I wasn't in there, Brett. I was never in any danger. You can't hold it against her that you were scared."

"Yes, I fucking can. She could have told me you weren't in there. She could have not shot at me. She could have had a discussion like a normal, rational person that didn't involve a gun and breaking and entering."

"See, this is your problem. You keep waiting for her to be a normal, rational person. You've waited for years for something to change with her. Maybe she isn't the person who needs to change."

I close my eyes and let Jesse's words sink in. She's right. I loved Sarah once. I do care if she dies. I just wish it weren't always so fucking dramatic with her.

"Can you get someone to take them back to my apartment?" I ask Eli before turning to Caleb. "I need you here. This might get...interesting."

"I'm here." He nods, walking back towards his truck to presumably get his gun.

"I'm not leaving," Jesse says beside me.

"Yes, you are. I already died once tonight when I thought you were in there. Gorgeous, I don't want you anywhere near her."

"I'm not leaving," she repeats. "I'll stay back here, out of the way. I also don't want you near her. You need to talk to her, but she already shot at you once. You aren't the only one who died tonight. Can you talk to her from around the corner?"

I didn't even think how she must have felt when she heard the shot fired then watched me fall back. All I could think about was the fact that she was alive. It never even registered to me why she was so frightened.

"Yeah, babe. I can do that. I've got my vest in the car. I'll wear it if that will make you feel better."

"Much better," she sighs, leaning her head into my chest. "I know I just encouraged you to do this, but now I'm kind of scared."

"Jesse, look at me. This is getting finished tonight. The fog vanished last night. It's nothing but you, me, and clear skies from here on out." Then I say my famous words from all those years ago, but this time I actually believe them. "Just hang on. It's all going to be okay."

Chapter
THIRTY-FIVE

Brett

"SARAH!" I call from around the corner.

I managed to secure Jesse a bulletproof vest and placed her a good distance away. I didn't want her anywhere near this. There are two officers flanking the door. If Sarah decides to come out, she won't make it very far. The last thing I really want is for Sarah to get hurt in all of this. Somewhere inside, she is still the hell-on-wheels, hilarious woman I met twelve years ago. But before this can get any further, I do what I should have done years ago—I start talking.

"Sarah! Please talk to me."

"Why are you doing this to me, Brett?" she asks, defeated.

"What am I doing to you? Because from where I'm standing, you are doing this all to yourself. Please put the gun down. Let's figure this out."

"You love me, Brett. You've just forgotten it."

"Do you love me?" I ask, but I don't care about her answer. Not anymore. But she needs to say it. Admit it to herself.

"It doesn't matter how I feel. You love me!" Her scream echoes off the surrounding apartments.

"No, I *loved* you. Every crazy ounce of you. You have to know that. You stormed into my life, and in one night, you wrecked and ruined me. Then, seven years later, you did it all over again. I loved you, Sarah Erickson, and wherever she may be in the heavens tonight, I'll always love her. However, I don't love *you*."

"It's still me. I'm just different."

My heart breaks at her admission. She has no idea how many times I told myself that over the last few years. Those words are the main reason I held on as long as I did.

"I can't keep trying to fix you. I have to accept that maybe you aren't really broken at all. This is who you are now. I just wish you would stop trying to kill this new person, too."

"I can't stop," she whimpers. "I don't want to live this life anymore. You're all I have left after the accident, and now you're leaving me, too."

"I'm not leaving you, sweetheart. We both need to move on from the accident. I can't take care of you anymore. I'm sorry I forced myself into your life. That wasn't fair to you, but I couldn't walk away. I felt like you needed me when, in reality, you just needed space."

"I don't need space. I don't know what I need, but I know it's not more space," she says in a voice so broken that, any other day, it would have me reaching to comfort her. Not today though. Not ever again. "I heard her screaming for you, Brett. The minute she called your name, you were gone. How can you say you're not leaving me? That's exactly what you're doing."

"This isn't about her. This is about me and you, Sarah."

She switches gears again and begins to laugh. "You can't honestly say that. You think that little girl is going to make you happy? I've seen y'all together. She might be a quick fix right now, but it won't last. You might forget it, but I know you. You'll get bored. I saw y'all at the ball. You had to drag her onto the dance floor. You love to dance."

"No, Sarah. I loved to dance because you loved it. I actually hate to dance. And why the hell were you at the ball?"

It suddenly dawns on me that Sarah has been watching us all along. The picture that mysteriously appeared on my desk was her way of letting me know it, too.

"You took the picture?" I ask in disbelief.

"Yes, and I broke it today too. I can't believe you had Caleb frame it for you. That was something special he only did for Manda, and you had the audacity to put a picture of *her* in one of Manda's frames."

"How the hell did you see the frame? Were you in my apartment?" I ask in shock. Suddenly, all the details of the day snap into place. "Shit, that's one of my guns, isn't it?"

"Oh, don't sound so surprised. I really thought you would have changed the combination to your safe over the last four years. Before you go and get all 'officer of the law' on me, technically, I didn't break in either. You gave me a key years ago."

"So you decided to do what? To use my gun to hurt Jesse? Destroy me once again? What the hell is going through your mind right now?"

"She won't make you happy!" she screams, breaking down all over again.

"And you will? Listen to yourself. You don't want me. You just can't stand the idea that I don't want you. This whole situation sucks because there is no one to blame. Not you. Not me. Just the crazy fucked-up universe. If I could just point a finger at someone, I think I could have handled this a little better. I'm pretty sure that's the only way Caleb has been able to survive losing Manda. Blaming you."

I hear her sobs from around the corner. I need to see her. I know it's going to scare Jesse, but I need to look into Sarah's eyes when I say these next words. She needs to know I mean them with every fiber of my being.

I turn to lock eyes with Jesse and whisper, "I'm sorry for this, too."

Just as her eyes go wide with fear, I step around the corner, coming face to face with the barrel of Sarah's gun.

Her hands are shaking and her eyes are wild. Despite the fact that she's already shot at me once tonight, I know she won't do it again. I don't know why I know that with such certainty, but I do. I slowly reach forward and push the gun down.

"Sarah, I don't blame you for the wreck. Not even a little bit. Even if you were drunk that night, I know you never would have chosen this life for any of us. You were—you *are*—a good person. Give me the gun, sweetheart."

"No." She begins to frantically back away from me.

"What would Manda say if she were here? Jesus, she loved you so much. She would lose her shit at the idea of you hurting yourself. She was so tiny, barely even reaching your chest, but that never kept her from getting in your face." I can see the memories flood into her mind, making her smile before overwhelming her and knocking her to the ground.

She drops to her knees and throws her hands to her face, desperate to scrub the memories from her mind. I take the moment of weakness to quickly reach forward, pull the weapon from her hand, and pass it out the door to one of the officers waiting. Finally, with the threat gone, I begin to say all of the things I should have said in the beginning.

Here, on an unusually warm evening, with the true love of my life listening around the corner, is where it ends.

"Sarah, look at me. You have to get some help. For me, for Manda, for Casey, for your sister, for everyone who loves you, but most of all, for yourself. Even Caleb needs to see you get better."

"What would have happened to us?" she whispers, still covering her face.

"I have no idea what could have been with us, but I finally know what will *never* be. You can be happy again. I never thought I would get there, but I have, and I know you can too one day."

She lifts her head and stares into my eyes. "What's it feel like, Brett? To

241

be happy again?" Her chin quivers at the question.

"It's indescribable. I feel alive in a way I never have before. After all of the hell we have been through, we know how rock bottom feels. But when you find happiness again, those lows only make the highs even higher. You have to understand—you're not stuck. You've just stalled. You can still move forward, figure out who you are, and eventually find someone who will complete the picture."

"Is that what she does for you? Complete the picture?" she snaps in angry tone.

Her sudden shift startles me. Her anger doesn't seem real though, and I begin to realize that she lashes out as way to protect herself from the answer.

"Yes, it is," I say as calmly as possible, not wanting to put her back on defense.

"I don't even know how to be happy again." I know this isn't one of her games. I can feel the fear in her voice.

"Look at me, beautiful." Her sad red eyes rise to meet mine. "There will *never* be another Sarah Kate Erickson Sharp, but that doesn't mean you can't choose to be someone better. You're so angry all the time, and that's enough to make anyone miserable. You just have to open yourself up enough to let happiness in."

She begins to laugh, but there is no humor in it. "Yeah, happiness worked out so well for us," she says sarcastically.

"You and I weren't meant to be together. We were fated for failure from the very beginning. This was never the course I intended to take, but there is no doubt it led me to where I was supposed to be. I'm in love with Jesse. I'm sorry if that hurts. I really am. But you have to understand there is nothing I would change from the last six months. Not even the ability to go back in time. As much as you were my life, Jesse is my future.

"This is the end of any 'us' that you might think still exists. I loved you once. If you remember what it felt like to love me, I'm begging you to please get some help. Find your own happily ever after. Find someone who will love you—not for the person you were, but for the person you are. Just give it a chance. I swear to you, life won't always hurt this much. One day, the sun will appear, and when it does, I promise you won't want to miss it."

And with that final sentence, I walk over to Jesse, curl her into my chest, and walk away. I can still hear Sarah screaming my name, but I can't bring myself to care anymore. Surprising the shit out of me, Caleb is the one I see rush to the door and carry out the shattered woman. Her arms are curled around his neck as he whispers words into her ear. I take a deep breath and focus back on the only woman who really matters to me.

"You okay?" I ask as we walk away, Jesse tucked tightly under my arm.

"I love you too," is all she says.

Six months ago, it would have destroyed me to watch Sarah self-destruct in front of my eyes. But because of the beautiful woman in my arms, the one who didn't comment on all the ugly that just happened back there, I'm alive again. All she heard was when I said I loved her.

On a night that should have ruined me, Jesse saved me with four little words. I can't stop myself as I let out a quick laugh, dragging her into a hug.

"I love you. I love you. Fuck, I love you. I want to go home. To our bed. To our life together. I want it all and I want forever. Tell me it's forever, gorgeous."

She looks up at me with big brown eyes and nods, saying the most incredible word she has ever uttered. "Forever."

Chapter
THIRTY-SIX

Jesse

BRETT AND I have spent the last few hours lying in bed. We're naked, wrapped in each other arms, but there is nothing sexual about it. This is two people who are just thankful to still have each other to hold. Today was hell. There are no other words to describe it.

When I heard the gunshot and saw Brett stumble backwards, I thought my life was over. I'd just witnessed Caleb heartbreakingly try to let go of Manda, and all I could think about was having to sit on Brett's grave and do the same. When he stood and walked towards me, my heart exploded in my chest. I didn't know if he had been shot, but I knew I would at least be able to hold him again.

I've witnessed firsthand the way death paralyzed Brett and Caleb, but it wasn't until that moment that I understood why. It was the most painful experience of my life. When Brett explained what he'd thought had happened to me, my heart broke for him as well.

Every few minutes, Brett mumbles something I can't quite understand. He's not talking to me, but I can tell he's replaying the day in his mind. When the memories get to be too much, I feel his heart begin to race just before he gives me a deep, agonizingly slow kiss. Each time, he grows hard against my leg, but he never takes it to a sexual place. He doesn't need that connection tonight. He just needs to feel me in his arms.

Occasionally, he will roll us over, but he never lets me go. He drags me over with him, keeping me curled tight against his chest. We must stay like this for hours before he gets to a point where he can actually talk.

"How did you end up at Manda's grave?" he asks with a small quiver to his voice. It's so unlike Brett. Even in stressful situations, he's always cracking jokes. It worries me a little, but I give him the time to figure it out on his own.

"Caleb showed up to check on me. He said you told him we split up, and he wanted to see how I was doing. He looked so sad, Brett. I could tell something was eating away at him, but he still made time to come see how I was doing. He's a good guy."

"Yeah he is, gorgeous," he says, running his fingers through my long hair.

"I told him what happened when you showed up last night, and he smiled the most painfully fake smile I have ever seen. So I did what I always do—I begged him to take me to meet Manda."

"Of course you did." He half-smiles and rolls us over again.

He uses the tips of his fingers to ever so gently stroke up and down my side. Goose bumps immediately spread across my skin, and he pulls the blanket over me.

"He's worse than you know. Caleb may act like everything is fine, but he really needs help," I say, gently placing a kiss on Brett's collarbone.

"You know, he's never taken anyone there before. I once showed up to take her some flowers and he got up and walked away without a single word. That's his private place. I owe him my life for taking you with him today. I can't imagine…" He trails off then reverently kisses me again when he can't bear the thoughts that invade his mind.

"I'm okay, Brett," I whisper against his lips. He nods, but even though I couldn't get any closer without melting into his body, he still tries to close the invisible gap. "I love you."

"I love you too, gorgeous. Forever."

Forever. It's a single word that hold so much promise. It means, no matter what, we will always fight for each other.

The last six months have been a roller coaster. It's been nothing but a struggle from the very beginning. Between Sarah, Brett's guilt, and my insecurities, it's been one road block after another. It's never been easy, but we are stronger because we overcame the struggles we have faced together. The fact that we are here in this moment—together—speaks more about our relationship than anything else.

"Do you hear that, gorgeous?" Brett asks, rolling me to my back, finally trailing kisses down my chest.

"Hear what?" I ask on a breath.

"The silence."

Epilogue

Brett

Nine months later...

"JESSE JAMES Addison," the announcer says into the microphone as the love of my life walks across the stage to receive her diploma.

A few days after everything went down with Sarah, Jesse walked into her advisor's office and officially declared a major. She has just received her bachelor's degree in counseling, and she will start on her master's degree next month. Eventually, she'll earn her PhD and become a licensed grief counselor. She said that it was the first time in her life she saw the path laid out in front of her. I know she'll be wildly successful. After all, she rescued me.

We all jump to our feet, clapping and screaming as she shyly walks across the stage. Jesse didn't want to do the whole cap-and-gown graduation thing, but I insisted. I also rented out the entire bowling alley for a surprise party afterwards. She is going to be so pissed. I laugh every time I think about the angry face she'll make when she realizes what I did. She'll have to get over it. This is something to celebrate.

Sarah has spent the last nine months in a court-mandated recovery center. It specializes in traumatic brain injuries, but they are also working her through all of her guilt. It's where she should have been all along. Her sister moved up from Savannah, Georgia, to take care of her.

I haven't seen Sarah since that night when I said goodbye. The very next day, I filed a restraining order so she couldn't see Jesse ever again. Jesse had Caleb go behind my back and have it temporarily lifted so she could attend Sarah's trial. She even spoke on Sarah's behalf when it came time for sentencing.

I can't forgive Sarah. I don't know that I'll ever be able to. The fear I felt that day was too intense for me to ever truly get over. But the way Jesse has taken Sarah's back has only reinforced why I fell in love with her to begin with.

"Where are we going?" she asks for the hundredth time since we left her graduation ceremony.

"Stop asking, gorgeous."

"No, start answering, Brett."

Did I mention that Jesse's sass factor has increased over the last nine months? Gone is the shy, insecure girl I first met. I might be biased, but this woman is even sexier.

"Do you love me?" I catch her off guard.

"Of course. Why would you ask me that? Oh my God, what did you do?"

"Forever. Right?"

"Brett Sharp, what did you do?" she yells.

I just smile to myself and turn into the bowling alley parking lot. "I bought you a graduation present."

"Please tell me you didn't buy me a bowling alley," she says, looking more concerned than angry.

I throw my head back in laughter. "Remind me later that we really should sit down and have a talk about our finances. I definitely did *not* buy you a bowling alley."

"Oh thank God!" she rushes out on a breath, causing me to laugh even harder.

"Come on, babe. This is about to get better." The familiar words cause her eyes to go wide before closing completely. "Jesse, let's go inside."

When she opens them, her eyes dance with pure happiness. I might have given her too much with that one sentence, but the look on her face is worth it.

"Okay," she whispers.

We walk into the bowling alley as everyone around us screams, "Surprise!" Jesse stumbles back into my body as her family and friends rush to greet her. I catch her eyes as she disappears into the crowd. There is no mistaking the smile on her face or the, "I love you," she mouths as she's pulled away. I stay behind, talking with Caleb and the woman he can't seem to take his eyes off.

"Brett!" I hear Jesse scream from the other end of the room.

Even all these months later, my heart skips a beat in fear. I relax and head her direction when she holds up the custom bowling bag I had made for her. I had them monogram 'Tiny' on the outside to remind her of our first date in this very same place.

"You found it." I pull her in for one last kiss before everything changes forever. "Well go on. Open it."

"Brett," she whispers, staring up at me, her eyes sparkling with tears.

I know, based on my words in the car, that what she is hoping for is not what she's going to find when she unzips that bag.

"Wow," she says, pulling out a blue-and-white-swirled bowling ball. It's brand new and wrapped in plastic. She searches the bottom of the bag but comes up empty-handed. "I love it. Thank you," she says, but her eyes say otherwise.

I try not to laugh at her disappointment, but as always, I fail. "I'm glad to hear that, gorgeous. It took me forever for me to pick it out for you. You ready to get your ass kicked?" I tease. "I'll even give you a warm-up tonight, Jess. Who knows? I may have just been hustling you for the last year." I grin as she gives me the eye roll I was half expecting and half hoping for.

I take the ball from her arms, unwrapping it, and place it on the ball return. A seasoned veteran at this point, I type our names into our lane and push play on the game of my life.

"You're up, Jess," I say, interrupting her conversation with Caleb.

"Go ahead, baby girl," he says with a wink.

Jesse walks forward, picking up her new ball, trying to push her fingers into the holes. She struggles for a minute before looking up at me. "There's something stuck," she says, holding the ball out for me to fix.

"Just pull it out. Quit procrastinating! I know you're afraid of losing tonight, but really, stop blaming it on the ball," I say with a false confidence as my heart threatens to beat out of my chest.

"I'm trying. It's stuck."

She toys with it for a few more minutes before it shifts loose. She pulls out a diamond solitaire engagement ring and her eyes snap to mine. Everyone knows but her, and they all stand behind us, clicking pictures and smiling.

"Brett?"

"Gorgeous?" I respond, walking the few steps to meet her.

"Um…" She holds up a diamond that is nowhere near worthy to sit on her finger but still far bigger than anything she would ever allow me to buy her.

"I love you. I think we've covered that part by now." I smile as tears start to slide down her cheeks, but her smile never wavers. "I don't think words can adequately explain all the reasons why I think you should marry me. For now, I can only offer you one, and it's selfish as hell. Jesse James

Addison, I can't live another day without calling you my wife. We have wasted too much time already. I should have married you that day at the football game fifteen months ago."

She starts laughing—just as I hoped. As the magical sound washes over me, I drop to a knee.

"Marry me, Jesse." I pull the ring from her hand and slide it on her finger.

She doesn't say a word as she drops to her knees beside me. She throws her arms around my neck and buries her face into my chest. I hold her for a few moments, waiting for an answer that never comes.

"You didn't answer," I whisper as the large crowd looks on.

"Shhh. Do you hear that, Brett?"

"Hear what?" I ask, thoroughly confused.

"The silence." She mocks my words then bursts into laughter.

I can't help but join her as I fall over backwards, dragging her with me. Without shame, I kiss her indecently on the filthy bowling alley floor.

"Yes," she finally whispers against my lips.

It's more than a word. It's a life, a future, and more than I will ever deserve. It's forever.

The End

Stolen Course

Caleb Jones' Story

Available now

**Support indie authors by leaving an honest review.
Positive or negative, all feedback is appreciated.**

Acknowledgements

So let me get this straight. I get as many pages as I want and no one will turn on the music and play me off the stage while I'm thanking people? I'm kind of scared this might be longer than the actual book. Well, here we go.

To my amazingly sexy husband Mike: I love you. Writing *Changing Course* might not have been "work," but thank you for letting me pretend it was. Thank you for picking up extra wine at least twice a week and for not complaining about the dirty house and seven bazillion piles of laundry. Oh, who am I kidding? It always looks like that. Thank you for not complaining about that too. Thank you for staying up all night and actually reading your wife's sexy book. You have always been the silence in my crazy world. MMmmMMMmmmMM!

To my kids Lunny, Toots, Grey, and Hoppy: Yes, Mommy wrote a dirty book. I hate to say it, but I'm pretty sure this won't be the most embarrassing thing I ever do to you. I love you more than words can ever express.

To my mom: Thank you for agreeing to read the abridged version of *Changing Course*. You know, the one where Brett never says a bad word and never goes further than holding hands. Most of all, thank you for always supporting me, no matter what wacky idea I had. I may not always be the most thoughtful or the easiest to get along with, but the fact that you put up with me unconditionally means more than you will ever know. I love you.

To my dad: Oh jeez, thank you for NEVER reading this book. I won't even send you the abridged version I sent Mama. Trust me, for the sake of awkward Christmas dinner conversation, it's better this way. But thank you for always being my daddy. I love you.

To my sister Lori: Thank you for giving me shit and always having my back when I need it—and even when I didn't know I needed it. Oh, and thank you for the one-star rating you will surely give me...ya know, just to keep me in check. ☺

To my sister Jennifer: Thank you for editing the crap-tastic first draft of my very first book. Seriously, you deserve an award for that, but all you are getting is this three-sentence acknowledgement. Don't let it go to your head.

To my brothers Jay and Matt: If y'all ever open this book, I will never speak to you again. But thanks for letting Mama read this little part to you over the phone when she finally tells you that I wrote a book. Random, right? Don't worry. I won't mention the championship underwear in any of my books. Oh, wait. Never mind.

To the whole Martinez family—Juan, Wilma, Telisse, Anthony, and Ashley: Thank you for being my second family and supporting me every step of the way.

To Autumn: Without you, Changing Course would be a drag, and I'm not talking about the good kind of drag. There would be no sexy without you, so I'm sure Brett and Jesse thank you for that almost as much as I do.

To Ashley T: Thank you for reading every agonizingly rough chapter along the way. Seriously, that was a tough job. I can't thank you enough for the endless amount of hours you spent brainstorming with me. I can honestly say Changing Course is better because you were involved.

To my AMAZING betas Bianca, Bianca, Adriana, and Lakrysa: I have no words. Changing Course would never have been the same without y'all. You ladies kept me laughing with your emails and made me get down and dirty with the ending (ehm…mean B). I'm so thankful to have such an incredible group of smart, funny, and beautiful ladies to help me on this crazy journey.

To Ashley B: Thank you for making me an amazeballs cover! And for putting up with my fifty phone calls asking you to change things. Most of all, thank you for being my friend through thick and thin.

To Biz: What should I say? You have had my back since middle school. It is no surprise you encouraged me to write as well. As long as you swear to never release our high school notes (sp), you will forever be one of my best friends.

To Crystal and Juanita: The ORIGINAL Regina and Anastasia! Thank you for providing me with a million hilarious stories to write about.

To Stacey: The best sprinting partner to ever exist. Thank you for answering all of my drunken questions. Hopefully you will one day be able to use your superhero ability to translate "drunk Aly" to make some money. Your inspirational pictures were always the best! I can't wait for book two! Goooooooooo!!! ☺

To Tessa: You inspired me in the middle of a Walmart parking lot. You know what? Walmart sells wine! Ennis, I understand it now! Thank you for taking me under your wing and helping me every step of the way.

To Danielle: I was so nervous to tell you I was writing a book, but you became one of my true champions. Thank you for always being just a text message away. I miss you every day!

To Ash and Fall: Yes, I know I already "thanked" y'all, but my White Zin Bookends partners deserve to be thanked again. Thank you for picking up my slack while I was hiding in the writing cave. Thank you for the endless hours of texts, debating the finer points of Brett and Jesse's relationship. And most of all, thank you for encouraging me to take this giant step. Without you ladies, I never would have had the courage to actually do this.

To every member of The Hen House: Thank you for always supporting me even though I live over a thousand miles away now. We can always have long-distance wine nights!

To all of my IRAC ladies: Look, a squirrel! I never would have finished this book without y'all urging me to drink more wine, look at hot guys, and pretend to sprint, when in actuality we just giggle and chat. Best writing group ever!

To Adriana: Thank you for doing a final edit when I was about to lose my mind. You really saved me from a nervous breakdown. Who knew writing a book would be so stressful? ☺

To Love Between the Sheets: Thank you for being the best promotional service a new author could hope for. I can't express how much owe you ladies for organizing my cover reveal, blitz, and tour. Most of all, I owe you for answering every one of my random emails.

To all the bloggers: Your endless support and positive words mean the world to me. Thank you for taking a chance on a new author.

About the Author

Born and raised in Savannah, Georgia, Aly Martinez is a stay-at-home mom to four crazy kids under the age of five, including a set of twins. Currently living in Chicago, she passes what little free time she has reading anything and everything she can get her hands on, preferably with a glass of wine at her side.

After some encouragement from her friends, Aly decided to add "Author" to her ever-growing list of job titles. So grab a glass of Chardonnay, or a bottle if you're hanging out with Aly, and join her aboard the crazy train she calls life.

Facebook: https://www.facebook.com/AuthorAlyMartinez
Twitter: https://twitter.com/AlyMartinezAuth
Goodreads: https://www.goodreads.com/AlyMartinez

CPSIA information can be obtained at www.ICGtesting.com
Printed in the USA
BVOW05s0438190316

440968BV00005B/193/P